Cave Dreams

A. R. Donenfeld-Vernoux

Library of Congress Cataloguing-in-publication data
A.R. Donenfeld-Vernoux
Cave Dreams: a novel /by A.R. Donenfeld-Vernoux
ISBN 978-09888853-0-1

MANUFACTURED IN THE UNITED STATES OF AMERICA
:
ISBN: 0988885301
ISBN-13:978-0-9888853-0-1

This book is dedicated to:

Melinda Bates, who not only believed in me, but also trekked up the mountains, down the mountains, and around the mountains of Corsica with me—even climbing alone to the highest scary peak so she could take photos of a Neolithic village where Aldo might have lived.

Lynn Doiron, my inspiration and mentor—who spent so much time and effort keeping my writing and characters honest and on the straight and narrow, and then created the perfect cover art. Mere words are not enough to say 'thank you' sufficiently!

My friends and fellow bridge players, Patria and Nancy who supplied moral support, and forgave my hiding at the computer all the time I was writing.

And to my grandson, who I predict to become the greatest baseball player ever—keep those home runs coming. Take a bow Parker Foss!

Table of Contents

Acknowledgments

This book couldn't have been written without the help, support and nagging of a lot of wonderful people.

Those who contributed so many helpful insights into the character of Aldo— the late Dr. Herb Weber, the members of the Orange Country Advanced Fiction Meetup: Dr. William Young, Dirk Sayers, Gregg Hanour and Niloo Sarabi who took turns both praising and beating me up. I'm so lucky I found you.

The Baja Writers Group, led by Marsh Cassady who taught me the meaning of 'show' not 'tell.'.

To my friends who waded through drafts checking typos and punctuation along with holes in the story:

Thanks to the kind people of Corsica for answering endless questions about flora and fauna, wines, cheeses, music, knives, cuisine and hunting; and to those kind and pleasant ladies at the Musée Départementale in Levie, Alta Roca for being generous in sharing their knowledge of local prehistoric sites, habitations and artifacts to two bedraggled and rain-soaked American ladies.

To Les Lauriers Roses— Jerome and Christian and family, for making us feel so welcome in Corsica we never wanted to leave.

Thanks to you all—no way could I have done it without you!

Chapter 1
Corsica

Aldo wanted to forget, if only for a moment, why he stood by the pyre he had built with such care. The brush and branches stood tall below the overhead opening allowing air currents to enter, catch funereal smoke and twist its escape to the heavens. To Dia. It was the ancient way for souls of the departed to be released. The way of the clan.

His hand found the sore spot low down on his back. Hauling rocks up the steep mountain track to contain the fire, then cutting dead branches to build a great blaze was hard work for a man past his youth. No one else was left to help him do such demanding work. The few young ones left the clan years ago; the elders too old and frail to help. This last honoring for his wife, Raina, was a task he completed himself and the aches showed his own time might be shortening too. But this day, he was beyond all feeling, beyond even the grief consuming him.

Fog clung to the mountains, and its dampness penetrated deep into the sacred cave. The cold it brought always seemed to last forever. Aldo looked forward to dry warm spring air but his instincts told him it was weeks off. Without intense sun warming the air for several days the cave wouldn't dry enough for the spring odor of old paper to return and mix with wood smoke and lost essences of the beloved and not so loved.

Three elders stood next to him as he set a torch to the heavy logs he'd dragged uphill for the pyre. His wife lay on top, lifeless and pale. He'd folded her hands across her chest to hold the small stone carving of Dia and a bouquet of early wildflowers, everything in place for her journey. She wore her best dress; one given to her by people in the village. The gay flowers once decorating the bodice and skirt had faded into obscurity.

The infant, a tiny girl, rested on her body, next to another small bouquet. Aldo had bathed the birth fluids off the cold babe and swathed her in a bright pink cloth in preparation for her journey with her mother.

Raina's health had always been frail; then worn down further with five stillbirths. This last child arrived living, but only for an hour. As his wife held the dying infant in her arms, Aldo stood at her side helpless, watching her give up her desire to live as she left him forever with the last breath of the tiny girl. Death won again.

Part of his grief was his knowledge the clan would end. If he survived the elders, which seemed likely, he would be the last. He had prayed to Dia for a son. A son to follow him, a boy he could teach to become le Maître, Dia's consort, and, like all the men in his family before him, the Signadori, a healer, one who releases *L'Occhiu*, the Evil Eye, a practitioner in the path of life to carry on the old ways and spiritual beliefs.

A tear glided down the brown crag of his face. He shook his head and sent a silent prayer to Dia. He'd little hope she'd hear him. The fire grew in intensity, moving toward the worn dress and faded flowers. The orange fuzz on the infant's head shined with false life in the flames.

Aldo looked at the dark smoke curling to the ceiling and out the hole blackened by so many other passages; his clan, his family. He studied the walls of the cave—too painful to watch the flames leap around the bodies of his family, the remnants of the artists who painted the decorations on the walls; ancient animals, vivid in ochre and rust, fleeing from the stick figures of hunters chasing with spears raised high. The paintings looked almost alive in the flickering soft yellow and orange caress of flames. But the power of fire wasn't strong enough to bring his wife and child back.

The elder Mazzeru, the clan dream hunter, had known. He foretold Raina's death. Aldo remembered the dream as it was told to him.

Sitting outside around another fire, those weeks before, the Mazzeru recounted the hunt in his dream vision. He told Aldo of traveling through a familiar landscape, following on the trail of his prey; a small hare not ready to die. The Mazzeru moved his hands in the firelight, acting out his dream, showing how he took his small spear, tested the point was well fixed to the shaft. He crouched next to Aldo showing how he had hidden behind a bush, waiting for the hare to appear. His arm poised backward to mime the fatal throw. Clapping his hands together, he showed the final impact. Then, turning his hand over, palm upwards, he acted out turning the hare onto its back. Pulling back in surprise, he told how the head of the hare become the face of Raina.

It made sense to Aldo. The clan believed the hare was the symbol of fertility, something eluding Raina. Yes, she could become pregnant and carry a child, but none survived. It sorrowed Aldo to admit it, but it was fitting for a hare to be her symbol of death. A dream hunter was never wrong.

But what of the death the Mazzeru had seen the next night? In the second dream hunt, the Mazzeru told of being in an unknown place, a forest of metal and stone he had never before seen, where he dreamt of spearing a stag. The animal was drinking at an unfamiliar stream along a flat path made of solid stone. When the Mazzeru turned the stag to see, the crushed face of a strange man appeared. The man was someone he didn't know; had never seen before. It was a mystery to the dream hunter. What could it possibly mean? Aldo couldn't spare the mystery man his grief. He only had enough room in his heart to mourn Raina. The unknown man would be mourned by his clan. The Mazzeru's dream nagged at Aldo. He didn't know why it had anything to do with him, but he felt somehow it did. Maybe it was his way to stop the pain of thinking about Raina?

He came back to the present with a start. The elders were looking at him. It was time for his part of the ceremony—time for him to perform the rites for Raina and his child—time to help their spirits move to the otherworld. Dia had claimed them. Now they were hers forever.

He moved toward the pyre to begin the chant in the old tongue.

It comforted him to remember the sounds and combinations of the ancient prayers. The fire, the smells of burning wood, lavender, immortelle, and asphodel evoked so many memories: sitting together with Raina, the clan, around so many fires, so many years. Then the acrid, cloying smell of seared flesh crept up his nostrils to remind him why he was there. The words of the ancient chant rolled off his tongue; his mind wandered and he thought, if I remember, I'll ask the Mazzeru later what the dream of the unknown man meant.

Aldo turned and in his chant howled his pain to the gods of the sky, of the air, and the woods, wherever the tricksters might be. It was over. His peace was gone and the clan finished.

It wasn't fair. After surviving for millennia to have it all end like this, a dead woman and child, three elders, and a worn out and despairing man.

The fire out, the night vigil over, Aldo turned and walked the rugged track back to the casteddu, all that remained of the village the clan had called home since Neolithic times. He climbed over the rough hewn rocks shaped into steps, and looked out across the mountain range down to the sea. Inhaling the rich scent of the maquis, the musty, sweet immortelle that gave his home, the mountains of Corsica, its own special fragrance, he wiped his hands on his worn out blue jeans and climbed the last boulder protecting the casteddu from the world below.

The hum of cars on the motorway below was more than he needed as evidence of what the island was becoming, a tourist attraction for the indolent rich of Europe. The azure beaches filled in summers with bikini clad swimmers. The clan fishing grounds were now the home of windsurfers and hang gliders.

Perhaps it was time. Perhaps the clan had run its course.
Perhaps he had too

Chapter 2
A Year Later, Connecticut

"My life is a mess!" Lenya confided to her twin sister, Lotte. As if Lotte didn't already know.

Lenya must answer the phone whenever Lotte called. If she didn't, her sister got into her car and made the hour and a half drive from New York City to Lenya's home in Trumbull, Connecticut "to make sure Lenya was all right."

Lotte was annoyed, "Ellie calls me daily for the first draft of the book. She says the publisher will sue you if you don't turn it in within the next three months. Now she calls *me*...since you don't answer the phone anymore. Thank you very much, sis!"

Lenya shook her head for at least the ten thousandth time this month. Since the death of her husband, Andre, the year before, she was stopped in life.

She took a moment to look at herself. *Ugh,* her tee-shirt was stained and she was wearing ratty ripped jeans. It seemed every day she lifted the same pair off the floor and shrugged into them. She bent down and sniffed. They really do need to be washed. There was a smell redolent of old clothes piled in musty thrift shops. Maybe worse, maybe girls' gym lockers. She wrinkled her nose in disgust. She knew this hadn't been her style, but now it seemed to be.

Lotte's exasperation mounted. "Sis, please get the hell over it! Move on and finish writing the friggin' book. I'm your sister and I love you. But I am *not* an intermediary between you and your agent."

Lenya heard a sucking, exhaling sound. Oh my god, is she lighting up a cigarette? Her twin must be really angry. She'd given up smoking months before.

Lotte continued, "Ellie loves you, but there's only so much she can do. Agents are having a tough time these days. New media is socking the hell out of print."

"I know, I know. She's the greatest, but she has to stall them a little bit more." Lenya looked at the frayed athletic clogs she wore, now a dusty gray never to see white again. She crossed her ankles and moved her feet back out of sight. She knew Andre would be horrified, but then, he wasn't around to chide her.

Maybe she should go to a shrink? Nothing was important to her since his accident. She got up in the morning to feed her tri-color Jack Russell terrier, Tom, and let him out. She sat mindlessly in front of the computer playing solitaire and, once in a while, ordered something online she didn't need or wouldn't wear. She often didn't even bother to open the boxes, only piled them in a corner. The television blared and she obediently stared at it with no idea what she was watching. Life went on. Lenya had stopped participating. The only thing she maintained was her daily Tai Chi. For an hour or more she lost herself in the movements that helped her block out the world.

Lotte's voice continued. "Ellie told me in confidence, if they don't get a draft shortly they're going to turn the matter over to legal. Lenya, they *will* sue you to get the advance back. Do you have it?"

Lenya laughed, "Hell no. What do you think I've been living on for the last year?"

Tears started to well up again. "Lotte, I don't give a fuck about the book, the advance, the money or Ellie!" As she slammed the phone down she didn't give a fuck about her sister either. *No one knows or cares how I feel.*

As she reached across the kitchen counter to the ever present box of tissues, she flashed back to the day she opened the door to find a tall, broad man on the step.

"I'm Detective O'Brien from the town police. Can I come in? Please?" He proffered his badge and she let him enter. There were home robberies in the area recently and she assumed he wanted to advise her to be vigilant; make sure her home was locked and alarm on.

"Mrs. Lecroix, please sit down," He reached over and put his hand on her wrist. "... girl and her car went through a guard rail... landed on Mr. Lecroix. I'm very sorry for your loss...to be bringing you this news m'am." He looked sorry. His eyes seemed sad.

"... Mr. Lecroix died instantly, crushed on impact. The girl... texting... banged up. I'm very sorry for your loss, Mrs. Lecroix." Hadn't he said that already?

Lenya crumpled into the chair. His hand gripped her wrist tighter to steady her.

"Are you all right? Is there someone I can call for you? ...family?"

Lenya felt as if he had punched her in the stomach. Her head was light, she thought she was going to be sick. An unfamiliar voice was ululating and she looked around for it, dazed, until she understood those sounds were hers. Wailing, she started to topple and the officer reached out for her.

Lenya had looked around the familiar room as the man held her, sobbing in his arms. He patted her back like he had done it many times before.

She became conscious of a lingering smell from the cigarettes Andre loved so much. The French cologne he liked wafted through the room. I'll never smell his cigarettes or cologne again. He's gone. Forever. How can he be gone if I can still smell him?

And the fucking little bitch who killed him walked away. Life is so stupid it's almost comical, Lenya thought, a bad joke the gods decided to play.

A year ago. She knew it was time to move on, but she couldn't. She hadn't. Lenya caught herself in the same obsessive memories roiling around in her head. She was the one dead, both in life and in work, an effort to remember to breathe.

She tried to get up a little anger to kill the sadness, push the depression away. Sometimes it worked. Not then.

Lotte knew her too well. The phone slamming led to darker days and she wasn't going to let Lenya go there. The phone rang again. Lenya knew Lotte was calling her back. There was no point in refusing to answer. Her sister would keep on calling until Lenya picked up, or she'd be banging on the door.

Lotte's voice was insistent and Lenya heard her impatience. "Listen, why don't you take a trip somewhere, get a change of scenery and change of heart. Gotta go, love ya', bye." Listening to the void from the phone as Lotte hung up, Lenya knew no one understood her inability to move on, get over it, get back to life.

She looked at her fingernails. Ragged. When was her last manicure? In the past she had standing appointments. She ripped at a cuticle before going to sit at her computer to play her interminable solitaire.

Instead, she clicked on the Expedia Travel site. She had no interest in going to Cancun or the Caribbean. Paris wasn't an option, there were too many memories on every street corner, no way she was going to visit Andre's family. She scrolled through tour packages to the Orient, South America, Alaska. Maybe a cruise? There seemed to be a lot of good deals. Then she visualized couples cruising together and the thought of sitting by herself at a table with paired up strangers was inconceivable.

She'd almost clicked off when a pop-up caught her eye.

"Visit Mystical Corsica.
Fly to Nice and cruise to the magical Island of Corsica.
Five nights in Ajaccio, Five nights in Calvi,
Includes:
Land Tours,
Snorkeling on stunning beaches
Gourmet Mediterranean dinners at Calvi and Ajaccio
Book now for last minute 35% Discount."

She thought of the famous Corsican Brothers, an image of bandits came to mind. Wasn't Napoleon a Corsican? It must be a wild place.

In a fog, Lenya found herself dialing the number in the advertisement. After all, she owed nothing to anyone except herself and Tom, and he always traveled with her.

He was sitting at her feet looking up at her with a quizzical doggy expression. The brown and black symmetrical markings made his face look like he was worried with furrowed eyebrows. His head cocked to one side as if waiting for her to say something. Lenya bent down to scratch him under the ears, "What do you say, buddy, can you stand one more adventure?" His tongue lolled out of his mouth in expectation. He was always ready to go, even though he was slowing down a bit at twelve.

There was a flight leaving in four days and the travel agent was overly cheerful, "If you book now, you'll have the last seat. Imagine ! You get a thirty-five percent discount. It's awesome, I wish could take the time off, I'd do it myself." She chirped on as Lenya recited her credit card number and security code. She booked a round trip for Tom to fly in his travel case at her feet.

"Oh, he'll love the French." The agent continued, "They let dogs into all the hotels and restaurants." Lenya didn't mention her husband was French and they visited his family in Paris several times a year. Tom was an old hand at French canine customs and cuisine.

As she hung up the phone she looked around. No lingering scent of Andre's cigarettes or cologne...all gone.

For a moment she closed her eyes and imagined him sitting opposite her at the table with a glass of wine in his hand. "There you go again," he'd say, "off on another one of your caprices. Don't you ever think about something before you act?"

"No, I don't!" she thought in their imaginary conversation. "You never cared before. How many times over the years did we go someplace crazy to sell whatever crap you were marketing? We'd pack up and go in an instant. Why should life be different now? Because you left and I have to do it alone?" She felt both anger and tears rise.

He looked at her, "Okay, you win, you're correct. Go ahead, it'll be good for you, stop moping around being depressed. You're even boring me...and by the way, you look like shit. Get out into the world again, find life. Oh, and try some of the wines of Corsica. I hear they're quite all right."

She smiled to herself. She could hear and see him so clearly in her head it was hard to believe he was dead. Typical Frenchman, he'd go anyplace if the wine was good. And she did look like shit.

This time she called Lotte. "Can you imagine? I'll be in Corsica... maybe even find a bandit." They laughed together. She realized it was her first laugh in a long time.

"I love you, but you need to pull yourself together before you leave. You're a total mess." Lenya felt a pang.. Her sister seldom hurt her.

Ten minutes later, Lotte called back. "As a going away present, I'm treating us to lunch and a day at the Red Door. Tomorrow. Get into the city by ten AM. I've already booked you with Raymond who does my hair and he's going to give you the works. You're having a mani, pedi, style, weave and facial. Afterwards, we're off to Bloomingdales for a new travel wardrobe. How do you expect to catch any fish, sorry, I mean bandits, if you don't bait the damn hook?"

Lenya looked at herself in the hall mirror after she hung up. Lotte was right. They were both about five feet seven, trim and shapely with dark blonde hair and blue-gray eyes. Both had been well coiffed and manicured as befitted the Upper East Side New York City women they were brought up to be. The similarity ended there. Their styles were different and suited to their personalities, not their professions. Each elegant in her own way. Lotte, the determined businesswoman, fashionable in the latest mode, often even ahead of the game. Flirtatious and sexy with wardrobe and grooming to enhance her appeal, Lotte made the most of what she had. Long, wavy hair, superbly cut with woven honey and gold highlights, framed her face and fell into her eyes. It was her signature ploy. Lenya always teased her about the way she constantly tossed it back off her face when she was on the prowl. To complete the picture of the urban seductress, Lotte liked low cut blouses, tight skirts and very high heels.

Lenya, the romance novel writer and creative twin, was conservative. Hair precision cut and short, clothes classic and running to well cut suits or blazers, tailored monogrammed blouses and Italian mid-heel shoes especially made for women on the go, comfortable, elegant, and not too stylish.

When either one of them walked into a room, their presence was felt. But now Lenya looked at herself and admitted, yeah, I'm a presence all right, I'm the presence of a bag-lady.

The Red Door was a success. Even Lenya confessed her sister was right as she caught her reflection when she arrived back home. Her hair was in its usual short cap style, the blonde weave a miracle of highlights. She waved neat cuticles and bright red nails in front of her face as she told Tom. "Well buddy, looks like you've got a hottie as a date for a change.'

The days flew by. She packed flash drives with her unfinished manuscript, her laptop, and one medium size check-through suitcase. It wasn't going to be a long trip, only two weeks, she thought as she packed her new purchases of drip dry underwear, tee-shirts, a dressy blouse, one sweater and a blazer, jeans, comfy shoes, nightgown and toiletries. More comfort than style to trek around a wild island.

Time to leave. Her handbag, Tom's travel case and an umbrella rested in the hallway next to her suitcase. E-ticket in hand, she waited for the taxi to take them to the airport when she finally awoke from her fugue state.

What on earth have I done and why am I leaving?

The horn honked and she walked down the driveway to the taxi, leaving her past behind her. Tom ran ahead, bouncing in anticipation of another adventure.

The scent of lilacs followed them out to the waiting car. She had a fleeting memory of Andre buying her a bouquet in Paris. She had sniffed them all during lunch in the square in front of Saint Chappell. He was right, she needed to taste something different, if only the wines of Corsica.

A year passed since Aldo placed the cleaned bones of his wife and child in the clan necropolis and now he put the remains of the last elder inside. The stones making the dolmen were large and rectangular, hewn millennia ago; three uprights on three sides, the largest rectangle over the top. The fourth side closed with smaller boulders easily removed to add new bones. The remaining elders would sleep for eternity next to his family and the rest of the clan.

When he was a child, the clan numbered well over a hundred souls, his father recalled several hundred people in the casteddu when he was a boy.

Aldo himself learned to hunt in parties of twenty or more men, healthy, in their prime, enjoying the chase of the hunt. Some were beaters, others hunters; all skilled and working as a team. As a young boy, Aldo sat with the women, all ages together from adolescents to elders, skinning and dressing the catch of the hunt as they giggled and poked each other, gossiping, telling stories of their love life and laughing. It was a fond memory. The girls liked his red hair and pushed and shoved each other for the chance to show him how to braid it to keep it out of his eyes. And to please Dia.

Where have they all gone now, those giggling women, those girls who knew how to make such intricate braids? Aldo placed the remains in the ossuary, folded in the positions they were before birth. He gave the respect they deserved. Anything less was an offense to Dia. Difficult as it was, he crawled into the small dark space to honor his dead, even though his own bones ached with the effort.

So far, strangers, archeologists, recent despoilers, had not found this dolmen, the only depredations were from long ago invaders looking for jewelry or anything worth looting. Burial places were the first stop for pirates, the loved ones were often honored with gifts to pay their way into the next world. Aldo had left a few pieces of jewelry next to Raina for her journey, simple things he carved from bones or made from pretty shells, things she had worn with pride.

The structure was crammed with bones. He could not have built another dolmen to house a larger clan. Marveling how his people muscled the huge rocks into place, managing the task of fashioning and moving such boulders, he wondered how it was accomplished. Each stone must weigh hundreds, maybe thousands of pounds, crafted to fit together and then pulled and pushed into position to build a place to honor the dead. He thought it must have been a very large clan with time to spare from simple survival to create such a building. The clan, as he knew it, had never been big enough to create such a monument.

He thought again of the giggling women. Some had died, other left, wanting their children to be educated and trained in the ways of the present world. Others went to find someone in the outside world to marry and have a family with. There were too few choices for them if they stayed. So each year the clan shrank.

His work finished, he sat on one of the rounded stones and looked out over the valley below. The tops of the far mountains were white with a shawl of mist. Inadvertently he shivered, thinking of more cold, empty nights to come.

Aldo had loved Raina. They grew up together, played like brother and sister since they were toddlers. She was a beloved partner, his wife, his responsibility, his duty to protect her always.

On reflection, he admitted he had felt something missing; as if there was more for him, another mate, one he might share the wild passion he imagined, a special power for Dia.

Now he was free to find her, this mate he imagined. He dreamt of soft breasts pressed against his back as she spooned against the length of him, arms weaving a cloak of security and love as his soul filled with the warmth of his devotion for her. Imagining her breath on his neck, her fingers caressing his face as she walked by him, the touch of her hand, he dreamt about her, this woman, his woman. He could feel her in his mind, soft to the touch but strong, capable, a willing partner in their lives together, the scent of her, the salt of her on his tongue, his face engulfed in the tantalizing perfume of her, a special essence all her own.

How could he find this woman he dreamt of, their life of pleasures shared, breathing as one, the gentle undulation of her breasts as he gazed at her sleeping beside him at night?

Who was she, this woman who eluded him? His other half. He yearned to complete her as she would complete him in all things, not only the pleasures of the body, but the bliss of sharing a spring morning, a quiet evening watching the sun drop over the horizon as it turned the mountains purple with afterglow. The enjoyment of a cooling breeze on a warm day. Laughter together as a puppy tumbled across the grass. And maybe, if they were lucky, they would share the joy of a child in both their images. A gift from Dia.

Almost two years passed since Aldo performed the *hieros gamos*, the holy marriage of goddess and consort. He once filled with pride to think about his skill, his restraint, his knowledge of how to give pleasure to his woman and through her, Dia. He hadn't forgotten how.

Aldo shook himself. It was too long since he had thought about these things. He wasn't even sure he could perform. He looked down at his crotch. Everything was there, but quiet. Soft. Too quiet. Much too soft. He sighed. So much for all his knowledge. He hungered for his special woman, thought again of her warm, soft body as they fell asleep together. The thought made him smile, but only for a second. Did something below stir a little?

His options were limited and he knew it. For centuries men and women chose their mates from within the clan. There were old legends about other clans on the island, but those stories were from the distant past.

Aldo turned and retraced the path to the casteddu. He looked out across the mother mountains to the sea. They were old but Dia was older, she, the mother of all.

The hum of cars on the motorway below reminded him the island was being conquered once again. Tourists. Aldo saw them fill beaches, race along the roads in a rush to get somewhere. What could be so important? Did they even see the beauty of the island? Care?

He inhaled the rich scent of maquis, the musty sweet immortelle. It smelled the same as always, but it made him sad even though he was resigned. Dia's will.

The elders understood it was better to marry outside the clan to keep the next generations from weakening. Interbreeding often resulted in children not right either in appearance or in the head. When such babies arrived, they were left in the woods for Dia to decide what to do. If they lived through the night, they were brought back to the clan, if not, well, they were with Dia.

There had been no contact with other clans during Aldo's lifetime. His father told him stories about clans living on the other side of the island, but father never saw them. The stories might be centuries old. Maybe he could explore and see if they existed? A last resort. Aldo was familiar with his own territory and wasn't comfortable going very far from it. He wasn't exactly frightened of going to new places, but fearful of being seen by people, by outsiders. He would speak of this to his friend Sirio, the next time they were together.

The clan always lived in the casteddu. Legends passed down by word of mouth from prehistoric times told the story of the clan settling on their mountain.

After many years, another group of people arrived, more families, a friendly people crossing the sea to seek safety. They liked the clans site on the top of a mountain and built their castle, or casteddu, as a walled fortress nearby. Both groups depended on the other for survival, eventually becoming one people, the walls extended to incorporate the clan. For protection, they remained hidden from the rest of the island.

Now the casteddu, Aldo's home, was mostly a pile of rocks. The way up the mountain was steep and treacherous. No road, access only by a narrow track even donkeys couldn't climb.

Over the centuries, while its inaccessibility protected the clan from invaders, it also kept them away from the changing influences on the rest of the island.

These days no one came along other than a few from the closer villagers, people from old families who followed the old ways, petitioning the Maître for healing or counsel, for curses or the evil eye to be lifted. There were fewer with each passing year. Aldo could hardly remember when the last villager came for his blessing.

Hikers passed far from the casteddu. They were frequent in the mountains closer to the sea, especially in warmer months. Climbing with their walking sticks, they exclaimed in many languages over the beauty of sea and its clarity.

Once in a while a hiker was foolhardy enough to make their way up the rough track winding its way up the clan's mountain. On those rare occasions, Aldo would show himself and glare. Few were brave enough to venture closer, or come back.

Some tales were told about a strange man in the mountains, but few paid attention and the old families kept his secret.

Mostly tourists of any kind annoyed him; especially those who dropped their garbage and papers to mar the beauty of the nature Dia provided.

One group in particular tossed their smoking sticks to the ground and as they left, he ran over and stomped on the butts before fire caught in the dry grasses.

This behavior made him so mad he wanted to hunt them down and kill them with the sharp knives he always carried. It was not right for people to come and treat his home, Dia's gifts, with such disrespect.

Every time he thought about it, he was sorry he didn't kill those disrespectful people. He knew no one would ever find the bodies in the dense wilderness where they were hiking. If by chance they were found, the corpses would have been destroyed by the elements and animals.

Whenever he saw a fire in the mountains, he wondered if it was started by those same disrespectful people. Then he felt a moment of guilt, perhaps he could have prevented the fire if he had killed them. Murder was not the way of the clan so he forgot about it, or tried to.

Other outsiders came to live, like those in the villages he foraged through at night. Some knew of the clan and sometimes even left things out for him, like the dress for Raina, but they seldom ventured up the treacherous trail to the casteddu.

Sirio let him know the local people told many stories about a hidden clan—people who built the menhirs, the guardians of the island.

The last worshippers of the goddess. They laughed together about this, both men knew the stories were about Aldo's family.

If Aldo came in contact with older villagers, they treated him kindly and with great respect. They knew Aldo was le Maître, consort of the goddess.

A few made the sign of the cross when he passed by, but they meant him no harm. Very few made the sign of the horns, protection as if he was a *strega* or witch. They understood he was a Signadori, or a healer, one who could remove the evil eye or a curse cast by a *strega*. Aldo's way was the way of light, of life, not that of death like the Mazzeri or evil like the *strega*.

He and Sirio attended the local markets from time to time. It was his main contact with the villagers these days. They would set up a small stand with some of Sirio's wines, and their charcuterie— artisanal hams and sausages made from wild boars that Aldo often hunted.

Locals accepted him as part of Corsica, part of its ancient heritage.

Aldo's fear of strangers extended mainly to tourists. He had several very unpleasant encounters with angry, skinny women in strange clothes with stranger faces when he was younger.

They shrieked when they saw him, didn't understand his rough clothing or long hair. He meant them no harm, just was foraging in their discards and saw some brightly colored toys he liked. He had no intention of frightening anyone and tried to run away but the lesson he learned was when the women screamed in needless fear, their men folk struck first and thought about asking questions later.

As he grew older, he kept to the shadows and out of their way.

He knew they were summer people in the holiday villages or the big houses on the coast overlooking the sea. They had no idea about the deserted casteddu nor did they have any respect for the old ways. No, he learned to keep well away from them.

Often over the years, the clan took in runaways—people who couldn't stay in their villages because of vendettas, prejudice or other reasons. The clan was forgiving. It was a rule of Dia to succor those in need of help.

Even the older villagers weren't always gentle in their treatment of ones who broke the unspoken rules. The island was small.

Sometimes people needed a place to hide.

Chapter 3
Aldo & Sirio

Sirio was Aldo's best friend. Sirio might be old enough to be Aldo's father, but their relationship was more like brothers, good friends. True, Sirio was a man born of outsiders, but he had spent his childhood within the walls of the casteddu, taken in by the clan.

Together, the men chatted companionably in Corsican. They both spoke French and Italian, but conversations seemed more comfortable in the language of their childhood.

Aldo also knew the ancient language of the clan, but it was secret and not shared with outsiders, even those like Sirio.

Sirio's mother, Adriana, was one of many Corsicans who found refuge within the clan. His father was an American from the base on Corsica established during World War II.

As was their habit, the men sat outside one of the many deserted shepherd's huts dotting the mountains and shared a bottle of good red wine and rest after a day hunting wild boar.

The easy familiarity of their evenings was a mainstay of their enjoyment. When a chunk of boar sizzled over a makeshift fire, it was time for Sirio to tell stories. The one about his American father was Aldo's favorite.

Sirio would lean back against a convenient tree and take a sip of wine before he began. "First the Italians came, then the Germans were crawling all over the island, turning Corsicans into slaves to build their filthy bunkers. In the villages people met in secret with the Americans to plan attacks and exchange information." He stopped for a moment to tamp more tobacco into his pipe and re-light it.

"One evening, some of the clan were hunting in the high mountain range and saw a plane go down in smoke. They knew it was American, a P-38.

"They could tell by the big silhouette and deafening roar of the engine. They ran to get to the wreckage before the Nazis."

Sirio stopped and turned to Aldo, "If it had been a fucking Bosch Messerschmit or Stuka, they would have stood around and applauded as the bastards fried."

They both always laughed at this part. Sirio continued, "instead, they pulled the surviving American flyer out of the wreckage and took him away to hide and care for his injuries."

Aldo knew the young American aviator was Sirio's father, and he was taken to the clan until his wounds healed enough to get back to his unit.

The haunch of pig cooking over the fire was ready to eat; Sirio stopped his story while the men ate the succulent meat seasoned with garlic, wild onion and a small bunch of savory herbs—rosemary, thyme and oregano—Aldo had found nearby.

The bottle of wine was almost gone by the time dinner was finished and the men watched the sun set over the distant ocean. When the mist began to gather around the crest of the far range, a breeze picked up from the west.

As stars grew visible in the darkening sky, Sirio pulled a bottle of sweet orange wine from his pack. He pointed it at Aldo. "I think we need some dessert with the rest of the story. What do you say to some of this?"

Aldo grinned his assent. Sirio prised the cork out of the bottle with his Swiss Army knife and handed the younger man some of the potent mellow brew in a small paper cup as he continued with his story.

Sirio and his mother, Adriana, eventually inherited her family farm and turned it into a successful vineyard. During her lifetime, Adriana never forgot the kindness of the clan when she had become pregnant by the young aviator.

Her father threw her out and her village was scandalized, but the clan took her in.

Aldo grew up knowing Sirio when he came often with his mother to visit their old friends. The difference in their ages didn't seem to matter.

Sirio never married any of the succession of beautiful women he courted, nor had he any children, at least who he spoke of. He took to the young Aldo as if he were a beloved nephew.

When Sirio and Adriana brought the clan simple necessities they might need—work clothes, warm blankets and jackets, knives, farm implements, flour, salt, fabric, pins, needles and thread, he always made sure to spend time with Aldo as the boy grew to manhood.

Sirio understood what it was like to grow up in the clan, isolated, unschooled, stuck in a time before memory. He tried to bring Aldo into the present as much as possible with magazines and newspapers; he taught the boy to read, even to speak a few words in English.

He brought photography books to acquaint him with the world outside the casteddu.

Sirio feared someday, with the clan dwindling as it was, Aldo would have to face the world of the present alone.

In later years, Sirio brought piglets for Aldo to raise and one time even a litter of puppies the clan trained to hunt when they grew up. The dogs gave several generations of excellent hunting dogs, but they died out like the clan when there were no other dogs to breed with.

The piglets roamed free around the casteddu eating wild chestnuts and became a source of both food and income when they bred with the local *sanglier*.

Aldo and Sirio made sausages and dried hams with their ancient recipes and sold them at the local open air markets. The two men thought of themselves as more than friends, as family.

Once, Sirio even brought a radio that didn't need batteries but was charged by turning a lever. Aldo listened to what was going on in the outside world, but mostly it frightened him with words and ideas he didn't understand.

He liked the music, and sometimes played it well into the night, searching for songs appealing to him, even finding local broadcasts of polyphonic concerts.

Now, more than a year since Raina died, the subject of their conversations had changed.

Aldo had something on his mind this night. He wanted to discuss it with Sirio, but had held his tongue, afraid his friend might not understand.

He knew the older man never married, perhaps he might not agree with Aldo, but there was no one else to speak with since all the elders died.

He leaned towards Sirio and began to open his heart. "I've been dreaming of a woman, special. A women who completes my soul. One who, knowing I am last of the clan, will make a family to carry on my line."

Then Aldo sighed and looked into the dying embers of their fire before continuing. "I'm certain such a woman has to exist somewhere. I've prayed to Dia for her. But no one has come. Now I must find her."

Sirio shook his head. It was strange to him when his friend, large, strong, bearded and looking like what he was, a throwback to a time before memory, spoke like a romantic. He understood it was Aldo's training in the ancient secrets, woman as goddess, holder of power, beloved as well as honored.

Wrapping his mind around the concept of his friend finding a twenty-first century woman who'd live in a stone hovel on top of a mountain in a deserted Neolithic village did not come easy. But Sirio knew enough to keep his peace. He had compassion.

Aldo had been through enough pain, and any hope keeping him going after all his suffering was a good thing. Sirio worked hard to generate positive suggestions.

"My friend, I think you have to spend more time in the villages, maybe think about finding a job. You could always work with me at the winery on a regular basis, rather than only doing carpentry and helping out at the harvest."

Many people came to visit the winery in the warm months. Maybe he might meet someone.

Who knows, Sirio thought, stranger things have happened. Also, Sirio had no other family and he enjoyed the younger man's company. He liked to listen to Aldo tell the old legends of the island; stories he learned as a child from the elders.

Aldo was always uncomfortable when the subject of leaving the casteddu came up. "You know I can't leave, other people might know about the clan." It was a secret the clan guarded beyond memory—a hard culture to leave behind, even if Aldo was now the only clan member.

Sirio understood Aldo's reluctance and his difficulty in overcoming it. The clan had made a decision to stay out of the "world" centuries ago when the island was rife with bloodshed, wars, banditry, violent religious conversion, the Inquisition, and blood feuding.

As soon as the Catholic Church determined to stamp out paganism with constant threats of death to non-believers, the clan knew they had to stay out of sight.

When the Inquisition came to Corsica, all those who believed in the old ways went into hiding. The villagers who still were believers professed in public their adherence to Catholicism. The fear of being branded with the taint of witchcraft, even though it was a far cry from their ancient beliefs in Dia, only re-enforced the need for the clan to stay hidden.

Once the choice was made, each new generation became more xenophobic than the one before. Aldo was no exception.

Sirio was sure, without going out into the world, there was no way to find the life Aldo dreamed of.

"Yes, I understand the need for secrecy. But, my friend, we're in a different age, a new time. Perhaps Dia wants you to stop hiding. Perhaps it's time to come out into the open."

He knew Aldo was stubborn like the rest of the clan before him, but since he was totally alone, Sirio felt he had to at least try to make him understand.

Sirio also had some of Aldo's fears as well as a few of his own. This was a big problem, what can happen to a man who doesn't exist according to the paranoid government of the present era?

How could anyone prove Aldo and his forbearers had been on the island long before any of the arrogant bureaucrats who now made the rules?

Sirio looked at the ocean spread out below them. Then he turned and thought about the deserted casteddu and the ruins of clustered houses now only piles of rubble, large stones piled together, no roofs, nothing to show they'd once been inhabited.

Only the stone dwelling Aldo lived in had a roof, a door, the look of habitation.

He thought for a moment about those French bureaucrats. How would Aldo ever be able to get papers, claim his family property, show his existence? He scratched his head.

Maybe it wasn't such a good idea after all. Would there be back taxes to pay on the property?

Aldo had his home, the skill of his hands and his honorific as Maître. Money was never important to him, nor did he really understand it.

What would happen if he couldn't pay? Would they make him move? Take over his beloved home?

Some sleazy developer could pay back taxes and claim all the clan property, valuable now in a world of summer houses and rich people avid to live on top of a mountain with the ocean spread below.

So far it had been saved by its inaccessibility, the sheerness of the rock face it was perched on, the rocks had protected it from marauders for millennia.

Now the marauders were different, nouveau rich Euro-trash with more money than brains, Arabic oil moguls, Russian mafia, high-tech billionaires, Hollywood superstars, all who might not care about the cost of building a way to get up there.

With horror, Sirio imagined a funicular groaning up to the summit. He had to admit the view was probably one of the most spectacular on the island.

Sirio sensed and sympathized with the younger man's unease. He also had no idea what might happen in cases like this.

Were there even other cases like this? Could Aldo fight losing his land, prove he and the clan had been there for eons?

This was a problem Sirio had to consider. For the moment he put on a smile to comfort his friend.

Maybe Aldo was right. Better to stay in hiding.

Chapter 4
Vive La France

Lenya's heart sank when she saw the crowd of people pushing their way onto the plane. Filled to capacity she was told at check-in. And I've got one of those damned middle seats she thought. The booking agent reserved an aisle seat but once at the gate, the overly cheerful agent notified all passengers the airline changed equipment. Lenya's seat number was now one seat off the aisle in the center section. Resigned after no amount of pleading had any effect, she crammed her carry-on in the already jammed overhead bin.

Between her and her seat was a large man mopping his florid sweating face. She cringed in distaste as she crawled over the immovable pile of lard to squeeze into her seat. He looked angry. So was Lenya. She gave him a meaningful look as she pushed against his large shoulders, beefy thighs and upper arms, all spilling over onto her. It was almost impossible to wedge herself into the small space, not even remotely possible to sit with any degree of comfort. *Crap, I knew this trip was a lousy idea. This may end up being the worst eight hours of my life.*

It took all her willpower not to jump into the aisle, grab her valise and flee the plane before it took off…anything to avoid unwanted contact with the moist mountainous man. She bent over and placed Tom in his travel case under the seat in front of her. There was barely room for her feet to fit next to him. *I swear they make the seats smaller every year…I know they do!* Tom moved around a bit in his pet carrier as he made himself comfortable for the long trip. *At least you always have the same amount of space, buddy. Maybe I should travel in a case too.*

One of the air hostesses came towards Lenya as she tried to wedge herself back into her seat.

Mrs. Lecroix?" the hostess asked.

Lenya nodded assent.

"Please come with me. I'll bring your carry-on if you let me know which one is yours." Lenya tilted her head as she looked at the attendant.

"Follow me. I'll explain." She took Lenya's bag from the overhead and walked toward the front of the plane. Lenya dragged Tom in his carrier out from under the seat in front of her and crawled back over the man, but this time was to freedom as she followed the woman.

"Here you are, a bit more comfortable, don't you think?" The hostess pointed to an aisle seat in business class. "There was a request from management to upgrade you. We weren't sure we'd have space but we had a last minute cancellation."

Sometimes it's good when your sister handles ad campaigns for airlines, Lenya thought as she relaxed back into the much wider and more comfortable seat. Another air hostess arrived with a tray filled with small plastic glasses, "Champagne, orange juice or water?" Now this is the way to travel, and Lenya reached out for the champagne. Tom looked up at her through the mesh at the end of his case. Even he had more breathing room and looked happier.

Lenya slept most of the way across the Atlantic, waking only for meals. It was early morning in Paris when she arrived at Orly. After she took Tom outside for his morning Parisian walk and pee, she had coffee and a croissant in the crowded airport bar while waiting for her flight to Nice to be announced. The tour included a night at a hotel in Nice before the short voyage on Corsican Ferries to Ajaccio the next morning.

The flight from Paris was short and uneventful, but the landing was abrupt when the pilot banged the plane onto the tarmac and rammed on the brakes to avoid the rocky breakwater holding back the Mediterranean at the end of the short runway. Thank you Air France! She knew the landing in Nice was always problematic, but she didn't remember such a bump, or maybe it was more like a smash. By the time she disembarked in Nice she wasn't looking forward to another airplane ride and was grateful the next part of her trip was by ferry.

The bus ride with the tour group to the Negresco was thankfully short. The hotel always reminded Lenya of an ancient courtesan who has seen better days. She might be aging on the inside, but she's decked out in satin, velvet and lace and manages to get it together—if you don't look too closely.

When she arrived, she was pleased to see the hotel had been renovated from top to bottom in gracious Art Deco and Victorian styles, lots of dark wood, marble and lush velvet. Andre would have been happy, she thought. The hotel had been one of his favorites. He was disappointed when they were last there; it looked a bit down at the heels with shabby lobby furnishings and worn carpets. It had smelled like damp decay, old dust and decades of beach sweat and sun tan oil. Now the old girl was shined up with a good face lift and a new wardrobe. The lobby smelled good from the ornate and colorful bouquets of roses, tulips, lilies and greens gracing every appropriate surface. If you can't have exotic bouquets in Nice, than where can you? Delicious.

The hotel faced the *Promenade des Anglais* and the Mediterranean for more than a century, one of the most famous of the "wedding cake hotels" of the Victorian Era. Lenya's room had a four-poster queen bed, well kept Art Deco furniture and everything was shiny and spotless. She gratefully took in the renovated bathroom as she slipped into the large modern shower. The bed was firm, the pillows plump and the sheets were smooth and cool she noted as she lay down for a nap. A wake-up call sounded at three PM giving her and Tom plenty of time for a walk around the city.

Whenever she visited Nice she made it a point to stroll the walking street, wandering into shops to admire the latest French fashions. The prices were no longer manageable for most Americans since the conversion to the Euro, but she found a pair of shoes on sale she couldn't live without and the price was surprisingly reasonable. Tom got a new collar and leash, all the better to impress any French Poodles he might meet.

The next morning, after coffee and croissant, *I've missed these edible pieces of heaven* she blessed the French as she devoured them, the bus took them to the ferry for the trip to Ajaccio, the first stop on Corsica.

She stood at the railing as the ferry pulled out of the harbor and rounded the promontory into the *Baie des Anges*. She looked back on the Negresco proudly shining in the morning sunlight, all its gingerbread decorations sparkling like a many faceted diamond. She watched the constant parade of joggers, runners, dog walkers and sun-sitters on the *Promenade des Anglais* diminish as the ferry headed off towards the island. The Mediterranean sun felt good on her face and she didn't miss for a second the hat her dermatologist insisted she always wear. Screw it, she thought, the body needs some Vitamin D according to the latest reports.

The minute Lenya set foot in Ajaccio she heard the voice calling to her. A sweet, soft voice, whispering in the wind—entreating her to live, to breathe. Running her fingers through her short hair, she looked around. There was no one standing near her.

She looked up at the old city beyond the harbor and the more modern buildings up the hills behind. It might be another interesting old Mediterranean port, but it felt like she and this place had forgotten memories, unfinished stories together. Try as she could, she was unable to brush the feelings away, they tugged at her viscera.

It was her first time on the island, where did these emotions come from? Tears started to rise, like the emotion of seeing an old friend again after many years.

Trailing her small bag along behind, she stood on the cement quay and craned her face to the ancient buildings crowding up the hills.

Lenya was quiet for a moment listening; she knew no one was speaking to her....but the voice? She wiped her eyes on her shirt as she heard a susurrus over the wash of the waves against the quay, insistent with its mantra of "Stay, stay Lenya, stay—breathe. Stay. Stay Lenya, stay—live."

Afraid she was hallucinating; she tried to ignore the voice. But she kept hearing it during the first week she toured the Island. She leaned over rock walls to see down the steep cliffs at stops along the coast, marveling with the rest of the tour group at crystal clear waters in coves below. They "oooohed" and "aaaahed" together at the brilliant turquoise sea lapping at secluded white beaches.

She was sure she was the only one who heard a siren's voice above the whisper of the waves calling her name. "Lenya, stay, live, breathe, stay."

It was time to get a grip. Let's face it, if I'm wacko enough to talk to Andre all the time, who's to say I can't hear voices calling me…and I've got to stop talking to myself!

Chapter 5
Calvi

Ajaccio might have been the first city to begin the Corsican seduction of Lenya, but Calvi was the closer. The *Tour de Sel* rising out of the harbor, open air restaurants looking over the water to Lumio on the other side, the Citadel and the old city perched above, all sang to her heart. Calvi sealed the deal. She was in love with Corsica.

As Lenya traveled outside of Calvi, she noticed an odd scent in the air. It was salty, but there was an underlying tang hinting of wild and untamed life, something savage and primal...a little musky. She tried to give it a name, a description. For a writer it was frustrating.

Their tour guide, a tall Englishman with an unruly mop of wiry gray hair and a slight stoop as if he was always imparting a secret, seemed ready to please by answering questions. Standing next to him, she turned to ask, "What is smell in the air? I can identify the salt, but there's something else, something not quite floral or sweet, but green.. herbal...maybe acrid."

He laughed as he replied, "You and Napoleon. You've got a good nose, you have—mustn't be a smoker. You've found the scent of the maquis, the wild plants covering the island. When old Nappy was finally sent to Elba, as he stepped off the ship he's reported to have said 'I can smell my home from here.' And he was referring to the unique fragrance of the maquis on Corsica."

"What's the maquis? I keep seeing term and thought it was a plant."

"Not at all, it's an ecosystem—like a savannah or a swamp. I believe the distinctive scent is from immortelle, the most common plant. You'll recognize its tiny yellow flowers. They use it all over the island to flavor things from honey to liquors to oils."

Lenya stepped back for a moment and looked around as she took a deep breath. Can this be what my new home smells like? She gave herself a mental shake. *Where on earth did come from?*

The guide walked the group around explaining "Calvi is a resort town first and foremost." Lenya moved close to him, not wanting to miss a word.

"Built originally as a fortified city, the citadel lifts skyward from the top of a promontory guarding the harbor entrance. The citadel isn't open to the public anymore...most of it's used as a base for the French Foreign Legion."

He paused to surreptitiously point out two tall and imposing men in spotless uniforms and kepis walking out of a small store. "Now you can say you've seen the French Foreign Legion."

Every head turned to goggle at the handsome Legionnaires. "The old part of the city encompasses parts of the citadel and its rock base." He turned and pointed to the crest, "St. Maria church is home to mass and the city's cultural events." They started up the hill to look at the church and the old city.

Lenya was not so enthralled by the huge blocks of stone that served for streets in the old city. Puffing like a locomotive and grumbling to herself, she bent over to hold her knees and catch her breath before entering the church. *Damn, I thought I was in shape.*

She looked back and caught a glimpse of the steep grade below. The crescent shape of the harbor and beach spread out to her right and directly below was the Tour de Sel, its rotund façade reaching toward the sky and cut off abruptly at its flat top. Maybe I'm not so bad after all. It's a lot farther up than I thought. Her breath was smoothing out after the exertion. Note to self, no climbing on a full stomach again. The large plate of pasta eaten pre-climb lurched about in her stomach.

No matter, she straightened up, huffed a few times and opened the stout carved wooden door to the church. The stained glass windows were lovely; the cobalt blue, brilliant yellow and red variants reflected off the stark white walls and vaulted ceiling. It was a bit odd, she thought, most of the churches she had seen around Europe had colorful religious scenes painted on the ceilings, but the flat white she found comforting in its simplicity.

Lenya relaxed for a moment in one of the straight wooden chairs at the back of the church and began to breathe.

There was familiarity in the scent of ancient stones, burned candles, furniture wax and humanity woven together in the salty fragrance of the sea below. It was the first time she remembered breathing in more than a year, or maybe it was the first time she had been able to breathe without thinking about it, forcing herself to do the unconscious act. She rejoiced in the simple pleasure of taking a time to enjoy the moment, contemplate—not mourn.

Lotte was right, getting away was the correct move, and Corsica had been the perfect choice.

On the way out of the church, she put several Euros in the donation box and read the notices on the board in the small entryway. There was one for a polyphonic concert of local singers. The date was a few weeks off. Polyphony was an ancient art practiced by local men singing intricate harmonies *a capella*. She had heard a few pieces from the Corsican group, 'I Muvrini,' who added instrumental accompaniment to appeal more to the mainstream; but she would have enjoyed hearing the original form. She felt a pang...regret?...to miss the event.

The tour stayed in Calvi for two more days before moving on. She went with them to Bastia, then Aléria and down to Corte. After reading the guide books on her flight across the Atlantic and on the ferry, she was most interested in seeing the early man sites. Archeology was one of her passions, and an idea for a new book was rolling around in her mind. Yes, she wanted most of all to see the Neolithic sites.

At the end of a long hike into the forest, near Alta Rocca, she came to her first menhir. The group grumbled along the rough road, but they grew quiet as they entered a secluded grove at the base of a mountain.

Actually, it was Tom who found it first. He bounded ahead of her and ducked into the underbrush. She went after him, praying for no poison ivy or sumac in the dense hedgerow. Or snakes. Lenya did not approve of snakes. Tom emerged from the brush as the guide pushed aside some overgrown vines to see what he discovered.

An oblong standing rock, about six feet in height was obscured by lichen and brush. The top of the stone had a barely discernible carving which, on close inspection, Lenya recognized as a stylized human face. The features were rudimentary but clearly human. As she stood a bit away from it, the light caught the shadowed indentations of a strap around the figure's neck and a clear image of a sword hanging from it. An ancient warrior. Lenya's mind spun into all the possible reasons for this representation.

The guide came and pointed at the find. "This is a menhir, one of the many artifacts of early man in Corsica. Some archeologists speculate there are more than five thousand such sites on this island, many of them unexplored."

The guide's British accented English droned on as the retired don gave his memorized spiel. He was a pleasant man who obviously enjoyed the tourists he guided around. "There are groups of these stones, often numbering in the hundreds. They are menhirs, the groups are referred to as 'alignments."

"How do you know they're early man? Couldn't they be left over from the Phoenicians or some other peoples who cavorted around the Mediterranean?" Lenya got a remote feeling of pleasure giving him an opening to show his erudition.

"Good question. Archeological societies have done carbon dating on similar artifacts, and they're convinced many of the carvings date from the Stone Age. I, however, think this particular piece is Copper Age. It has a certain refinement pointing to a more cultured and sophisticated society. Also the sword is from a later period than Stone Age."

He winked surreptitiously at Lenya. He knew she cued him in so he'd get a bigger tip at the end of the tour. They'd chatted companionably over a few glasses of wine together the night before. She patiently listened as he complained the tour before were all English, notoriously penurious about tipping, even to their own countrymen.

As the rest of the group left the grove, Lenya moved up face to face with the stone. As Tom sniffed at its base, she placed her hand over the carved features and traced them with her fingers. It was as if all the pieces of her life clicked in her head and shifted into their proper places. She felt a connection to all those hands, the bodies of those who came before her for millennia to put their imprint where her hand and fingers now rested.

At that exact moment, Lenya knew she had found her place, at least for a while. There was no way she'd go home with the tour.

When she arrived back at the hotel, she called her sister Lotte. Their mother had been a "Three Penny Opera" buff and couldn't resist naming her twin girls after Kurt Weil's wife, Lotte Lenya, in homage. *Or who knows, she might have been in love with "Mac the Knife."*

The phone conversation was long, but with Skype and her new laptop, the call was free.

"Lotte, I need your help. I know you might be angry, but I really need this from you."

"Anything you want, baby sister. Ya know I got your back" Lenya was seven and a half minutes younger than Lotte. Lotte being the wiser older sister was a lifelong running joke and she often signed her name as L1 to Lenya's L2.

"I want to stay here in Corsica for a while."

"'Kay. What d'ya think, another month...two? Le'me know and I'll touch base with Ellie."

"No Lotte, longer. I think for at least a year. I don't really know ."

The other end of the phone went silent.

"Hello, hello, are you there?" Lenya knew when her sister was quiet, something was wrong. Disapproval oozed through the silent airwaves. Lotte couldn't get in her car and rush to Connecticut and shake Lenya lose from whatever problem she was having. It had to be driving her sister wild. But this time, there was no problem.

"Please, Lotte, hear me out. I have an idea for a new book, but there's a lot of research I'll have to do. The idea came to me as I've been wandering around this island. I'm in the middle of a proposal to send to Ellie right now...think she'll like the premise." See, no problem.

The tension on the other end subsided a bit. It didn't seem as much like she was talking into a vacuum sucking up her words. Lotte's breathing sounded less forced. Lenya imagined her brow smoothing out as she continued. "Please sister mine, I need you to go to the house and clean out my refrigerator. Make sure there's nothing to draw ants in the cabinets. Turn off everything, water, electric, cable... telephone. Tell them I'm away for an indefinite time on assignment and I'll notify 'em when I return."

Lenya thought for a moment. What've I forgotten? Oh, yeah... "Have the mail forwarded to you until I give you a permanent address. Tell Ellie I'll be in contact with her as soon as I have the proposal finalized." Lenya figured if she rushed it out, it might sound more planned than half-cocked.

"Look Lenya, I'll do anything for you, but are you sure this isn't another wild goose chase? Andre always teased you about being capricious. I don't want you to jeopardize your career." She was quiet for another moment. "...and don't forget about sending in the last manuscript. You do not need a lawsuit!"

"Don't worry. This is a great new direction for me. I'm starting to feel like I'm coming alive again. After Andre died, I was trapped...a fugue state...couldn't move myself. Here, on this island, I feel like there's something alive for me." She snorted a short laugh towards her computer. "Kind'a like Snow White waking up. Who knows, maybe there's a prince out there for me...as well as a story?"

She knew Lotte was bugging her to start socializing again, maybe even dating. Lenya had hardly been able to drag herself out of bed in the morning to brush her teeth and hair...dating? Impossible to even contemplate.

"All those historical romance novels I churn out are fine, but I'm getting stale...my motivation went with Andre. How many times can the same type of heroine fall in love with a tall, handsome, big-chested man with flowing locks of black, brown, or chestnut? I'm boring myself!" She paused to catch her breath, "Truthfully, I'm not much into love stories at the moment anyway." Even she could hear the ring of sadness in her voice. "And I will deliver the book under contract. She'll have it in a couple of weeks."

"Okay, okay, I get it. As your sister and most fervent fan, I admit I was impatient... a bit anxious to have some of your heroines actually get it on. I wanted to stop with the 'she felt movement low in her groin as he swept her off her feet and into his strong manly arms' shit. I'm ready for a good true blue sex scene about now. It'd be the perfect thing to wake me and the rest of your audience up. Your restraint has been admirable."

"It's not my restraint—what the publishers want. Can't offend the ladies who buy the books. They sell big-time in the Bible Belt. Their readers' imagination is better than I can write, and they don't feel they're reading smut if I leave the details of the juicy sex bits for them to fill in."

"What's the new book about? Can you give a hint without stopping the creative flow?" Lotte always teased about how easy it was for Lenya to write, being the anointed creative arm of the twinship.

Lenya looked on for years as Lotte flitted from one love affair to another, each new lover Playbilled as the 'one' and then unceremoniously kicked to the curb for the next. Lotte passionately involved herself in a different cause every month from saving baby seals to feeding the homeless, changed her style and hair color to suit her mood and dabbled as an artist from time to time. But ditzy as she seemed, she was an excellent and no-nonsense businesswoman. It always amazed friends and family how fashionable and frivolous, free-wheeling Lotte was the star businesswoman. Her mind actually ran to more pragmatic, rather than artistic, directions.

Lenya—methodical, studious, and conservative was creative. The women themselves seldom thought about it, but for a moment it flashed through Lenya's mind she was doing something Lotte-like while Lotte was taking over Lenya's usual mind-set.

"I'm not exactly sure, but I have an inspiration to write about the pre-history of this place. The mountains are studded with these mystical dolmens and caves. Historians know early man settled here. Some sites date as far back as the Neanderthal man but most are Neolithic. The big mystery is no one knows what happened to the first settlers who left these traces, or even how they got here—or from where."

As she spoke, Lenya could feel her excitement build. Maybe she was doing what the voices wanted? It did have a certain ring of rightness to it. "I want to study the local archeology and history to come up with a unique story. The books, I want to write a few of them, will follow several families from early man through the French Revolution, sort of a modern version of what Michener or Jakes have done in the past."

I'm on a roll, let's go for it, Lenya thought as she continued. "There's so much mystery and history mixed up here, you can feel it everywhere. Napoleon Bonaparte was Corsican, and the island's been shuttled back and forth for centuries between Italy, the Venetians and France. They even like Americans here because when they built the air base here during World War II the Yanks sprayed the area and killed all the mosquitoes in the swampy area. Malaria had been a real problem. The island...it's French now... has a separatist movement to this day."

Lotte was silent on the other end while Lenya sprinted ahead. "... and today I met a nice man, a warrior, probably around seven thousand years old. A bit worn around the edges, but someone I'd like to get to know better." Lenya held her breath until she heard her sister on the other end. "Sounds like an interesting project, but not an easy one. How long do you think you'll stay?"

Lenya knew Lotte would do anything to help bring her twin out of her melancholy and she also knew she was imposing. But this one time she needed freedom, new air to breathe, an adventure of her own. Hell, she'd gone this far on her own, she wanted more time.

"I've no idea, but I know the research will take a while. Please, I need you to take care of paying taxes for my house on time and I can take care of the rest on-line while I'm here. Thank god for the Internet!"

"All right, I've got your back. You stay as long as you need. I'll contact Ellie and tell her to expect both the overdue book and a new proposal.

"In the meantime, she can deposit royalties in your bank as usual. They should be enough to support your lifestyle in Corsica and pay for the house here as long as you don't go spend crazy. Please, get her the other book before the lawyers come calling.

"And by the way, I understand the Euro is knocking the hell out of the dollar so things are probably expensive. You'll need the rest of the advance."

"You know me too well, you're right as usual."

Lenya smiled as she clicked off Skype.

Chapter 6
The Cabin

Lenya made up her mind. She wanted to stay in Corsica for at least a year. Then, she'd decide on her next step, maybe stay longer...maybe not. All she was sure of was she wanted... needed... this hiatus from her regular life, or what had once been her life.

She said her goodbyes and left the tour group, rented a car for a month and drove back to Calvi. It was where she wanted to find a more permanent place. She booked a rustic furnished apartment at Les Lauriers Roses outside Calvi. The two brothers who ran the place, their mother and their families made her feel so comfortable and at home she was tempted to stay and not move into her own place.

After a week she knew she needed to be alone in order to finally come to grips with life without Andre. There no longer was any choice—she had to admit he was gone.

She haunted local real estate offices, at least those open off season and hoping for a last minute renter in search of the prefect place. They greeted her as if she were a godsend.

Originally she had hoped for one of the centuries old stone houses in the tiny villages hanging off the mountains. But once she was inside she found them cold and dank as well as lacking the modern basics.

It hadn't occurred to her before how technology had moved from innovative and interesting to requisite until she realized she couldn't make do without Internet access and sufficient electrical outlets in convenient places for computer, printer and satellite television.

Modern plumbing was also another essential. But after the third exquisite and inconvenient stone house she'd visited, she gave up idea and went decidedly more modern.

Most of the newer rentals she saw were in holiday camps, lonely and deserted in the off-season and packed for July and August. She was looking for isolation all year long, not easy to find close to the coast.

She was about to give up the whole idea when an estate agent took her to an A-frame built in the 1950's in the style of a ski chalet or cabin.

The owners had elder care responsibilities and couldn't come for their usual six week summer vacation. The place was always vacant the rest of the year.

The cabin was only a fifteen minute drive from both Calvi and L'Île-Rousse, near the Route des Artisans. Lenya almost liked the fact it was rather inaccessible. The approach was an uninviting and narrow old road twisting upward to a turnoff onto a treacherous and deeply rutted dirt road stretching even higher. She decided she could live with it, even though the journey wasn't for the faint of heart. There certainly wouldn't be hundreds of summer people trooping around during the high season.

A spectacular view greeted her on arrival. The cabin was near the edge of the forest on a promontory branching off the side of the mountain. Perfect for a writer who needs to write.

As she walked up to the cabin, a large wooden deck beckoned her to come, sit, relax and enjoy the fresh mountain air. The dark brown weathered-shingle exterior was softened by gay white and red painted trim. Walking across the deck, she entered through sliding glass doors and paused to take it all in.

The interior was inviting—charming, and homey—a great room combining both living and dining areas greeted her.

Lenya found the basic furnishings comfortable though not lavish. An antique carved wooden farm table and chairs had an aged patina hinting at contentment, perhaps even joy.

A sofa, covered in softly faded pink, blue and green floral chintz and scattered with matching solid color pillows was the perfect size for afternoon snoozing. The sofa was flanked by two navy tweed upholstered club chairs with ottomans. Small tables were casually scattered around ready to perch wineglasses on—everything quite acceptable, utilitarian and well-used but not abused.

The people who owned the place obviously cared about it. She would take care of it for them she thought, and nodded to herself.

The wood walls and ceilings, reasonably well equipped kitchen with open cabinetry displaying local blue and marigold color pottery dishes completed the look of familiar country comfort. A pleasant woodsy aroma permeated the atmosphere. A few added touches of her own would make it her home...at least for now.

On further exploration, she found a bathroom off to the left and a small bedroom in the back, the entire space almost taken up by a double bed.

A large sleeping loft guarded by a substantial dark wood balustrade overlooked the main room. She chose the loft as her sleeping space as soon as she saw the king size bed perched under its high peaked wood ceiling.

The idea of being close to the wood was appealing, but the deal maker was the view. The loft faced a triangular window extending from one side of the cabin to the other looking out on the valley below and the tops of trees dancing in the breezes drifting by.

In the distance, the sea sparkled in the sunlight, tossing diamonds of light carelessly to the sky. She could barely make out the white sails of a few sailboats enjoying the light breeze. Perhaps a small regatta, or a sailing school?

It was magic to her, a flatlander from the East Coast. The mountain roads were a bit hairy and would take some getting used to, especially the rutted dirt part, another part of the adventure.

She had reservations about the winter—heating in the cabin was rudimentary, a stone fireplace in the far wall. While the Mediterranean climate was generally mild, guide books warned about snow in the mountains covering the higher peaks towards the center of the island, rather than those near the coast. She'd tough it out, cold seldom bothered her.

Tom seemed to like the place, sniffing out all the corners, and finally settled himself on a round scatter rug in front of the fireplace. "Okay little guy, it looks like you've already moved in." Lenya said as she examined what the owners had left for her to work with in the kitchen. Whatever else she needed she could pick up at the big supermarket in Calvi.

Lenya signed a year lease. The owners were delighted to rent to a widow with good references who paid in advance.

Lenya understood why, she'd cringed when the agents took her into beat-up vacation houses, some with broken doors and cabinets, torn upholstery, one with filthy walls and the stench of overflowing cat litter boxes; all trashed by careless summer renters.

The broker agreed to arrange for her telephone, internet connection and satellite television. Everything was installed and working by the time she moved in.

Chapter 7

Cave Dreams

The first night in the cabin, Lenya stretched out on the king sized bed in the loft. She'd made it up with a new flowery sheet and comforter set she couldn't resist, even at Calvi's extravagant tourist prices. The pinks, soft greens and lavenders were French-estrogen and calling to her—tiny embroidered rosettes and leaves trellising over the comforter, the trim of the sheets and pillowcases. She had to have it for her new home. The only male she was living with was Tom, and she knew he didn't care.

She laughed to herself as she thought of Andre scoffing at the lace and flowers she had always been drawn to for their bedroom. It was odd even to her when she longed for very feminine bedding. Her clothes were always traditional, conservative, no frippery, but she wanted lace, frills and flowers on her bed.

He'd say, "Remember, it's my bedroom too, love. Don't make me feel like an outsider in our own home." So she'd succumb and buy stripes and geometric or nature designs, rosettes for their bedrooms in both France and the States were excluded. It was a very small sacrifice.

Smiling to herself at the memory, she traced her fingers over the crisp white sheets with the flowery embroidery as she moved to ruffle the fur on the neck of her faithful bed companion. Tom snuffled and rolled over onto his back for his evening tummy rub. Probably wasn't the best idea to get fancy expensive sheets with an active terrier sleeping in her bed. But she didn't care. Muddy paw prints came out in the wash.

Since Andre died, the warm body and sounds of Tom breathing next to her calmed her sleep. Before, he had been relegated to his own bed in a corner next to theirs, but now he slept with her. During the night, he snuggled against her back and made small woofing sounds as he chased prey through his dreams. Those signs of another life close-by kept her sane all the months she hid from the world.

The new sheets were cool and smooth against her body as she luxuriated in them, stretching out as if making a snow angel. Tom stayed put at her waist as her arms and legs shuffled between the sheets. She looked up at the slanted wooden ceiling overhead and inhaled the cedar and pine freshness of the air as she fell asleep.

Drums. The drums were incessant. The rhythms repetitive and melded with odd harmonies...a flute? More than one?

And chanting...many voices singing...no...chanting...the same words over and over in some strange language. Flames licked stone walls, carved and painted, ceiling a vaulted space leading to a hole where stars shined through smoke fingers waving across their brilliance.

Where am I? Her hands moved to find a soft fur beneath her body, maybe several layers cushioning her from the hard stone she knew she was lying on.... have to go, get out of here...but no clothes...naked as she felt her body, exposed... must go...must...sounds of drums incessant, feet pounding rhythms in time slapped on bare stone...go...

She moaned in her sleep. Turned fitfully. The new sheets bound her legs as she thrashed about. Tom moved to a far corner at the foot of the bed. Lenya almost woke, but something pulled her back into the dream.

Voices, men, women, clapping to the drums...words?...grunts and words, odd clicking sounds and then howling like a wolf...snarling like a bear and shadows jabbing with sticks...spears? High pitched sound...something close to birdsong but rhythmic pierced the growling as voices raised together in almost harmony.

She struggled to turn her head...see what was happening...where...but didn't want to move or even wake...something inside her knew all this, knew this rite, this place, an inner memory? A hand...large, strong...gentle...caressing her body...knowing...touching, first tracing the line of her neck, then moving down

*to her nipples and circling the aureoles as fingers gently flicked the sensitive tips...
she moaned...and then again...*

*Light flickered on walls of stone...a cave? She forgot the walls and felt
again the hand...insistent...parting her legs it cupped her sex...arching her back,
she brushed her hand over her face...go...must go...please go. But she knew she
wanted to stay.*

*Something warm and moist and...soft laved the length of her body...soft
hair tickled the inside of her thighs, pleasure intensifying with every slow move...
while the hand continued its exploration, touching her face, the skin of her neck,
under her ear... below, on her private places...it was warm, insistent... exploring
her sex before plunging into her.*

*She screamed at the gentle invasion... quieted as it moved around and
around...brushing against and inside her. She forgot about screaming... gave herself over to the thrill of pleasure...arched her back...moved her legs further apart.
Movement... intimate... fur...a beard? Hair shining in the flames between her
thighs, moving...ohmygodohmygod...her voice...over and over...body pulsing...
thrilling... sensuous ... in time to the music?...her nerves thrummed with delight...*

*She twisted her head to see who was between her legs...saw only flames
flickering along a stone wall illuminating a hunt... men ...chasing an aurochs
across...across time?*

*Unseen voices kept up their incessant chanting... saw only shadows ...
shades of men and women joining the frenzy of the hunt...arms raised clapping...
stomping ... lunging over and over with imaginary spears...clubs...killing their
prey as they sang to the pounding beat of the drums. Her back bowed once more
and she came again and again...and again.*

*Scents of herbs, lavender, patchouli and sage filled her mind, smoke from
the fire blended with them, and something musty, familiar from long ago...can-
nabis? But she wasn't drugged, only a dream...she fought for a surface further
than she could reach.*

*And, when she could take no more, he moved, loomed over her and spread
her legs further apart...thrust his body up and over to penetrate her, and she knew
she wanted him inside, would give her life to have him pierce her...desperate for
the feel of him...his skin against hers...inside...this unknown man playing her
body with such skill... but she gasped as he pushed gently to enter because he was*

a stranger and she was Lenya who didn't do this kind of thing with unknown men...in caves...and people dancing.

As she struggled to run, to flee her dream, she felt a light hand on her brow and heard a soft woman's voice above the chants—calling to her as before—the special voice. She opened her eyes—which she didn't remember closing—and saw a woman looking down at her. Tall, strong body wearing a diaphanous robe, her long dark hair blowing in a breeze Lenya didn't feel. The woman smiled and nodded in assent as she put the index finger of her other hand to Lenya's lips as she caressed her brow.

Permission given...Lenya understood and gave herself over to the man moving inside her, her legs up and hooking over his shoulders for the full feel of him deep inside. Moving...moving in time to his thrusts...to the chants...to the drums, to reclamation of life she howled her bliss to the heavens.

Looking up once again, woman nodded and silently mouthed "Grazie."

Tom was licking her face as Lenya wrenched awake to the sound of her own screams. Soaked with sweat, her pajamas and the new bedding was drenched from her ecstasy.

Embarrassed and stunned, she clutched the sheets to her chest as she looked around the loft. She was panting, out of breath like a runner, but alone with Tom, his the only living presence. No cave, no dancers, no music or drums. Alone. Completely.

It had been so real.

Shaking and breathless with the yank from climax to reality; as suddenly and as real as they had appeared to her, the images of her dream began to fade.

And then she remembered a long ago night when she was sitting with friends over too many bottles of wine. Someone asked *the question.* "How do you know if you're in love?"

One of the guys was quick to respond, "My father always told me it was the touch of the skin. The first touch tells you all you need to know. If it's electric, it's right. Lenya never forgot. It spoke to her— exactly the right answer. The first time Andre took her hand, she had felt the electric connection between two people.

Still under the spell of the dream, she could almost feel the man's skin against her skin, his body against hers, their legs entwined and his skillful hands, searching tongue, the thrill of his hardness as he penetrated her.

But no matter how hard she tried to remember, no matter how real he felt in the ecstasy of their union, his face eluded her as she knew she had felt that special touch. *Who was the man?*

A chill shook her, and she felt alone as the dream slipped away.

Sitting on her damp bed hugging Tom for solace, she regretted the end of the dream. 'Bereft' came to mind as she longed for the feel of his skin—please—once more.

Chapter 8
Routine of Life

Lenya and Tom fell into a comfortable routine: Tai Chi on the deck in the morning, then shower, work at the computer, lunch, an afternoon walk, more writing, dinner and some television. Lenya watched both French and Italian programming to improve her language skills, but it wasn't easy when there was no one with whom to practice. Her only contacts with people were occasional trips to the village where she bought her supplies.

The strange erotic dream hadn't disturbed her nights again.

It was her third week in her rental house. Lenya got out of bed and stretched. *Am I imagining it, or am I getting stiff? Maybe older?* She walked down from the loft and looked out the sliding glass doors to the deck and forest behind.

Soon she was brushing her teeth as coffee dripped into the glass pot. Tom had already scarfed his breakfast. Out past the deck, the sun was breaking through the usual morning clouds drifting to the edge of the mountains. She put her hand on her hip and bent over sideways. One complaining muscle needed a tad more stretch.

Looking up at the wooden ceiling and dark beams, she sipped her coffee and planned her day. She was going to spend the morning in further reconnaissance around her new neighborhood.

The first stop was the small Spar market in Calenzana for a few groceries. Then she was going to take the *"Route des Artisanes"* which she hoped promised all sorts of intriguing adventures. According to her map the road looked like the ruching on the hem of a ruffled dress—an irregular pattern of squiggles she knew indicated a breathtaking climb up and around the mountains.

She enjoyed small ateliers where the ancient crafts of knife making, pottery, glass blowing, weaving and basket making were practiced. Other ateliers might offer local wines and cheese, especially the *bracciu* cheese made in baskets to allow the moisture to drip away.

After parking the rental car and entering the market, Lenya was again struck by the incongruity of the efficient and well lit market snuggling to the base of the ancient town.

The chain of Spar markets dotted the island with almost everything one could want in the food department. Cans and bottles were well displayed on modern shelves; fresh refrigerated meat was shrink wrapped in plastic trays.

She could choose from steaks to *viande hâché* to rack of lamb. It was all so clean it looked as if it had been placed in the case only moments before she entered. She replenished her supply of *Mâche*, the small round green leaves called Lambs' Lettuce, if and when it could be found in the states. Her favorite salad was *Mâche* with baby lettuce and tomato, Roquefort cheese and a simple vinaigrette dressing.

She tried some of the local artisanal pâtés, but found them too salty for her taste, so she confined herself to the pre-packaged store brands. They were delicious and quite a bit less expensive. So were the paper thin sliced hams from Spain, Italy and Bayonne.

The hams were so enticing to choose wasn't easy so she decided to go in alphabetical order and try them all. Today was the ham from Bayonne. Lenya added a baguette and some Caprice des Deux cheese, a double cream that took Brie to new heights. Two bottles of water, an apple, a pear and a demi of red wine rounded out her purchases. It was enough to hold her through both a day of adventure and dinner at home.

There were few people in the store; most of the tourists already gone for the season. Those left were smart laggards who took advantage of the off-season rates, or people who lived in the area. As she checked out, the man in front of her turned back and smiled. He had graying blonde hair in a brush cut and nice blue eyes. Obviously another tourist, although the woman at the cash register greeted him like a regular.

Hoping someday to also be greeted like a regular, at least after a few more weeks of shopping there, she smiled broadly at the woman who took her money.

Everything fit in the soft cooler she had bought for jaunts in the mountains. Since the tourists left, stores weren't always open and finding food could often be an adventure in itself. The boulangeries closed from noon to two, sometimes three. Trust the French to close when you needed them the most. Sorry, Andre.

Her rental car was underpowered, but reliable. There were some mountain inclines she had to encourage the car to take with both prayer and first gear.

Pigna was her aim—an artists' community hanging off the side of the mountain. Dying until recent times, a new mayor with foresight made it a walking village, brought in more artisans and a few entrepreneurs and touted it as a Mecca for tourists in search of Corsican crafts. Lenya had been told it was a "must see" by the estate agents and put it first on her list.

So here she was, winding her way up the mountain and down the mountain. She almost missed the first hairpin turn leading to the village, but managed to ask some cyclists stopped by the side of the road if they knew what road to take. As she got out of her car to ask, she turned to see why they'd stopped. Below, the Mediterranean was spread before them, a brilliant blue with hint of green, then blending into an eye-searing turquoise as it neared the shore, only to be frosted with whitecaps before it brushed the rocky beach.

The four of them stood in silence. The beauty of the sea caught Lenya's heart and dried her throat. She found she couldn't speak. The moment passed, directions were pointed out and she was on her way up and up yet again.

The turn in to the village led to a parking area to leave cars as the village was walking only. Tom sniffed and was sniffed by the big Labradors lounging in the sun at the edge of the parking and then took up his post at Lenya's heel as they walked on cobblestones into the narrow twisted village alleyways.

The buildings were the dun color of old stones, pocked with colors of peach, rose, grey and tan. New patches, colors diligently matched, the patina slightly different from those softened by age, were easily spotted.

Every turn brought a new atelier into sight. A print shop, another with music and music boxes. Shutters painted what Lenya could only think of as Pigna Blue graced every window and complemented doors of the same blue or antiqued wood.

She took out her camera and photographed ancient ironwork locks and carved wooden doors. The roofs were tiled in rust colors faded through centuries of sun. There was a book shop, another selling glass figurines and assorted souvenirs. A sign pointed around a corner indicating local pork sausages and dried meats.

Disappointed, she found the knife maker was closed for holiday. She stepped up on a stone platform to read a poster for a polyphonic concert when she noticed a niche carved high up into the stone where the building wall was patched. It held a pitcher and a small figurine. Both were in clay. The door beneath opened to the potters atelier and as she entered she caught sight of the most amazing blue she had ever seen. The colors were so compelling; it was hard to see the objects they decorated.

The room was small, as if carved from the very mountain itself; a veritable cave with a vaulted ceiling. It was no more than ten feet by fourteen feet at most, the walls filled with handcrafted wooden shelves and openwork displays meandering down the center. What they held was magic. Pottery pieces of every size and description, mostly in blues.

As Lenya's eyes rejoiced at the sight, she understood she was looking at the changing colors of the sea captured on bowls, platters, cups, vases and serving pieces. No glaze was exactly the same, but each, in its own version, managed to catch the hues of the Corsican waters.

On some of the other shelves, the pottery was in yellowish mustard hues. They also captured the essence of Corsica, but this wasn't the sea, it was the wild maquis, the immortelle that gave the island it's special scent.

The potter was dressed in the traditional French workman's garb of royal blue cotton coveralls. He wore gold-rim glasses and his sparse, almost colorless hair, was cut short and combed tight to his head. But he was the magician who had managed to dig into the heart of his home and re-create it in his own way. Lenya was awestruck as she moved about the small shop, looking at the creations with reverence. This is what it's like to be able to create something you love; to distill its essence while leaving the emotions intact.

On the way home, the car coughed and groaned up the steep grade to the cabin. Lenya had to face facts. It was far too isolated, even for her, without a larger and more powerful car. It was time to buy something more serviceable.

The next day she stopped at a bar along the way and picked up the local classified throw-away paper to see what was offered and found a ten year old Toyota RAV4 with a few dents and low mileage. The main selling point was four- wheel drive. Driving up the rutted dirt road in the rain was going to be a lot less daunting.

Life was to be simple, the way Lenya wanted it. Once inside the cabin, she felt she was in command of the entire space. *Simple. Friendly.*

The house in Connecticut was too big, she'd rattled around in it by herself the last year. There were far too many memories to deal within its walls. She and Andre bought it with the idea of parties, friends, entertaining.

Without Andre, Lenya had lived in the kitchen and her bedroom. She hadn't gone in the other rooms for months as they reminded her of what they were supposed to be used for. Someday she knew she would have to deal with it, but not for the moment.

Selling the Connecticut house was exactly the type of decision she didn't want to make. For the moment, life was good, no stress, and she was finding a new point of view on this island so far away from her usual life.

She felt as if her lungs were expanding and she could breathe better, coming alive again. The hikes and Tai Chi building up her stamina, the new surroundings clearing the cobwebs from her mind.

Every day she and Tom trekked into the vast forest surrounding the cabin, exploring the world around her, enjoying nature. In the past, she had been so busy with deadlines and social engagements there had been no time in her life for walk-abouts.

This new freedom was a gift she was learning to appreciate. Looking back in time, she was also better understanding her old life. When she walked along the empty paths enjoying the beauty surrounding her, or relaxing in one of the cafes along the harbor watching the world go by, she realized the opportunities for pleasure she'd missed while racing through her formerly hectic life. Perhaps, she thought, I'm finally on 'The Road Not Taken.'

Down and on the other side of the valley, she found one of the many dolmens the island was known for. From the photos in her Corsican guide, she assumed it was Neolithic. No one knew how old it was when she asked about it in the village. Boulders surrounded the perimeter at a distance, like seats at a small amphitheatre. The structure was massive flat stones, some standing, others dug into the hillside to support the single larger stone placed on top.

Her other favorite place was a stand of chestnut trees with rounded boulders flattened on the tops and roughly spaced in a circle between the trees. Outside the circle and to the side, another rock formation festooned by trees and shrubs sheltered a grotto with a pool fed by a slow drip from higher up the mountain. A shaded large flat boulder appeared to be an altar or a table, several other boulders were close enough to use as seats. The place was silent and cool with the freshest air she'd ever breathed.

The grotto was high on a list of her favorite hikes and often, when she needed inspiration, she packed lunch and a bottle of water, donned her hiking boots and headed out with a long mop handle to use as a walking stick for balance.

Tom valiantly trotted ahead to make sure the pathway was safe. She had never cared for hiking before coming to the island, but since so many of the places she wanted to explore were otherwise inaccessible, she had little alternative.

As Lenya was walking away from her cabin, some distance away, Aldo leaned over to wash his face and arms in the cold water of a grotto pool. It was his daily ritual to come to this quiet place where he splashed in the fresh trickle flowing down from the mountain. He liked the crisp feel of the water and the way it made his skin break out in tiny prickles and bumps.

As Maître, he didn't believe the old superstitions about water breeding evil. It couldn't be true, water was the source of life, without it, life wasn't possible. While many on the island thought evil ghosts hovered nearby rivers and ponds, he thought they were gifts. Gifts from Dia, who loved all things in nature, especially wild animals. She would never allow her animals to drink if the water was evil.

The cold fresh water from the aquifer ran over him and he felt alive.

Thanking Dia for another day, he washed and rubbed himself with oils steeped with rosemary and lavender to honor her.

Aldo was a holy man, a consort of Dia, and as such, he took pride in following the required rituals. He kept himself healthy and, in accord with the rules of hygiene required to please his goddess, he anointed himself with scented oils variously made from saffron, lavender, immortelle and myrtle; daily he washed, combed and braided his hair and beard, prayed and placed gifts by her effigy and at her sacred places. But it wasn't enough. For whatever reason he was unable to fathom, Dia had not seen fit to find him a mate.

Alone, he had none of the living energy to pass to his goddess. He watched in sorrow as all around him the life of the forest celebrated the sacred rites necessary to the continuation of the cycle of life. What could he do?

He'd wait. Faithful to Dia's way, he'd try to understand. He told himself it wasn't so long since the last elder died; perhaps it was the time for him to reflect, worship Dia, learn to live by himself. Learn to live alone. There was no other reason he could think of as each day passed like the one before. No one to speak to, no one to share the gifts of life with.

He visited his friend Sirio when the solitude became too much for him to bear, but, much as he enjoyed Sirio's company, it wasn't the same as living in a clan, having a mate, someone to worship Dia with, someone to wrap his arms around and protect from the night.

As he reflected on his lot, Aldo heard someone singing. Quickly, he moved away from the pool, moving soundlessly into the surrounding maquis. It was late in the season for hikers and tourists, and surprising for anyone to be so far away from the usual hiking trails.

A person and a dog stepped out of the forest into the clearing and walked purposefully down the hill towards the grotto. At first he wasn't sure if it was a man or a woman. An aura glittered around the head, obscuring his view. But the stride was long and strong.

As the figure moved closer, he noticed blonde hair—short and cropped close to the head, and then the soft roundness of breasts. The woman was tall, taller than the women of the clan, and what he had thought was her aura was her golden hair reflecting the sunlight filtering down through the trees. His heart lurched in his chest. Was she his gift from Dia?

The woman looked young, at least she wasn't wrinkled like a clan woman, and she stood straight, walked with authority. It was obvious she didn't care if anyone heard her coming because, not only was she singing some strange song at full force, but the undergrowth cracked and snapped with each step.

Her dog was small and white with two black spots and a brown, black and white face. Its short tail stood at attention, clearly alert, and it began sniffing in his direction. Aldo hoped it wouldn't bark and give him away. Instead, the dog began to growl—not loud, but low in its throat, a warning to keep your distance. Aldo was silent and unmoving. Knowing how to not frighten animals was second nature to him.

He wanted to see more of this woman.

Where did she come from? He knew most of the people in the area by sight, at least the ones who came for more than short summer holidays. He thought of the summer people as a plague on the island and Aldo mostly stayed close to the casteddu for those periods, coming out only at night to hunt and forage. Dia wouldn't send him one of them?

This woman was alone and it was past time for the summer people. She was something different. He was curious. Squinting through the foliage he saw she was a bit thin for his taste, but well built and sturdy. The way a woman should be. Her complexion was the color of cream with a nice soft rosy color in her cheeks from the exertion of the walk.

She looked very healthy. Not sickly the way Raina had always looked. Did she have a mate? Has Dia guided her steps? She was, after all, in this place where he came every day.

There wasn't a sound as he crouched down. She looked like she was going to stay in the grotto for a while and he didn't want to miss anything. He felt a tiny spark of hope ignite as he watched her explore, stop at the altar and open the bag she had on her back. She took out a bottle of water and some food wrapped in paper. Was she making an offering to Dia? He hoped she wouldn't leave any trash.

She sat on one of the nearby boulders and began to eat. The dog sniffed around the grotto, finally came over to him. The little animal examined him thoroughly before deciding he posed no danger, and nudged its nose into Aldo's hand for a friendly rub. Aldo obliged and after a moment, the dog silently trotted off to sit at its mistresses' feet. Aldo'd passed the "friend not foe" test.

After the woman finished her meal, she and the dog left. Aldo noted with approval as she put the paper and water bottle back in her pack—not leaving garbage behind like the summer people. Respectful.

He wanted to see where she went, he followed at a distance. When he saw her go into the cabin, he stayed. He had to see if there was a man there with her.

Comfortable in the forest, he hunkered down on the balls of his feet to wait. He was in no hurry; he would stay as long as it took to satisfy himself she was alone.

Several hours later he woke with a start. The dog was licking his face. Luckily, the woman had stayed in the cabin. Embarrassed, he realized he dozed off and had curled around the tree in his sleep. Looking at the low position of the sun—he'd been asleep for several hours.

Stretching and brushing leaves and twigs off, Aldo remained hidden, studying the cabin through the surrounding brush. The woman was sitting on the deck with a glass of wine in her hand. She was alone. He heard her call to the dog, it's name was Tom, and he obediently trotted back to her. Two more hours passed and Aldo neither saw nor heard any sign of a mate. He would have to come back other days to make sure, but he was beginning to think this really might be the woman Dia had chosen for him. Otherwise, why had she put this woman so conveniently in his path?

If she was truly alone, how was he going to approach her without frightening her? This was something he'd have to think about very carefully. …and what was she like? Would he want her? Would she want him?

A few days passed and Lenya was antsy again. It was sunny and warm with a breeze wrapping itself around the island. Time for another walk. When Lenya last visited her favorite place, she had the impression someone or something was watching. It was unpleasant and creepy, but she didn't feel danger. After all, she had her mop handle with her for protection, and Tom would warn her if someone came close.

Lenya never considered herself a victim and had no intention of feeling like one now. At one point Tom had started to growl low in his throat, but it didn't last for long and then he came over to sit quietly next to her. She had thought it probably was a small animal in the underbrush and promptly forgot the incident.

Because of her writing, Lenya was often too preoccupied with her own thoughts to pay much attention to what was happening outside her periphery.

The walks and explorations were like moving meditation for her. Her surroundings drifted away while her body moved effortlessly through the forest, her subconscious free to rove to mysterious places of its own volition. It was like driving a car and suddenly realizing you had safely driven miles with no recollection of how you got there.

She wanted to visit the grotto again. The place was cool and secluded, not as if the rest of the valley wasn't, but she always had a special feeling in "her place." She'd worked on her proposal all week, but something was missing. Lenya needed inspiration.

The crystal clarity of the air in the grotto always cut through any cobwebs in her mind. Solutions to problems of plot and characters seemed to resolve themselves there. She could munch her lunch and let the grotto be her private muse as she breathed in fresh air and new inspiration.

Entering the silent grove she noted again the lichen growing on the flat grey stone, the coolness of the air; fresher somehow than air on the other side of the valley. There was a tranquility in the atmosphere, as if the place had its own micro-climate, especially unsullied.

Walking over to the grotto to admire the patterns where the water had worn a rut in the rock in places, and in other places ran free, sheeting the stone face as it made its way to the small pool where Tom liked to drink, Lenya noticed the waterfall grew or shrank depending on the amount of rainfall. It hadn't rained the past week and there was no smooth flow, an intermittent dribble of water adding a counterpoint to the ambient sounds of the forest and birds.

The grotto was filled with ferns branching out to impossible sizes as they greedily sucked up water constantly dripping into the pool. She thought the grotto carried with it an artistry landscape designers sought to achieve, but could never compete with the perfection of this mystical place.

Lenya leaned over the green lace of the ferns to see if any fish had suddenly appeared in the pool. She knew they hadn't, but always felt compelled to look. It was a perfect place for colorful koi to loll about and was always disappointed when only her own reflection looked back at her, the pool never disturbed by slow motion fins gracefully fanning the water.

The larger clearing was filled by wild grasses, and the spaces between the trees were home to low growing brush and bushes decorated with what appeared to be strawberries but which she had been warned by her guide books not to eat. In the center, as the focal point, the table and its large balanced stone top.

Walking around the surrounding boulders, she lightly traced her fingers over the rounded surfaces placed as if they were stools, smooth and slightly indented on the top. The first time Lenya came, she automatically sat on one of the stones and was amazed at how comfortably the indentation fit her derriere.

The flat stone in the arms of the grotto was her favorite. Not only was it shaded, it was smooth and rounded at the corners and edges, feeling like generations of hands had honed the surface to a mellow gray patina—the perfect place for a picnic.

About to set out her lunch, Lenya saw the flowers. Bright yellow, blue and pink, the small bouquet reminded her of those she used to pick as a child, a nosegay of wildflowers gathered and carefully arranged. Perhaps these were an offering to ancient gods? They were in a small indentation on the stone near where she usually had her lunch.

She moved closer to inspect the flowers and found they were fresh and crisp, as if placed there only a few moments before she arrived. She looked at the dog. Tom appeared calm as if he sensed no one; there was no other sign of any human presence.

Feeling like a Native American tracker, Lenya looked in the soil around the area searching for footprints, hoping for a clue about the flowers.

The only tracks she found were those of her hiking boots, but on her second round of inspection, she saw what might be part of a toe peeking out from under her more recent print. It was at the outside rim of the clearing, heading into the dense underbrush surrounding her.

As she looked around she felt a chill. The hair on her arms stood up. Was it a cold breeze? It could have been her imagination. Give it up, Lenya, you're no Sacajawea. She shook her head and moved back to the table and her lunch.

She tried to brush off the feeling, but no matter how she tried, something was creepy. Oddly, her hackles didn't rise again, but she looked around several times to make sure she was alone. It was the first time she had felt uncomfortable since she arrived on the island.

It felt cooler in the grove than usual, but she dismissed the thought. If Tom isn't worried, I won't be either. But she was. She ate her lunch quickly, then gathered up her trash to leave.

She didn't move the flowers, but bent to smell them, and left them behind. Again, she felt as if someone was watching her, but Tom was quiet and relaxed.

She made up her mind a child had gifted the grotto with flowers and wondered where the child came from. Probably a kid of one of the summer renters? Although by now, most of them had left the island. School started a few weeks ago in France and those families with children headed back to civilization.

Maybe it was a local child, one of the brood from the family who owned the little market where she shopped? Still, it was far from the store and she was a little concerned about the idea of a small child wandering around in the dense forest alone.

She dismissed her fears as she left the flat rock with the tiny bouquet behind her. I refuse to be frightened, she thought, instead, she gave a silent "thank you" to whoever left the nosegays to brighten her day and headed back to the cabin.

Aldo was pleased. The woman had noticed the flowers and seemed to like them. He'd remember to bring her more and wondered if she thought about who left them just on the spot where she liked to have her lunch.

He had no idea what such a woman might think about anything. Would that be a problem? He never seemed to know what Raina had been thinking about, and they almost never fought. Might it be the same with this woman?

She seemed exotic to him, not at all like the women of the clan. He found the difference exciting, almost mysterious. It made him want to know more about her. To get closer to her. To feel her skin on his.

Chapter 9
Tasting & Talk

Lenya's favorite drive was along the Route National between Calvi and L'Île-Rousse. Once the tourists left it was no longer packed with wild French drivers incensed at the thought of another car driving in front of them. The RN sometimes even had an occasional passing lane, uncommon on Corsica.

Her private mission: to explore all the small side roads along the coast, or at least as many as possible. Some were only dirt cart paths, winding upwards into the mountains away from the sea, often ending suddenly for no apparent reason. Others were part of the Route des Artisans, filled with hidden ateliers of local craftsmen.

Small, hard to read signs, announced potters while others pointed to the cheese fabricants and basket makers, sausage makers, boulangeries and wineries. Knives, essential oils, soaps, all were made in various workshops, some hidden in dense forest off the winding roads, others in villages perched over the sea.

On one of her excursions she had found a jewelry atelier and bought a silver and onyx bracelet, pendant and earrings to send to Lotte as a 'thank you' for taking care of all the financial arrangements allowing Lenya to stay in Corsica. Lenya was always ready for new treasures to be found on her next foray into the workshops of the local artisans.

From the wares she sampled, so far the saucisson and breads were superb. Lenya smiled to herself, typical of the French, eating as an art, and reminded herself not to call the Corsicans French. It was a hard habit to break.

Today she was on a hunt for wine. Tom jumped into his place on the passenger seat and Lenya fixed his harness to the seat belt. She didn't want her best buddy flying through the windshield if she had to jam her foot on the brakes to keep from hitting the typical Corsican driver treating the narrow hairpin roads like their private race course.

Leaving Calvi, she drove north along the coast, once more amazed at the blue clarity of the sky and the blue-green intensity of the Mediterranean. The mountains stretched north and south on her right, the sea on her left, the sun suffusing the turquoise water with variations of dazzling color. There was a lacy ruffle of whitecap as the ocean sloshed onto the occasional breakwater protecting the beachfront.

Everything on the mountain side was green, more shades than the eye could count as the maquis filled every scrap of ancient landslides. At the top on one of the turns, she noticed an interesting pile of boulders and wondered if they were natural formations, or ruins of some ancient village. She must remember to explore the place another time.

Several horns blasted her reverie and she realized ubiquitous Corsicans in miniscule cars almost nudging her bumper. The message was clear—get the hell out of the way. Why don't you slow down and enjoy your own country?—she thought as she pulled over. Corsicans!

Slowing down to let everyone behind her pass, she noticed a small road almost completely obscured by brush. It invited an exploration. She turned the old RAV4 and was started up the steep grade when she noticed an arrow on a faded sign announcing:

De Manzino Winery, Salle de Degustation,
Overt tous les jours sauf Lundi, 9AM-4PM

If the sign hadn't been left over when the place closed for the season, it was open every day but Monday and it was now Tuesday. It would be great luck if she'd found a winery. Andre would be proud of her. So far, she'd confined her wine purchases to what she found at Spar or the big Casino market in Calvi.

After twenty minutes of winding up increasingly bad roads, another arrow announced she was close to the winery. The road in front of her was a single lane and so rutted she wasn't sure even the RAV4 wouldn't bottom out and get stuck. Not a quitter, Lenya's interest was piqued. She refused to give up.

As she jounced along, Tom gave her what passed for a dirty-doggy look as the bouncing prevented his curling up for a snooze on the towel nest he made on the passenger seat.

Two tall tumbledown columns fashioned from local boulders marked the entrance. A cut iron sign, badly rusted and attached to a rough-hewn beam spanning the columns, announced she'd arrived. The rusted gate hung open and led to, if possible, an even worse dirt road.

Lenya looked at Tom, "Okay buddy, in for a penny, in for a pound. Let's go see what it's all about." Tom made his usual response. He picked his head up and set his ears at full alert as he looked around with his tongue lolling out of the corner of his mouth. There was always a chance there might be food.

After a short drive up the driveway, if it could be called such, they arrived at a cleared area marked with a weathered board nailed to a tree and hand painted with a single word "Park." A barn-like structure stood with open doors and another board with an arrow announced, "Entre."

Lenya stared at walls made of irregular stones, artfully and intricately placed. Someone created it to be pleasing to the eye and blend with the local rock formations in their variegated colors of grey, brown, chalk, beiges and peach.

The roof was ancient mottled thigh-rounded red clay tiles. Vines clung to the stones and crocheted swaying pathways up the walls and across parts of the roof. Trees overhung the structure, completing the illusion the building was a living part of the landscape. The air was different here, not the maquis, but a sweet fruity and vinegary scent mixed with a hint of must. A place where the wine was actually made. Lenya was impressed.

A small Jack Russell Terrier bounded up to the car barking out a welcome. She couldn't help laughing as a small white and brown head with bright black eyes kept bobbing up at the window as if saying to Tom "Get the heck out of the car, do it now, now, now!" At least Tom might get lucky.

As soon as Tom was out of his harness he bounded out to perform the usual two ended sniff, followed by a territorial pee on the nearest bush. Introductions over, the two dogs were off and running around the parking area. Lenya wasn't worried about them being run over by traffic in this hidden grove, so she stood for a moment laughing as she watched the wild abandoned joy of the two dogs racing together in freedom. She understood; Tom had been lonely too.

She almost missed seeing the man standing in the doorway of the barn. He was tall, slim, weathered like the building and smiling at the dogs racing around and around, soaring in abandon over any obstacle in their way.

Lenya got out of the car and walked up to the entrance.

The man took a pipe out of his mouth and pointed at the animals. "They need to have friends. She is Sophia—too young to be alone with just me for entertainment. Now there is someone to run with. Even dogs—it's not good for them to be alone."

It took a minute for her to realize the man was speaking English; obviously learned in America rather than England. How unusual. I'll bet there's an interesting story behind, she thought.

As she walked towards the barn, she held out her hand, "Hello, I'm Lenya." She pointed to the dogs, "and that's Tom. I hope we didn't disturb you. I'm looking for the winery."

"Well, you've found it...and me too, I'm Sirio. Please come in." He let go her hand and gestured to the interior of the barn. On closer inspection of the large structure, it looked decades old, perhaps even centuries.

Inside, the stonework was enhanced by wood darkened by smoke, fumes and use to a deep mahogany color. Huge beams, appearing hand hewn, carried the weight of the interior wood ceiling and exterior clay roof. Rustic pegs of both wood and iron kept the whole edifice together.

Lenya thought it was probably one of the most beautiful structures she'd ever seen. It was so organic, so much a part of the surroundings she found it hard to believe it was inanimate.

The building interior was divided into two areas. A small bar stood to the left of the entrance and to the right a table set with several bottles of wine, clippings in plastic and flyers announced prizes won by the various wines. The wall to the right was lined with giant wooden barrels stacked four high.

An archway far to the right was dark and shadowy. Through the gloom she could make out barrels, and some machinery she thought might be for bottling glinted in filtered sunlight through a vine covered clerestory window.

Sirio moved behind the bar and began to shine a wine glass with a clean towel. "Please, may I offer you to taste some of our wines? After all, you have found us; in and of itself a major feat of bravery. Now you must be rewarded."

Lenya looked closely at him as he spoke, his full head of hair and flowing moustache snow white sprinkled with a very few dark strands. His face was tanned—dark in the way only working outside will tan. An open collar shirt revealed a dark V with white skin at the edges, sleeves rolled up to his elbows. She was sure if he rolled them a bit higher there'd be another tan line.

Tall, standing straight to more than six feet, wide shoulders, trim waist, he seemed fit, strong and very handsome, even though his skin was heavily lined over a well formed bone structure.

She guessed he must be in his sixties at least. But what a hunk! He was silent, and in a moment of embarrassment, she realized she'd been staring.

"Uh, uh,...can you tell me a bit about your wines?" She was embarrassed by her stammer, sure he must think her a complete idiot.

"Certainly, I am *padrone* of this winery. My mother and I established it many years ago." He gave her a shy smile with an impish hint. "Now, what would you like to know?"

"My late husband loved wine and liked to find new ones. We spent a fair amount of time traveling the wine regions in Spain, France and Western America. He passed away over a year ago...an accident. It was hard... I'll be here for the next year... it would be great to find local wines... I don't know anything about them." *Oh shit, now I'm babbling.* She looked at Sirio and saw the imp replaced by kindness in his eyes.

He turned and reached under the bar, "All right, let's sample some of the wines." He handed her the freshly shined glass and began to pour in something resembling dark red liquid velvet. There was a twinkle in his eyes as he continued. "Don't let the smoothness of our wines fool you; they have higher alcohol content than the wines you are used to. Be careful, they sneak up and bite you."

He moved around from behind the bar to get a stool and brought it over to her, gesturing for her to sit. "Now you sit and relax while the dogs play together, and I'll tell you everything you want to know."

She looked at him in astonishment. What did he mean? Was there a hidden meaning in those words? I'm imagining things, she thought as she took a sip of the wine.

As the luxurious deep ruby fluid swirled around in her mouth, her tongue savored its taste and bite as her nose was filled with its smooth bouquet. She raised her glass in a silent toast to Andre, "Thank you, my love, for suggesting I sample the wines of Corsica."

After her first few samples, Sirio joined her and they sampled more wines and conversation while the afternoon passed smoothly by. Three hours later, they were sitting in comfortable chairs in front of the fireplace in the living quarters attached to the back part of the winery.

Sirio decided she should have dinner with him before attacking the drive back home. "Too much Corsican wine does not mix well with our terrible roads in these mountains. I don't want my new friend tumbling down into the sea."

Lenya was grateful for his suggestion. As soon she got off the stool and stood up, she started to wobble. She'd imbibed a bit more alcohol than she was comfortable with and needed some food to set her straight.

He prepared a meal of local cheese, dried pork sausage and a salad from his garden. The dogs shared a bowl of kibble and snuggled together on an old rug strategically placed in the warmth from the fireplace.

Afterwards, the humans and dogs sat together watching the fire dwindle while Lenya sipped espresso so strong she thought could it could be used as paint remover. "Sirio, if you don't mind my asking, where did you learn to speak English? You have an American accent...at least it sounds American me." Lenya said.

Sirio laughed. "You caught me. My terrible English, I know, and to add insult to British ears, I did learn it in America. It does not seem to hurt your ears." He said.

"*Au contraire*, my ears are happy, but not as happy as my tongue. It's restful to not have to wind it around French for a change." They both laughed.

"My father was an American flyer who crashed on the island during World War II. My mother fell in love. He promised, but never came back to her—the sorrow of her life."

He tamped more tobacco into his pipe. "My mother brought me up by herself, it wasn't easy, ostracized by both her community and her family. I realized the greatest gift I could give her was to find out why my father never came back."

She could see this was emotional for him, so she remained silent. He continued "So, I went to America and found him, or at least his obituary and grave...he'd been killed in the war. I stayed with his family—also mine, of course, for more than a year—learned your language.

Later, I brought my mother to visit, her first time off Corsica. It was important for her. He'd told his family he'd loved her, wanted to marry her, even not knowing she was pregnant. Sadly, his family didn't know her name and though they tried for years, had no way to find her."

He got up and rooted around on the counter for more tobacco. Once he had the strands glowing again, he sat down and coaxed both dogs onto his lap.

As he exhaled a dense cloud of smoke, he continued. "It was a healing time for us all, made a big change in my mother's attitude. After all the pain she suffered in her life, she knew the man she loved hadn't deserted her."

He looked off into the fire for a moment before continuing. Perhaps he was reading the memories in the flames, or just gathering his thoughts on how to continue.

"The family also gave her a letter they had received from my father. It was found in his belongings after he died.

"He had told them of a woman he'd met when his plane crashed. How much he loved her, his Corsican angel, as he called her. He had planned to go back to Corsica after the war, find her, to ask her to marry him, to bring her back to America for a new life with him."

Sirio stopped. It was obviously a painful memory. Lenya reached over, took his hand and gave it a gentle squeeze.

They were both silent, gazing together into the dying embers. A branch broke with a loud crackling noise. The moment was over, he regained control. Both of them surreptitiously wiping the corners of their eyes.

After a while, he turned and looked her over. "I think you are all right now, no?"

"Yes, I'm fine. The food was excellent. Exactly what I needed. I forgot about lunch before I left and your wonderful wine on an empty stomach did me in."

"Will you be all right to get home now? The roads are treacherous and there is no light on them." He got up and came close to her, "We don't want an accident...you can stay here. I promise you will be safe with an old fellow like me."

She felt safe, he was so like her grandfather in many ways, the smell of the earth, his pipe, the farmer tan and wrinkles. But Sirio also had a sophistication her grandfather wouldn't have understood.

She thanked him and left with a big smile on her face.

After all, he wasn't that old. And he was very handsome...more than just handsome, very attractive.

As she started the motor of the Rav4, something stirred, stretched and phoenix-like, breathed anew inside her.

Damn, I'm not dead after all!

Chapter 10
Final Edits

Lenya was almost out of American coffee. She pulled the small Italian espresso pot out from under the cabinet and decided to give it a try—go Corsican with real coffee like Sirio's; so strong and thick you can stand up a spoon in it.

The three mile drive down the mountain over rutted roads to the Spar market in Calanzana was always a challenge. Lenya was now a regular customer in the small market along with the rest of the year-round population living up the hills in the village, the newer houses in the flat area at the bottom, tiny hunting lodges and cabins dotting twisted paths through the high forests.

Today, the rain of the past few days had stopped, and she decided to go walking. It wasn't enough to do Tai Chi exercises daily on the small deck under the careful scrutiny of Tom. Better to not take the car for a change.

She made her way carefully down the dirt road avoiding the deep ruts and puddles. Misjudging the depth of the water in one of the larger puddles, she ended up with one of her boots stuck in the mud. The only way out was to roll up her jeans and pull her foot out of the boot, then bend over and yank the boot out. She balanced perfectly on one foot. So far so good. But when the errant boot released fast and nosily from the suction, her balance was destroyed, and Lenya ended on her butt at the edge of the puddle. Her jeans were soaked and her dignity muddied. She laughed so hard Tom came over to lick her face and comfort her. Got'ta remember to treat those puddles with more respect.

Lenya giggled herself all the way back home. While it was a nuisance to go back and change; it was too cold and uncomfortable to continue her walk covered with wet squishy clay all down her backside, not to mention wet jeans chafing in unpleasant places. It was a relief to once again find humor in mishaps.

The little accident had given her a big insight—she was recovering. Her first *contre temps* with a mud puddle when she first moved into the cabin resulted in a lost shoe and a burst of tears as she sat alongside the road next to the puddle sobbing. Anything going wrong had pushed her further into the abyss of depression.

Now she thought the little mishap was funny as she laughed about how she must look, butt covered in gooey mud, one boot on and one boot off. What a turnaround.

After changing into clean clothes she decided to take the Rav to the market after all. She left in clean clothes and high spirits.

The car tucked into a small space in the open village square, Tom walking at her side, Lenya looked again at the surrounding homes, cut stone facades darkened by time facing the tree overhung space.

As she arranged her purchases into the back of the Rav, she decided to take a road she noticed on the other side of the Calanzana village square. It might turn out to be a short cut to someplace interesting, perhaps the hidden atelier of some reclusive artisan, or another of her back road adventures. Her groceries wouldn't suffer from an hour or so in the car, she thought, turning into the narrow street guarded on both sides by the typical grey stone two and three story town houses.

In a few minutes the road narrowed to one lane and she realized a large black SUV with darkened windows was trailing behind her. It was too close to her rear bumper for comfort. For the first time on the island she was edgy. She looked ahead for some place to turn off, any street or driveway leading off the narrow lane—to get away from the menacing SUV. There was no chance to exit ahead. Now frightened, she passed a large wall and then through a gate into a private estate. The SUV was on her back bumper.

Lenya gulped as she remembered the stories about Calanzana told to her by the old gals who owned a small coffee shop there.

The urban legend, or maybe the truth, named Calanzana as the village of choice for retired Mafia dons from Marseille. Lenya figured she'd have to tough it out as she rolled down the passenger window and looked into the faces of four of the hardest-looking men she'd ever seen. Crap, I've done it now, she realized, I'm on the property of some don.

She batted her eyelashes and deliberately, in her worst New York accent, said in French, "Excuse me, I'm an American visitor, and must have made a mistake. A wrong turn? May I turn around here? And, please, can someone direct me back to Calvi?" She sealed it with a large, toothy-All-American-helpless-female-smile.

Two of the men stared at her stone-faced. The driver looked like he was reaching for a gun inside his jacket but only brought out a pack of cigarettes.

The fourth man, older and dressed in black suit, white shirt buttoned to the neck with no tie, smiled back at her, displaying a full set of shining white teeth, almost as white as his full head of hair. In slightly accented English, he said in a surprisingly high raspy voice, "Sure lady, turn around. No problem. When you get back to town, turn left and go down the hill, it'll take you where you want to go."

She had a curious feeling he knew who she was as he motioned to the driver to go ahead into what Lenya realized was a compound with several buildings circling an open driveway area. She turned her car around, relieved to be getting out of there, and made her way back to town and down to the familiar roads.

Once back at home with two of her prized Carte Noire coffee packages in her voluminous hand bag, she stood in front of the sink and let the tap water run cold. It was wonderful, coming from icy peaks above the cabin. It made the best coffee ever and once she had even tried to imagine Andre was there to share it with her. But now, she fully acknowledged he was gone.

I must be more careful on my explorations, she thought. I have to accept I'm a woman alone in a strange country. Might have had a close call today. What if they thought I was spying? Or worse, from what I've heard, working for the government?

Corsica was rife with rumors of old vendettas carried on, kidnappings, bombings, violence directed against newcomers, especially the pied noir, or French Algerians, who settled in Corsica after the Algerian war. Last week a pharmacy in Lumio burned down, supposedly an accident, but the rumor persisted it was set by someone in town who had a grudge against the new owner.

Several holiday mansions had been burned down last summer, supposedly a message to the French to stop building McMansions along the coastline and making real estate too expensive for the offspring of the local Corsican population. The same problem around the world.

As she moved from the sink with her fresh steaming cup of coffee, she heard the familiar Skype ring telling her she had a call. When she got to her computer, Lotte's voice and image were there, keeping her company from the other side of the world. "And how is my roaming twin doing these days? Are we getting over the blues finally? Have any arguments with mud puddles lately?"

"Yeah, not only did I end up butt first in the mud today, but I think I've finally come to grips with the pain of losing Andre. And I promise to be more careful about avoiding the puddles." She laughed; her sister never let her forget anything klutzy. "It's been really good for me to get away." Lenya sighed as she looked around the cozy cabin she made her home. "Sometimes I think Andre's around, and we have occasional conversations, but now we joke and have fun. I know it's nutty, but it makes me smile, not cry." Lenya caught herself starting to cry again as she said it, "Really, I'm okay, I'm not delusional or nuts, I promise you." She giggled a bit, "In fact, I laughed myself silly after ending up in the mud this morning...realized it was funny to me rather than upsetting...big change."

"I always knew you were a little eccentric, but you've been pushing the envelope this past year." No matter how cheery Lotte tried to be, Lenya heard concern in her voice. They were all was left of their little family, and they took care of each other.

"I think I made a friend yesterday. I met an interesting man... owner of one of the local wineries. Sirio. He speaks English; his father was American. We had dinner last night and talked for hours."

"Damn sis, I knew I couldn't leave you alone!" Lotte's voice sounded back to usual. "So, give, is he a hottie? Did'ja get lucky?"

"It wasn't like. He's much older, we talked. He has a dog, Sophia, a Jack Russell like Tom and they were like puppies playing and running around together. Sirio made me dinner and we sat in front of the fire talking." Lenya said. "Then I went home."

"Just because he's older doesn't mean anything. I'm sure they have Viagra in Corsica. Those oldies can be as randy as the young ones now." Lotte chortled on the other end. "At least it shows you're alive."

"Well, don't get your knickers in a twist, it wasn't like that at all...simply friends. But he is an amazingly attractive man." Lenya continued chuckling, "and today I almost got kidnapped...took a wrong turn and ended up in what was probably a Mafia compound...spoke to the don himself...in English."

"By God, you do have a fabulous imagination. I gotta go, back to work...but now I'm happy."

Lenya could hear the sound of Lotte laughing in the background as Skype clicked off. It made their life so easy to keep in contact. They could see each other and talk, and it was almost as good as being together ...almost. It was Lotte's morning and Lenya's afternoon when they spoke. One starting the day, the other ending it, and laughing together again. Lenya knew her life was getting better. She remembered the telephone call from the police, the accident, the horror of the morgue, but it was dimming. She remembered more and more of the good times together with Andre. Maybe it's all a part of healing.

Lenya took her coffee out to the small deck overlooking the side of the mountain down into the valley. Tom was at his usual place by her side. She put the coffee on the top of the porch rail and breathed in the air. Pollution-free, one of the many miracles of Corsica. The loamy, piney smell on top of the constant underlying scent of the maquis; an air filled with growing things, salt and now, the faint snap of ozone foretelling the coming of fall.

Lenya began her routine of Tai Chi. First stretch the arms, then her legs and lower back. Raise the arms to greet the sun and fold down to touch toes. Slowly, she began the form, the pushes and strikes, yin and yang, tiger hands, catch and push the ball, twirl like leaves in the breeze, steal the black pearl. It was soothing and the movements came so naturally her mind went to its own quiet place.

Today, she her job was concentrated on finishing the final edits of the damn book the publisher was dunning her for.

In a few hours it would go off to Ellie, always an amazing feat to her, the child of another generation. Her manuscript would go from Corsica to New York City with a click of her mouse. Ellie would read it over one last time before she e-mailed it to Kinkos to be printed and sent to the publisher, all the requested changes made.

From her computer to hard copy to editor's desk in less than twenty-four hours. And then, she would finally be free to start on the new book.

She felt like a kid who had to eat her dinner before she could have her dessert. Smiling, she remembered her grandfather telling her about the Irish nanny he and his brothers had growing up who used to say to them "If you don't be eatin' your Charlotte Russe you can't have no bologna." It became a family joke.

Humming to herself, she went into the cabin for another cup of coffee and turned on the radio. Might as well have some music with my coffee. When she poured a cup, she heard the haunting strains of "I Muvrini," the famous musicians who brought Corsican polyphony alive in the modern world. Stopping to listen, the hair on her arms stood up as the sensuous music swirled through the cabin.

Her heart beat with rhythms reminiscent of Syria and Arabia of old, early Mediterranean sounds, Gregorian chants, and something primitive and ancient beyond memory hinted at through the harmonies. The music hit her hard and she felt tears roll down her cheeks.

Unfamiliar emotions stirred in her. Odd, I never had kind of response to music before. And then she realized what she felt was joy, peace—contentment. It had been a long time coming.

Back inside, she worked on the last edits, content to be at the computer after her trip to the market and tai chi.

Humming from the music when she returned to the deck hours later, she saw a tiny bouquet of fresh flowers. It was in the exact place where she stood to drink her coffee and look over the mountain.

Tom was sniffing nearby at a new bone.

Chapter 11
Pre-History

Two days later, when Lenya turned on the computer, the top e-mail on the list caught her eye—it was from her editor. Fearful of what it contained, she didn't want to open it before her coffee.

What if it was a rejection? If she had to scrape up the advance to return to the publisher she wouldn't have enough money to stay in Corsica for as long as she might want.

Seven e-mails later she could no longer delay. She knew the damn e-mail could send her one way or the other and she hated the thought she might lose control. Scrolling back Lenya clicked on the message and shut her eyes as she saw it come up on the screen.

Tom licked her ankle and nudged her a bit as if he wanted to be picked up. Maybe he already knew what the message was and was prompting her to read it?

Eyes closed, she inhaled the scent of the cabin. Her brain registered the woody, smoky fragrance laced with olive oil, garlic, and underlying hints of the dried lavender she placed in every possible container.

Today there was a slight trace of green. Hopefully it forecast new beginnings.

She read the first lines of the message.

There are a few minor changes to be made, but we expect the book to be on our winter/holiday release list.
As to the new proposal, we are very interested, but want to see the first three chapters before we commit. Personally, I think it's about time you took on a project like this; you've outgrown your genre and have been wasting time with the last two books.

It took two more readings to understand she was finally free in the truest sense of the word, to write what she always wanted and stay in Corsica. No advance to return, instead, more money coming as soon as the manuscript was accepted.

Lenya danced out onto the deck, hoisting Tom in jubilation and waltzing him around as her dance partner she laughed into the fresh cool air. I'm back, she told herself. It had been a long time coming. Lenya savored her sense of completeness and hint of renaissance it represented.

Corsica is good for me. As she put Tom down, she thought she heard the faint sound of music in the woods. A flute? One of the local warblers? It had the same haunting quality reminiscent of the music of "I Muvrini" she'd been listening to inside the cabin earlier. Maybe the group took their sounds from the local birds? As soon as she stopped to listen, the music stopped. She forgot about it immediately as she gloated over her news.

Have to tell Lotte right away, she decided. Her fingers flew. She typed a message to Lotte and attached the mail from her publisher.

'Here's what the editor sent me.
Your little sister is free, free, free!
Me, your loving twin, L2 (as if you didn't know - LOL)

Lenya decided to celebrate with a filet mignon and open the bottle of dark red Sciacarellu she had bought at Sirio's winery. The next afternoon Lenya finished the last edits requested and e-mailed the book to her editor. In a few days she should have her acceptance and a check following shortly after.

Humming, she pushed "send" on her laptop. Gone! Done. On to the next. She sat back and felt relief push away the tension in her neck and shoulders.

Chapter 12
Pasta and Polyphony

Lenya was singing off key as she pushed the dust mop into hidden corners of the cabin, astounded at dust bunnies collected since her last foray into cleaning.

Tom suddenly became alert. There was a faint tapping outside. What? No one knows I live here. Must be a branch somewhere. But Tom ran to the door and scratched at it with wild barking. It was Sirio. As soon as the door opened, Tom flung himself at Sophia, wagging tail stumps quivering in greeting.

"Sirio, how nice to see you. How on earth did you find me? Come in, come in." He was the first and only visitor to her house. "Can I get you some coffee? Shall we leave the dogs outside? Is everything all right?"

"Lenya, everything is fine. One question at a time. Please." Sirio put his hand up as he looked around. "Very nice place. I am glad to see. But the road to get here..." he slapped hand to forehead. "... a challenge when the rains come."

"I know, I know. Now you understand my 4-wheel drive. Also have to remember to keep the larder stocked up."

Sirio shook his head and smiled at her.

"How did you find me?"

"You forget you are on Corsica." he said with a laugh. "Everyone knows everything about everybody."

"You mean someone told you where I live?"

"Of course. As soon as you sign your lease, the whole island knows. You are a famous writer, we are proud you are here."

"I don't understand."

"You buy your groceries at the Spar in Calanzana, no?"

"I do."

"You drive a Toyota Rav4, old."

"You saw it at the winery."

"Yes, but I know who you are as soon as you drive in."

"How is that possible?"

"This house you rent is owned by a cousin's family. Their son-in-law told me over a nice orange wine." He got up and walked to the window. The afternoon shadows were lengthening on the deck and the green of the near woods was intense. The dogs continued chasing each other around the clearing, pleased with themselves as they spun in circles in their mad dashes.

"You must learn it, Lenya, there are very few secrets in Corsica." He turned towards her. "And those that exist, you don't want to know." He put his index finger against the side of his nose as he turned away. "And, by the way, be careful where you drive, don't get lost if you can avoid it."

She was silent for a moment. Did he know about her taking the wrong road? It was such a tiny thing, too small to mention to anyone. "I'm sure you didn't come to tell me secrets, Sirio." She stopped for a moment and studied him. "May I offer you something to drink?...wine?"

"No thanks. I come to kidnap you for the evening. There's a polyphonic concert at the cathedral in Calvi I thought you might enjoy." He looked down at his shoes. It was becoming a familiar mannerism; she'd seen it before. "The music is typical Corsican, no musical instruments... men singing a capella...our tradition."

The invitation was a surprise. Before she could answer, he continued, "We can have an early dinner at an Italian restaurant I know at the Port and then walk up to the Citadel. The cathedral is there—no strings, as you Americans say." He looked down again for a moment and then at her. "Sometimes it is much nicer to do these things with a friend. I am tired of enjoying such pleasures alone. If I had your telephone, I would have called first. Sorry."

Lenya nodded. She understood completely. "I'd be delighted. I'd seen the advertisement, made a mental note I wanted to go and then forgot about it. What time do we go?' She started wandering around the cabin, trying to think what she needed to get done before she left. Certainly get presentable. "I need to feed Tom first. He gets cranky and nips my ankles when he doesn't eat at his regular time." She was nervous and couldn't stop talking. It was her first time alone with a man in many years.

"I get cranky too." Sirio said. "But I promise…I do not nip ankles." They both laughed. It broke the tension.

She looked down at her ripped jeans and the ratty tee-shirt she'd been cleaning house in. "I think it might be nice if I wash up and change my clothes. What do you think?"

Sirio laughed. "I think would be all right as long as you are quick about it. The concert starts at eight o'clock… if we go soon, we will have time for an aperitif at the Port before dinner."

"What do you want to do with your dog? Sofia, isn't she?" Lenya said.

"We can either leave her here to keep Tom company… or they can come with us. It is Corsica; they can join us for dinner, they only have to sit in the truck while we go to the concert. Cathedrals have not understood it is dogs who are truly God's chosen creatures." He took out his pipe and rubbed the bowl against the side of his nose before putting the stem in his mouth. The movement was comfortable; it was reminiscent of grandfather telling her it was how he kept the wood bowl of his pipe oiled.

In twenty minutes she was back looking fresh, showered, hair combed, clean clothes, scented with a whiff of Coco Chanel and enhanced by a modicum of make-up.

They piled Tom and Sophia into Sirio's big Toyota Tundra.

"I like the color of the truck, I've never seen such a deep burgundy color." Lenya remarked.

"It's the color of my excellent Sciacarellu wines." he explained with his finger alongside his nose. De Manzino Vinicole was emblazoned in gold script across both doors. "It's a reminder to all my patrons when they see me driving around. Free advertising—always a good thing."

Lenya was grateful to find the suspension in the big truck better than her Rav4 and it took the rutted dirt road with less discomfort. Lenya brought a small bag of dog food, a bottle of water and plastic bowls. The dogs would not miss their evening meal.

They settled into one of the many open patio restaurants rimming the Port of Calvi. Tom and Sophia curled up together on a nearby chair.

As she and Sirio sipped their Kirs and looked up towards the Citadel, he pointed across the bay to the small village perched on a steep hillside. "Look over at Lumio. We are here at the perfect time to watch the sunset. Keep your eye on it."

Lenya looked towards the whitewashed village. It was barely discernible.

"Now, now, look at it change color."

As the sun set behind the Citadel, the buildings of Lumio turned a soft peachy pink color.

"It's breathtaking. I've never seen anything like that view anywhere else," she looked at the pink of the village, the green of the surrounding hillside and the turquoise of the water below. "Corsica is truly the island of beauty."

"This is one of my favorite views," he agreed. "But there is an interesting history to Lumio. It is said to have been the ancient site of sun worshippers and they built the village angled especially to collect the last rays of the setting sun." She saw him twisting the ends of his moustache.

"Let's toast to the builders of Lumio." She raised her glass.

"Thanks for the view," they said in unison and clinked glasses.

At the restaurant, she studied the large menu. Italian food was Lenya's favorite and her stomach was growling. She realized she'd again forgotten lunch and looked around to see what other people were having. Everything looked good.

Sirio seemed to sense her hesitation. "How about the angel hair with Puttanesca sauce, and linguini a la Carbonara. We can share, okay? Then a salad and some fried calamari. They all go well with the house red. It's a bit rough, but nice." He laughed and shook his finger at her, "but we will share only a demi carafe so we don't miss the concert."

She tried not to look embarrassed as she remembered how tipsy she was at the winery. Sirio waved the waitress over to order. Tom and Sofia were sleeping together on the banquette. Lenya looked down at the them and thought how well behaved they were, better than most children at restaurants.

As soon as the food arrived, she tucked into it with gusto.

"Tell me about the concert, what will we hear?" Lenya asked.

"Corsica is famous for the polyphonic tradition. Some think it goes back to Neolithic times, others think it has African, Eastern influences. Men generally, singing with no accompaniment. Now sometimes women too."

"I've heard 'i Muvrini' on the radio. Like them?"

"Yes, but they have modernized the traditional form and made it more mainstream...more popular...a good thing to my mind."

"I love their music, I have it on my iPod and listen to it for inspiration when I write."

"You have a good ear, my dear. Tonight you will hear some of the original, perhaps more of the ancient church music and more traditional. Hopefully a good group. I've not heard them before."

Sirio checked his watch. "We must leave now to see the concert begin."

Lenya looked at her half-finished bowl of pasta. She was so busy talking she didn't do her usual New York style gobble of everything on the plate.

As Sirio waved for the check, she managed to scarf down a bit more of the remaining pasta. Delicious.

Tom looked up at her from his spot next to Sofia. Lenya could almost read his mind. "Don't tell me I eat too fast. You're a dog and you bolt everything down without chewing." He almost shrugged as he snuggled back down next to Sophia. "Don't get too comfortable, you get a fast pee and then into the truck with you. I'll bet you'll like being alone with your new girlfriend."

Sirio had the check in hand. Lenya leaned over, "Please, let me pay my share."

He looked offended. "Lenya, this is not a 'date' as you Americans call it, but a night out with friends. Next time, you invite me and you can pay." He chuckled. "This way I'm assured of a return engagement."

"Okay, it's a deal, but don't forget—my turn next."

They cracked the windows in the truck for Tom and Sophia before locking it. Sirio turned toward the Citadel. "Take my hand and we will hopefully make it in time." He pointed up the incline rising beyond the steep hill they'd already climbed after leaving the restaurant.

Lenya was already out of breath. Damn, shouldn't have rushed those last bites but too good to leave. Remembering the first time she made the climb, also after a big meal, she thought she'd at least be in better shape now after hiking in the mountains.

Sirio marched up the carved stone ramp leading to the Citadel at the pace of a speed walker. Lenya dragged behind him like a stout anchor. By the time they came to the steps led to the place d'Armes she was sweating and dinner was roiling around inside. "Stop. Give me a moment...have to catch my breath." She bent over and once again put her hands on her knees.

As she looked up Sirio was laughing. "You rest here a minute. I'll go get the tickets. Meet me at the top when you can. Don't worry, you'll find it." He turned and hiked up the steep steps.

The bloody old man must be part mountain goat, she grumbled to herself.

By the time she made it to the top, Sirio was standing at the entrance to the Cathedral St-Jean Baptiste.

With tickets in hand, he directed her inside. It was smaller than she remembered. The white walls set off the stained glass windows and handsomely carved altar in the 13th Century building.

Then Lenya remembered her brief introduction to Calvi's history. The cathedral had been partly destroyed during the Franco-Turkish siege and never completely restored to its prior grandeur. She rather liked it the way it was, rougher, more rustic.

Sirio leaned over during a break between songs. "Look, no fresco or painting behind the altar, everything white. Maybe the artwork destroyed by British cannonball when Admiral Nelson helped Pascale Paoli the revolutionary leader."

He put his finger alongside his nose.

Lenya finally understood it was the signal for a questionable story coming next.

"Maybe stolen—no one knows for sure." He shook his head and grinned, "...very Corsican" and leaned back in his carved chair with his hands folded over his stomach as the music started up again.

The singers, five young men, the oldest no more than early thirties, stood in front of the altar. They were casually dressed in dark clothes, black shirts and neatly pressed blue or black jeans.

No musical instruments accompanied their voices as their harmony soared into the ribs of the groin vaulted ceiling, magnified and came back down to fill the hearts of the spellbound audience.

Lenya knew she was sharing the authentic polyphony of Corsica, a musical tradition passed down through the centuries. Some of the sounds were clearly reminiscent of Gregorian chants she had heard, but other parts were more primal, more dangerous in finding hidden places of her consciousness.

African rhythms reminded her she was on an island anchored in the Mediterranean in an area criss-crossed throughout time by the seafarers of three continents.

The cathedral in its chunky simplicity provided the perfect acoustical stage for the traditional nasal voices. Lenya soaked it all in and almost pinched herself to prove she was really there. Life is wonderful, after all.

A tall, young man broke away from the group and stood alone in front of the altar. Lenya smiled; he was so heavily muscled, broad shoulders and thick neck, he looked like a longshoreman or a stonemason rather than a singer.

Holding his hands stiffly at his sides he lifted his face and began to sing. The strains of "Ave Maria" filled the building in the voice of an angel.

Lenya felt the hair on her arms rise as the familiar hymn enveloped her. She had to look again to confirm the sweet music was coming from the strong young man with the pink cheeks. Magic comes in all forms, she thought as the Cathedral erupted with wild applause.

At the end, Lenya and Sirio made their way out with the small crowd. Going down was easier—and dinner had settled.

When Sirio dropped her off, he took her key and, walking across the deck with her, helped her open the door. Then backed out of the doorway and took her hand. "Thank you for a most enjoyable evening. You are very good company, my dear."

"Sirio, I'm the one to thank you. It was a delightful evening. And, you're pretty good company too."

He turned and made a small bow and waved as he walked down the incline to his truck.

Aldo was in his usual post to watch the cabin. He was shocked to see his friend's truck pull into the long drive. It couldn't be. But then he saw Sirio go around to the passenger side and help Lenya down the long step, take Tom in his arms and place him on the deck.

She and Tom were both absent when he returned to his post after hunting even though her car was in its usual place. He had no idea 'his' woman, as he had begun to think of her, knew Sirio. Was she now the woman of his friend? He was relieved as the big truck pulled away after Lenya opened the cabin door, turned and waved goodnight.

Life was beginning to become very complicated. He had to speak to Sirio about this. He left his post and made his way back to the cast-eddu. He knew the track well, even with no light.

Chapter 13
Aléria

Once free from finishing the overdue book, Lenya decided to take a short holiday. It was time spread her wings, explore further reaches of the island, to leave the safe haven of the cabin.

Aléria was going to be her first foray. Etruscan artwork piqued her interest, especially the erotic art on bowls and vases in the 15th century Genoese Fort de Matra, now the Musée d'Archeologie. It was also reputed to have prehistoric artifacts from the Neolithic Age to the Iron Age.

Lenya was always fascinated with archeology and this was exactly the right place to start her explorations. Her solitary adventure made her feel like a kid in expectation of a longed for chocolate dessert and she reveled in the realization she had no trepidation about taking the short holiday alone.

Corsica had been occupied continuously for over 8500 years through the Neolithic, Chalcolithic, Bronze and Iron Ages. Artifacts from these ancient civilizations, hidden for centuries, were now often uncovered due to the rapid development on the island and some found their way to the Musée in Aléria.

An ancient Roman city was a short walk behind the museum. Perched on the crest of a hill it overlooked present day Aléria and the sea. She wouldn't see any of the dolmens or menhirs she was so fascinated with, but Etruscan porno was enticing and maybe she'd rent "La Cage Au Folle" again after seeing the real thing.

She'd daydreamed for hours wandering in the fort-turned-museum, only quitting when it closed. The prehistoric artifacts were disappointing, With the current fad for muscled superheroes tainting her imagination, she had expected macho representations of warriors and gods and the proliferation of effete men in feminine poses surprised her. Several were obvious pornography, and it was clear the Etruscans had no problem with homosexuality.

It gave Lenya food for thought as she remembered the acid political battles going on back in the states between the ultra conservative religious right and the more liberal thinkers over gay marriage. She lamented the new fundamentalist religions demonizing behavior existing since the beginning of time. What was it the ancients knew? What have we forgotten in America...or never learned? How had the strident certainty and acrimonious polemics of conservatives and fundamentalists co-opted natures organic tolerance? Another mystery to ponder.

One afternoon in the unsullied sun of the island, she sat on a block of stone in the ruins of the Roman forum outside the museum and munched on a cheese and ham baguette. It was a wonder how a single layer of cheese and an almost transparent slice of ham slathered with butter could taste so good. Was it the bread? Americans had to have a mound of both cheese and ham in their sandwiches while the French seemed to get by very well on much less. Cultural differences again, like the Etruscan art.

You didn't have to agree with the differences between people, to accept them. It occurred to her maybe taste alone was at the bottom of culture—social decisions and expediency. Perhaps civilization had little to do with moral imperatives, real or invented by imaginary friends, but should be looked at in the context of the personal choices of those who yelled the loudest. She didn't know, but the deeper she immersed herself in the culture and history of what she now considered her home, the more she questioned the culture she had been brought up in.

The sea and the harbor of Aléria were filled with ships in ancient times. But the Etruscans had picked a hill quite a ways in from the port to build their city. Perhaps it was easier to defend against pirates. Maybe they wanted to keep from being easy pickings where the marauders could hit and run back to their boats with whatever they were able to grab.

Then she remembered visiting Aigue Mortes, a massive fortification on the Mediterranean near the Camargue. Once having direct access to the sea, the guardian of the port now squatted in a swamp silted over with mud and time. Perhaps was the case in Aléria, as it had been with Ephesus also. Time and weather could change everything, even seemingly move cities away from the sea.

Cultures could change in time as well. New religions, beliefs, ethics and rules. All made by men—perhaps those who shouted the loudest, the strongest, held the most weapons, or had the most followers.

From where she sat, Roman temple columns and steps were visible in mounds of rock. If she squinched her eyes, she could make out the forum as it had once been, almost see the stalls selling multicolored fruits, grapes, cheeses and dried meats. There must have been fish, caught earlier in the morning, fresh for the table. Hawkers selling their wares, amphorae of wine touted to be the best in the region. Aléria was a quiet city in the present. In Roman times it bustled with trade from all over the Mediterranean. Was the Etruscan pottery sold in the marketplace? She wondered if it was made to order or painted at the whim of the artisan and offered at their stalls. Was it commonplace to ask for the obviously homosexual themes, or was it something to be kept secret and private? Different cultures again, or just pre-Christian?

She remembered sitting with Andre years ago in a similar spot in the ruins of Volubilis in the Atlas mountains of Morocco. The Roman city was built to overlook and guard the pass leading to the Sahara. At the time she marveled how small the city had been, the ruins of the grand homes demarcated into rooms appeared tiny to her. Perhaps it's difficult to guess space from only an outline?

Getting up from her stone, she stowed the remains of her lunch in a pocket to dispose of later and strolled around the remains of the ancient city once more. The archeological recovery of the ruins had been discontinued due to lack of funds. She wondered what other historic projects around the world suffered because of the world financial crisis.

Standing in the middle of the old marketplace, Lenya looked around before leaving, wanting to memorize the scents in the air, the feeling of the breeze from the ocean wafting over the mounds of the deserted city. As she leaned against a wall covered with moss, she closed her eyes to listen to the chatter of the ancient streets. Almost.

She was filled with cheer as she walked to a small restaurant on a side street near where she stayed. The owners were an English couple who fell in love with Corsica and moved there when they married. Twenty-four years later, the love affair with the island and each other continued strong as ever.

The husband was the chef and waiter. His wife bustled around the dining room, her sphere of influence. Her mission was to be sure everyone was happy, glasses filled, and food satisfactory. In her spare time she collected money and found out as much as possible about all her customers. The lower reaches of the dining room were the domain of a pug who followed the wife around, always close to her ankles. Lenya wondered how the woman didn't trip over the small stout animal.

They adopted her, the American writer, as she was referred to. It was pleasant and relaxing to speak English as they queried her about what she was working on.

The wife was fond of Tom. So was the pug. Tom was always on his best behavior and was rewarded with a water bowl and his own dish filled with a bit of potato and some meat culled from plates going back to the kitchen. He was already full and snoozing under Lenya's table as she attacked her favorite meal—lamb laced with garlic, flageolets and a demi-carafe of the strong local red wine. It was superb, *comme habitude.*

"How did the research go today?" the woman asked as she looked under the table. The pug had decided hanging out with Tom was more agreeable than following ankles.

"Interesting," Lenya said, filling her wine glass again. "The pottery in the museum never ceases to fascinate me. We are so prudish about sex in the States I'm constantly amazed by cultures so open they eat off dishes depicting what many would call an 'abomination' back home."

"You Americans—always obsessed with sex and repressing it at the same time." The wife laughed. Lenya was so used to hearing about sexually repressed Americans it rolled right off her back. Having a French husband had injured her to most of the anti-American slurs Andre's family was prone to throw at her. She'd learned since the war in Iraq anti-American sentiment wasn't limited to the French, the English had jumped on the bandwagon too. She wasn't going to join in this war of words and, ignoring the missiles, let them fall short of their intended target.

"We Brits have much wider thoughts about the subject. Everyone knows the boys have at it with each other in the schools and no one pays any attention. Probably half the men are closet poufs and we don't bother ourselves about it." She flicked an imaginary piece of lint off her immaculate black skirt. "Let's face it, if we got bothered about the occasional homo hump, we'd not have a man available." Lenya glanced at the husband behind the bar, rolling his eyes as he dried a glass.

"What do you think the ancient Corsicans thought about it?" Lenya asked.

"Probably didn't give it much thought. It was considered the norm in the ancient armies. Greek for sure. Roman too I think, Janissaries, certainly. Women in short supply, easier to have a boy at the ready who you can later train into a soldier when he gets of an age past the taste of his lover." She shook her head. Lenya could hear the "harrumph!" trailing behind as she went into the kitchen.

The coffee was the usual tiny cup and only half full, a swallow at best, but Lenya wasn't ready to go back to the pension. "I found some archeologists in the museum today who think some of the carved stones found on the island date back to the end of the Neolithic Age. They might be from at least 4000 BC, or even further."

"I'm not surprised. A customer of ours is a professor from Scotland. He frequently comes to the university as a guest lecturer." She bustled around Lenya's table scraping up the crumbs from the crusty bread. "He suspected there are many more undiscovered sites in some of the wild mountainous regions. Whenever he has the chance, he treks through areas where there are no trails." She rubbed energetically at a spot refusing to give up. "Everyone is afraid he'll fall or have an accident, won't come back and they'll have to go and look for him. The hunters around here call him the 'Crazy Scott' and tell him to wear a bright red shirt so they won't mistake him for something to eat when they go boar hunting."

Lenya wondered if he had come upon the stones in the woods behind her cabin.

Soon the wine took hold, she realized she was tipsy and time for her to gather up Tom to go to their nearby room.

The next morning she spent communing again with the ancient Romans in their excavated city. By the time she photographed the remains of the various temples, the forum and some private homes, she was ready for the torturous trip back home. The RN was fine but side roads were narrow, filled with switchbacks and no lights. Not much fun in a car with a stick shift.

The drive offered plenty of time to think about the past evening's conversation. The Brits anti-American stance was expected. It was odd to find on the island. The Corsicans had been surprisingly welcoming to her, especially when they found out she was American. Since Corsica was part of France, this was a mystery until Sirio explained the Corsican affinity for the USA. "During World War Two, in order to build their airbase, the Americans rid us of mosquitoes. Malaria was a huge problem so the Yanks sprayed all the swampy areas and the disease has never came back. Corsica once had a high death rate from malaria...every family on the island effected at one time or another."

Lenya had been even more interested when he continued, "Also, in WWII, first the Italians came to the island, followed by the Germans. The French did nothing. The damn Vichy government sold us out and we were starving and being shot and killed at will by the Germans. Everything changed once the Yanks came to build their airbase. They supplied us with food, kept the Bosch at bay and saved a lot of lives. Corsicans have long memories. We don't easily forget—either cruelty or kindness—we remember."

Halfway home she was ravenous, but every eating place was closed during the off- season. About to give up, she spotted a light in the distance. Hopefully, it looked promising. As she pulled up in front, she found it was one of the ubiquitous bars serving both coffee and liquor. Generally, they also had sandwiches and snacks for aperitifs. As she walked in the door, a chill hit her. The hair on the back of her neck stood on end. This was the wrong place to be a stranger.

At a small table off to her right two men were seated, one wearing a black cowboy hat, an odd thing to find in Corsica, let alone in this out of the way place. The other man was dressed in the traditional old-fashioned blue workmen's coverall.

They appeared to be deep in conversation, but stopped the second she put her foot in the door. Behind them, there was a tiny alcove with four men seated at a table, all dressed in dark, non-descript clothing and older than the two men in front. Again, their conversation stopped. Oh-oh. This is not the place to be. All six men looked at her with a combination of both suspicion and malevolence.

Her foray into the don's compound hadn't frightened her as much as this place. She could tough it out or run screaming out the door. Lenya was not a screamer.

A middle aged woman behind the bar stopped washing glasses, wiped her hands on her apron and looked up with both a question and a warning in her eyes. "What d'ya want?" she asked, not very cordially in French.

"I'm looking for something to eat. This place has the only light I've seen since leaving Alèria." Lenya felt a tension the room so palpable she thought she could almost reach out and touch it. "I'm going to Calvi" she continued.

"Where you from?" the woman asked in her gruff manner, "hear some accent in your French...not from around here."

"Yes, no,...sorry, I'm an American...New Yorker." she heard a brief and barely audible sigh of relief from the men as tension leaked from the room.

"Ah well, okay. Can give you a coffee and baguette with some cheese, nothing else to eat in the place. You'll have to take it with you." She cast a sideways look at Lenya as she inclined her head towards the men.

"That will be fine. Thank you. I only need something to keep me going until I get to Calvi." Lenya read the message loud and clear: get the hell out as soon as possible!

As she waited for the woman to make her sandwich and coffee, she saw off to one side the stuffed head of a mean looking *sanglier*.

What then caught her attention was a photograph behind the bar. It was blown up to the size of a large poster. A French police car, doors open, was in the background. A young man, wearing a cap and dressed as a farm worker with a sullen look on his face was being handcuffed by two policemen. Lenya thought it was odd to have as decor, but she knew enough to keep her mouth shut.

The woman handed her a small sack containing her coffee and sandwich. She paid and left. As she clicked the lock open on the Rav she heard the conversation start up behind her and she felt the tension leave her spine.

She felt if she had walked into the middle of the men planning a bank robbery...or even something worse. With a sigh of relief and a sip of good hot espresso, she got back on the road. The realization she might have put herself in real danger was frightening, not something she was used to.

She was exhausted by the time she finally arrived at the cabin. For the first time since moving in, she felt she was coming home as she made her way up the familiar dirt road.

Her flashlight illuminated the steep track studded with rocks and roots—dangerous going; especially for someone who lived alone. Neighbors were much further than a shout away.

Still frightened from the menace she had felt on the trip home, it made her think about other dangers she had unconsciously been facing.

Her main fear was falling and breaking something that would prevent her from moving. It could be weeks before someone noticed the crazy American woman in the cabin was missing. At this time of year, they'd probably assume she'd given up for the winter and left like the rest of the tourists.

It might be spring before she was found, stiff and cold with pieces missing after the resident wildlife took a nibble or two. Tom could easily starve to death or be eaten by something larger.

He didn't seem worried as he trotted along at her side, tail wagging as his rump rolled with its springy terrier gait. His nose was in the air.

"What's up Tom? Smelling something good?" She wasn't embarrassed talking to him. If someone heard her they might think she was dotty, but too bad. They wouldn't understand he was the only familiar living being she had in this strange place. She often found herself singing to him, talking to him and asking his opinion, which she obligingly supplied for him in response. Then she thought of Sirio. She felt she might have finally found a friend. A human one.

Tom's ears stood up, he was alert, but not running off to chase whatever he scented. It mustn't seem a threat to him. When they were back in the States, he knew all her friends and greeted them with tail wagging, but he barked at strangers.

Lenya trusted his ability to know the difference and to keep her safe. She kept along the path but held the heavy flashlight a little more securely, in case he made a mistake. Maybe his nose was as questionable as his hearing.

The beam from the flashlight made the large deck circling the cabin into a ballroom for shadows created by surrounding trees dancing and bowing, pirouetting in time to music only they heard. She realized it was the first time she'd come home after dark, and chastised herself for being a fraidy-cat.

It did look desolate without lights on, blank black windows with no hint of what might be lurking inside. She must light up the house and make a fire in the fireplace right away to cheer herself up and take away the primal fear of the dark.

The flashlight beam illuminated a burst of color on the deck. It shouldn't be there. She brought the light back over the spot again and saw a small, colorful bouquet of wildflowers like the ones she'd seen before she left for Aléria. These were wilted now and looked as if they'd been there for a few days.

Odd for a small child to have been at the boulders and then found their way to her home? Did I bring the flowers home with me after lunch? She clearly remembered she left them as an offering to the ancient god who inhabited 'her' grotto.

She entered the empty cabin with trepidation, but found all as she had left it. Empty. Alone.

Yes, she thought as she turned on every lamp in the place, lights make a huge difference. Relaxing in front of the stone fireplace, the tiredness and fun of the last few days returned...but the flowers on the deck made the hair on her arms stand on end when she thought about them!

Tom's ears perked up again at a soft scurrying sound outside. Lenya thought she saw a shadow swiftly cross in front of the large uncovered picture window.

Someone or something was on her deck. She put on the bright outside light and got up to look. Standing at the sliding glass doors with her heart beating a vigorous tattoo, she saw nothing.

Then she remembered a night her first weeks in the cabin. She was watching television and had a feeling like someone was behind her. Eyes seemed to burn against her back like searchlights and she turned quickly—catching two small deer huddled together on the deck wide-eyed as if caught in the act of watching her television. Their hooves clattered across the wooden deck as they sped off into the night. She remembered laughing and feeling sorry she'd scared them away before the end of the program. They might have wanted to know which ladies the bachelor gave the rose to.

This sound was not the same as the deer noises, but she dismissed it as probably one of the many critters who inhabited the dense woods on 'her' mountain.

If Tom wasn't afraid, then she wasn't! But odd... Must remember to ask if there are any critters in the forest to watch out for the next time I go to the market.

When she went to bed, she took her mop handle with her, propping it upright between the bed and the night stand so she could grab it quickly if needed. She laughed to herself as she imagined brandishing the pole like a weapon and scaring the daylights out of one of the millions of squirrels who inhabited the surrounding trees.

Later that night, Aldo caught his breath as she took off her sweater and stretched in front of the bed, idly scratching her midriff where her jeans had rubbed an irritation into the tender skin. Throwing her nightgown over her shoulder, she made her way down from the loft into the bathroom to brush her teeth and change for bed.

She had a strong and healthy looking body, he thought to himself, admiring her curves and the round fullness of her breasts. Her skin looked soft and smooth.

The thought of touching her made him stiffen a little. He knew it was too soon to think like that, and he willed such thoughts away.

He hoped he hadn't frightened her when he placed a fresh bouquet on the deck. The ones she found had been wilted, but he hadn't wanted to replace them until her knew she was back home.

Aldo made himself comfortable in a pile of pine needles under the large tree nearest to her loft. Because of its elevation, he could see into the top half of her bedroom window.

Tom greeted him like a long lost friend when Lenya let him out for his last pee of the night. He gently nuzzled Aldo's hand as he took the offered piece of dried meat. Reluctant to go back in the house and leave his friend outside, Tom looked back once as he went through the door into the cabin. Knowing the dog's name made Aldo feel closer to the woman. Tom was a friend she obviously held dear.

Aldo pulled the rabbit skins closer over his shoulders before settling in for the night. Joy filled his heart at the thought they were home again.

At first he had been afraid they wouldn't return, but she hadn't taken all her machines with her so he'd thought they probably weren't gone for good.

He'd keep watch until the first light and then slip away into the woods. He'd already found her some pretty fresh flowers to make her smile when she let Tom out in the morning. In the meantime, when she put her lights out, he could play her some music. Fingering the small flute he carved years ago he began to play music.

But what had she been doing with Sirio? When she wasn't home these last days, he waited for a while in the woods near Sirio's vineyard, but the man was there as always, alone except for Sophia trotting next to him as they greeted visitors to the tasting room.

The woman was nowhere in sight.

He'd speak with Sirio and find out what was going on between him and the woman.

Maybe Sirio would know where she went when she left for a few days. It worried Aldo. He didn't think he could stand the bad prank if the gods fooled him by putting a woman in his path who wasn't really meant for him.

Dia wouldn't do such a thing, of that he was sure. But the other evil tricksters? They could do anything.

As *signadori* he had lifted enough evil eyes placed on innocents by the *ammaliatrice* or *streghe* and their evil-doing gods to know anything was possible.

Chapter 14
A Phone Call

Modern technology is wonderful, Lenya thought as her cell phone rang first thing in the morning. The tiny France Telecom model gave its familiar digital rendition of the theme from "Mission Impossible" and Tom barked along with it. For some reason, the ring irritated his failing ears. She reminded herself to change the tune.

Lotte was on the line.

"Hey sis, what are you up to? And by the way, congrats on finally getting the book done." Lotte liked to know what was happening at all times—couldn't stand the notion she might be missing out on something.

"I'm okay, how are you? What's up?"

"Remember Francis, the gal who handles my accounts at the bank? Well, her brother is on a walk-about sabbatical from his company. He designs computer role-playing games involving medieval combat."

Lenya rolled her eyes. She could feel it coming. Lotte was trying to fix her up. Her sister suffered from an odd compulsion. She wouldn't let Lenya alone, even if they were thousands of miles away. At three feet or three thousand miles, Lotte had spent most of her life 'managing' her. *Why?* Lenya wondered. *What is it about me whispers 'help me?' Or is it Lotte?*

Lotte continued, "He's with one of those new techie companies who treat their employees with kid gloves...nice guy, but more importantly, Francis says he's a real hunk. A few years younger than you, you dirty old woman...anyway, he's going to be in Corsica." Lotte couldn't help it. Her voice always rose up a few notes when she was getting ready for the denouement. This time she was reaching a new pitch. "And— he lives in Los Angeles." Lenya had no idea why her sister thought LA might be a selling point.

"Francis called me. She remembered you were in Corsica and wants to know if you might be willing to meet her brother, Terrence, and show him 'round the island. Unless you have something better to do—like take Tom for a walk or something." The irony was stiff with more starch than needed.

Not the first time she's tried to fix me up—Lenya remembered high school and college. But she's outdone herself this time—sending someone to Corsica is over the top, even for her. Lenya sighed, there was no way to get out of this, she'd have to meet this guy or she'd never live it down. She imagined Lotte telling the story, left eyebrow at full tilt, "Sure, I send her a guy all the way from Los Angeles to Corsica and she's too busy to even meet him for a drink….and you should see him, a real knock-out, blah, blah." Lenya shook her head, it was better to meet him than to deal with the crap if she didn't. She laughed to herself as she imagined Lotte getting in her car and trying to figure out how to drive to Corsica to bawl her out.

"Okay, I'll meet him. When's he coming in and where? You know I'm in the sticks and it takes a while to get anywhere on this island, even though it isn't very large." She made sure her voice was flat—not a hint of interest. It wasn't easy to make a point; Lotte was as thick as a brick when she wanted.

"He's coming in the day after tomorrow and he'll be staying in Ajaccio for a couple of days. I'll e-mail you the name and number of the hotel. Why not give him a day to get cleaned up and smell good and you can meet him the next day for lunch, that is, if your schedule's not too full."

Okay, okay, I get it! Lenya thought. "No problem; it'll work for me. But keep in mind it will take me almost a full day to get to Ajaccio. It's south and on the other end of the island from where I live. Give him my French cell number so he can call me if he's delayed...or his plans change."

"Will do. Give Tom a pat for me and an extra doggie biscuit. Has he met any randy French Poodles he can't live without?"

"No, and he doesn't want to be fixed up with any either, so don't go making dates for him too." At least they both had a little snicker over that barb.

"Speak at ya later. Love ya." Lotte was laughing her little victory laugh as she hung up quickly so Lenya couldn't change her mind.

Looking at the silent phone, Lenya made plans in her head. Tom behaved with the distinction of a true Englishman. He could go with her to any hotel in Ajaccio, and sit on the floor or on a banquette next to her when she had her obligatory lunch with this LA video games designer. Then, after the requisite lunch, she could say her good-byes and be off on her own. Terrence. She had to remember Francis' brother's name was Terrence. Nice name, she thought.

She hadn't been to Ajaccio since she arrived on the island with the tour; two days of being whipped around the city in a bus was enough to whet her appetite for more.

The idea was starting to appeal to her. She could take Tom on a long walk around the seaport, have a relaxed dinner in one of the restaurants fronting the water, and take a couple of days to explore Ajaccio's nooks and crannies. She had no schedule to keep, no meetings or appointments to cancel, no one to account to. She and Tom were free to do as they wished. Lenya waltzed around the deck and air punched the sky. *Yeah! Freedom!*

Guide books spread on the dining table, she began to make a list of places she wanted to see in Ajaccio. The first day she arrived on the island she almost drooled passing an open market with local Brocciu and Tomme cheeses, fig jams and chestnut and Clementine blossom honeys. Everything looked delicious—she wanted to buy it all, but of course didn't. Now she could stop to gather some delicacies to bring home, maybe even share with Sirio.

The *Musée Fesch* was on her bucket list, reputed to have an excellent collection of Italian art. She heard rue Cardinal-Fesch, a pedestrian street filled with chi-chi boutiques calling her name.

When she thought about it, it was a long time since she'd gone shopping for herself, with the exception of being shoved in and out of Saks Fifth Avenue by Lotte before she left the states, and the hour or so she and Tom strolled around in Nice. Certain she owed herself more time than that for shopping, and since she was due the final advance from the book she delivered, she added on an extra day to wander in and out of classy French boutiques. It was about time she checked out some of the current fashions, at least those suitable for polyphonic concerts and dinners in Calvi.

She might even be ready to consider a social life on the island and she wanted to be dressed for it. The few things she had packed for her original trip were getting slightly worn and seedy by now and she always forgot to ask Lotte to send her a box of clothes from the Connecticut house. As a matter of fact, she hadn't even thought about her appearance.

Most important of all, she was anticipating with pleasure rather than dread the thought of getting out of the cabin and doing things to please herself—things she was happy about doing.

Leonidas! Oh! She almost forgot. She would go on-line and see if Ajaccio had a boutique selling her favorite Belgium chocolates, a visit to Leonidas alone was worth the journey. Calvi didn't have any and it was probably a good thing. Lenya could easily scarf down a pound of the delectable pieces of joy. Then her clothes would not only be worn, they wouldn't fit either.

Soon she was wiggling in her chair in expectation of a fun excursion. When she went to Aléria, she had been in her studious research mode. This trip was going to be fun with a capital 'F.'

Decision made, she continued putting ideas on her list. If the weather was good, she might go look at the Îsles Sanguinaires, named for their dark red granite cliffs as they turned blood red in the sun.

The route back home would take her past the famous Ajaccio beaches. The Towers dotting the coastline fascinated her, ninety-one of them built by the Genoese during the fifteenth century to provide early warning of pirate raids and other attacks. As soon as an enemy was in sight, fires were lit on the sighting tower and could be seen by the next, who then lit their own fires to signal on down the line until the whole island was warned.

Thinking about the call, she decided, after all, she was also looking forward to speaking English with an adult human being from home.

Sirio was good company, but sometimes it wasn't so easy to communicate with him. His English, while correct, wasn't very current.

She had no idea what a video game designer—Terrence, she must think of him by name—talked about, but it certainly wouldn't be in French or Italian, definitely a plus.

Out on the deck to finish her coffee, she spotted the new bouquet. How did that get there? Was it the noise she had heard the night before, the shadow she saw moving so quickly across the deck? For a moment she was frightened again before thinking how irrational her fear was.

If whoever was leaving the nosegays meant her harm, then she would have already been confronted. But no one approached her, threatened her, or came near. Was someone watching?

Maybe it was a good idea to leave again for a few more days. Whoever was playing these tricks might get bored by the time she came back and leave her alone.

In the interim, she'd stay close to the cabin and try and catch whoever or whatever was leaving her flowers.

Could someone be stalking her from the woods? She thought of all the television programs about serial killers who went after women in isolated places. Very nasty to think about.

She stood on the deck and looked out over the green of the surrounding woods, inhaled their fresh scent and noted touches of red and orange—leaves already turning color. It looked very safe to her, but perhaps it was only because she wanted it see it that way.

Maybe it was time to look forward to meeting a nice man. And why not? she told herself.

Chapter 15
The Interrogation

Aldo never found it easy to start conversations. To ask Sirio about the woman—thinking about it was worse than torture. Should he be direct and ask what Sirio was doing with her? Or was it the wrong thing to do, impolite? While the clan had rules of etiquette and ways of communication, Aldo understood the world outside had different ones. He was at a loss.

Should he claim this woman as his and tell Sirio to keep away? But it wasn't true, and anyway, it might make Sirio mad. He didn't want to anger him. They were old friends. It took three days of thinking and planning for him to find an acceptable approach. He would visit Sirio; tell him he'd found a woman who might be the mate Dia chose for him. He'd not mention having already seen Sirio with the woman.

Every time he thought about it, he was more and more uncomfortable about the omission. Deception was improper and against his moral code. It probably wasn't the best plan, but it was the best he could come up with. Still, it made him feel awkward. He wasn't actually lying, only omitting things, but...it was...unethical. It was when he realized how much this woman meant to him—what he was willing to do for her. Maybe at the last minute he could come up with a better idea.

Aldo arrived at Sirio's winery late afternoon with a brace of wild hare slung over his shoulder. When Sirio saw him striding up the dirt road he waved and smiled.

"What have you brought me? Something good to eat?" Aldo always came with some fresh game, fish he caught, or ripe fruit or vegetables. Their routine was long established. Sirio cooked and the two of them ate and ended their evening relaxing over a bottle of the special orange wine he made only for friends and family.

Sirio cleaned the hares, covered them with a mixture of olive oil, grainy Dijon mustard and *herbes de Provence,* setting them aside to marinate while he made a fire in the outside stone fireplace; letting it burn until the correct amount of ash showed on the wood. Only then he placed the meat on a spit over fire, and two potatoes nestling below in the hot coals.

They had a while to wait for their meal to cook and started with an a aperitif of dry aged wild boar sausage complemented by fresh goat cheese. Sirio added a large pitcher filled with red wine from a barrel ageing at the back of the winery and chunks of baguette to slather with cheese.

What a well fed pair we are, Sirio thought, I make the wine, he hunts, and together we have made both the cheese and sausage.

After dinner, Sirio brought out their favorite orange wine. The sweet liquor slid over the palate complementing espresso while they relaxed outside in the cooling night air.

Aldo looked at his friend. Sirio's face seemed as relaxed as an open book. Uneasy, Aldo leaned over and put his elbows on his knees before he began. "Sirio, I've found...met *her.* The woman. My woman. But...a problem...she is one of the new people...I think." He put his head in his hands and looked miserable.

Sirio poked the fire to collect his thoughts, sighed. "Have you now? What makes you think she is the right one for you? Have the two of you spoken?...met?"

Where had Aldo found a woman he liked? What flashed through Sirio's mind was the influx of summer people, their false laughter, the women in *maquillage* and bikinis, all worried about their weight, their hair color, the latest fashions, the best plastic surgeons.

Sirio wondered what would happen if his new lady asked "Do you think these slacks make me look fat?" Aldo would probably say "yes" and be delighted about it. He hoped his friend wasn't in for a nasty surprise. He couldn't even begin to put an image of any of them alongside Aldo, try as he might.

"No. No, I haven't spoken to her. I don't know how to start...what to say."

"Well then, is she French? Italian?"

"I don't know... English?...sounds like when she talks to her dog."

"She has a dog? What kind?" Sirio asked.

"It's small—white with black and brown marks, looks like Sofia. She calls it Tom."

Sirio couldn't believe it. Aldo was talking about Lenya. His friend Lenya? "Is she tall with blonde hair and lives in the old A-frame cabin at the top of the crested mountain?"

"Yes. You know her?" Aldo's stomach lurched at the lie. He had seen them together, now desperately wanted to know if Sirio would admit it. As soon as the words left his mouth, he felt bad for deceiving his friend.

"Yes, I know her. We are friends." Sirio topped off both of their glasses with the orange nectar and continued, "Let's go inside, I'm getting a bit of a chill."

They doused the fire and took their glasses inside, making themselves comfortable.

The move gave Sirio some time. It looked like it was going to be a long night. "A few weeks ago she came to the winery. Her name is Lenya and she is an American, of all things. So few of them come to visit our island."

He turned aside and took out his pipe and then found some Old Tavern English tobacco he had been saving for a special occasion. This was as good an occasion as any, he thought, as he tamped it carefully into the bowl.

He needed to consider how to explain this to his friend. It would take delicacy. "I think she's very much alone, as I am. We've spent a little time together. She is, as you can see, much younger than I am, but she seems happy to have a friend. We had dinner and enjoyed a polyphonic concert at the Cathedral. It is all."

Aldo was pleased to see Sirio didn't have any problem speaking openly about the woman. It had to mean Sirio had nothing to hide. It made Aldo feel even worse about his deception but it wasn't easy to learn about a person spying from afar. He was ashamed to admit how much time he spent looking at the woman, tracking her. "Tell me about this Lenya. What is she like?"

Sirio paused, it wasn't easy to tell a man locked in an era of thoughts, customs and a way of life millennia past, what a modern woman was like. He got up and walked around the room, the room he and Lenya had spent a companionable evening in.

The sky was darkening earlier, the hint of winter not far off. He had hoped to spend a little of the cold weather enjoying the warmth of Lenya's company and conversation. This was an obvious complication, he thought as he lit a match and began to draw on his pipe before he turned and faced Aldo.

There were things to be said. "You, my friend, have chosen to be on your mountain with the clan for most of your life. You know the ways of the clan—have rejected the ways of the village and people who live in the modern world to keep true to the traditions, the worship of Dia—your role as her priest, her consort, le Maître. This has been your choice and I respect it."

He stopped and looked at the old beams supporting the ceiling in the winery, the wooden and metal pegs, the cobwebs collecting in the corners.

How do you explain the new and modern to the old? How do you bridge centuries with words? It was a puzzle he understood had to be put together gently.

"You must understand she had far different experiences." He stopped there. Aldo was hanging on his words, but Sirio was stumped on how to make the differences clear. There was no help but to forge ahead. "She is a famous writer...born and raised in New York City, one of the busiest and most modern places on this planet. Her education and travels give her a wide perspective on life." He bent over the ruffle the fur on Sophia's neck...anything to get away from this conversation he knew he was trapped in.

He continued, "She too was married, and her husband was killed in an automobile accident...I think it was about the same time Raina

died. I don't know her beliefs or her religion, those things are not a matter of discussion between us. I do know she is sophisticated in the ways
of the world."

"But then, why is she here?" Aldo moved closer and bent forward
in his eagerness. "She lives in her cabin in the woods, no neighbors...her
little dog for company...in a place very hard to find."

Sirio could see the rationalization. "Yes, but she is a writer. Perhaps being alone in the country frees her mind to fly to the places of her
stories. Perhaps she must be alone with her thoughts to be able to put
them on paper." He was almost desperate to make the other man understand his differences with this woman. Perhaps it was also an insur-
mountable task.

His pipe had gone cold and he rubbed the bowl thoughtfully
along the side of his nose before tamping the ash down and lighting it
again.

Aldo clasped his hands over his knees and sat back. "She walks
in the mountains. I see her take her meal at the grotto of the gods. She
is respectful of their power. I left her flowers, both at the grotto and on
her deck. I play her music at night and watch over her. But I don't think
she knows I'm there."

Sirio faced a conundrum. He now realized his friend was stalking
Lenya and wondered if she felt it...found it... disturbing? Frightening?
Maybe she didn't think about it or hadn't noticed. But he didn't believe
it. She was smart and observant. She must have sensed something. He
realized Aldo must have seen him pick Lenya up to go to the concert. Sly
fox, he knew all along I was friends with Lenya. He's craftier than I gave
him credit for, and I always knew he was smart.

Sirio decided the straight on truth was the right way. "Aldo, what
are you thinking about? This isn't a woman to live with you in the
casteddu. She may be in a small cabin now, but she's used to much
more. Every modern convenience available. You have to think of her as
if she was one of the *nouveau riche* ladies living in the big houses by the
beach." He didn't want to hurt his friend, but he couldn't help shaking
his head.

Then Sirio tried to put Aldo and Lenya together in his mind. Aldo was younger than she was. A plus. Women reached sexual maturity later than men.

Thinking about Lenya and sex made Sirio smile. If he were a little closer to her age he would certainly have wanted to make love to her. It had passed his mind several time how she might rejuvenate him. As old as he was, a woman like her could bring back the lust he had lost over the years. But now he discarded the thought.

Lenya was a woman at her sexual prime and needed a young lusty man to keep her satisfied. Sirio lived with the clan long enough to know Aldo's first sexual encounters would have begun as soon as he reached puberty. As consort-to-be, he had been under the careful tutelage of the clan priestesses, their duty to assist, oversee and train the boy, later the man, until he could play a woman's body with the finesse and skill of a virtuoso violinist. His instruction wasn't complete until he learned to bring a woman to total ecstasy in all the varied and sacred ways craved by the goddess.

The sacred marriage, the clans gift to Dia, secured the clan's harvest, their health, the hunt and their fertility. It was the duty of the consort to provide fruition—anything less for the woman who became the vessel of Dia was failure. Sirio smiled to himself and wondered what Lenya would think if she knew about all his training and expertise.

Aldo cleaned up the remains of their dinner while Sirio watched him carefully, now assessing him in a very different light.

Perhaps Lenya would enjoy a strong, younger man, especially one who knows what he's doing. Aldo was certainly attractive with his powerful body, sculpted face, shining red hair and beard.

Sirio knew Aldo faithfully adhered to his duties as consort of Dia, paying careful attention to his personal hygiene as required by the daily rites. His clothes were always clean, even if tattered. Sirio looked at Aldo in blue jeans dotted with patches and worn through in places. Yes, he thought, ripped jeans are very haute couture at the moment, but not paired with an ancient white linen tunic, sleeves rolled up to hide worn cuffs, and a vest crudely made from rabbit skins. Lenya is probably used to bespoke suits.

Aldo's red hair was rolled into a long coil, then twisted into a knot at the back of his head, and held in place with several long bones smoothed and shaped into picks. A few errant strands curled around his ears and down his neck. The light in the kitchen turned the locks into a brilliant bronze crown. Sirio didn't know if such hair would appeal to a woman or not. To him, it was innocent and endearing. A deep unwanted sigh escaped. Aldo turned at the sound. Sirio knew he had to think about this carefully.

Lenya appeared to be a woman with no hidden agenda. She spoke about her deceased husband with obvious love. Clearly they'd had a good marriage and she missed him deeply. She never gave a hint there was another man in her life.

Maybe it was time for her to take a lover. And why not? It would probably be good for her, help her put her grief aside. But he couldn't wrap his mind around how Aldo might fit the image. Also, his friend was looking for a mate, quite a different scenario than a lover and Sirio didn't want Aldo hurt.

They continued their discussion long into the night. Exactly two more bottles of orange wine later, they fell asleep where they sat.

The next day, Sirio woke up in his chair with the telephone ringing. He got up to answer it and realized he was stiff from a night of sleeping in a most uncomfortable position. The sun was shining. Much too bright. Aldo was nowhere in sight.

He picked up the phone and heard Lenya's voice on the other end chirping through the wine pounding in his head. His mouth tasted like the inside of a birdcage. Nasty.

Rubbing his forehead to try and clear his brain wasn't working too well. Lenya was chattering about men in Calanzana and something about a bar on the way back from Aléria.

A. R. Donenfeld-Vernoux

"Wait my dear, it was a long night last night. Please. Stop. Let me put myself back together. I promise to call you in a short while."

Lenya laughed, "Ah-ha. My friend sounds like he had too much of his own grape. Of course. Call me when you want. I am home all day."

An hour later, instead of calling, Sirio was on the front porch with Sofia, a baguette, and a small bottle of local honey.

"A peace offering in apology for any rudeness this morning. I had a very long night with a good friend. It entailed quite a bit of wine...as I am sure you figured out." He looked down at his shoes for a second then looked up to give her a brilliant smile. "Actually, it was quite interesting. In its own way."

Lenya hugged him and brought him inside, "Sirio, you are a rogue, but a delightful one. I'm glad you had a nice evening."

"So tell me, or ask me, my dear...whatever your heart desires." He said as he sat on the couch. Tom and Sophia immediately leaped onto his lap and after a little pushing and shoving curled together like a rolled Danish pastry.

"I've had a few adventures since we've last been together. I think I may have walked into two hornets nests and you are my source of everything not quite in plain view on the island."

"So, am I your 'deep throat' as you Americans might say?"

Lenya figured his hangover must be dissipating. The twinkle was back in his eye.

"Yes. Sort of like that—you are my reliable expert for all things Corsican. I think I might have met the local don and then walked in on some kind of conspiracy."

First she told him about her adventure in Calanzana and the strange men she met. Before he could interject, she went on to her stop for coffee in the odd bar on the way home from Aléria.

When she finished recounting both stories, Sirio looked at her and shook his head. "Lenya, you amaze me. You absolutely have a penchant for finding all the mysterious characters on our island. I can't think of anyone you've missed."

"What do you mean? Tell me everything."

"There is not much to tell. The man from Calanzana is in fact a don. He is a very good and dear old friend of mine, who has now retired to live out the rest of his years here in this beautiful place with his family. Your guess was right and it is all you safely need to know about him." He sounded brusque even to himself and immediately knew it had been the wrong thing to say.

She started to respond but he put his hand up. "Lenya, stop. I have nothing further to say about this matter. I think it is a good idea if you no longer take this particular 'short cut.' Do you understand?"

"Okay, I get the picture. But what about the men in the bar? What was it all about? Planning a heist or something?"

"Not at all. I think you might have walked into a get together of one of the local cells of the Corsican Brotherhood or perhaps the FLNC. The first is a semi-religious, semi-political group active here for many, many years. They are partly under the wing of the Catholic Church, but their main and unspoken goal is to kick the French out of Corsica."

He took the cup of coffee she offered him, put a sugar cube in his mouth and took a sip through the cube before he continued. "No, wait—the photo with the police car and the man in handcuffs is the key. You probably disturbed the FLNC—the *Fronte di Liberazione Corsu.* They have also been fighting to get out from under the French.

"Maybe you walked into the middle of them planning something. Maybe as simple as spray painting out the French names on the road signs...or something bigger, a bombing, a fire...who can tell. But I strongly suggest you find another café or bar to stop at on your adventures. The next time they might be more suspicious."

They finished their coffee in companionable silence.

Lenya had food for thought. She was going to have to give more time to consideration of what was really going on beneath the surface of the ancient 'isle of beauty,' as the Corsicans called their home. *Now my home too.*

She also forgot to tell him she would be leaving in several days to go to Ajaccio.

Chapter 16
The Grotto Speaks

Two days later, Lenya was up at her usual six-thirty facing a new chapter and a full pot of coffee. After the sun rose, she watched the mist shrouding the mountaintops dissipate. It was going to be perfect—warm and sunny; the kind of weather the island was famous for. She strode out of the cabin, determined to enjoy the gifts of the day. The guide books warned winter was the time for rain and even the possibility of snow in the higher altitudes.

This might be her last chance for a while to take Tom for one of their long walks. Early tomorrow morning she was leaving for Ajaccio to meet the mysterious video game developer. Who knew what the weather would be like when she returned?

After all her lists and plans, she was actually looking forward to the excursion, and if the guy—Terrence—turned out to be all right, it would be an unexpected plus.

✿

The path before him glistening in the sun, Aldo walked back to Lenya's cabin. He didn't like to be away from her for very long, no matter what Sirio might think. Too much wine and the talk with Sirio a few nights ago made his head spin.

Perhaps Sirio was right, she wasn't the one Dia had provided for him, but he couldn't make himself accept it.

He watched his woman—Lenya—he must remember to think of her by her name, step out of the cabin with her mop handle and Tom trotting at her side. He was sure he knew where they were going; the grotto where she liked to eat her lunch.

If he hurried, he'd get there first and leave her some more flowers. They were hard to find now, the season passed and it was too chilly for blooms, but some fragrant immortelle, rosemary, orange and yellow strawberry bush branches and pines made a colorful bundle. They would not only decorate the stones but give her a pleasant aroma while she ate.

After these weeks of watching her, Aldo felt he knew this woman. She was no longer strange to him; he knew what her body looked like, how she moved. He knew her scent. When Tom came to visit him, her essence clung to his fur and Aldo would pick him up and inhale her personal fragrance. He wondered if she knew he was watching her, always nearby. Keeping her safe. Protecting.

The discussion with Sirio came back with clarity. He thought long and hard about what his friend said. He couldn't even imagine the world the woman came from. What if she felt the same about him? The thought was depressing.

He had seen photographs of the outside world all his life, when he was a boy, Sirio had brought him picture books to acquaint him with life and places far from the casteddu. As he grew older, he often picked up magazines from the trash in the villages and studied the photographs. While he couldn't read many of the languages, he was fascinated by the cities, the tall buildings built of stone, brick, metal and glass. He wondered how people got to the top, did they climb stairs? It seemed a very high distance. One day he asked Sirio about it and then understood there were small boxes people could stand in, and by a pulley system of ropes and wheels they were hauled to the top. It sounded dangerous but Sirio explained it was commonly used. Did Lenya live in such a place? Did she get hauled to the top? He would like to know.

Aldo studied the fashions, the furniture, the pictures of colorful places with strange trees and smooth beaches. There were pictures of machines like the one she sat at every day, many of the others were a mystery. He looked at what he knew were called "automobiles." They had been on the island since he was born, and he hadn't realized how many different types they could be. Pictures of many hundreds of them packed together on roadways were both terrifying and interesting. Someday, he thought he might even want to learn how to command one. His arthritis was giving him trouble and the idea of not walking up and down hills was appealing.

When he thought about it, Lenya's life on the island seemed very much like his. She ate, walked, played with Tom. The only difference was she played music on her machine and also sat in front of it most of the time, working—her writing?

Did she hear the music he sent to calm her dreams in the night? He sat outside her cabin and played the flute. As he fingered it, he remembered carving it with care, wanting to get the sounds sweet to soothe dreams of the children he hoped to have, but never did. Now he played to a women he wasn't even sure knew he was there. But she would. Someday. It was meant to be. *No, it had to be!*

He roused himself from his thoughts and made his way to the grotto, stopping only to gather his offering.

Crisp and cool air surrounded Lenya as she made her way to what she now thought of as "her secret" place. The weather was changing; soon it would be too cold to have lunch in the shade of the little grotto. It was time to find a new place in the sun, warmer—perhaps overlooking the sea. She wanted at least one more meal here before the weather stopped her. Last week when it rained, she saw snow covering the tops of the mountains in the distance. It was still there two days later when she went to the store in Calanzana. Maybe there'd be warm sunny days when she could try again, but she figured if it couldn't melt snow, the sun might not be strong enough to warm this spot until late spring. She could at least visit during the winter if she didn't sit too long in the shade.

Pushing past the last bit of foliage hiding the grotto, a small splash of green greeted her on the flat rock. This time it was fragrant herbs. She smelled basil and immortelle, inhaling the scent of the island as she examined the bouquet. The sight of bright crimson berries from the strawberry bush reminded her the holidays were nearing. The basil should not have lasted so late into the season—the gatherer obviously knew a sunny place out of the wind. Her only plausible explanation—an offering to the gods of the dolmen? But why were they leaving gifts on her deck too?

She spread her lunch as Tom went sniffing in the underbrush. The fragrant little herb bundle mixed with the cool air to perfume it with a tang of the special warmth born from sun grown things.

Her reverie came to a sharp close at loud sounds of snarling and thrashing coming from the underbrush. Tom yelped in pain and Lenya jumped to the rescue, grabbing her mop handle ready to do battle. Off to her right the foliage shook. Dirt and pieces of brush were flying into the air, but it was too dense and too high for her to see. She couldn't lose Tom. She wouldn't let it happen. He was her best friend, keeping her tied to sanity and the rhythms of life this last year. Without a thought for her own safety, she charged screaming and shouting through the leaves and brambles.

A thorn tore at her face; she didn't feel the small trail of red course down her cheek—a tear of blood. Somewhere deep in the recess of her mind she realized she wasn't wearing gloves as another thorn ripped open a gash across the back of her hand. She was so intent on rescue she felt no pain.

The branches parted in time to see Tom leap into the arms of a large hairy creature. *Apelike?* An angry raccoon menaced in the stance of an enraged boxer as it batted paws topped with long claws at Tom and the other...animal?...ape? The battler—in protection mode over something...food? ...babies?

Lenya got the picture fast enough. Tom's terrier heritage made him to go after something the raccoon was protecting, not knowing the other animal was within fighting distance. Everything was happening too fast for her to be afraid. How do I get Tom away from the hairy ape? *And, what the hell is it anyway?*

What, or whoever, was holding Tom waved her off and, no question; it was trying to get away too. It was retreating and making a quite sort of shushing noise. The angry raccoon stopped advancing. Tom didn't seem to be in imminent danger so Lenya slowly backed through the bushes towards the clearing, and the furry thing...*a yeti?..* slowly followed her, Tom clutched protectively in its arms.

Once they were both in the clearing, she took a closer look. It wasn't an ape, it was wearing—old blue jeans, of all things. A soft looking fur pelt she thought was its hide covered its back and shoulders. Then she realized it wore a vest of skins crudely stitched together—a simple covering—no shirt underneath, muscular arms tanned and bare. She was even more frightened when she realized...he?... human...maybe? Then he began to laugh in relief! A man.

Tom wasn't the least bit afraid. He was licking the face of his smiling savior as if they were old friends.

The man saw her confusion, and the mop handle she brandished. He nodded and reached out towards her, carefully handing over Tom. His hands were strong looking, clean and weathered, the skin darkened and fingers callused—the hands of someone who worked outside.

He seemed to not only understand her fear, but wanted to show he meant her no harm. She took Tom and nodded assent.

The man pointed to blood on Tom's rump. She saw a ragged spot where the raccoon had raked open a nasty looking cut.

He nodded to the bottle of water sitting on the dolmen and cocked his head as if asking her permission. She automatically nodded assent.

Taking the water, he poured some of it on the wound, cleaning it with his hand and handed her back the bottle. Turning, he rummaged in the underbrush for several leaves he tore off, crushed, and rubbed into Tom's fur. The bleeding stopped and the man smiled at her. He pointed at the leaf he'd rubbed into Tom's wound. "Immortelle" he said in a deep gravel voice. Lenya found it hard to keep thinking of the strange apparition as a man and "he." But when he spoke, she noticed he had nice white teeth.

Who on earth was he?...or what? He was taller than she, maybe a little under six feet, maybe more if he stood straight.

He was broad shouldered and heavily muscled, but looked thin, as if he hadn't eaten well in a long time. Muscles and veins showed as distinct ropes on his arms and neck. A broad and strong chest was evident beneath the crude fur covering. His face was hollow eyed, a long, russet beard hung almost a foot below his chin. She saw high cheekbones, a prominent brow. A strong jaw hidden beneath all the beard? She couldn't tell. Grey-blue eyes were gentle looking even though deeply set. His nose was large and slightly splayed; an orangey- red moustache flowed into his darker beard. Red hair cascaded in shining waves down his back and she noticed two long narrow braids framing either side of his face. Must be to keep his hair out of his eyes. He was a collage of reds, hair a brighter, more definite red than moustache and beard. His light russet chest hair blended with the fur of the homemade covering to make him look more animal than man at first sight. The broad smile showed again.

As Lenya gaped, unable to take her eyes off the man, she noticed his hair looked clean and soft, as if recently washed and his long beard was well-kept, braided in two neat strands at the sides and tied with leather thongs. A strange combination of savagery and sophistication marked his appearance, wild and barbaric, yet at the same time—well groomed?

She felt an errant desire to reach out and touch his hair... *Touch? My god, I want to sort of pet this person? What am I thinking?*

The scent of rosemary and mint wafted from him, noticeable in the clean air. Does he perfume himself? She felt like she was looking at an Early Man diorama from the New York Museum of Natural History she had visited so often as a child. The only real difference was the man was wearing pants, albeit old and tattered—oh, and this time, she was the one carrying the spear.

After he finished rubbing the leaf on Tom, he motioned at her face and hand. It was only then she realized she too was bleeding. He took the water back from her and moved closer as if to cleanse her wounds. She inadvertently hopped backward. Like a frightened animal.

He put his palms up and then pointed to her scratches and handed her the water, again making a pouring motion.

She poured the water on the back of her hand and, wetting a paper napkin from her pocket, dabbed at the scratch on her face. The napkin turned bright red from her blood. He foraged in the underbrush and came back with a strong smelling leaf and made rubbing motions, once again pointing at her hand and cheek. It was what he had patted on Tom's wound. Understanding, she took the leaf and trustingly rubbed it on her face and hand. Couldn't be poison ivy, sumac, something nasty, could it?

He hadn't done anything out of order or made a move to frighten her...only acted with kindness. But she was alone in the grotto with him, no one around for miles and certainly not in shouting distance.

She surprised herself by not being frightened. In fact, she felt drawn to him. He seemed to only want to help, almost taking care of her. She wasn't completely comfortable, but she sensed a sad and kind quality about him. It quieted her fear.

Tom wriggled to get loose from her grip. No sooner had she put him down then he went immediately to the man, jumping up and down waiting to be picked up. Lenya watched him bend down, pick up Tom and gently soothe him, careful to avoid the wound.

Looking directly at her, the man nodded in the direction of the herbs on the stone and said. *"Vous piace?"*

She thought he asked if she liked them in Italian, or was it French – *oh, both*. She was surprised at the mixture of French and Italian in the same short phrase. His voice came out as a deep guttural croak. It sounded unused.

She nodded back. *"Si, me piace."* The mystery of the flowers was solved. *But it also means he knows where I live.* The thought gave her a tremor of fear.

She hastily packed up the remains of her scattered lunch and turned to leave. But first, she thanked him by pointing to Tom and holding her hands in front of her with palms together and bowed her head towards him. *"Grazie molto."* He seemed to understand both the words and the *namaste*, a universal gesture of thanks.

He was the strangest person she had ever seen, but if you liked a thick chest and muscular strong arms, with a lot of very red hair, almost fur, then he was a fine looking specimen. On further consideration, he was almost handsome—a primitive beauty. Something in the structure of his face reminded her of a National Geographic series on the development of modern man through the ages.

Turning once and waving goodbye, she left. She turned again, expecting to see him standing in the glen, but he was gone.

As soon as she and Tom entered the cabin, she wanted to sterilize their wounds with peroxide and alcohol, but Tom's wound was clean and healing already from the herbs the man had used. She checked his papers to confirm he had his rabies shot only a year prior. There wasn't much rabies on the island she had heard of, but it never hurt to be sure. Looking in the mirror, her face showed no redness of infection, and her hand was the same.

Later she wrote an e-mail to Lotte.

Lenyascribe:

U won't believe it, but after I spoke to you, I think I either met a Yeti or a real honest to goodness caveman. I was eating lunch with Tom at our favorite spot on top of a dolmen and Tom got into a fight with a raccoon. He was rescued by the oddest man I've ever seen. He was wearing tattered pants and a fur thing over his shoulders—looked like he made it himself. U had to see his face, beetling brows and sharp cheekbones, looks like prominent mouth structure—bright red hair all over—at least what I could see—face, arms, chest. He rescued Tom—put leaf stuff on a wound on Tom's butt—my face and hand too.

Luv ya'. L2

Almost as soon as it was sent, she got a reply from Lotte. She must have been bored at work or busy sending e-mails.

Lotte469:

Now aren't you glad I sent you a real guy? Don't get desperate on me and go around picking up Neanderthals. Was he at least sexy looking?

Lenyascribe:
Actually, he wasn't too bad looking if you like a bit rough and furry 'round the edges. We even talked...a few words, and he spoke a funny sounding combination of Italian and French. I think he's the one been leaving me flowers.

Lotte469:
Be careful Lenya, he might not understand. I keep seeing these programs about serial killers and some of them look like underdeveloped cavemen.

Lenyascribe:
Yech! You sound like Mom — stop it! I'm OK

Lotte469:
You know I worry about you, you're all I've got left. And you know what they say about taking presents from cavemen?

Lenyascribe:
No, I don't know and I'm sure I don't want to know.
I'll be fine, he seems kind and was gentle with Tom.
Anyway, it was interesting.
Please tell Francis I called Terrence. I've got a date with him when he gets here. He sounds nice on the phone and at least he has a sense of humor. Gotta go now, it's late and I need my beauty sleep. Luv ya!

Lotte469:
Take care and let me know how it goes with Terrence. Luv ya too and even more! Oh, and caveman saying... you might have to put out to repay the presents sometime, like with the modern guys. LOL L1

Lenya could almost hear Lotte laughing at her last words as she clicked off and prepared for bed.

Later, alone in her bed in the loft, she couldn't get the strange man in the woods out of her mind.

Even though he laughed freely, there was also a melancholy quality about him. She found herself worrying where and how he lived. I'll inquire about homeless people when I go to town. If there are a lot of them, must remember to be more careful when I go out for a long walk. I'll ask Sirio next time I see him, bet he'll know. But she wasn't really afraid; the man didn't set off any of those warning signs. She remembered seeing an Oprah show about the "uh-oh" moment when you knew you were in danger. Tom's rescuer set off other signs, and they weren't warning.

Chapter 17
Aldo Takes Stock

He talked to the woman! The one he thought of as 'his' woman.

Lenya. Now he knew she was Lenya. Sirio had told him. He should have told her his name, but he forgot in the excitement of the moment.

She saw his face and even smiled at him. She wasn't afraid of him like some of the new people. He had taken the first step and it hadn't been as difficult as he imagined. Maybe Sirio was wrong. They were able to understand each other. He was delighted.

Aldo decided to leave his watch post and go home for the night. As he walked up the steep track to the casteddu, he felt more strongly than ever how alone he was. He had always known it, but this night was painful.

Being near the woman, his Lenya, outside her cabin, keeping watch over her, had given him a feeling of being connected to her...part of her life. Going back to his home, spending the night away from her seemed to increase his loneliness.

He thought about what Sirio told him, where Lenya came from, how she had been brought up, what she was used to. Then he looked around the ruins and saw with a new eye where he lived. The top of the mountain. The winds howled around the stone walls at night, and in storms, found every little crack to worm cold fingers into his bones. True, he could look to the sea and it's brilliance in the sun.

Beneath his mountain, the valley rolled a verdant emerald carpet towards the sparkling sapphire and turquoise of the water. Roads dotted the once pristine landscape, but he was used to them. They were part of life now.

The entrance to the casteddu, in past times secured and guarded, was now a tumbled down open space in an old wall protecting ruined buildings. Once a fine village and home to more than a hundred souls was home to him now. Alone.

His house stood roofed and secure. The only one. The walls were made of large boulders, several menhirs fitted in with the rough stone blocks—spaces filled by mortar made from earth and water.

The floor was dirt covered by reeds carried from the nearby estuary. A window high on the east wall let in sunlight and air. He covered it with blue painted wooden shutters in winter.

No real door closed off the entrance, only branches woven within a frame and a skin secured on the inside to cut the winter wind, taken down in summer to let the breezes enter. It faced towards the outside wall so the prevailing strong winds were blocked.

Several of the crafted stones making up the west wall protruded from the smooth face and had boards placed across them forming shelves. Three carved wooden dishes and several glass jars culled from village discards made up his meal service. A few bowls of various sizes, reminders of his mother and Raina, were once used for storing vegetables and mixing things. There was a large wooden spoon; two forks he had also foraged.

Knives of various sizes were stuck in a block of wood to keep from rubbing together and blunting their blades. They were used for cleaning fish, cutting meat and skinning game. It was all he needed, apart from the cast iron pot he used to cook. Herbs and savories were easy to find in the woods when you knew where to look.

He grew a few things in the rudimentary garden Raina started years ago. Aldo maintained it from habit. Basil, tomatoes, rosemary, zucchini and green beans continued on. His collection of dried herbs and flowers hung in profusion from the ceiling and blended into a special perfume to permeate the walls.

His bed was a stone slab smoothed by the bodies of generations past as they slept or created the next generations to come. The slab was covered with fresh reeds, then piled with skins for sleeping, some to soften the surface of rock and reeds against hips and backs, others to keep out the cold winds of winter.

He thought of his parents sleeping on the rough pallet and later, he and Raina slept there.

Sometimes at night, when it was quiet and the winds usually breaking the silence of the night with their whistling rush up from the ocean were still; he could imagine the sounds and feel the power of ancient generations of lovemaking. His forbearers, honoring Dia with the sacred marriage. An act of devotion and respect continuous and constant from the beginning of time.

The rest of the casteddu was empty. Houses tumbled down around him and he took what he needed from them to repair his own. Roofing beams and slats were always needed when the high winds made their depredations. Rain bothered him and he hated it to drip on him when he slept so his roof was always the first thing he mended.

As he looked around, he had to acknowledge Sirio was right. It wasn't a place for a woman used to the trappings of modern life.

He kicked at the pile of reeds and skins he slept on. No creatures scurried from them. He smoked his house often to keep at bay the small predators who might otherwise have nipped tender parts at night while he slept.

As he pondered how he might make his home more suitable for a modern woman, he walked to the wall and looked out at the setting sun. The far mountains were capped with snow and turned shades of pink and peach and mauve as the sun sank into the sea.

There was no sound other than the wind. Nothing mechanical. It was too high up the mountain for much of civilization to impinge on the natural silence. He could hear his feet scuffing against the rock and dirt above the whisper of the breezes. Without the sun it was getting cold.

Time to light a warming fire in his hearth. Time to sleep alone once again. Perhaps tonight he might dream of Lenya. The thought cheered him as he made his way back inside.

Chapter 18
Games and Designs

Thursday arrived. It was time to meet the mysterious computer game designer. Terrence. Lenya had dawdled along, taking more than five hours to make the drive from Calvi to Ajaccio the day before. She wasn't in a hurry. The ride was lovely and there was time to spare and enjoy the countryside. It might only be early fall, but several of the mountains in the distance had peaks already mantled with snow. While it had rained before she left the cabin, making driving treacherous to get through the muddy obstacles to the main roads, the rest of the drive was dry and clear.

Signs for a shop selling hand spun wool caught her attention and she followed them across a picturesque babbling stream, past a group of well fed sheep, and on to a rustic stone building.

Luckily, it was open. On entering, she was taken aback by every possible shade, hue and color of tan, brown and gray from the natural color yarns as well as the stone and wood decorating the interior walls, displays and shelving. Skeins and balls of wool in a profusion of muted colors and weights, handmade knitted, woven and crocheted sweaters, hats, bags, shawls and throws filled the shop. Everyplace Lenya looked shelves overflowed with yarns of all weights and colors, all natural fibers.

The sun streamed in through the large windows and created an air of magic. Giving in to temptation, she purchased a wildly expensive cardigan sweater in bands of natural grays and oatmeal colored wools she was sure had been donated last spring by some of the sheep she'd passed.

The temptation to take up knitting again, a skill she had learned as a child, was overwhelming, but she had too many other things to do now, she thought as she drove over the bridge and back on the RN towards Ajaccio.

She spent the night at one of the small hotels along the way. Most were already closed once the tourists left at the end of October. She wanted to arrive fresh, not at the end of a long drive.

Lenya kept forgetting her cell phone worked all over the island. The mountains didn't seem to be the same obstacle they were in the states.

In Ajaccio, the hotel operator was pleasant when she called.

"Yes, Monsieur has already checked in. Would Madam like to be put through to his room?" Actually, Lenya wasn't sure. She was so close she was having misgivings, but she said "Yes."

His deep American voice answered the phone. Before she could say a word she heard, "I'll bet this is Lenya." There was a laugh underlying the basso as she, flustered, admitted it was. When she spoke to him the first time at the cabin, the connection had been poor and she hadn't realize how sexy his voice sounded.

"How about you come to my hotel? Call me from the lobby and we can have a coffee and make plans from there. I have no idea where to go, and since you're the expert, I'll rely on you."

Okay, he did sound pleasant over the phone. There was a mischievous quality she found immediately appealing. Maybe this was going to be fun after all. "It'll take me about an hour to get there. I drove down from Calvi last night so I'm pretty close."

"I'm sorry, I didn't realize you had such a long trip. I thought the island was small."

"It's only about a hundred and fifty miles long and fifty wide, but there's a lot of up, down and around to get from one place to another— very little is direct."

"Well, then you will be hungry and at the very least I can feed you well!"

Lenya couldn't help laughing. "Is there anything special you like to eat? I'm not that familiar with Ajaccio. In fact, maybe you can ask the hotel to suggest something."

"Good idea. I'm up for anyplace, as long as they take dogs. The girls were telling me about your traveling companion and I've been hoping to meet him." There was underlying smile in his voice again. "They said he was the one I had to make friends with; your most important protector."

"Don't worry, he's easily had, a bone and a pat or two and he'll be your friend for life. See you in a little while."

As she turned off her cell, she realized she was looking forward to meeting this Terrence with the smile in his voice.

The weather forecast was for storms. Lenya knew her decision to stay several days had been correct. She wasn't thrilled at the thought of driving back over narrow mountain roads after dark in the rain. Corsica, like most of the Mediterranean, was subject to torrential downpours. Blinding rain didn't stop local drivers from careening along the two lane RN at top speed in their constant quest to pass the car in front, no matter the consequences.

There was also the little matter of the treacherous road to the cabin, not to mention slopping through the mud driveway in the dark. It was better to be prepared. Since she planned to stay a few nights she would rent a room in Ajaccio and leave for home in a few days, or at least after the rain stopped. There was no one waiting for her at the cabin and she had no pressing deadline.

She had packed dry food and bowls for Tom. For herself, several changes of underwear, clean shirts, a pair of jeans toothbrush and a little makeup. Since she had already planned shopping was in her future, it was enough. Everything was stowed neatly in her big traveling shoulder bag when she and Tom left for their adventure.

As she put the last touches on her makeup in the badly lit motel mirror, Tom looked at her appraisingly, his black eyebrow markings quizzical as always. Well, she thought, I'm not too bad for forty-two – okay – almost forty-three. My hair's starting to get a little grey but my butt is almost back to where it started, thanks to all the Tai Chi and the damn walking I've been doing.

Lenya knew her five feet seven inches were well proportioned, her features regular, and her short blonde hair cut in a becoming style—*as good as it gets at my age.*

She was a Connecticut oddity, not overly concerned about her appearance. The guy came from California, the other side of the world. He probably dates only nubile nymphets. Not that she cared; it was only a meal, after all. She harrumphed, grabbed Tom's leash and was out the door. *I may not be a beauty, but no one's thrown me out of bed either,* was her thought as she turned the key in the Rav.

Before she had left the cabin, Aldo watched Lenya as usual. This was something different. She packed things in a big bag and put Tom on a leash, but she wasn't dressed for a hike. She had on black leather shoes with small heels. Not good for woods.

He became concerned as he saw her get into the car. She couldn't be leaving for long; her big machine was on the desk where she closed it up. She took a smaller one with her, bright pink and slipped easily into her large handbag. His life depended on the big machine. She sat at it all day when she was home. He was sure she wouldn't leave it behind.

She must be coming back.

He curled up by the tree and pulled his furs close around his shoulders to wait. Later, rain pelted leaves overhead and trickled in drips on him in an irregular rhythm. He hated rain and would never get used to it. It made his bones ache, but he wasn't going to go back to the casteddu.

Chapter 19

Lunch in Ajaccio

Lotte was right. He is a hunk. Lenya watched the man rise and come towards her as she entered the hotel, Tom bouncing along at her side. He was well over six feet tall, slender with wide shoulders. She noted unruly brown hair framing a face appealing in its slightly irregular masculinity. Handsome actually, nice sculpted nose, high cheekbones and firm chin...and looks fit too. Maybe I'll forgive Lotte after all. Not bad, not bad at all. Probably has ten women after him in LA and all of them twenty years younger than me. She sighed. Ah well, it's just lunch.

"Hi, I'm Terrence, and I'll bet you're Lenya." He bent to give her a casual one arm hug and she smelled fresh aftershave with notes of citrus and balsam.

Ummm...smells wonderful too. So far so good. "Yes, it's a pleasure to meet you. My sister had very nice things to say about you." There, nice and proper. Mother taught me right...she'd be proud. Her nervousness didn't show. It had been a very long time since she had been on a blind date. Actually, she couldn't even remember when, or if, she had one before.

He bent down and held out his hand for Tom to sniff. "Hey old guy, you're as cute as your advance notices said. Are we going to be friends or what?" Tom dutifully sniffed, wagged the stump of his tail and seemed to smile. "Well, at least one of you seems to approve of me already."

Interesting, Lenya noted, he's a bit insecure. She was used to Andre. He was short and not so handsome, but never doubted his appeal for a moment.

"I remembered there were several restaurants by the sea, but the weather man says it's going to be stormy, so I thought we might eat in the old city instead. I'm sure we can find a restaurant with a fireplace and stone walls. Unless you happen to like watching storms." she said. As she looked out the window, it was already starting to drizzle. Close would be better...easier to run to the car in the rain.

She was conscious of him looking her over. Her mind was racing. Mustn't babble under scrutiny. Damn! I'm out of practice... alone too long and lost the knack of flirting. Lotte would kick me under the table if we were sitting at one. I'm not comfortable with men any more, at least, suitable ones.

"Whatever you think best...this is your island...I'm along for the tour."

He really did have a nice smile. It came from the eyes and worked its way down into the corners of his wide mouth. There was something about California men. They had a special well groomed air about them, and regular well-kept teeth. She approved.

Do I want to be with him near the water in a storm or in front of a fireplace? Both were quite romantic and she was suddenly angry to even be thinking in those terms. "Let's go into the old town. The concierge must know a few nice places there and you can make your choice. I'm not really familiar with this city." She realized she sounded brusque. *Too bad, it's the way I am these days.* She turned, leaving him standing in the lobby and walked to the reception desk. He came up beside her and inquired about several restaurants from a list the concierge had given him earlier. He spoke very serviceable French. She was impressed and pleased; then angry at herself. There I go, selling everyone short. Why shouldn't he know French?

She pulled her raincoat close around her shoulders and headed toward the door.

He caught up with her and took her arm with authority. "Okay, I've got the low down and a map. The concierge says it's only a five minute walk and he's marked several places he's sure are open. Most of the city seems to be closed until spring. What a strange place."

The drizzle was light as they left the hotel but the sky was a dark and threatening grey. Squeezing under her small umbrella, they made their way up the hill to the old city. Lenya found herself enjoying the solid feel of his arm laced through hers.

As they walked up the narrow streets, almost all the stores were closed and shuttered, heavy metal security gates pulled down over empty windows. Only a few sported dressed windows, those obviously catering to the locals. They passed yarns, synthetic this time, warm looking underwear, reasonably priced shoes and every day clothes, rather than the high fashion tastes of the summer tourists.

They weren't near the pedestrian street and she hoped she wouldn't be disappointed later when she went shopping.

One lone stationer was open displaying newspapers, magazines, and several shelves of tourist ware: ashtrays, salt and pepper shakers, olive oil flagons, and small garlic grating plates, all emblazoned with "Ajaccio." And probably made in Taiwan, Lenya thought.

The store window displayed allegedly local knives with horn or wooden handles. Terrence tilted towards the entryway and they went in to peruse the meager offerings. He looked at the pocket knives and she went to check out the tee-shirts.

She was on a hunt for a tee-shirt she had seen, the front with a picture of a typical road sign with the name of a village in both French and Corsican. The French name was crossed out with black paint and riddled with bullet holes, leaving only the Corsican name visible. It was the pre-eminent "fuck-you" of the Corsicans to their French "occupiers" and Lenya laughed every time she saw one of the signs. The tee-shirt said it all! The shop didn't have what she wanted, but she was sure she'd find it someplace and refused to give up looking.

Terrence found a small knife with an olive wood handle and paid for it, asking her if there was anything she would like. A real gent. Nice. She demurred.

As they left the store, he nodded to a white flag with a black profile of a curly headed man with Negroid features. "What's that about? I've seen the same image several times since I've arrived."

"It's the Corsican flag."

"You're kidding, right?"

"No. Seriously. The story is, it's the head of a Moorish pirate who preyed upon seaside Corsican villages. He was caught and beheaded for his crimes. There are several other versions of the story...one is he fell in love with a beautiful Corsican maiden. He captured her on one of his forays...back and forth fights to bring her home to Corsica, he still lost his head, but in this version he lost it twice." She smiled at her own joke. "No one is actually sure who he was. The image is a message to the outside world: don't mess with Corsica. Look what happened to this guy!"

Terrence laughed. "Now I see why everyone is afraid of the Corsicans. They get right to the point."

"Don't believe all you hear. I've found them to be a wonderful people, hard working, family oriented and very warm once you get to know them. But it takes a while. They have a long history of cause to be wary of strangers."

They found the recommended restaurant. It was, of course, small and intimate. The owner was a woman in her sixties who ran the business with a younger man Lenya assumed was her son. The owner surveyed Lenya speculatively, giving her an approving nod and wink as Terrence turned to look around the restaurant.

Ancient stone walls were broken up by dark wood beams; wooden doorways and shelves looked hand carved and very old. The sky outside darkened as the storm moved over the city. They'd made it into the restaurant as rain began to pound the streets, beating a deep irregular tattoo on the tiled roof of the single story building.

Lenya shivered unconsciously as Terrence helped her off with her coat. Damn, this place is romantic. But it was too late to change.

Terrence was very nice, but she didn't want to look like a desperate woman on the make, but he had chosen the restaurant. All she wanted was a meal with this man to get her sister off her back. Then she could go on her short adventure with Tom before heading home. Alone.

Terrence looked around with interest. He studied the shelves filled with old copper cooking pots and iron hooks used for turning meats over an open flame. Then, his attention was caught by two swords crossed over the fireplace. Standing close to the mantle, he looked at the blades.

"Would Monsieur like to see the swords...more close?" the young man said as he stepped from behind the rustic bar running along the back left side of the restaurant. "They belonged to my great, great grand uncles...alleged to be Corsican bandits. Mother doesn't like them... reminders of...older...perhaps not so pleasant days. But...after all...we are Corsican." He shrugged and a big crooked smile lit his face.

Reaching up, he took one of the swords down and handed it hilt first to Terrence. Lenya could see it was artfully worked with the hilt sculpted in intricate geometric patterns and the blade engraved with swirls and vines its entire length. It was obvious it had a lot of use as the blade was badly nicked and marked. The engraving around the hilt was worn smooth as if a hand had held it in many battles. She didn't want to think too much about the blood the blade might have tasted in its heyday.

Terrence moved into the center of the empty room and swung the sword a few tentative times. "It's well balanced," he said admiringly. "Do you mind if I take some photographs of the designs on the hilt and the blade?"

"Not at all. As you wish." The young man was clearly pleased by the request. He pointed to the empty room and gestured at the tables set with pristine white linen, small pots of flowers, a rustic and heavy dinner service. "Do as you like, today this restaurant belongs to you. It looks like the rain chased everyone else away. Sadly, there is very little bravery left on this island." He shook his head as he walked back behind the bar.

Terrence took a few photos with a digital camera he had in his jacket pocket and then carefully placed the sword back in its position of honor.

Lenya sat when Terrence pulled out a chair for her at a table against the wall, not too far away from a fireplace with a low fire. Tom ambled over to check out the broad hearth. At his age, he liked to get as close to warmth as possible.

"Would you care for an aperitif?" The young man was obviously not only part owner, but also waiter and barman.

"Yes, please," Lenya said, "I'll have *Kir vin blanc*."

"I'll have the same," Terrence agreed, and then, leaning over towards her whispered, "What the heck is it?"

Lenya couldn't help but smile. "It's white wine with a bit of *framboise* or raspberry liquor. Most people prefer it with champagne, then it's called a *Kir Royale*, but I don't particularly like champagne. It gives me a headache."

The aperitifs arrived in tall slender wine glasses and were set on either side of a small bowl of olives. After a few minutes, menus were placed on the table with a wine list on top. Lenya thought of Andre and his admonition to try the wines of Corsica. She had been here almost six months and other than Sirio's wines, hadn't really explored much more than the plonk they sold at the small Sparr near the cabin. This was as good a time as any to start, she thought.

After the Kir, she felt herself begin to relax. This wasn't a torture she had to endure; she was in a beautiful city, in a charming restaurant with a very appealing man. What more could a woman ask for? You really are an ungrateful bitch, she told herself, enjoy the moment; who knows how many more of these you'll have in your life the way you've been going.

"So, tell me what a video game designer is doing in Corsica?" Her mother always told her the best way to start a conversation with a man was to ask him about himself.

"I mostly design role playing games and I want to do one with a medieval theme this time. I'm sick of the ones with car thieves, hookers, robots, aliens and gangsters. Maybe I can teach the kids some history at the same time."

"The only thing I remember about role playing games was the sword and sorcery of 'Dungeons and Dragons.' Do you mean like that?"

"More or less, but the technology has gone through the roof since then. The kids can play on their computers, laptops, X-Box, and all the new technology the Japanese have in the pipeline.

It's all we can do as game designers to keep up with the new players. They eat the games up and spit them out faster than we can design them. The virtual habitats are coming out soon in high definition and have to look so real they need to be researched to be believable. Every detail accurate." He pointed around the restaurant, "Like this place—it would be perfect as part of a village. Then, the characters, or avatars the players use, need to have attributes realistic for the theme and setting of the game. Their clothing, weapons and styles have to be accurate for the era to have the game work."

"It's a lot more complicated than I thought. I've never played any of the games so I had no idea."

"Think about researching an historical novel and you'll understand. You want it to be as accurate as possible to have the reader immersed in the era, the story and the characters."

He seemed much more relaxed as he talked. It was the first time Lenya had been with a man who was involved in a creative type of work even remotely similar to hers—she was finding the experience pleasurable.

The owner stood by the table to take their order. "I'll have the rack of lamb, rosé please, with flageolets." Lenya closed her menu and turned to Terrence. "I can't help it, it's my favorite dish." The woman had an approving expression on her face.

"What are flageolets?" Terence leaned over the table and whispered again. "Sounds like they're either kinky or gaseous." He couldn't contain a wide and naughty grin.

"They're sort of like lima beans but better. The whole thing is divine and the garlic will drive away any vampires lurking in the general vicinity." Lenya found herself liking this man more and more. She was always a sucker for a good sense of humor. Even her body language was changing as she leaned towards him.

"Okay, I'll have the same thing the lady is having."

"Excellent choice, Monsieur." The owner couldn't suppress a slight smile. She turned to Lenya, "and to drink?"

She looked at Terrence, "What would you like?" She consciously kept her sentences short as she realized she felt like babbling.

"So far you're doing okay. I'm a fan of French wine—spent some time driving around the Rhone and Burgundy areas, but I'm not familiar with the wines of Corsica, so—your turf, your choice." He closed the *carte de vin* and handed it to her.

"Do you have a preference in wine? With lamb... red, rosé or white? Anything goes." She was fiddling with her silverware and wondered why she was so nervous with this man?

"I'll leave it in your hands. I like almost anything—other than California Chardonnay and Cabernet." They both laughed. Conspirators together.

"What is your house wine?" Lenya couldn't keep her eyes off him. He had an intelligent quality to his rugged face she found very appealing.

"We have a very nice wine from Corsica goes quite well with the gigot. Most of my customers enjoy it. I have an open bottle at the bar. Why don't I bring you each a small taste—see if you like it? Then decide."

"Great idea," Terrence said as he looked at Lenya, "I almost always go for the house wines too, usually the best deals."

The wine was pale and slightly more orange in color than a traditional rosé. "Here's to the wines of Corsica." Lenya toasted.

A soft, rich flavor with a mildly fruity overtone filled her mouth. *Delicious—a perfect complement to lamb.* Both of them nodded in assent. "Let's make it a full bottle." Terrence said. The young man brought the wine to the table and showed them the bottle. "It's a Domaine d'Alzipratu, from Zili in the Balagne—near Calvi."

Lenya laughed, "aha, one of the wineries in my area. It's delicious, I'll have to pay them a visit when I get home."

"Yes, do, it's worth it. They have one of the better wineries on Corsica and it's served in all the fine restaurants." He bent over to pour some into their glasses. "This is a blend made from grapes grown here, Sciacarellu, Nielluccio and Grenache. The vintner is famous for not using any pesticides so it is also organic."

It was going to be a long wet afternoon and what better place to spend it than here? She looked around the restaurant again as she sipped the smooth wine. The stone walls, the rough hewn wood and tables with the fresh flowers dotting the place with color were all so inviting. It was cozily dim; the fire brought warmth. The restaurant smelled of fragrant wood burning, warm bread fresh out of the oven, a faint hint of lamb cooking in garlic and *herbes de Provençe*. She snuggled down into her chair. She hadn't noticed before, but the son had placed an old cushion in front of the hearth and Tom was curled up on it sound asleep. Obviously she wasn't alone in her pleasure.

It was so homey and comfortable she felt her shoulders relax. This was one of those places she could stay forever. Then, she thought for a moment of ski lodges in Italy with Andre and immediately pushed the idea away. *It's a different country, a different man and a new place and time.*

Lenya smiled to herself as she rolled a sip of d'Alzipratu around on her tongue.

Nectar fit for gods.

Chapter 20

The Man In The Woods

Aldo was cold. The rain drenched him through to his skin. He was stubborn—refused to go back to the dryness of the casteddu. It was a long hike, but once home he could light a fire and dry off. Instead, he worried about the woman. When would she come back? Was she out of the rain and dry, or was she wet too? She left the day before. It was already after dark. Maybe she was away for a long time? Gone?

The first time he saw her, he sensed she was special. She, not caring who heard her walk with surety through the forest. She, grounded to the earth as he was. The golden aura shining around her head—the goddess light.

The more he studied her, the more he was convinced. Solitary, except for Tom always at her side. A creature of nature, like the small fox who slept at his feet most nights. And she showed respect, careful to never sully Dia's gifts. No smoking or leaving burning things behind. No trash. A knowing and respectful woman. He nodded his head in approval. It was so. Definitely his other half—his spirit-earth mate. He thought with a smile of all his prayers to Dia, rather than those *dios peligrosos* he didn't trust, those tricksters of the old Pantheons who played with a man for their own entertainment. Not so with Dia, she was the shepherd of her own flock, protecting their clan all these centuries, giving them good harvests, successful hunts, and making them fruitful... or...at least she always had in the past.

He admitted to himself present times were different...hard. Ever since the new god and his followers had taken over the island, his priests trying so hard to stamp out—burn out—the ancient mysteries. The Inquisition. The banning in towns of the worship of Dia. All her believers speaking the words of the new god in public and praying at hidden altars to Dia, powerful in her secret grottos and groves. It made his stomach clench to think of it. *Painful.*

Fewer and fewer villagers made the difficult journey to the cave during the times of solstice. To leave their offerings. To ask him as Maître for blessings, for cures, to remove the evil eye. To join their voices and bodies in ancient chants and dances to honor Dia. To offer their flame painted shadows to meld with the hunters on the walls. Ancient rites enacted for millennia. *Mystical. Powerful. No longer.*

Aldo was sure she sent this woman to him. *Maybe it was hope?* No matter, he knew. Now he had to find a way so she too would understand. *They were meant to share a life together.* He prayed to Dia for her understanding, prayed so Lenya would understand too. He knew her name. Lenya. He liked the way it sounded. Fluid, smooth..*suave.* Like the fur of a kit fox. He no longer had to think of her only as 'his woman.' He must tell his mind to use her name. Lenya.

It was cold and wet and the second night she had been gone. Maybe it was time to give up and go home. Get dry. Tomorrow see what happens. Maybe she is back by then.

For three moons past the hunters moon he'd waited for the chance to meet her. He'd been...not afraid exactly... maybe not quite comfortable. He had never been rejected. It was difficult for him to admit he might fear anything. Especially approaching a woman Hadn't he been Dia's consort since puberty?

He understood she might not understand. *Different ways.* Now, once he had made contact with her, she left. It was puzzling. *How long might she be gone. Forever?* It bothered him Sirio found it so easy to meet Lenya. She walked into the winery and they started talking. Why did he, Aldo, find it such a problem? Could it be what Sirio had told him—they came from two different worlds? She was a person...even under all the clan decorations of her people. He couldn't believe Dia would bring him this woman and then have her be...inaccessible?

He stood tall among his clan and those who remained believers in the old ways. He, Aldo, was a revered member of the clan, an elder. Above all, he was the consort of Dia. Maître. He wasn't timid in front of a woman. But he was reluctant to approach her. Afraid she wouldn't understand how Dia destined them to be together...preordained. *He knew.*

She was a different woman—big and strong and smart. She commanded machines, the small ones in her house, the bigger ones like her car. It showed she wasn't ordinary. She was a woman to respect. A woman with her own power. A fitting mate for him.

Then he felt a moment of doubt. *What would a woman of respect want with him? He would not give in to such doubt. No Maître, consort of Dia and elder of his clan ever doubted.* And he was the last one alive. He took a deep breath and straightened his back.

He cursed himself for a fool. *What was an elder without a tribe?* He felt ridiculous claiming, even to himself, he was worthy of respect as an elder of a non-existent clan. *Would the woman...no, Lenya,... laugh at him?*

Aldo huddled under the tree where he usually sat to keep watch over the house and couldn't be more miserable. *Tomorrow every joint would hurt.* Looking at the empty cabin again, he sank deeper into blackness. The dark windows felt like they were staring back at him. *Lenya wasn't there.* If she were, there would be music and light filtering out those windows to fill the air with life and joy.

A small covered porch, at the back of the cabin—hardly more than a wide step, was under a portion of roof built out to cover it. A large white machine she used for washing clothes was in the corner of the porch next to the wall—butting up against an open railing. It would make a good wind-break if he squeezed in next to it. He stood up. Even from a distance he could see it was dry. The wind came from the front of the cabin and pushed the rain away from this little spot of refuge.

Lenya wouldn't even know he was there when she came back. He could be dry and wait for her someplace she wouldn't see. When she came home, she always went to the front door... walked up the stairs to the deck and straight in through the wooden door across from the big glass sliding door. She only used the back door when she did the wash or let Tom out. He would hear her then. It took her some moments to unlock the two locks on the door, one was sticky. He watched her do it enough times to know.

He crept up to the tiny back porch. *Yes, enough space to curl up out of the rain.* He put his head on his arm, curled into the fetal position with his back against the white machine, arranged the soggy fur vest over himself as best he could to keep out the cold. *Even though it was damp his body would warm it... would give him protection from the wind and the cold air.* He stayed motionless and a layer of warm air built up under the vest and between his body and the machine.

As he lay in his tiny shelter, he thought back to his life, to the clan. It was meant to continue. The clan had existed in the mountains forever. The elders passed on the old stories of their survival, hidden from the rest of the world.

No one knew how long the clan had lived on the island. The stories told of when the clan came to settle Corsica was not yet an island. And, they did have visitors. Outcasts, people running from the world or thrown out of it came to be welcomed into the clan. They brought stories of the world outside, the world of violence, different religions, machines and wars and strange customs. When the clan foraged, they brought back magazines and newspapers. They saw what it was like outside the casteddu. They wanted no part of any of it.

He remembered some of the new people. Some stayed and bred with the clan. That was good. It made the blood stronger. Others left when they were ready to go back into the world. Some came back from time to time. They'd brave the steep hidden track to the casteddu. Bring gifts and thanks for sanctuary. Bring unwelcome news of the outside world. They sometimes brought blankets. Those were welcome, especially for the old ones. They could be wrapped in warmth in the cold of the casteddu on those nights when even a fire wasn't enough to keep the chill from their bones. And some brought knives, sharp with strong blades forged by the artisans in the mountains.

Some the clan had taken in were escapees from vendettas. Hiding so as not to bring further danger to their families. Others were people with nowhere else to go—homeless and tossed out by society for reasons they didn't understand. All were given food and shelter. The clan turned no one away unless they were dangerous. Murderers or rapists weren't welcome—tainted people. The clan wouldn't put their own in jeopardy. As hunters, they had their ways of dealing with those tainted ones. They were treated like rabid dogs. Put down.

Some of these visitors brought interesting news, current events... what was happening in the world. Often, the elders didn't understand it, they nodded and appreciated these former "guests" visited and cared about them.

Someone once even brought a story there might be another clan on the other side of the island. It was exciting news. Aldo wanted to investigate. Before he could make the journey, the elders started to die...Raina fell sick. He stayed and took care of everyone... his duty. Maître. If he had left, maybe he would know where to find another mate to continue the clan, not wait here in the rain for some strange woman to return. *Lenya.*

It was late at night. She wasn't coming back, he was sure. In all the time he watched her, she never stayed out late... didn't like coming home in the dark.

As he drifted into a fitful sleep, Aldo tossed and dreamed. Visions of open fields, hunters alive and chasing game raced across the rocky surface of his nightscape. He saw another time, when only the clan lived in the casteddu. The game looked different to him. He didn't know why. The hunters used weapons he hadn't seen before. But they felt familiar in his dream hands, as if he was used to hunting with them. The clan looked different too, eyes deeper set behind a more protruding brow, smaller, bow legged. Some had red hair like him, others dark eyed with tight curly black hair. He knew these hunters in his mind were ancient. How ancient, he had no idea.

In one of his waking moments, he remembered the treasures the elders kept in the cave—hammers made from sharpened stones tied to heavy wood with leather, now rotted and stiff with age, pots and bowls of clay, arrowheads and spear tips fashioned of stone and metal. They honored the old things, those relics crudely made and shaped by ancient hands—not machines. The elders kept these implements on a shelf in the cave with some pottery, beautiful red clay shapes decorated in black and ochre with the same stick figures as the caves. Animals ran from hunters with spears across jugs and bowls. Sadly, there were few animals to run from hunters these days.

Small figures carved from stone, wood or bone stood among the other memories from the past—smooth carving of a woman, her belly filled with child, large breasts to feed new life.

Fitfully turning in his sleep, his dreams went to the carvings and he saw her, Dia, Goddess of Heaven, Magna Mater. She was beautiful, her face framed by long dark hair blew around her. Tall, stately—not like the little round stone goddess. Diaphanous robes caught in the wind, swirled and molded her, outlining her body—full figured with life and strength—breasts swollen with milk and ample hips to carry a child—fruitful. A light filled cloud of sun rays surrounded her, misty and blinding his vision as she leaned over him. As she touched his face he became instantly erect. Smiling, she kissed him gently on the lips. In his sleep he felt himself stiffen. He awoke at the moment his seed spilled.

He grunted and felt ashamed. Seed should only be spilled inside a woman to put her with child or in her mouth to share his strength. This was how the clan continued life for millennia. No seed wasted. It hadn't mattered, for decades no one had birthed a child who lived.

Dia gave them no more gifts. *What had they done to offend her? Had he not fulfilled his role as consort? Did he not give her enough pleasure?* He tossed and turned; ashamed and mumbling prayers in his sleep—prayers in a language so ancient no one now living had ever heard it.

He worried Dia had forsaken both the clan, and him. The game had died out and so had the clan. *His failure as consort?*

Their island was filled with strangers. More and more people came, houses and cabins built on clan hunting grounds. Once quiet coves where the clan fished in secret now filled with men and women wearing tiny pieces of cloth barely covered them as they swam and lay in the sun. The clan wouldn't fish where they could be seen. It didn't matter, there was no one left to fish anyway. He couldn't stop the sadness remembering what had been and what now was. He hoped Lenya would be back before first light. He drifted off into sleep to the sound of rain thrumming its eternal melody on the roof overhead.

Chapter 21
Carcassonne And Terrence

Lenya was glad she came prepared to stay. Terrence was surprisingly good company. They talked through lunch, tea at the hotel and then dinner in the hotel dining room. Seldom had she met someone so comfortable to talk with.

Lotte, thank you. Now I'll have to admit you were right this time. She'll think she's the greatest. Lenya smiled to herself as she contemplated Lotte's bragging rights if this meeting went anywhere. *What was I thinking? Did I expect a West Coast surfer dude with the attitude and charm of a computer nerd?*

She ended up taking her own room at his hotel so they could meet early the next morning for breakfast. There was no hint of anything more than friendship. Lenya was grateful and found it appealing. Her Andre was a gentleman but had been very assertive in the romance area. Lenya was glad Terrence wasn't; she had mixed emotions about having a physical relationship .

Terence explained he planned to spend ten days following in the footsteps of the Templars and the Cathars as soon as he returned to the mainland. He wanted them for some of the characters in his new game.

The night before, in the process of downing their second bottle of d'Alzipratu with dinner, he told her his theory. "I'm convinced they're connected. At the battle of Mount Segur, the Cathars were defeated. I think the Catholic Church believed the Templars stashed the Holy Grail and their fortune with the Cathars for safekeeping. It wasn't they hated the Cathars so much, the Church wanted the Templar treasure...simple greed" Eyes bright; he ripped up pieces of bread and rolled them around in his hands.

"What safer place could they have found? The Cathars preached against the richness and ostentation of the Church so they wouldn't care about the gold and jewels the Templars were supposed to have amassed. It would be safe with them, or so the Templars thought." Terrence leaned back in his chair, a bit flushed from the wine but obviously pleased to have an interested audience.

Lenya hadn't read too much about the Cathars, but she remembered legends about the Templars hiding their treasure in the South of France. There were hints the treasure was stowed somewhere in the mountainous Gorge de Verdun, not far from the center of the Cathar faith. She made a mental note to do more research when she returned to the cabin.

He continued, "I want to visit the Templar sites as well as Mont Segur, where the Catholic Church massacred the Cathars in their last battle. It was in March of 1244 after a twelve month siege. I'm convinced what the Church really wanted was to find the Templar treasure. The common belief is the battle wiped the Cathars out." Terrence leaned forward, obviously into his theory. "But I'm not so sure. The Cathars were offered the option of recanting their beliefs or burning at the stake. Two hundred of them chose to burn—no record of what happened to the rest. I'd like to see what the locals say about anyone having survived.

I've already made reservations on the ferry to Nice and plan to rent a Renault Espace on the other side to do some nosing around."

She noticed he was a bit nervous and uncomfortable. *Did I say something to upset him? Is he trying to get the hell out of here? Dump me?*

He moved around in his chair and fiddled with his wine glass. He looked about the restaurant as if he was studying the architecture and décor. Finally, he waved to the waiter to bring the check. Lenya stayed quiet—he had something to say and she wasn't going to help him out.

Terrence squared his shoulders and reached out to take her hand. "Would you like to come with me?" She must have looked surprised, because she was. He continued, "no pressure—friends." A sheen of perspiration stood out on his forehead. "Not as if I don't think we could be more, but I don't want you to think I'm trying to make a pass...at least not so soon." There was a tease in his voice and even in the dim light Lenya saw he was blushing. *I haven't made anyone this nervous since my junior prom. What is going on with this man?*

Lenya looked him in the eye. "Oh, that wasn't what I expected. Sorry. I thought you were going to tell me you were getting married when you got back to L.A." This time she gave a nervous laugh. She liked him, but wasn't sure how much and it might be uncomfortable traveling together. It was surprising he seemed so...shy?... with her. *How odd, he's such an attractive and successful man.*

"Lenya, I really don't know how to say this correctly, but it would be great to have you as a traveling companion." He paused for a moment, "...and whatever else you might be comfortable with. But don't worry; we'll have separate rooms or separate beds, or even separate hotels. It's up to you. I'm enjoying your company and I think it would be a lot more fun to travel with you than by myself."

It was clear to Lenya the little speech had cost him. She didn't know how to answer. The idea of a jaunt off Corsica sounded interesting; she hadn't been off the island for months.

She watched Terrence frown. "I have to leave tomorrow and I'm sorry we don't have more time to get to know each other." Lenya realized with a shock he was not only shy, but was as reluctant to commit to anything as she was. "I don't think I've ever found someone I could talk to the way we did tonight and I really liked it. In fact, I liked it so much I don't want it to end when I leave tomorrow."

He leaned over and took her hand before she could answer. "Look, I know you are a recent...widow. My sister told me about your husband and what a shock it was to you and I get it. But I think you and I have a nice rapport, and I'd like to see where it goes. You make of it whatever you want. I'm not pushing you"

She found his discomfort with his own sensitivity endearing and was liking him more and more.

Lenya felt something inside her open. It was creaking with a rusty hesitancy, but it was definitely opening.

Why not? Since I'm on one adventure, why not go on another...and I certainly enjoy this man's company. Who knows where it might go?

Before she could change her mind, words were out of her mouth, "How about this, I'll book my own room in this hotel, stay here tonight, and over breakfast tomorrow, in the cold light of day—and sober, we can see if we want to do this." She smiled at him as she said it.

Terrence was clearly relieved. Maybe he was going to be lucky enough to have a very interesting traveling companion. "Agreed. You and Tom have a date for breakfast tomorrow at seven sharp. The ferry leaves in the afternoon so if we want to make it, we need to decide early."

She laughed, "You are not only a man of decision but you also have a seven AM date."

At seven sharp, they were both in the small breakfast room dunking crusty butter-slathered baguettes into huge bowls of *café au lait*. It was decided. She would go with him for a ten day tour of the south of France. They were on a mission to hunt down the elusive Templars and try to find the last of the Cathars.

Terrence requested the concierge to change his ferry reservations to include Lenya and her car on the overnight from Calvi to Nice instead of leaving from Ajaccio.

Lenya was filled with a sense of freedom, mixed with a bit of the excitement that comes from playing hooky from school, as they piled Tom and Terrence's luggage into the Rav4 next to her small bag. They headed back to the cabin to pack a suitcase for Lenya, pay her rent and utilities and then be off on their adventure.

Even the weather seemed to agree with her decision. The storm had blown off the island and they were treated with a drive under a clear sky and glorious sun.

Aldo heard the car stop at the foot of the walk to the cabin. After hours of tossing and turning, he'd finally fallen into a deep sleep. Panicked, he didn't want her to catch him soggy, dirty and sleeping on her porch.

Making himself as small as possible, he waited until she entered the house, and then melted into the safety of the nearby woods. Tom raced around the outside of the house, sniffing the porch where Aldo had slept. He knew his friend was near and followed Aldo's scent into the woods to greet him. As Aldo ruffled the dog's ears in joy, he saw a man come out on the deck and stretch. Where had he come from? He must have gone into the cabin when Aldo turned his back to run into the woods.

A man. She had a man with her! Aldo was sure she had no mate. Sirio never mentioned another man. Who was this? A brother? Was the strange man going to stay? Had she come alone at first and now the man came to join her?

Aldo thought back in time, she'd been in the cabin alone for two seasons. Was this a new man? What if he, Aldo, was now too late and another man claimed her? He hugged Tom to his chest and groaned. The shock was like a punch as he fell to his knees. Tom yelped and jumped out of his embrace, standing and looking at him with funny quizzical expression. Even Tom looked worried, but he quickly ran back to the cabin when Lenya came out on the deck and called his name.

Aldo shook himself. He had to see more. It couldn't be true, could it? She was leaving? He crept closer to the cabin and watched through the open sliding glass door while she packed up her machine and handed it to the man. She had a big travel bag as well, and a case for Tom. She was going away with man!

He screamed silently at himself. Aldo is too cautious, too late to assert himself to the woman. Is this what I deserve? As he watched them load her things in her car, he beat himself mentally for being so slow. How could he have been so stupid? He didn't deserve to be consort of Dia, elder of the clan. No wonder Goddess had forsaken him. Dia, forgive me for being too slow to declare myself to the mate you found for me!

Aldo watched as Lenya's bags were stowed in the car. Tom eagerly jumped into his case and was secured across the back seat. Aldo couldn't believe it was over.

Anger welled up as he watched his Lenya ease into the passenger seat. The smiling man closed her door, got into the driver's seat and pulled away. Dia, what have I done to deserve this? Did I disrespect you so much you do this to me, or is it another game the fates play on me? She has a new mate and once again I fail.

Aldo stumbled blindly back to the sacred cave. He was so angry with himself he couldn't go back to his home, the casteddu. He needed the comfort of Dia in her home.

Curled into a ball on the cold stone floor, he didn't even bother to light a taper to illuminate the only companions he had left—the hunters and their prey on the walls. Shadows no longer danced across the stone to keep him company and comfort him.

What can I have done to make Goddess so angry? Is this the price I pay for spilling my seed in my sleep? Have I not fulfilled my duties as consort? Did I not give Dia my ecstasy?

He went back in his mind to what he had done in the past. He could think of no disrespect. As the clan always ruled, he cleaned away the charred flesh from the bones of the elders, his wife, and family. Then, he placed them in a basket to take into the burial dolmen—send them on their last journey. No one was left to do for him. He hoped Dia would forgive him... not think it sacrilege on his part, because he finally came to a decision. He willed himself to die.

As he drifted into sleep, he hoped there was a Mazzeru left somewhere on the island, one lone dream hunter dreaming of a kill. Then, when the Mazzeru turned over the dead game, it would show Aldo's face and he could finally leave this world and its pain.

The next morning he felt the sun with joy. Outside, it warmed his flesh and soothed as it crept into his bones and joints. He was happy until he remembered Lenya. Gone. Aldo turned to the sun and as it blessed his face he screamed with wordless anger, frustration, despair, mixed together. It wasn't enough. He picked up a rock and hurled it at the rock wall, happy when it split into pieces, one of which bounced back and cut his shin. Grateful for the blood running in a rivulet down his leg, he hurled another rock and another until at last, tired and his anger assuaged for the moment, he sat down on a boulder and howled. It was too late. The one he had been sure was *his* woman was gone. There was nothing left for him...and it had been all his fault.

Stupid!

Chapter 22
Meeting Goddess

Aldo lay on the cold stones where the dead were placed for their final rites. Since there was no one to perform the sacred rituals for him, it was the best he could manage. He had made up his mind to stay there until death, even though he knew the elders would have thought it desecration of their sacred place.

According to the legends, his ancestors had placed the stone warriors in the woods and mountains, heroes ready to protect the island, no matter the cost. Now, the clan was gone. Each generation grew weaker, more prone to disease, fewer skills to survive, the old ways forgotten. The elders knew it was not good to mate within the tribe for so long. They needed new members, new blood but were afraid to search outside for mates, the same as he had been. Now it was too late.

Only the cave and the relics so lovingly saved, and the eternal hunters chasing their prey would remain to show the clan ever existed. Aldo turned his back to it all and faced the end of the wall where it met the floor.

For days he remained in the cave. There was no Mazzeru to dream his death. Something inside him refused to give up. While he took no food, he couldn't refrain from drinking the cool water from the stream below. He tried to stop filling the gourd when it was empty—but his resolve wasn't strong enough.

He lost body weight, muscles and tendons prominent on his legs and arms. His beard matted and filled with twigs. Before, he was vain about his appearance and hygiene—to honor Dia. He had bathed daily in the chill streams and rubbed himself with fragrant herbs afterwards. Plaited his hair and beard in the old manner. Now he stank. The foulness of his own rancid pelt was offensive to him and certainly to Dia.

No hunter could be accepted by the gods in this condition, perhaps this was why he didn't die. Even the god of the Underworld didn't want him.

One morning he woke up with the realization he wasn't going to die so easily. Dia had given him a great store of energy. As he lay in the cave, defiling the memories of the ancient hunters with the smell of his own excrement, Dia came to him once again in a half-waking dream.

This time she was in her stone form, rounded and small with her pendulous breasts prominent and resting on her enlarged belly. Between sleep and waking, he realized he was very uncomfortable.

Something dug painfully into his backside. He reached down to remove the obstruction. It was one of the goddess sculptures. The little Venus figurine must have fallen from its shelf and he had rolled over onto it in his sleep. With no meat left on his body, it hurt.

As he held the little statue in his hand to study it, the sturdy little woman looked disgusted with him. She appeared to be wrinkling her face up over the *ordeur désagréable* he had surrounded himself with in her cave. The stone woman was looking at him like his mother did when she was angry. He remembered her poking him with her broom when he wanted to stay in bed to sleep.

Mother's voice rang in his head, "Aldo, get up you lazy boy. Life is not going to come to you if you sleep it away. The deer doesn't find you in your bed and the herbs don't jump into your gathering bag." He could almost feel the broom handle pushing at him with more vigor when he turned away from her. "I mean it boy! Get out of bed and do it now or you'll get more than this little nudge from me." His mother hated when he was lazy.

His mind tried to connect his memory of her with his excuse to now lie in his own filth. Maybe she was right; maybe he was lazy.

Aldo hurt—inside. His hopes were gone; the pain was more than he could stand. Didn't she understand? He looked at the statue again and found nothing in its face willing to allow him an excuse.

He knew he had to do something to make it right. For Dia. He had never before thought the little statue might have its hands on its hips. Dia had to be obeyed. He got up from the floor of the cave and recognized the aches in his body had worsened—muscles and tendons unused for so many days.

Painfully, he pushed all the waste into a basket and took it out to bury in the woods as far from the cave as his weakened body could go. Next, he carefully swept the stone and dirt floor with a broom—his mothers, made of fine branches tied to a stout stick. Then, he put a covering of new pine needles and eucalyptus leaves to freshen the cave. As he worked, he found some dried meat and berries to eat slowly while he drank his water. The food brought energy to his starved body and made his stomach rumble after being empty for so long.

Later, he walked to the stream to bathe. For once he looked forward to the pain of the cold on his body. It was what he deserved for letting the clan and Dia down. Afterwards, he took the time to comb and braid his hair and beard before moving and stretching his muscles. As the blood coursed through his veins, his ego took control once again—he would regain his strength for what life called him to do next.

The urge to go towards Lenya's cabin once more was too strong to resist. As he neared it toward dusk, he saw a spark of light through the trees. He felt a moment of joy, then thought, maybe someone else was living there and she had gone forever. To make sure, he trotted up to his usual sentry post.

Chapter 23
Living Goddess

Lenya opened the door to the empty cabin, put her suitcase by the door and walked out on the deck to smell the familiar air she now identified as home.

Her trip to the mainland of France was over. She was on her own again—and relieved.

She and Terrence enjoyed each other's company, and discovered an easy friendship. They were each researching similar periods of time and shared information. Within a day or two, if they had been worried about being compatible, worry was long gone.

One night during dinner, Terrence asked her if she'd made any friends on Corsica. "Yes, I have a good friend who owns one of the wineries. Sirio. He's quite a bit older... we're platonic friends. We go for dinner from time to time and have been to a concert."

"Do I have to worry?" Terrence asked with a serio-comic frown and wiggled his eyebrows.

"Perhaps. If he discovers Viagra and his memory kicks in." As soon as she said it, she was sorry. It was a bad raunchy joke at a good friend's expense. Lenya was ashamed of herself.

The first few days of their trip they reserved separate rooms. All physical contact was limited to holding hands and a chaste double cheek kiss goodnight in the hallway in front of Lenya's door. She and Terrance kept studiously away from each other.

Then, they checked into a small hotel in Carcassonne looking over the ramparts. Lenya's room was small, whitewashed walls, dark wood door and window frames. As she looked up, there was the familiar wood ceiling like her cabin. A "matrimonial" bed dominated the room.

French doors opened to a tiny wrought iron balcony with a view of the ancient ramparts and the neat rows of grape vines radiating into the distance like spokes on a wheel.

It's magic here, she thought. This has to be the most romantic spot on earth. Why the hell not take advantage of it? Lenya, you are a fool! Look at the gorgeous man you're with. Get a grip, honey! Her own voice sang in her head and she knew it was right. She knew he was growing fond of her, Terrence made it clear. He was both understanding, and a real gentleman—kind, considerate. She realized she actually wanted him...and felt good about it. *What in heaven's name are you holding out for? Virginity? A little late for that, my dear, don't you think?* And she laughed at the thought.

That night, they dined in a small restaurant outside the ancient walled city. Terrence had asked where the locals ate. The place was modern, none of the familiar stone walls and fireplace. The tables were set with the traditional bright blue and gold cloths of Provence. Walls covered with photographs of excavations done throughout the 1900's followed the history of the city to the present. Terrence was fascinated and studied them with interest while Lenya studied him. Before she realized it, she drank two Kirs before dinner, the Cassis a velvet heaven on the palate. Her resolve grew stronger with every sip.

"Hey, babe, look at this one." His enthusiasm was infectious and she went over to see what he was pointing to. As she moved next to him, he automatically put his arm around her shoulder and drew her close, breathing into her hair. It was surprising to her how right it felt. He caught himself in the familiar embrace; dropped his arms and pulled away.

"It's okay Terrence. I liked it," Lenya whispered. As she turned towards him, she realized it had been an automatic reaction and he looked relieved she didn't mind. She took his hand as they stood together looking at the photographs, and at one point she even squeezed a bit. Lenya wanted to make sure he understood he hadn't breached their unspoken and reticent relationship.

The large picture windows in the restaurant faced the ramparts and showed off the ancient city lit up like a movie set. Carcassonne remained as one of the largest standing walled medieval cities in Europe and the tourist office knew how to make the most of it.

After dinner, she took a sip of a fifty year old Martell Cognac he ordered as they sat on the patio watching the Sound and Light spectacle detailing the city's history.

Later, they strolled back inside the ramparts and stopped at a sidewalk café. From their rooms they could see the vineyards, so they decided to enjoy some more of the bounty and shared a demi-carafe of local red wine. Lenya hadn't had so much to drink since Andre died and she could feel it glowing inside as it shredded all her inhibitions into tatters.

On their return to the hotel, instead of their platonic-goodnight-cheek-kiss ritual, Terrence moved his mouth over hers and held her for a long, deep kiss. Her response was instantaneous as she melded her body against his. They practically had their clothes off by the time she fumbled open the lock on the door to her room.

She had dreaded a Beverly Hills male response—the quick blow job and 'good-night' she and her girl friends always joked about. What she got was something else entirely.

The next morning she awoke with her body glued to his. His face was nestled in her hair and she inhaled the maleness of him while her nose was tickled by the curly dark strands on his chest. As she peeled herself off, trying not to sneeze and wake him, she remembered an hour or more of considerate, gentle lovemaking. Exhausted, they had slept in each other's arms—sweaty, smiling and satiated.

Creeping to the bathroom, she almost laughed aloud at her image in the mirror. Hair askew, cheeks and chin red with stubble burn, her eyes glowed. Remembering. Sex and laughter. My favorite mix.

She had forgotten how lovemaking made her feel afterwards. The mirror couldn't lie about the pleasure her face radiated. Lenya girl, she thought, a good fuck is a lot better at bringing back the bloom of youth than plastic surgery or all the face creams money can buy. Looking back at her was a happy well satisfied woman. Not quite...everything...but super fine.

From then on, they took one room, preferably with a king size bed.

Lenya found him acrobatic and fun, sharing and gentle. I'm not in love...maybe sincere like and respect? ... all right with me...really perfect... She remembered the title of the Meatloaf song "Two Outta Three Ain't Bad." It's okay for now, she thought. Even Tom agreed, snoring companionably at the foot of the bed.

Terrence was going to continue his trip and would be on the move for months doing research. She breathed a sigh of relief realizing there was no possibility for a serious relationship.

One morning over breakfast, she felt Terrence studying her face. "What's up? Are you taking a mental picture or have I got toast crumbs on my mouth?" She asked.

"I was thinking how nice it is to have breakfast with you. I'm going to miss you a lot when I have to leave."

"Don't worry. I'm sure you'll find plenty of company along the way...handsome guy like you...no problemo!"

"How about you babe, going back to your old geezer vintner when I leave?"

"Don't call him a 'geezer!' He's a great guy and wonderful company. Sirio keeps me from being a total hermit and hanging out with a caveman for company."

"Caveman? You have to be kidding. What do you mean?"

Lenya was instantly sorry she brought it up. Now she owed an explanation. "I met a man in the woods. Actually, he rescued Tom from a very pissed off raccoon when I was having lunch at my favorite grotto." She looked down at her empty plate and paused for a moment. "I think he's been bringing me flowers." She plunked her folded napkin on the table as if to accentuate the end of the conversation.

Terrence wasn't letting her off so easily. "What do you mean, caveman, and...flowers?"

"I find little bouquets of flowers and herbs on my deck and on the rock where I like to have lunch sometimes. At first, I thought it was a small child...maybe offerings to some of the carved deities in the grotto...this odd man, he looks like something from a natural history museum diorama...like a caveman...sorta." She picked up her napkin again and twisted it. She didn't want to talk about the strange man in the woods. It made her uncomfortable.

Terrence pressed on. She had piqued his interest. "What does he look like? What made you think caveman?"

"He has long red hair and a long beard and wears a fur vest looks like he made it. There's something very primitive looking about him. And, he speaks in a combination of French and Italian – together, some English words too." It had all come out in a rush. She sighed. "That's it."

"Sounds to me like you have another new suitor. I'd be careful— he might be after you...and I thought it would be safe to leave you alone on the island."

"I don't think it's a problem. He's been very polite and he seems quite gentle. I do think Tom has a crush on him since the rescue." She got up from the table abruptly. Conversation over.

Later in the day, over a glass of wine, Terrence told her of the next part of his trip. "I'm going to visit Prague and Warsaw...spend a few weeks in Russia, first Moscow and Leningrad, then to the countryside. After —Asia." He refilled their glasses and took out a map of the world filled with yellow magic marker and post-its and spread it out on the small table. "Look, babe, I want to see the Great Wall of China and the Imperial City." Both had yellow circles. "But most of all, I want to follow some of the routes Marco Polo took...photograph the stone army... clothing and weaponry." She nodded at his enthusiasm as he continued, "Then to Tokyo to study the samurai... customs, costumes and armament." His last stop before going back to Los Angeles.

Who could know how many exotic and interesting women might cross his path? Lenya hoped he had a fabulous time. She knew she would enjoy seeing him again—but she was also content with the idea it might only have been a wonderful vacation—nothing more than a delightful moment in time. She'd learned a lot from Terrence, and she was grateful. She enjoyed sensual closeness—it hadn't died with Andre as she had feared.

Lenya knew she was coming alive, reclaiming herself. Every time she looked in the mirror she saw a glow she hadn't realized she'd lost. Funny how those things are, you convince yourself part of your life is over, and when it comes back you realize how much you'd missed it all along!

The rest of the trip seemed to fly by. For a moment she had felt a pang of regret as she dropped Terence off at the airport, but it slipped out of her mind as she headed for the port. Before she even realized it, she was on the ferry, once again alone with Tom; this time watching the lights of Marseilles fade into the distance.

Now she was glad to be home, as she considered the cabin. Opening the doors and windows to let in the clean mountain air, she thought how much she'd missed her solitude, and secretly welcomed the idea Terrence was on his way across the globe.

She'd hugged him goodbye, resisting his offer to continue the journey with him. She was glad to be back to her own life in Corsica. For now, Tom was company enough.

As she lay in bed, sleep was elusive. She studied the wood ceiling and inhaled the familiar forest scent, a living presence surrounding her. It had been so good to sleep pressed against the length of Terrence's body...and the lovemaking...

Terrence was attractive, intelligent and interested in many of the same things she was. He was a thoughtful and considerate lover. What in hell more do I want? The mere fact she was happy to be without him shook her. Her old perception of herself said she wanted, maybe even needed, male companionship. Was a new Lenya emerging?

She took half a sleeping pill and went to bed feeling oddly safer in her little cabin than she had anyplace on their trip, even though she had slept spooned next to a delightful man. What's wrong with me? Anything...? Maybe 's the way it is now. Maybe it's called growing up.

Before Lenya drifted off to sleep she thought, tomorrow I need to have a long conversation with Lotte about this. Before Andre, I would have been delighted to keep company with a man like Terrence. He has everything, and I mean everything, going for him. I need Lotte's take.

Then, some errant thoughts passed by. Wonder if he was so nice to me because there were no Beverly Hills Barbies around to entertain him? Maybe 's they're the type he really likes and I was what was available. Talk about being insecure... Ugh!

I must be losing my mind! She decided as she finally drifted off to sleep.

❦

She was back! Tom had sensed Aldo's presence and scratched at the door to get out. When Lenya opened the door he rushed into the woods, greeting Aldo like a lost friend. Aldo hugged the warm wiggling body to his chest and felt his heart lurch into life again before Tom squirmed out of his grasp.

Aldo heaved a sigh as the lights went off inside. As he looked up at the cabin, he imagined her sleeping on the other side of the triangular window.

He wrapped his skins more securely around his shoulders and burrowed into the base of the tree to keep as much wind as possible off his back. He didn't mind the cold. His muscular body had been used to it, but now he'd lost most of the layer of fat that kept him warm and he felt the cold more than usual. He was happy. She was home. There was no man.

❦

Lenya woke up well rested and content to be home. When she let Tom out for his morning constitutional, she saw a small green offering on the deck. Nestled into the greens as if in their own tiny nest were two small speckled eggs and a handful of chestnuts. Wrapping her robe tighter around her body she studied the woods around the cabin. .. no sign of her friendly neighborhood caveman. She wondered for a moment what he was doing while she was gone and how he knew so fast that she had returned, but other things were on her mind and she forgot about him as she got back to work on the new book.

Good news came in an e-mail from Ellie, her agent.

Last payment arrived on the book—publisher ready for
Christmas release. They plan big promotion. Please be
available for Skype interviews as publisher already advised
you won't be in the States.
Check bank account for payment.
Enjoy Corsica and keep writing!!

Lenya got on-line and there, in her bank account in all its glory, was the nice fat payment. Less Ellie's commission, of course. Corsica was secure for at least another year, and more, if she was a tad careful.

She had an e-mail from Terrence. It was his usual up-beat style.

BevHlsGamaster:
Hey, Babe! How's Corsica treating you? Been researching where I'm
going next and found a photo of a little wall I thought I might copy for my
place in LA. Do you think I need to bring in a million Chinese to build
it or will a few Mexicans do?

There was an attachment with some photos of the Great Wall of China.

He went on in his usual chatty way, full of humor and observations of life around him. She felt as if she was sharing the journey and for a nanosecond was sorry she hadn't gone along.

She looked again at the green nest with its eggs and chestnuts. November was three weeks away and the chill in the air was already more pronounced. She thought for a moment of her friend from the grotto and hoped he was keeping warm.

Chapter 24
...back at the Winery

Her first stop once she unpacked and stocked up the refrigerator was a visit to Sirio. Lenya felt guilty about leaving in such a rush. She hadn't told him she was going and hoped he hadn't worried about her. He deserved an apology.

As soon as the Rav began to bump up the long drive to the winery, Tom anxiously pressed his nose to the window to look for Sophia. His rigid stance of anticipation told Lenya he had missed his pal.

And there was Sirio, leaning against the barn like a part of the structure, his pipe in his hand and a big smile on his face. When she parked the car and walked up to him, he held out his arms to embrace her, but she could tell he was disturbed.

Hugging her, he began, "You are a very naughty girl, Lenya." Then he smacked her butt with a nearby newspaper—hard but not painful. "You have to learn here, on the island, when we leave we always tell our friends...so no one worries. When I didn't hear from you for a few days...no answer on the telephone...worrisome to those of us who live alone...we imagine...things. Anyway, I drove to the cabin...in the bloody rain...to make sure you hadn't fallen or had an accident."

He finally let her go, a bit crushed but nevertheless intact.

"I'm here to apologize. You're right and I'm so sorry." She could feel a blush start up her neck. "I had only intended to go to Ajaccio overnight to meet a friend from the states for lunch...but...." A bright rosy color suffused her face as she continued, "an overnight turned into ten days in Provence on a historical mystery adventure. I was so rushed to make the ferry in Calvi I forgot to call." Now she was looking down at her shoes. "Please accept my apology."

Sirio laughed at her discomfiture. "Don't worry my dear, you are allowed one mistake in your perfect life." He gave her another hug, this one gentle and friendly. "Now though, you have to pay the price of mistake and tell me about the trip...and what mystery you were trying to solve. There is one thing I know already. You had a good time, and realized once again you are a woman."

Lenya thought she had blushed before. This time she turned bright red. "Huh-huh...how...what?"

"My dear, I am neither blind nor stupid. I am only old. A woman who has been well pleasured has a certain look about her...contentment...serenity perhaps? Whatever. You have the look...and it becomes you. Now you must tell me who this lucky man is."

He opened a bottle of light and fruity white wine and the two sat outside with the dogs in the freshening air as she told Sirio about Terrence and the pleasant time they had together.

"I really enjoyed his companionship," she paused for a minute and rubbed her finger around the bowl of her glass before she looked up at him, "but it was a relief to come back to the cabin and... solitude."

He nodded understanding. "And that, my dear, is why, at my very advanced age, I am *un solitaire*, perhaps not quite *un ermite*...but...alone." Looking down at his feet he continued, "But I hope it is not how you end up...I mean alone, like me."

"At least we have each other." She said with a smile.

"Yes, we do, but I am not sufficient for you...your age...you need more."

"Enough. Let's speak about a more interesting subject." Lenya told him about her adventures with Terrence; twisting through the Gorges de Verdun driving at breakneck speed, the hairpin turns going on forever, and the trek up the mountain to the tacky souvenir shops and bad food of les Baux de Provence, even though they later decided the spectacular view was worth it. Their search for the Templar treasure and the Cathar connection. Not very successful but certainly both entertaining and interesting.

As the afternoon faded into dusk, they chatted about the wines of Carcassonne and the sadness she had felt visiting Mt. Segur, standing on the site where the last of the Cathars were massacred.

Sitting together in the warm evening, Tom and Sofia sleeping between them under the old table where they placed their wine glasses, she realized she'd finally come home.

Chapter 25
Peligroso Dio

Terrence e-mailed Lenya almost every day. The story she told him about meeting the caveman stuck with him and he often asked if she'd seen the man again.

BevHlsGamaster:
Hey, Babe! How are things? Seen your Neanderthal boyfriend recently? I'm worried he's beating me to the punch with courting you. Got any good presents lately?

Lenyascribe:
Hey T! Been quiet around here lately, only presents have been some nice greens and the pickins' are getting thin by the looks of them, or maybe he's losing interest...and if anything...he's Cro Magnon—remember?
Did some good stuff on the last chapters and I'm on a tear.
Thanks for the links on DNA studies...very interesting. Maybe the explanation for my buddy, plenty of early man sites in this neck of the woods. Wish I could ask more questions but conversations are limited.
Bye for now...Lenya

While Terrence was fascinated by the possibility she met the last of the island's Neolithic residents, Lenya was reluctant to speak about it to him—as if she was talking about one boyfriend with another, a real high school no-no.

Oddly protective, the only response she gave when Terrence brought the subject up was reminding him a Cro Magnon was more likely than a Neanderthal because they were closer in time and species to modern man.

In the course of Terrence's research, whenever he came across an article he thought might interest her, he sent the link. Discover Magazine quoted an expert on a new DNA study who said Neanderthals had not really disappeared; they only merged into the rest of the humanoid population. So why not Cro Magnon? But she'd read other studies claiming Neanderthals had been a separate species and were more likely to dine on Cro Magnons than mate with them.

She and Terrence corresponded back and forth by e-mail, but she couldn't shake the feeling he was being guarded about something. Whatever it was didn't concern her. She liked him, enjoyed his company, but didn't have a deep emotional attachment.

Lenya settled back into the rhythms of life in her cabin. It was harder and harder to remember life before Corsica—life with Andre. The island had taken her over, it folded her into its arms and she happily followed its lead in the dance.

The weather was changing. The Foehn blew in from the south to bring its strange headaches. One morning she woke to mild Indian summer weather at least fifteen degrees warmer than it had been all week. For a few days there'd be unseasonable warmth, but Lenya knew it was only a short respite—a gift to be taken advantage of—time for a nice long walk with Tom.

Strolling through the pines and chestnut trees on the way home, she gathered a pile of twigs and branches for the fireplace. The next morning, she discovered a stack of logs on her deck along with the usual small bouquet of herbs. No one was there as she searched, trying to see into the dense woods. She felt sure of his presence, but standing on the deck rubbing her arms against the cool air, she could find no trace.

Strange, she thought, where can he go, and where does he live? She didn't know if she should feel creepy about his secret visits, but she felt an odd kind of comfort at the thought he was around. She forgot about him and went inside for her second cup of coffee. There was a lot of work to do on the new project and she was anxious to get started.

The book was coming along well. She had the first several generations in outline form and was working on the 18ᵗʰ Century. This was where she had decided to place a major romance. She was annoyed because it didn't ring true and she needed to make it feel realistic. When she found herself stopped in one place, she went to another section and worked on other chapters and other generations of characters. But the 18th Century was haunting her.

Lenya decided she needed inspiration. A visit to the grotto for lunch generally worked its magic by taking her mind to other places more relaxed. By the time she came back to her computer, the solution to most problems didn't seem so important and easily appeared.

Sunlight filtering through bare branches warmed and brightened the damp loamy air as she sat at the dolmen and nibbled her sandwich. Looking across the clearing and into the brush, she noticed for the first time several tall, slender elongated stones standing upright. Usually obscured with leafy vines, they were now visible since the concealing leaves had fallen after the first frost. Curious, she looked closely. They were in the crude shape of figures...menhirs. Leaving her lunch aside, she went to the stones and cleared the brush from one of them, a menhir. The head was indicated by hewing the top in a rounded shape. The face had eyes and nose faintly carved. It was hard to see details, but if you looked at it from a certain angle the features appeared. A few feet on either side, she found several similar stones; one barely upright and two others on the ground.

An alignment. She hadn't known there were any near the cabin. None of her guidebooks referenced such findings in the vicinity, but then, they didn't mention the dolman she had found either.

She took her camera out of her pocket and began snapping photos to send to Lotte. E-mail with attachments was her favorite. Lotte like to share her sister's discoveries and it kept Lenya from feeling so far removed from home.

The stones had carved almond shaped openings for eyes, the iris defined by a hole. The mouth, if visible, lifted at the corners in what could have been either a gentle smile or an evil smirk. She pushed and pulled at the carving on the ground, it was too large and heavy for her to stand upright. Kneeling by it, she began to scrape away the lichen and dirt obscuring the face. If she was able to get the right angle and lighting, she might capture the expression with her camera.

On her knees, with attention focused on cleaning lichen and dead leaves from the image, she wasn't aware of anyone coming near until feet encased in hand sewn moccasins appeared next to her. She looked up and there he was. Tom hadn't made a sound. He's really is getting senile not to have warned her.

The man looked concerned. He shook his head as she reached again to touch the stone face. *"No, no! E malevolo Dio."* he said in a guttural voice. She quickly took her hand away so as not to offend him. *"Peligroso. No toca."* Italian? Maybe Corsican? He was telling her it was a malovelent god, dangerous to touch. He reached down and took her by the arm to pull her up and away from the fallen image. His grip was firm, but not threatening, guiding her away from danger. Protecting.

As Lenya stood brushing dirt and leaves off her jeans, she remembered Corsica had been under Italian rule, or more particularly, both Venetian and Genoan, for centuries. The Italian language had then been the language of choice on the island, before being replaced by French for the last two hundred years. The Corsicans, stubborn as always, spoke Corsu or Corsican, a language with close ties to Italian.

For whatever reason, she preferred speaking to him in Italian, even though she was perfectly able to converse with shopkeepers and merchants with her serviceable French.

As she looked him over, it was obvious he had lost weight, his face was gaunt and his bones more pronounced. Maybe there was less food available to him this season? Then she recalled the fall harvest. He should have looked better. Had he been ill? How was he going to make it through the winter like this? And why do I care?

He looked at her sandwich neatly placed on the rock table. What the hell, I might as well feed him.

She motioned for him to sit at the rock with her. He pointed at his chest and put his head to the side in question. She nodded. He came over and sat on one of the rock formations opposite her. Lenya handed him half of her sandwich. Motioning for him to eat, she picked up her half and bit into it. She felt a moment of self-consciousness as she realized he was studying her intently. Did he want to see if she died from eating the sandwich? Or prehaps he wanted to see if she ate it or if it was an offering. He nodded and picked up his half as she did, watched her for a second and then took a huge bite. After a few moments of chewing, he swallowed and smiled. *"C'est bon, me piace."* There it was; French and Italian together. His voice was so guttural she had to concentrate to understand what he was saying.

She pointed to herself, *"Me chiama Lenya."*

He pointed to himself and announced with a huge grin, *"Me chiama Aldo."*

Well, that bridge was crossed. Now what? It was hard enough to think of something to say to a stranger when you speak the same language, but this was near to impossible. She wasn't sure which of the two languages, if any, he spoke or preferred. Maybe he was some sweet but slightly backward local? She didn't want to get more involved than sharing a sandwich, no encouragement. She subconsciously pulled her sweater closer around her shoulders as if for protection as she looked him over.

His looked clean except for a few pieces of brush clinging to his beard. It wasn't braided this time, but his hair was—a single thick plait trailing down below his shoulder blades. Lenya found the sight of it exciting, long hair on a man was always exotic and sensual, but she brushed the thought away immediately. With his hair away from his face, she could see him clearly. Prominent cheekbones and high forehead, blue-grey eyes and a rather large nose. Each feature distinct, strong. She had to admit to herself this man, while very odd, was also masculine and appealing. He smelled pleasant, like eucalyptus and immortelle and some other scent. But she couldn't imagine hygiene being one of his long suits. He probably lives in a cave and sleeps on pine needles.

She had no idea how close to the target she was.

He didn't seem to need conversation. He ate his half sandwich and looked at her from under slightly beetle brows. Tom snuggled into his lap and snored contentedly. The man occasionally stroked Tom and made little murmuring sounds to him. Lenya's camera was sitting on the table in front of her and she surreptitiously turned it on video.

They all sat in easy silence, breathing in the fresh, pine scented air and listening to the sound of the incessant wind singing in the tree branches that presaged the coming of winter. They might be enjoying the last bit of warmth for months.

She surprised herself by relaxing and enjoying the moment. The man's presence was comforting in a companionable way and she found herself not at all fearful of him. She had to stop thinking of him as "the caveman" now she knew his name was Aldo.

Sun through the foliage turned Aldo's hair a glistening rust color with highlights of gold and bronze. His beard was darker in color— auburn, almost brown with glints of red; moustache of strawberry blonde and brilliant orange mixed with red—all the hues of autumn. Beautiful, she thought. Something about him was familiar to her, but the memory was elusive. Other than the one time they met at the grotto when he saved Tom, she couldn't recall seeing him before. She looked again at his face, the carved cheekbones, strong teeth with a slight endearing space between the two front ones. He's really handsome.

She picked up the camera and fiddled with it, turning off the video. He was smiling at her and holding Tom in his lap. Tilting her head as a question she pointed it at him; she remembered to turn the flash off, she didn't want it to frighten or anger him. He shrugged his shoulders and seemed unconcerned so she pushed the button. His image appeared on the screen and she turned the camera around to show the photo of him holding Tom. He looked surprised at the image appearing so quickly, but he wasn't afraid. He seemed pleased and interested.

Then she moved around to stand next to him and holding the camera out at arm's length, snapped a photo of the three of them. Again, she turned the camera around to show him. He looked at the photo and this time he laughed—loud—and long. Lenya thought it was the best laugh she'd heard in years, pure uninhibited joy tossed to the air. She found herself laughing along with him. It was fun. They were having a good time together. She'd heard stories about native peoples thinking cameras stole their souls and becoming agitated and violent when their pictures were taken. This was certainly not the case with Aldo.

She took some more photos of the menhirs and in one, he even went over to stand with his arm around it.

Then she showed him the button to push, and how to sight what the photo would be and handed him the camera. The thought never crossed her mind that she might have trouble getting the camera back.

She picked Tom up and went to stand between two of the menhirs and indicated he should push the button.

He looked at the image in the finder and seemed to be carefully lining his shot up like a professional photographer before he pushed the button. He obviously understood the concept of capturing what he saw in the finder. She had no way of knowing he enjoyed studying photographs in magazines since he was a boy. He always wanted to be able to capture such images himself. To have an actual camera in his own hands was a miracle...and to see the picture appear in a window as soon as he clicked was magic he never dreamed of. As he looked at the picture on the small screen, he laughed again, pleasure unbridled.

She thought how wonderful it was to laugh with someone when she came around to look at the image he had produced. He had taken pains to get her face well lit, and the features on the menhir were enhanced by the shadows. Have we got a budding photographer on our hands? Was it intuitive or by chance?

He handed her back the camera, hugely pleased she'd let him take a picture. She indicated he could take more if he wished, and he took several of her sitting with Tom. Again, they showed a choice of light and shadow more creative than she would have imagined. The man seemed to have the eye of an artist.

Shortly, it began to get chilly as the sun moved to the other side of the trees and draped the clearing into shade. It was time to go. She packed up the camera and the remains of lunch, carefully putting the wax paper from the sandwich back into a small brown paper bag she stuffed into her pocket along with the empty bottle of water. As she got up to leave, Aldo started to follow her home, walking slightly behind but keeping pace.

Lenya imagined a conversation with her mother, "Hi Mom, look what I brought home. It followed me from school. Can I keep it? Please, Mom? Please. I'll take care of it, feed it, clean up after if, take it for walks every day, I promise. It won't make a mess. I'll be sure it's housebroken, it won't be any trouble, honest Mom." The pained expression on their mother's face and the inevitability of her capitulation came back in a rush.

No, she was *not* going to keep him. The sooner he understood the rules and the faster they were laid down, the better it would be. She didn't want to have problems with this man in the future and it was best to be up front and firm at the outset. Clearly, he already knew where she lived as he'd been leaving her presents.

As they came to her path, she had figured out how to tell him to go away. *"Allez vous en...chez vous...maintenant."* She could manage it better in French after a futile search of her memory for the phrase in Italian.

But when she turned around to speak to him, he was already gone—vanished as if the dense maquis had swallowed him. She sighed in relief. She hadn't wanted to be aggressive; lunch and a few photos were as far as she was willing to go. She didn't want any strange man hanging around.

But he had been good company...in his own peculiar way.

Before bed, she turned on the computer and downloaded the photos from the afternoon. She e-mailed them to Lotte with a note.

Lenyascribe:
Hey Lotte: Had a lunch date today with my new boyfriend. Here are some photos we took together. He's the one with the skins, not the one on

the ground with the flat round head. I even showed him how to take pix and he took the last ones. Seemed to have a flair for it, don't you think?
Love, Sister L2

Within seconds it seemed, there was a ping indicating new mail from Lotte.

Lotte469:
Hey You! Actually, he looks rather handsome. If you look at his eyes, they have a real sense of intelligence. I think you're wrong about him being childlike...although you might be right about him being a missing link or something...don't get involved, I know you have a thing for strays...
Love ya sis!

Lenyascribe:
Don't worry, I prefer my men less furry and more metrosexual. Tom, however, is smitten and spends as much time as possible in ape-man's lap.

Lotte469:
He's no ape-man honey, he's a real hunk. Don't sell the boy short.

Lenyascribe:
Did I ever tell you you are a certified horn-dog? I can't believe you have the hots for a fur-ball.

Lotte469:
If 's a fur-ball roll it my way baby! Gotta go to work — love ya much!!

Damn Lotte, she always has to get the last word in!...and why did I refer to him as my new boyfriend. I'm regressing.

Chapter 26
Turkey Day

Thanksgiving loomed two days off. Lenya stood on the deck looking towards the mountains and listening to the fallen leaves rustling as they blew across the path in front of the cabin. The desolation of the once green-robed trees suited her mood in their somber colors. Not only was she alone, but this strange place didn't even celebrate her favorite holiday.

The bare branches reminded her of witches' fingers beckoning to her. It was a far cry from Thanksgiving dinners with Andre and Lotte and mother.

They always made it a point to be together as a family on Thanksgiving. It was mother's favorite occasion because it wasn't connected with any religion—simply a celebration of life and giving thanks for what they had. Lotte and Andre came home from wherever they were in the world to celebrate with Lotte and mother. Now both mother and Andre were gone. Lotte announced in her last e-mail she was going to the Hamptons for the long weekend with friends. Lenya was alone and feeling sorry for herself.

She brushed her hair and looked in the mirror. Am I getting to be a lonely old woman? Naw, I'm way too young! She was glad her sister was going away to have fun with friends, but wished for a moment she was going with her. Then Tom started barking and she walked outside to the deck to see what was causing the racket.

Terrence was at the end of the walkway paying a taxi, his luggage piled in a neat heap with a large brown carton on top. Usually Lenya did not like surprises, but this was very welcome. She ran down the walkway to give him a huge hug.

He broke into a grin, arms open for her attack. "I'm so glad you're here – and happy to see me. Otherwise I would have had to cook this bird in the woods with your nature boy buddy!" His smile was a mile wide and he was delighted at being able to pull off a surprise.

"You really took a chance. What if I had gone to Paris to spend the holiday with some American friends living there?"

"Listen, if you don't swing, you'll never hit the ball. I thought it was worth the chance if I was lucky enough to catch you here." He couldn't resist a wink. "And, if you remember, yesterday's e-mail did have a little grouse about being alone for the holiday." He pulled her over to the brown box and wrestled it open. She peeked in. There was a huge frozen turkey, two boxes of Pepperidge Farm Seasoned Stuffing, cans of yams and chicken broth. On top of it all was a pumpkin pie.

"How on earth did you ever find this stuff in Europe? They don't even celebrate Thanksgiving."

"A friend ... officer at the US base in Ramstein, Germany ... asked him to do me a favor... wife went to the PX for Thanksgiving feast ... he schlepped it to the airport for me." He stopped for a moment to enjoy his own resourcefulness. "...I met him at the gate before I took off et voila!" Terrence beamed with pride.

Gotta' love a man who can bring off something like this, let alone even dream it up, Lenya mused. She couldn't help giving him another hug. "You really are the best!"

He looked a bit rueful for a minute. "Hey Babe, I hope you know how to cook?"

"No problem, I've been preparing the family feast for years. Lotte is not a cook, and Mom never bothered to take the time to learn. Her idea of holiday meals was to invite us to the local restaurant until I took over the holidays and did the cooking. I guarantee you the best Thanksgiving ...and with great Corsican wine to boot!"

They both laughed at his victorious surprise as they took his gear inside the cabin.

Chapter 27
The Other Side

Aldo couldn't believe his own eyes. The man was back! And with suitcases! ...and a big box that seemed to be filled with food. After Aldo had worked so hard to start to make friends with Lenya. Why was the man there? Was he going to stay? In the house with Aldo's woman?

No, she wasn't really his woman, but he was sure she should be. Maybe he should challenge the man. He could kill him. Aldo was strong and knew how to fight. Hadn't he spent his childhood where any contact with the new people meant fighting off those who made fun of him ... teased him...called him ugly names and threw stones at him? He could kill the man if he had to—he knew he could.

He thought about it for a while. He pictured the man with his throat slit and the blood coloring the fancy clothes he wore. But Lenya might be angry with him, the man might be her mate. Aldo didn't think the man was, but maybe Lenya did and would hate him afterward.

Such a horrific thing as murder was against the spirit of the clan; a peaceful people who never attacked first. As Maître and consort, such a thing was unthinkable, shameful to kill without cause. The only fighting to death was to defend clan, family, and loved ones. Violence only for defense.

He had a dilemma. He could defend what was his, but was she already his? He didn't think so. Not yet. It was complicated.

From times beyond memory, battles were always when others started them. If forced to kill in battle, they honored the dead and set their souls free.

The vendettas plaguing the island for centuries were not acceptable in clan culture. Instead, the clan often provided safe haven for locals running from vendettas over some stupid slight. They looked with scorn at the foolish vendettas of the villagers. Stupid basic emotions—revenge for imagined slights, greed, hate, anger, envy. The clan had no use for such silly things, their intent was to keep the spiritual balance of nature in harmony. Vendettas were disharmony.

He remembered stories about those in the clan who killed for greed, or in anger, or to steal another's woman. The penalty was banishment. Naked, with no clothing or weapons, preferably in the coldest part of the winter, the transgressor was sent out into the world. If the killer survived, it was the will of Dia. If their bones were found in the spring, picked clean by the creatures of the forest—Dia willed it.

No, he wouldn't kill the man. The deed would shame him. And Dia. He grumbled to himself as he went back to the casteddu.

But he couldn't believe his bad luck. Could Dia be angry at him—but what had he done? It was all he could think about—there must be another solution—another way to find a mate.

Sitting in front of the fire, head in hands, the smoke and flickering light calmed him. Aldo remembered old stories about another clan. They were supposed to live on the southern side of the island, or perhaps even on the other island to the south. He might have to make a boat to get there. The legends told it was not so far away but the very idea of having to swim across a large amount of water terrified him.

Since dying was out of the question, now would be the perfect time for him to go. The tourists had gone home; the woods were free of campers, hikers and hunters. He could make his way across the mountains to the south end of the island before the snows came and with them the bitter cold. He would see for himself. Maybe there was another clan in hiding. He had no idea how to find it, but he prayed for Dia's help.

He watched the flames of the fire flicker and die as he made plans. He had work to do tomorrow, gather his belongings, some weapons for hunting, and enough food to last him for at least a week. He wasn't sure if food was easily found once he left the woods and mountains he knew so well.

The idea of action cheered him and, almost happy, he fell asleep in the warmth of the casteddu. Maybe the strange man coming was a good thing. It would be better for him to find a woman of another clan. Better than this odd woman.

He didn't understand why he felt so strongly about her, this Lenya who commanded her machine all day. But when he thought of giving up on her, her scent of flowers, soap and dog, her shining hair and clean body, the assurance as she walked and lived alone, her slow measured movements each day on the deck, he felt a pain in his stomach. Lenya was as he imagined Dia to be—strong. Brave—and cold. But was she as grounded to the earth as he was? He admitted to himself he really didn't know. Wasn't sure.

He stiffened his resolve. A clan woman would understand him, know how to behave, know what he wanted, and be happy to bear him children.

It was decided.

He would take a few days to prepare and then begin his journey in search of a wife, a mate, the mother of his unborn children—children to continue the clan. A woman who would appreciate him—his knowledge, protection and strength—enjoy the ecstasy he knew how to give.

Chapter 28
Solitude and Solace

The turkey arrived still frozen despite its journey, but it finally thawed as Thanksgiving morning dawned.

Lenya spent most of the morning preparing the meal. Every so often Terrence called out "If you want me to do anything, give a holler!"

She wanted the kitchen to herself. "I've done this for years, trust me...honest!"

Terrence felt as relaxed as a lizard in the sun watching Lenya bustle around in the kitchen. There weren't too many Beverly Hills Barbies who knew how to cook, or at least, if they were around, he hadn't met them.

The fire was warm. Tom curled up by his feet. Terrence alternated between dozing off and keeping an eye on the progress in the kitchen. He had offered to help but Lenya shooed him away. "Out! You're in the way. Your time will come when the dishes need to be done."

The aromas wafting across his nose lulled him into a soporific state, lazy and hoping everything tasted as good as it smelled. He was working up a fierce appetite.

The feast was set for early evening. As the bird cooked in the oven, giving off fragrant whiffs of onions, garlic, *herbes de provence* and stuffing, Lenya grabbed Terrence by the hand and dragged him upright.

"Come on with me. I want to show you my neck of the woods and some of the most amazing places." Terrence slowly moved, unwinding his long frame from where he had draped himself over the sofa. Lenya thought it looked uncomfortable but he seemed not to mind. Tom went to inspect how things were doing in the kitchen.

Tom tore himself away from gazing at the oven door and sniffing scents of the cooking bird to leap up and down at the first sign there might be movement to outside. The only thing to distract him from the kitchen was the hint of a walk.

Terrence gave in to the obvious enthusiasm of both Lenya and Tom as he stretched and yawned.

"Okay, okay. I'm up. Hold your horses."

At least he was good natured about it, Lenya thought. Andre was always loath to go for a walk; he preferred a comfy chair, his cigarettes and lifting a glass of wine for exercise. She almost had to beat him outside as she had often teased.

"We have at least two hours before I have to do anything more to the bird. Come on, let's get moving."

Terrence groaned at the idea of walking for such a long time but gave in graciously. He liked exercise, but he had been so comfortable in front of the fire with Tom warming his feet and Lenya moving about in the kitchen. He sighed as he looked longingly back at the sofa.

Lenya hitched a small backpack over her shoulders, closed up the cabin and headed off towards the large rock where she usually had her picnics.

Terrence took her hand and Tom bounced on ahead, exploring to see if there was anything good to hunt in the bushes. Lenya yelled, "Tom, get back here. You're too old to be chasing around, remember the last time you tried it." Somehow he seemed to understand and came back to walk in front as if he were blazing a trail rather than chasing game.

Terrence smiled at her. "Seems like you have all your men well trained."

She had the good grace to blush. "Well, he was attacked by a raccoon... and he's a little old to be getting into fights. He should know better." She huffed at the thought. Tom looked back at her with his quizzical expression. "Okay old guy, I won't talk about you anymore."

Terrence squeezed her hand a bit. "Do you think we might see your caveman? Does he hang out around where we are going?"

"I doubt we'll see him, he seems shy of people… seeing you could frighten him away."

"Gee, I didn't think I was ugly." Terrence pulled a scary face.

"That's not what I mean, silly…he seems…wary of people in general… don't know why he isn't afraid of me."

"Hah! I knew he had the hots for you. I'll bet he's got a crush."

"I don't really think he's my type…hmmm… he is handsome though, at least as cavemen go."

They reached the edge of the grotto and Lenya pulled aside some of the brush so Terrence could get through. He looked around in wonder. "I'm amazed you even found this place, it's so well hidden."

"I wouldn't have without Tom. He was chasing something and I followed."

Terrence leaned over to scratch Tom's ears. "You are some guy, not only a hunter, but a finder of secret places. She should have called you 'Indy' instead of Tom."

They walked over and sat around the large stone Lenya thought of as her table. Taking a bottle of wine from the backpack; she handed it and the opener to Terrence. "Here—you do the honors." She placed two plastic glasses and some napkins on the rock.

"My, my, you really are a scout."

"Always be prepared, it's my motto too."

He opened the bottle and they sipped the velvety red.

"Got anything else in that pack?" Terrence asked.

"As a matter of fact…" Lenya rooted around and found a piece of cheese and half a baguette. "Thought these would go with the wine…" Some more rooting and a Laguiole knife appeared and a sausage dangling from a string.

"… remind me to always be with you if I plan to be lost in the woods." He helped himself to a slice of cheese and sausage with a torn chunk of bread. "You sure know how to prepare a feast… and what a setting!"

Their silence was companionable as they sipped the wine and shared the food. It was enough to listen to the soft music of rustling leaves, water dripping into the nearby pool and forest creatures trying so hard to move stealthily in the underbrush. Lenya thought she had never been so tranquil on Thanksgiving before, and she gave silent thanks for Terrence's company.

Then Terrence became serious. He reached over and took her hand. "Lenya, I need to be truthful with you."

Uh-oh, I knew something had to be up, he's been much too insecure to have it be me. I'm really not in the mood for a confession to mess up this wonderful day.

"I haven't really been honest with you. I'm not married or anything, but a long term relationship I was involved in broke up very recently."

Okay...damn, here comes the story now. Lenya figuratively girded her loins.

"...been involved with a much younger woman for the last five years... almost half my age." He took a large swallow of wine. "Not perfect, but happy enough..." He paused again. "...truthfully, I'm so damn busy with work I didn't want to deal with it or rock the boat." He took another gulp of wine as if to fortify his courage. "Anyway, the long and short of it is, she dumped me for someone else. She texted me at the office a couple of weeks before I was to leave on this trip. That's why my sister was so pleased you and I could get together."

Lenya gasped. She had heard of text break-ups but this was the first one she heard of up close. Talk about cold...

"Seems she's met a guy her own age...decided to marry him... she was moved out by the time I got home."

So that's what he's been uneasy about. Hmmm. Lenya took his hand. "Listen Terrence, you don't have to explain. You've no commitment to me. I'm okay with the way things are. I've been fighting my own demons since Andre was killed. Let's relax...have a nice holiday together. Friends?"

His relief was obvious. She continued, "I'm glad you're here and that's enough for me right now."

"Thanks. What a relief. I guess I'm used to hearing about internal clocks ticking… expectations…way more than I'm willing or able to give. You're a true breath of fresh air."

Yeah, I guess I am, she thought, since they both seemed to be commitment-phobic…and as for internal clocks, that train left the station a while ago.

Lenya was silent as she started cleaning up the mess from their picnic. She and Andre tried to have a child for a while with no luck. Finally, they decided a baby would interfere with their life-style and passed on fertility clinics. Lenya never used the pill or other contraception—assumed she was unable to conceive. They had each other; which was always enough.

Terrence automatically used a condom and she never said anything about it. Better safe and all …and there are all those nasty STD's around…not to mention HIV.

They ate the last of the cheese and bread, fed Tom the end of the sausage. Lenya drained the bottle of wine and they started back to the cabin.

So that's the story of this guy. No wonder he's been so jumpy, not insecure, but hiding something unpleasant. Even if he wasn't totally committed to this woman, he obviously wasn't pleased about having his trophy girlfriend dump him for a younger guy. I'm sure there's more to the story, but at least part of the mystery is solved.

Aldo watched from the thickness of the brush around the grove. He watched as they drank their wine and ate their meal. They seemed companionable but he didn't feel the man was her mate. Maybe he was family? No, she wouldn't have kissed him the way she did when he arrived. Aldo didn't care anymore; he would go to the other side of the island and find a mate of his own who would understand him. No more wasting time.

But the pang when he thought of Lenya was there. He could almost smell her special scent.

The turkey was cooked to perfection, the stuffing was excellent blended with the vegetables Lenya had put though a food processor and added to it, and the gravy came out thick and savory. They gorged themselves on the familiar food and lolled in front of the fire.

Terrence turned to her. "Lenya, I want to thank you for a wonderful Thanksgiving dinner." He sounded formal, mimicking an announcer. Then he continued, this time with a laugh in his voice, "I want to be clear up-front. If I fall asleep on the couch, it's not the company; it's the L-tryptophan in the damn bird." His voice had ended low and warm—almost slurred with wine, relaxation and too much food.

"Don't give it another thought. I'll wake you up in a while for pie and ice cream...and to do the dishes!"

Terrence gave a groan of pleasure. "Cool, babe." He sounded like he was almost asleep already. Lenya laughed to herself.

She snuggled up next to him on the sofa and found herself dozing off too.

A few hours later, they both awakened with a different hunger and made love in front of the dying fire. Then made their way into the kitchen to satisfy their next hunger—warm pumpkin pie and ice cream.

Lenya put both arms around Terrence and looked up into his face, "Thank you. This has been the perfect Thanksgiving. In fact, I've given thanks you're here...and especially you were resourceful enough to bring turkey...and pie...and I had vanilla ice cream in the freezer!"

She dodged his reaching arms, eluding an embrace and ran into the bathroom laughing so hard she was snorting.

He laughed at her snorts and the moment changed from a soupy romance to good friends teasing each other. It was perfect for both of them, he thought as he turned to attack the dishes.

Chapter 29
Sirio and Terrence

The Saturday after Thanksgiving shouted island road trip with its Mediterranean salty-soft air and brilliant sun. Lenya couldn't wait to get out of the cabin. After breakfast she grabbed Terrence's hand and propelled him across the deck and into her car. "Come on, we've got some sightseeing to do...show you around......places to see...friends to visit."

Terrence acquiesced in his usual good-natured way. Tom vaulted into the back seat as soon as Lenya opened the car door. No way was he going to be left behind. They bumped down the rutted road and out to the RN along the coast. It wasn't long before Lenya turned off to the right and up the narrow winding "Route des Artisans."

As they climbed the steep road, the Rav's engine whining a bit at the strain, Lenya turned to Terrence. "So, big guy, how do you like the color blue?'

Terrence looked at her with head tilted and one eyebrow quirked up. "I like blue fine generally, depending on what it's on or attached to. For instance, blue, like black and blue isn't one of my favorites and blue balls are certainly not my choice. I like Picasso's Blue Period and Nat King Cole singing "Blue Moon" and light blue shirts, navy blue blazers... blue jeans are at the top of my list."

Lenya laughed at his off-the cuff compilation. "Well, you're about to see another kind of blue from those you mentioned. I call it 'Pigna Blue' because its the color of the shutters on most of the buildings in Pigna, the village of artisans we're heading for."

"Hey babe, you're driving. I assume we've got a full tank of gas, the sun is shining...what more do I need?" He grinned, opened the window, stretched his arms and arched his back. One hand rubbed Lenya's neck, the other unfurled out the window to feel the wind. "Life is good,

I'm with you. . .drive on o ye intrepid pathfinder. Let's do blue!" He closed his eyes for a moment and stretched again.

They were silent for the rest of the drive up the mountain. Lenya liked the silence, the companionable kind where nobody needs to chatter.

She pulled the car into the parking area at the foot of a *village perché* and were immediately greeted by the two large dogs guarding the visiting cars. Maybe it's their job and they take it very seriously, Lenya thought. The dogs were friendly and knew Tom from prior visits, but they wandered over so the three of them could perform their perfunctory 'hello' and 'how are you' sniffs. Then they gave the humans a sniff. Everyone must have passed muster because the dogs turned and moseyed off to their preferred napping places.

Lenya took Terrence's arm as they walked up a steep path to the narrow curved walking streets of the village. Stone walls in every possible shade of gray to beige crowded narrow walks winding up the mountain. Flower boxes drifted tendrils of green overhead, windows opened on the narrow byways, and doors of vintages spanning well over a thousand years broke the monotony of the stone facades.

"See," she said, pointing at the blue shutters. Myriad shades of similar blue hues and various stages of disrepair ranged from new and shining to multiple layers of paint—some peeling, some fresh, some decrepit with the color barely discernible. "Pigna Blue, a special blue with a *soupçon* of green. I think it's exactly the color of the water in the island coves when it glistens in the sun." It was fun to be in one of her favorite places with Terrence. She was enjoying watching him look around with interest at the picturesque village.

Camera in hand, she began photographing the various shutters they came upon as they strolled through the twisting alleyways, now out of season and practically empty. It was like having the tiny town all to themselves, except for cats they came upon who made a point of studiously ignoring the visitors. Especially Tom, who they sneered at with distain as he passed by at a safe distance from any possibility of extended claws.

She hoped her favorite atelier was open. As they turned a corner, the door to the pottery workshop was ajar. They walked up the steep steps in front and Terrence stood for a moment to admire the wall, patched and repaired, obviously over the centuries to the present, each repairman adding their own special touch. Differing grades and sizes of stone, various types of cement, showed the progression from neglect to repair. Several clay figures watched silently from carved niches, other lintels held a pot or a plate with artless beauty.

Lenya peeked into the open door of the workshop, "Are you open?...can we come in?" The owner wiped his hands on his potters apron and nodded his head in the direction of the showroom. They entered a roughly rectangular room carved out of sheer rock, a vaulted dome overhead and walls filled with shelves and displays of pottery.

Lenya nodded at a display of bowls, mugs, and dishes of various shapes and sizes glazed in a golden mustard color. "See those? They're the color of the immortelle flowers, the main scent of the maquis. The fragrance of the island." She picked up a small bowl and held it close to her heart before she moved over to the next display, similar objects, but more varied designs, and glazed in a vibrant blue.

Terrence found himself drawn to the blues and stared into the depths of a large bowl. "It's like looking down into the sea from the cliffs around the island. The potter even managed to get the rays of the sun as they radiate out into the water."

"Yes, it's the Pigna Blue I mentioned. Isn't it special? I've not seen the exact color before." She looked into the bowl he held and the design held her for a moment. "There's something very compelling and mystical about it, don't you think?"

They examined the pieces on display. The blues were sensuous and compelling in their beauty, daring the beholder to reach out and touch, to fall under their spell.

Terrence wanted to send Lotte, and his sister Francis, something from the shop as a way of thanking them both for their introduction.

They finally decided on a bowl and platter for Lotte in the spectacular blue. For Terrence's sister, they also chose the blue—three pitchers in various sizes and shapes. Francis collected pitchers.

The potter would pack everything in two packages for shipment to America. He assured them he sent his wares all over the world with no problem and everything was insured against damage.

By the time they paid and left the shop, a chill had come to the air and Lenya was ready for their next stop.

The big dogs didn't come to say good-bye as they got into the Rav to leave. Lenya turned out of the driveway and headed back down the mountain, by a different route.

Terrence leaned back and hummed along to French radio as he took in the view. After a half-hour of driving up one mountain and down another, they bounced up the rutted entrance to the winery. Sophia and Tom were joyful at seeing each other.

As Lenya opened the car door, she was engulfed in a hug by a man who looked like part of the countryside—tall, rugged, handsome and dressed in hues of browns, and green.

"Sirio, I'd like you to meet Terrence. From L.A.. Terrence, this is my friend Sirio who I've told you about."

The men shook hands, eyeing each other, both about the same height. Terrence urbane, casual but expensively dressed in the latest designer fashion, tailored to show off his slim physique.

Sirio, as tall and slim but garbed in rumpled corduroy a bit baggy around the knees and a plaid flannel shirt over a faded dark tee shirt, both worn thin in places. As Lenya watched them together, she realized each had a commanding presence of his own. Men to be reckoned with. Men of substance.

Sirio nodded at Lenya as if in approval. "Come in, you two. I've uncorked a new bottle in the tasting room for a couple who wandered in earlier and didn't buy a thing." He put his finger alongside his nose, looked down at his shoes, then smiled at Lenya. "It would be a shame to let it go to waste."

Terrence looked around the interior of the winery, carefully taking in every detail before he turned to Sirio. "This is probably one of the most beautiful buildings I've ever seen. It has a look...something ... almost alive... like it's part of the countryside, not manmade, something that grew here."

Sirio was obviously delighted. "Actually, you are almost right. My grandfather, great-grandfather and his father before him started building it more than two centuries ago. Each generation seems to have been compelled to add a bit of their own ideas to it, and so it has really grown. Sadly, I have no children," he paused and the tell-tale finger was alongside his nose again... "at least that I know of...so perhaps it will not be added to again. But let's not speak of those things. Tell me what trouble you children have gotten yourselves into today."

He poured wine into three glasses, handed them out while ushering them towards a table and chairs near the fireplace where he poked the embers back to life. Tom and Sophia got the message they were going to be there for a while and plopped down together on the rug in front of the fire.

The men began immediately to chat about life on the island, how to make excellent wine, what it was like to live in Los Angeles, had Terrence ever met Hugh Hefner or been to the mansion and other things of great importance to men of all generations.

After about ten minutes, Lenya dozed off. She'd had a full day of driving up the mountain, down the mountain, around the mountain and shifting constantly. The conversation droned like comforting white noise and the fire warmed her feet. At one point she dreamt there was a weight on her lap, at another time something seemed to shift around near her, but neither movement was enough to wake her until someone took her arm and shook it.

Terrence was standing over her. "Wake up babe, we need to go home. I think we've overstayed our welcome, our host has been very kind but it's time for bed."

Lenya looked down to both dogs sound asleep on her lap. It was dark outside and when she consulted her watch, she realized she'd been asleep for several hours. She shook herself, dogs bouncing off her lap, stiff and wobbly as she stood.

"Are you all right?" Sirio looked concerned.

"Yes. Sure. A bit cramped from sleeping in the same position with those little devils on my lap. Give me a moment to wake everything up and I'll be fine." She noticed the men were slightly less fine and saw three empty bottles lined up in front of the fireplace. "Hmmm, I see you guys have been enjoying a bit of the grape."

Both managed to look a little sheepish but Sirio took control. "Since we didn't have the pleasure of your company, my dear, left to our own devices we decided to take matters into our own hands and entertain ourselves as we saw fit. Any damage is certainly on you."

She couldn't help grinning at him as she leaned over and gave him a hug. "You are truly a rogue—but I find you irresistible." He returned the grin. She continued, "Now we must leave, let you get a good night's sleep and I have to get both my gents home and feed them before I put them to bed."

"The feeding of both has been attended to, you have only yourself to take care of." Sirio walked them to her car, bowed ceremoniously and with great care as he blew her a goodnight kiss. "Please be safe going home, you know how treacherous the roads are in the dark."

On the way back to the cabin, Terrence raved about how much he had enjoyed the evening with Sirio. "He has the most fascinating stories. He told me about his father, the family, the local Mafia, and some of the history of the island." He yawned loudly. "I could have listened to him for hours, if I could have stayed awake...and the wine was great too." He reached over and patted her arm, then he promptly fell asleep, loudly snoring the rest of the way home.

The weekend went by quickly. They were friends and they were lovers. No words...no commitment... no forever after.

As they got into the Rav to take Terrence to the airport, he leaned down and gave her a big hug. "You know this isn't the end of me. You can be addictive."

"Have a great trip and send me e-mails with photos."

"Are you sure you won't change your mind and come too? You know we travel well together."

"I know, but you have to do what you have to do and I have to do my thing."

"Yeah, okay...but if you change your mind, e-mail me where and when to pick you up."

"Will do. But I think we both need this time alone. Especially you. I've had a little more alone-time to adjust to the changes in my life. You need to do the same." He nodded but didn't look convinced.

Back home, she sighed, swept up the mess they'd made, returned everything to its proper place. Where *she* wanted to put it—and she was glad the remote to the satellite dish was back in her hands.

How crappy am I? I had a great time, fabulous sex, excellent company. What more can a woman ask?

But I'm happy he left.

Terrence was a great guy, sure, but there was no...no...special touch of the skin.

Chapter 30
One More Try

Aldo's preparations were finished. Everything was ready for him to leave. The pack Raina made of skins was filled with dried fruits and meats. He touched it reverently, remembering the effort she put into the gift, one of the few he'd received in his life. His favorite knives nestled inside. One for carving to entertain himself as he sat at night by the fire, one for hunting meant to deliver swift death, and another for skinning, cooking and eating. A bag made from a dried boar testicle held a few dried herbs, a small stone carving of Dia nestled among them. He thought she might like the fragrance.

He packed one shirt and a clean pair of patched jeans. He wore his other shirt and jeans and his vest-like covering of stitched-together skins. A carved walking stick made from a stout branch might also serve as a weapon if needed. He hung a water bag made from sheep bladder over his shoulder. The island had water in so many places he was sure it could be filled often during his journey.

As the time of leaving arrived, he felt a sting of trepidation. Seldom had he been away from the territory of the clan. When he was young, he went with his father to faraway places to hunt, but was a long time ago. Dia always protected him; he had given her offerings and prayers.

He was certain his purpose would please her enough to smile on his effort.

As he thought of Dia, he had an inspiration. What if the man left? Aldo hadn't been near the cabin for at least a week. Was it a way to avoid leaving, or might Dia be telling him to give the woman, Lenya, one last chance? Lenya seemed to like the man who visited, but Aldo had no feeling of a long-lasting connection after watching them together. Maybe it was only wishful thinking, but he wasn't convinced the man was her mate or if he was going to stay.

They appeared comfortable but it had the scent of friendship when they looked at each other. There was little or no touching between them. He thought they probably had sex at night because he saw the man slept with her in the loft. It didn't matter to Aldo, the fact they had sex was of little interest to him. Sex was a normal part of life. Making love was something different, a sacred rite.

He had to take one last look to make sure. After all, as far as he knew, there wasn't anyone waiting for him on the other side of the island—no reason not to delay leaving a little longer. There was always the chance the man had left.

Chapter 31
Sirio And The Don

Lenya was enjoying the peace and quiet of having the cabin all to herself once more. She and Tom went back to their familiar rhythms of morning coffee, Tai Chi and work at the computer. All of which was interspersed with looking towards the mountains and off to the sea—confirming the view was as beautiful and ever-changing as always.

Once again, her coffee supply was low; forcing Lenya to the market. She and Tom got into the car, and she realized it was the first time since she'd taken Terrence to the airport.

Another perfect day in Paradise. Trite and true, Lenya thought as she left the Spar market. Writing wasn't on her mind, it was too nice a day. Time for a small adventure, a visit to Sirio would be perfect, and the car almost turned itself in his direction.

Arriving at the winery, she was surprised to see a large black SUV next to Sirio's Tundra. It was the first time she'd seen another car in the visitor parking when she arrived. Customers? Maybe she should leave? But as the thought came to mind, Sirio stepped into the doorway of the barn. He threw her a kiss as he motioned her to come inside. Sophia raced the Rav, bouncing up and down at the window in hysterical invitation to Tom to come out and play.

When Lenya had passed the SUV on the way in, she thought it looked familiar. As soon as her eyes adjusted to the gloom of the old building, she remembered when she had seen it before.

Sirio was chatting with two men, one standing and the other sitting. Her attention first caught the standing man, memorably large, well over six feet tall and so broad he could have been a professional linebacker. His face was chiseled, nose tweaked to the side as if broken several times. Not a hint or trace of a smile on a face that looked carved from the local stone. Dark expressionless eyes stared at her from deep sockets.

Not someone I'd care to meet in a dark alley. A chill ran up her back as she felt hair rise on the back of her neck. Bad. A bad guy.

Then she looked at the man in the chair. It was the man from Calanzana. The man with the compound. Mafia? From Marseille? With Sirio?

Sirio put his arm around her shoulder, "Lenya, I want to introduce you to some good friends of mine." He pointed to the seated man. "This is Don Raphael Rizzoni. I think you two have already met. Briefly." He couldn't help smiling. Lenya blushed as he continued, "and this is his nephew, Michaele Cazzato." The huge man nodded his head. No warmth. The don stood and put out his hand. Lenya shook it and tried not to be obvious as she studied him. Once again he was dressed in a black suit, sparkling white shirt buttoned to the top and no tie—taller than she first thought. Perhaps because he was slightly stooped. He had a full head of white hair, thick black eyebrows framed dark intelligent eyes moving constantly, taking in every nuance. His skin hung loosely on sharp facial bones, almost transparent and mottled like the skin of a frog. She should have been repulsed, but there was something in his eyes she liked—a welcome and a feeling of a repressed sense of humor. All in all, a very interesting man.

The don was appraising her too. "So Sirio, this is the beautiful American writer you have been telling me about. I thought it might be her when she was lost in my driveway." He laughed at the recollection. "So sorry Lenya, you looked...frightened?...like you had fallen into a lion's den. I promise you, there was no danger...we don't bite. Any friend of my friend Sirio is also a friend of mine."

"Thank you Signore Rizzoni, I appreciate it...and apologize for the intrusion."

"Please, call me Rapha, all my friends do." He nodded to Lenya with a sly grin. Now more nervous than ever, she continued, "I didn't want to intrude on your home... I thought I found a shortcut... perhaps a new adventure." *Damn, I'm rattling off again. Stop it!* "I've been enjoying exploring the smaller roads into the mountains."

"It certainly could have been an adventure." Sirio couldn't resist the jab. Michaele gave him a dirty look before resuming his watchful stance, hands folded together in front.

Sirio continued, "Lenya has taken an oath to explore all the side roads up the mountains between Calvi and L'Île-Rousse. She has a penchant for finding menhirs, dolmen and hidden ateliers...preferably as many as possible."

"Please, be careful, or at least take a bodyguard with you; there might be things in those mountains you are not prepared to find." The don sounded serious, but he had a twinkle in his eye.

"Oh, she's already been introduced to the clan. Aldo gallantly saved her dog, Tom, from an angry raccoon." Sirio announced with pride.

"There you are, he is still amongst us then, and as usual, looking out for his people. I was not sure Aldo was here, I had heard perhaps the clan had finally died out."

"Not completely, but he is now the only one left. It is a very sad end."

Lenya wanted to ask Sirio what he meant about Aldo, who he was, what he meant about the clan, but as she was about to ask, Rapha took her arm and steered her to where the men had been sitting under the trees at the front of the winery. "So you have already found out, there are very unexpected things to be found in the mountains of Corsica... not only artisanal ateliers and stone warriors." The pleasure in his voice was obvious.

Sirio held a chair for her. "Come Lenya, sit with us. It's a perfect day, let's enjoy the gift...and Rapha wants to hear about our newest resident, a famous author. Since he met you, however briefly, he always asks about you. His daughter also wishes to be a writer, so it is a topic of great interest to him."

"Yes, she is a very smart one, that girl of mine. She knows what she wants and she goes for it." Lenya saw the pride in his eyes. "Now she is in your country, studying at Vassar College...a good one I think? No?"

"Yes, one of the best. It used to be all women but now is co-educational. Not far from my home in Connecticut." Okay Lenya, time to shut up. She squirmed in the proffered chair.

Sirio picked up the conversation. "Rapha has six more older children and now...how many grandchildren?

"Eight at the moment, two more on the way very soon." Rapha was grinning, overly white teeth shining in the sunlight. "Two of my boys are attorneys, and a grandson also, one son a doctor, one followed me into the family business, and the rest are girls—two married and one a school teacher who chides me all the time like I am one of her students...do this papa...do that... She thinks it is her job to boss me around ever since my wife...her mother... passed away."

Lenya liked the way he spoke about his family, such pride in his voice, animation in his face. How nice for a father to take such an interest in his family. Her father had been disinterested in his two daughters, and eventually his wife as well.

Rapha motioned several fingers at Michaele. The large man walked over and bent down while Rapha whispered in his ear. Michaele nodded and walked out of the winery towards the SUV. Sirio looked over and jutted his chin toward Rapha in question.

"I hope you don't mind, but I've sent Michaele to bring us some lunch. Please Lenya, I hope you can join us. We own a restaurant nearby... it's well known for quite agreeable food." Rapha looked towards Sirio and this time he was the one to put his finger alongside his nose as he ducked his head in mock deference. "...and I'm sure we can find some decent wine somewhere."

Lenya had planned on going home to work, but this was an unexpected treat. Lunch with a real live don? Fun! "Thank you, I'd be delighted. Nothing I have to do can't be put off. Lunch with such excellent company is a delightful surprise." She beamed at both men.

The three of them walked around the side of the winery to an area Lenya had never been before. A long wooden table, rustic and old, sat underneath an ancient grape arbor. It afforded a view of neat rows of grapes trailing down the hill, then across the leafy tops of the vines to the mountains in the distance.

As she stared at the view, entranced, Sirio nodded towards her. "Lenya, help me being out some chairs, glasses and a cloth so we are ready for lunch when Michaele returns."

Rapha joined them to help carry chairs, and when they had sufficient, Sirio offered Rapha the one at the head of the table.

Lenya brushed off some fallen leaves, spread a gaily colored oil-cloth patterned with grapevines on the table, and brought out glasses from the tasting room. Sirio arrived laden with several bottles of wine.

In less than an hour Michaele was back lugging a huge carton he placed on the center of the table. Lenya looked on while he unloaded a mound of round tins covered with cardboard circles. At the bottom of the carton were four large white dishes, napkins, flatware, salt, red and black pepper, olive oil and Balsamic vinegar, a huge chunk of cheese and a grater. The only thing missing were candles and Lenya wasn't about to mention them.

Lenya hadn't realized how hungry she was until a heady bouquet of olive oil, onions, garlic, cheeses, meats and herbs floated by her nose. As Sirio and Rapha began to open the tins, Michaele ran back to fetch another carton, this one filled with two roasted chickens.

Lunch was miraculous. Four different pastas, one with truffles in cream sauce, one spicy with olives and capers, another with sausages and peppers, and the last, cappelli d'angelo topped with fresh chopped tomatoes, basil, garlic and olive oil. The roast chickens were cut in pieces and surrounded with artichokes and mushrooms in a brown sauce. Two long loaves of crusty bread completed the meal. Lenya's eyes widened a bit more as each dish was unveiled. The aromas! Nothing in memory ever smelled so enticing.

"I hope you like Italian food?" Rapha said.

"Please, I grew up in New York City. To me, Italian food is 'home cooking,'" she replied.

They all laughed as she attacked the meal. Conversation stopped and was replaced with sighs of enjoyment. Lenya felt she had landed in heaven as she ate under the grape arbor and looked out at the mountains.

Afterward, Sirio brought out his famous orange wine for desert and they sat back to let the pleasure of the afternoon wash over them. Reluctantly, Rapha poked Michaele, who leaped to his feet. Rapha pointed at the table and nodded towards the cartons and plates. Michaele began to scurry around cleaning up the mess they had made.

Sirio put out a hand to stop Michaele, but spoke to Rapha, "Don't worry, we will take care of this...you have done more than enough." He looked over at Lenya, "I'm sure Lenya will help me put everything away. It will give us a chance to catch up on each other's news."

Michaele looked relieved. He hadn't seemed at all pleased to take on the alternate job of busboy. Driver and bodyguard were more his speed.

Rapha inclined his head at Sirio and waved his hand in the style of a monarch in acquiescence. "Thank you my dear friend. And don't forget, if you see our mutual friend, le Maître, please tell him Raphael sends his humble regards and asks for his blessing."

Sirio slid a look at Lenya out of the corner of his eye. She did not appear to have heard, and was busy taking the plates from the table. The men got up to leave shortly thereafter.

Before he got into the car, Rapha took Lenya's hand in both of his. "My dear new friend, don't worry about anything here...on the island. I'll make sure everyone understands you are a special friend of mine. You are safe...like a babe in her crib." With that, he kissed her on both cheeks, winked, turned and got into the car.

As the SUV headed out of the drive, Sirio looked at her. "Well, well my dear one, you have made another conquest. Seems you have a way with we poor men; we obligingly fall at your feet. You may not appreciate what was said to you, but you are now under the protection of the most powerful don in this part of the Mediterranean...not only Corsica. No one will dare to touch you or cross you."

He put down the empty wine glasses he had been carrying and looked out over the vines for a moment before he continued. "But you have to understand. What you have received is both a blessing and a curse. A blessing if you need it...a curse if you abuse it."

She was quiet afterwards as the two of them cleaned up the remains of the meal. There was enough left to fill both their refrigerators and feed them for at least a week, with plenty leftover for Tom and Sophia.

As the last glass was washed and put away, Sirio turned to her. "I liked the man you brought to visit. I liked him a lot...very real...a gentleman and quite kind, but I don't think he is the one you might be looking for. Something is missing between you both, some...I don't know exactly what...some...click?" He snapped his fingers. "He is good company and, I'm sure, an excellent companion...but ...maybe not quite... enough?" He brushed an imaginary crumb off the counter. "Some things are hard to understand. Me...I gave up trying a long time ago."

Chapter 32
Aldo And His Fox

Lenya was on Skype with Lotte. She had been at work organizing her research and needed a break.

"...so what did all the women wear to the Thanksgiving dinner? What is the newest look today in the Hamptons?" Lenya really didn't care, she wanted Lotte to keep talking, enjoying the so-familiar face on her computer screen.

"You wouldn't believe the get-up one of the trophy wives was wearing! ... remember November in New York? Well, she had a bare midriff and a belly-ring, short sleeve top and mini-skirt so tiny we could see her butt-cheeks every time she bent down...and she picked up a lot of canapés off the coffee table." Lenya giggled on the other side of the world as she saw her sister's nose wrinkle in disapproval.

"Where were they from, California?"

"Naw, worse—Vegas." Lotte giggled again. "And one of the girls said it was obvious she was cold, her nipples were at full tilt. It had started to snow outside. The guys loved it. Men! They never give up a free peep show." They both burst into gales of laughter.

"The hostess caught the whole act from the other room. When I checked if she needed help, she said she could have rented a pole for the occasion if she knew there was going to be an exotic dancer in the group."

Lenya was conjuring up the image of a pole dancer in the middle of a hoity-toity Hampton's Thanksgiving.

"Don't tell me, it couldn't have been bad."

"Bad?...my dear, worse...much worse. A gaggle of pre-pubescent rug rats ... boys... spent the day following her to see what flashed...

whatever... After all, there it was, real, waxed and literally in your face... better than Paris Hilton on the Internet."

"You mean she wasn't wearing underwear?"

"She was, barely, one of those thong-things, you know...butt-floss." The giggles started again.

This was what Lenya missed, the easy gossip, the laughing together. It was so good to be able to enjoy it through her computer. They hardly seemed so far apart.

"So, what's been happening with your caveman? Left any good presents lately?"

"I haven't seen or heard from him since Terrence was here for Thanksgiving. Maybe he got the idea I was taken and left for greener pastures."

Lenya felt a little pang at the idea; somehow his presence and his gifts were comforting. The idea he might have gone somewhere else irritated her.

"But I had dinner with Sirio at the winery and met the local don. You might be pleased to know I am now under his protection."

"Get outta' here! You're having way too much fun on your island. Tell me all about your new boyfriend."

"He's not a boyfriend!" Lenya corrected. "But it was an interesting afternoon." She proceeded to describe the men, the food and the venue. It was odd, but Lotte hadn't asked her about Terrence, and Lenya completely forgot to tell her about her Thanksgiving.

Once she clicked off, she rummaged around the kitchen, banging pots and pans harder than need be. The sound relieved some of her irritation.

The next day Aldo was standing on the path up to her deck. He didn't come closer, stood a short distance away watching her do her morning Tai Chi. When finished, she put her towel around her neck and sat on the edge of the deck, motioning him to join her. A grin split his face as he came and sat a foot or so away from her. Tom immediately plunked himself in Aldo's lap.

Aldo fumbled in his pockets. A few small apples and what looked like some kind of meat jerky appeared in his hand and he offered them to her. Lenya was suspicious of the jerky, she wasn't about to eat some mystery meat, but took one of the apples. They sat together on the deck munching companionably.

I have no idea how to make conversation with this man, or even what to say, she thought. She decided it was best to say nothing so they sat together in silence. The forest sounds provided enough music to make conversation unnecessary.

In their stillness, the sounds of the forest came to her with clarity, an ambiance she seldom paid attention to or even realized was there. As she relaxed and listened to what she had taken for granted as silence, she heard a constant buzzing and chirping of insects, the branches of the trees creaking in the breeze. Birds called to each other, small animals rustled about unseen and she could hear them scurry in search of food to put away for the coming winter. It was a veritable symphony of sounds, unheard as she rushed through her days.

She let her mind roam, smelling the cool air; the pine and green scents of the forest mingled with the earthy smell of decaying leaves.

After a while, Aldo touched her arm and she jumped, startled. He put his finger to his lips and pointed to the far edge of the clearing. As he did, he grabbed Tom by the collar so he couldn't race out to hunt. She saw several large rabbits, probably hares she thought, come closer. The nearest was the biggest—he was obviously in charge. The others hung back, partially obscured by the brush. The larger animal's ears and nose twitched as it searched for danger. There was no movement on the deck; Tom quiet but alert. An invisible signal was given and the smaller hares moved into the clearing. They must have found something to their liking as they foraged in the high grasses while she and Aldo watched from the deck. It was thrilling to Lenya, raised in the city so far from the realities of nature. Like an Animal Planet reality show, unexpurgated and in the moment.

Something in the brush made a movement Lenya couldn't hear or see, but the entire family of hares sped in unison into the dense ground covering; as if they all heard the same signal. Lenya felt a pang of disappointment for the disruption and then a moment of fear for the defenseless family.

Aldo kept his hold on Tom's collar. While the dog was old and couldn't see as well as in his younger days, fast movement attracted his attention.

At the edge of the now empty clearing, cautiously, a small red head with black tipped ears and white markings peeked from the bush. Large intelligent eyes studied the tableau on the deck. Aldo motioned for Lenya to take Tom and put him inside the cabin. Then he pantomimed covering his eyes. Lenya, understanding, got up slowly and went inside to put Tom in his travel case, out of view of the outside.

She took her seat next to Aldo as a small fox slipped up next to him. He bent down and gently ruffled the animal's fur. He pointed to the animal and himself, *"Siamo amici."* They were friends. She remained as quiet as possible so the fox wouldn't feel threatened. After a few minutes, Aldo pointed to the little animal and Lenya and made petting motions. He nodded assent. As she placed her hand gently on the soft fur, the animal turned it's amber eyes to her, an acceptance of her touch. She had the feeling she was being told quite clearly, "Any friend of Aldo's is a friend of mine. Now behave." As she explored the creatures body, she felt its ribs through the fur, and then a gentle swelling along the belly. Either the little animal was pregnant, or had swallowed something very large.

Lenya looked at Aldo and made a motion of a big belly and tilted her head as in a question.

He smiled back at her and pointed to the fox, *"Si, bambini subito."* How wonderful, soon a litter of pups. She hoped he would bring them to play.

The little fox got up, tired of so much adoration and petting, stretched, looked back at them and sauntered off. Lenya felt stupid she hadn't offered her new friend something to eat, dog biscuits, kibble, water? Something to keep her strength up.

After a while, Lenya got up and went in the house. Aldo looked at her for a moment.

She waved at him and shut the sliding glass door. She wanted him to know he was not invited inside. They had enjoyed a nice moment on the deck. It was over.

When she turned to see if he might be disappointed, he had already vanished into the woods.

Chapter 33
Conversations With Sirio

It was time to admit the truth. Lenya was fascinated with her new companion. Aldo showed up at the cabin every day or so. If he wasn't there for a few days, she wondered if he was ever coming back. She actually felt lonely without him around and it made her mad. How could she miss him? They hardly spoke, but his presence made her happy...no, the thought was too strong—he kept her company. Another adult person close by was comforting—nothing more.

One morning she came outside earlier than usual to drink her morning coffee. Aldo was already there, sitting on the deck un-snarling his damp hair with a bone comb. Silent, so as not to disturb him, she watched as his strong fingers deftly plaited the long red strands into an intricate French braid. Soon, neat plaits merged to intertwine into a rope of glistening red trailing down his back. It was wildly sensuous, something she'd never thought about before—watching a man braiding his hair. Something lurched deep inside her and she couldn't stop her mind from imagining what those skillful hands would feel like on her body. She had liked watching him braid his hair as much as she liked watching him laugh his free and unrestrained man's laugh, well, maybe she liked the braiding better...those skillful hands...better not to think about it.

Her life was so simple he had quietly become an integral part of it. She'd be on the deck doing Tai Chi or drinking her coffee and when she looked up, there he was, silent and waiting to join her in her break from work.

She didn't realize he waited, hidden, if she went to the local market. When she came back, he appeared, as if by magic, to help her bring the groceries up to the cabin. He carried them from the car to place on the deck outside the sliding door. It was as close as he got.

She had no idea Aldo was obsessed with her, every minute of his day consumed with waiting for her, spying on her, thinking about her.

Lenya was burning to know about him too. Who he was, where did he come from? What was his story? While her curiosity was unbridled, she was reluctant to ask him about himself. For some reason she thought her questions might offend him... might indicate she thought him strange? Maybe he doesn't know how different he is?

It took her several days to make up her mind how to go about a reconnaissance mission. She burned to know more about Aldo. It was time to ask Sirio what he knew. Maybe she could find out who he was and where he came from.

She left the cabin with a colorful Provençal print grocery bag filled with local sausages and cheese and more than an armload of determination. Tom bounced into the car, always ready for a road trip. They made their careful way down the rutted track to the RN and the turnoff marked with the ancient painted sign for the winery.

Sophia ran out to greet them. Sirio was not far behind with a big grin of welcome once he recognized his visitors.

"Halloo Lenya, what drags you away from the terrible jealous computer of yours? Is it time for a break?"

"I admit it. There's a moment when I must talk to a human rather than look at the mechanical monster. Sometimes, I feel the damn machine is alive and then I know it's time to get away." They both laughed as she gave him a hug and the cheek to cheek air kisses so mandatory in France.

"I've brought you some cheese and sausage. I went to the open market in L'Îles Rousse. They had a vendor I hadn't seen before and everything looked so appetizing, I couldn't resist." She held out the bright bag filled with small packages wrapped in butcher paper. "Everything was crying out for a good wine and it so happens I knew where to find one." She bent into the car and emerged triumphant with a baguette in hand to thrust at him.

"Well, this calls for a little celebration. I think I might be able to provide not only some wine, but perhaps a bit of kibble for my other guest? We must show good hospitality, mustn't we Sophia?" He bent to caress them as they jumped up and down in excitement at the smells of the sausage and cheese. They knew a good treat when they smelled one. Lenya looked at the two dogs; Tom always seemed to be a pup again when Sophia was around.

The four of them sat in the fading sunlight under a chestnut tree. The chestnuts covered the ground around them and a few dropped dangerously close. Sirio left her for a moment as he went into the winery.

"Help me please, Lenya," Sirio appeared with a bucket.

"What can I do?"

"Let's collect some of these chestnuts and I'll roast them. They make a great counterpoint to the feast you've provided."

They bent to their task and soon the bottom of the bucket was covered with the shiny brown nuts. When they went inside, she saw Sirio had started a few logs burning in the winery fireplace, and he brought out a large flat pan with small holes in the bottom attached to a long iron rod ending in what looked like a hand carved wooden grip. He spread the nuts out evenly over the flat surface and placed the pan on top of the burning logs. Soon the smell of chestnuts cooking blended with the garlic from the sausage and the strong sour smell of cheese.

Sirio arrived with two of the tasting room glasses half filled with a dark red wine and handed one to Lenya. They relaxed in front of the fire in chairs Sirio extricated from a dark corner Lenya had not yet explored. Dark wood frames carved in intricate designs of animals and flowers twined together were fastened at backs and seats with stout leather and bronze studs, the legs carved Xs crossed in the front and back like ancient versions of director's chairs, but more elegant and sturdy. They were surprisingly comfortable when she sat. Imagining they might be several hundred years old, Lenya thought them more at home in a cathedral or a castle with a moat around it.

Sirio pulled over a small table for the glasses and feast. Taking a horn handled knife out of his jacket pocket he began to slice the sausages and remove the casings.

How do I start? This might be a difficult subject for Sirio... I don't want to offend him either. I hope he doesn't think I'm crazy if I tell him I think there's a caveman living in his back forty.

She held her wine glass by the large round bowl and caressed it. "I have a question and I hope you can answer it. I've met a man...in the woods behind my cabin and...I was concerned about who he was... didn't seem dangerous to me, but you can't be too sure these days." She rubbed her index finger around the rim of the wineglass. "He seems harmless, but very strange...like he's a...a... caveman?... or something? Tom seems to like him a lot and he's a good judge of character. ...usually."

When she looked up, she realized Sirio was laughing so hard tears rolled down his cheeks. "Sirio, what's so funny?"

"I see you've finally met Aldo. I can assure you-—he's quite trustworthy. What's so funny? He has a crush on you. He's not dangerous—other than being smitten."

"What? Who is he? Where does he live? He's very strange." So many questions to ask. "And...what do you mean by 'smitten?'"

"It's a very long story, but I will try to make it short. If you look up to a certain mountaintop from a small road crossing the valley on the way to Bastia, you will see a large pile of rocks at the top. They are the ruins of an ancient settlement. A casteddu as they are called here on the island.

"There is a small and extremely difficult...I should say dangerous... track to get to it. Only one person lives there now. Your friend—Aldo. He is, sadly, the last survivor of a very ancient people; many think the only remnants of the original Corsicans. Perhaps even those who carved the menhirs, built the dolmens...no one knows. The very few archeologists—outsiders—who have been allowed to know the clan existed, think they might be the descendants of a Neolithic or Bronze Age clan. There are many theories, many versions of what might be the truth. A typical Corsican story.

"The casteddu, or the ruins, I should say...or at least a part of them, are possibly more than eight thousand years old. No one is sure.

Some of the casteddu is much newer, probably from the middle ages, and it incorporates the Neolithic village, and at one time, probably also its inhabitants. It is his home. Where his family and the clan once lived."

He looked into his wine glass and swirled the liquid around. "I grew up with the clan as a child. My mother and I lived with them until I was old enough to go to school."

"Oh my! I knew he was different, but not so different. What is... are...those people like? Are they civilized? Tell me...everything?"

"Oh yes, they are, or were...very civilized. They live by an ethical code of behavior, an ancient one. They worshiped Dia, the goddess—more or less a fertility cult...very common around the Mediterranean before the Judeo-Christian cults took over. Think of the old religions of Cybele and her priests. Remember Greek and Roman mythology, history? Their gods and goddesses? Especially the goddess cults: Aphrodite, Ceres, Venus, Magna Mater, Athena, Isis...probably hundreds of names for her. The sacred marriage of the gods. You understand?"

Lenya was stunned. She had never heard of anything like this existing today. "Sort of. But how have they survived? Why hasn't the modern world claimed them?...absorbed them?"

"Lenya, this is something very Corsican. Very protected. An almost sacred part of our heritage. Yes, we know of their existence. At least those of us from the old families. But we don't talk of them. They are not for outsiders to know about. In particular, not for the French." The last part was said with a sneer. Lenya recalled the road signs, the French names blasted with shotguns. Corsicans don't take well to outsiders. No matter how long they may have ruled over the island.

Sirio continued, "These people are no one's business, especially now. What would the bureaucrats do? Tax them? Make them serve in the military? Examine them like they were alien specimens from another planet. Poke them? Prod them with needles? Have them go to school and forget their culture, their language, their beliefs, their version of civilization?" He shook his head and violently jabbed at the fire. He harrumphed, "...like the fucking Spanish with the Basques? The Catalans?" The smoking logs burst into flames as if to punctuate his words.

He took the pan with the chestnuts off the fire to look at them. Satisfied they were cooking properly, he shuffled them around with his knife to make sure they roasted evenly. Once the flames subsided, he placed the pan back on the logs. "No, no, no! We do not tell anyone! We are, despite all attempts to civilize us, Corsican. We protect our own."

"But I don't understand how you can keep a secret like that. Don't people know, haven't they seen him...them?"

"Certainly. But we Corsicans love our secrets and guard them jealously, like original people from around the world. Life here exists on two levels, what we show to the world, and the secrets we know from our past. But it is less with every new generation. Stamping out the old ways, ancient beliefs and religions is never an easy thing to accomplish. Catholicism has tried for centuries, but these beliefs are like the glue, the cement, holding the souls of a people together, a common set of beliefs inherited from our father's father's father and back into unknown time. Here on Corsica, we have our Mazzeru—dream hunters, our brujas who cast spells and can give or remove the evil eye. They are no one's business but our own."

He picked his pipe up again, put it back and took his wineglass instead. "Haven't you heard about the yeti? Ever wonder what or who it is? Perhaps it's someone like Aldo, outside of the modern world, living the life they choose for themselves." He looked agitated as he got up and began to stalk around the large room. "When there is talk, questions, we say they have seen the phantom hermit from the woods. There are ghost stories we use to make children behave. Sometimes we tell people they have made a mistake, the stories are only legend or, don't believe your eyes. Other times we tell about a naturalist from Amsterdam, England, America, somewhere far away...who has grown a beard and is here to study our wildlife...or to live in the forest...or the ghost of a Corsican murdered in a vendetta...perhaps a pirate killed on a raid and walking the forest to find his home...whatever story comes to mind at the moment." He pulled the pan out of the fire again and examined his handiwork. He grunted in satisfaction and tilted the chestnuts into a nearby copper bowl and nodded at her, "Let them cool a bit before we try to eat them."

"He is hard to understand." She was embarrassed to ask the next question. "But... is he, I don't know how to say this in a politically correct way, but is he...is he retarded?"

"No, not at all, not at all." Sirio's expression tightened and turned serious as he leaned over and placed his hand on top of hers for emphasis. "In fact, he is quite intelligent...and both learned and civilized... only not in ways you might recognize."

"Sirio, he visits with me. Several times a week. Is that usual?"

"No. He generally keeps away from new people. He likes you. It is why he comes. You are special to him. His wife died more than a year ago and the few elders left in the clan followed her to the other side very soon afterwards. He is a very lonely and different person, Lenya. Complicated and complex. He enjoys very much your company and Tom."

"How do you know?"

"He has spoken to me about you. Aldo, he is my dear friend...from the time he was a child."

She sat silent for a moment, deep in thought. "Why have they stayed hidden all these years?"

"Don't think about them in hiding for years. More likely they have been hidden for centuries...more, even millennia. I know...I know it's hard to believe, but it's true."

Her mouth dropped open. "I don't understand. How can they not have been discovered?"

"You haven't seen where he lives. The approach is grueling and the path so concealed it would be difficult to find, even to follow him. It looks like a sheer cliff on both sides of the casteddu, but there are easier ways to approach, if you know how. Most people don't."

"But you say he's been seen in the villages. The local people, at least some of them, know he exists."

"Yes, of course they do, but they would never tell. He is sacred to them. They know him as a holy man, a priest of the old religion. He is the Maître, trained consort of the goddess, keeper of the old ways. Those ways die hard and take a long time in places like this...especially in the villages far away from the cities. Aldo is an essential element of the heritage of Corsica, a direct descendent in the line to the mother of us all. No one would give up his secret. There are those who might go to the casteddu for blessings, to give offerings—gifts to Dia and her consort, but to tell? Never!"

Sirio was worried about how to explain this, this man, this living phenomenon to her. How can a modern person understand the superstitions, the archaic beliefs, the faith breathed into the island since the beginning of time? He knew Aldo as friend and a beloved son. While his friend was a man, at the same time he was more, so much more—a living link with antiquity. Aldo was perhaps the only man alive who, because of circumstances, grew up in the past, a past so distant modern man had no way to wrap his mind around the ancient way of life. And now his friend had found a woman, the most modern of women, and he seemed to have fallen in love. Sirio shook his head. What a conundrum.

"Lenya, I don't know how to explain him to you. You have to take him on faith." She looked back at him, her expression blank.

He continued, "Close your eyes, imagine a glacier on the mountain over there," he pointed across the vineyard to the mist covered peak in the distance, barely visible in the dusk, "and it breaks loose from the top and crashes to the bottom where it melts. Inside is a man, frozen in time for a thousand years, maybe several thousand, but all during that time, he was actually asleep. In his dreams he hears sounds, the course of history, life, events taking place in the outside world as it moves around his glacier. But he can only interpret it against his frame of reference, his culture, what he believes, what he has seen, what he has been taught."

He looked at her, and, eyes wide, she stared back at him as though he posed all the questions of the mysteries of the universe—and she looked to him for answers.

He knew he had none and kept on, "So you see, while he might have heard what has happened while he slept, he understands it in a way different from your understanding. For instance, he abhors wars and fighting. From his prospective, it is the most vicious element in man's makeup. Dia, his goddess, has forbidden wars. So, anyone who incites them in the name of a god or goddess, commits blasphemy. There is no 'just' war in his mind."

She had her head in her hands, rubbing her scalp as if she wanted to push his words into her consciousness.

"So my dear, it is not easy, is it? Think of the old allegory about the blind men standing at different places around an elephant, touching and feeling the part where they stand and trying to describe the whole." He reached over to touch a chestnut and pulled his hand away quickly, then sucked on his finger for a moment, shaking it before he continued. "Aldo is a very interesting man, to say the least. Much more intelligent than you would think for someone who has spent their life hiding in the mountains. He has been well schooled in the old ways, such as they are."

For a reason she couldn't fathom, she started to cry—quietly with tears rolling down her cheeks. Sirio, surprised, bent over and dried her face with an old plaid handkerchief he fished out of a pocket.

"I'm sorry, I don't know why I'm doing this," she said. "I'm not unhappy or anything." She wiped at the last of the tears, sniffed loudly and sat up straighter. She was embarrassed at her reaction.

Sirio handed her several steaming chestnuts in a tea towel and looked down at his shoes for a moment before he looked up into her eyes. "Be careful not to burn your fingers. The heat on the inside is much more intense than it looks." Lenya wondered why he stared at her so long.

She spent the next few minutes intent on peeling the hard skin off the hot chestnuts while she digested this new information.

She remembered it was the same lesson her mother tried to teach her so long ago: things are not always as they seem.

Chapter 34
Lenya Reflects

Lenya sat on the deck alone and sipped coffee. The sky was a cerulean hue she'd only seen since coming to Corsica. No matter the time of day, it was always a more intense color then the sky back home. She wondered if it was the lack of pollution and thought again of the blue pottery and shutters in Pigna.

Corsica had its own special life and atmosphere, now painting itself indelibly into her psyche. She wondered if she would miss the island when it was finally time to go back to the states. It was inevitable, sometime, but at the moment she couldn't imagine ever leaving.

Would she miss the smell of the maquis, the yellow immortelle permeating the island? What else would she miss? Sirio, of course. The island itself. Aldo?

But she wasn't enjoying the morning with the same ease she usually felt. Sirio's revelations about Aldo disturbed her deeply, and she was exploring the reasons for her unusual disquiet. It was as if something in her life had tipped to the side. It was—disorienting.

Her life with Andre had been ordered. She worked or studied and did research for her next book. He worked and traveled for business, and with her for pleasure. She wrote, they had a social life with friends. It was all a very predictable pattern and one she had been brought up to accept as the way things were. Certainly they knew the world, or at the very least, she thought she did. Now, she was coming to the realization her knowledge was limited to a very small pattern of behavior. What had I been thinking? What arrogance to think I had seen...knew...it all.

In the past, the only way she made sense of life was a mental diagram. She thought of an area like a football field, but square. The world population was inside it, divided by a grid-like pattern keeping it neatly pigeonholed. On the top were the good people, smart, hardworking and, of course, liberal in their politics. They held a laissez-faire attitude and tried not to bother the rest of the world except in case of dire need.

The bottom held the rabid right wing conservatives, war mongers, nut cases, murderers and crooks. They rubbed shoulders with religious fanatics and all the others who limited personal freedom. Then there were serial killers, child murderers and rapists, and last, but not least— greedy industrialists whose only interest was to line their own pockets, no matter the expense to others. She would laugh and think of oil company executives packed in with the likes of raving religious fanatics and Jeffrey Dahmer.

In the middle was most of the world. They were neither good nor bad, average families trying to get along as best they could. They were susceptible to movement in either direction, up or down, depending on outside influences.

The patterns were neat, as was most of Lenya's life. It was a huge leap for her to comprehend the lives of these who had become such an integral part of her life since coming to the island. Talk about enigmas!

Sirio had been brought up between two worlds, or perhaps better said as between two time frames, but he had made his choice and now lived in the present. She could relate to him, his perspectives were understandable relatable.

Try as she might, there was no way she could imagine what it was like for Aldo, growing up in an ancient village with a clan—a throwback to millennia past, not a mere century or two, and living his whole life to date in the same continuum. His religion, his language, all foreign in a way she could never relate to. It was the same as if an alien spaceship landed and dumped him in the middle of a foreign planet. What caused her the most angst was considering what it must be like for him? How can he comprehend the insane modern world surrounding him?

Thinking about it made her head hurt. Then, she remembered a prompt from a creative writing course. The professor had drawn a square and placed a dot outside it. "Do what you want with this," he had said as he plunked the paper in the middle of the table.

She remembered looking at it. What the hell? At the time, she wrote something about an ant colony with a lost member trying to get back inside. The little guy was frightened in a strange place and wanted to get home.

The idea made her sad. Aldo was never going home. He was outside of the grid, lost in both time and culture. An image of his face came to mind, the sadness in his eyes as it disappeared when Tom jumped into his lap. The image of him braiding his hair on the deck in the morning—a sensual, moment of joy, sun shining, dog in his lap, strong fingers weaving patterns in the molten bronze locks. She had to shake her head to draw her thoughts away.

Refugees from wars, people displaced by floods and tsunamis are uprooted from friends and relatives. Homes destroyed; families flung to far corners of the earth, but there's always hope of finding someone with a familiar culture, a common way of life. At least they're all in the same time frame.

Not so with Aldo. His home was centuries past and, unlike her lost ant, or a displaced refugee, had no hope of ever reconciling with his kind again. The closest he could find was Sirio, a man of the present but understanding Aldo's link with the past.

How can a man exist out of time? Again, her mind slipped back to the prompt and the dot outside of the square. And more important— why did she even care? Was she feeling sorry for him? Tears coursed down her cheeks again as her chest tightened. It was like contemplating infinity—another idea she couldn't wrap her mind around.

The image of him braiding his hair irresistibly spilled into her thoughts once again as she tried not to admit to herself why she was so emotional.

The phrase crept stealthily across her mind...'touch of the skin'?

Chapter 35
Can It Be...?

Mid December arrived with a small flurry of snow and lasted on the ground for less than an hour—gone as soon as the sun came out. The rest of the afternoon sparkled with warmth and sunlight. *Ya gotta' love 'da Mediterranean* she thought to herself as the trace of New Yawkese slipped into her mind. *Maybe my sense of humor hasn't completely deserted me.*

To promote her book, she conducted Skype interviews almost every day; mostly at odd hours because of the time difference. She sat at the computer facing the webcam with her hair combed, make-up, her best black cashmere turtle-neck sweater and pearls, pajama bottoms and pink fuzzy bedroom slippers hidden below the desk.

Her book was selling well and Ellie was delighted. The publisher had almost recouped the advance on Christmas sales alone and there was talk Oprah might mention it on her show. In a couple of months, she went from a bad child to a pampered author. Lenya had no illusions; it was 'what have you done for me lately' in the publishing business. Success meant little to her other than money coming in. Starting the research and outlining for her new project was more interesting. Finishing up the old book was merely the end of a part of her writing career.

Aldo sat outside on the edge of the deck with Tom snuggled in his lap keeping each other warm. Aldo seemed to enjoy keeping Lenya company while she did Tai Chi. He watched her go through the movements as he idly stroked Tom's fur. What she couldn't know was he liked watching the play of her muscles beneath the soft fabric, and entertained himself by imaging ways of using some of the movements as part of their eventual conjoining.

Lenya studied her two "men"—or were they different kinds of pets? She had no idea and hated herself for the awful thought as soon as it surfaced. She knew it demeaned Aldo and it made her feel small to have so disparaged him. But she was frightened of her own feelings and did everything in her power to try and give herself peace.

Aldo's deep set eyes always looked sad to her. At first she attributed it to his facial structure, but then she acknowledged it might be a bone deep sorrow she didn't want to penetrate, even if she had the communication skills to do so. Tom had his own quizzical worried expression, but Lenya knew it was simply the design of his markings, now changing as the jet black and dark brown fur on his muzzle turned white with age.

This morning, as she went through the calming movements of the ancient form, bundled in sweat shirt and pants, she looked at the two of them. They watched her every movement with intensity, but it no longer embarrassed her. She accepted the fact the three of them had become an odd sort of group, or was this what it meant to be part of a clan? They did everything together, and there were no arguments even though they were learning to communicate quite well. She had been surprised to find Aldo had learned quite a bit of English from Sirio over the years, so with three common languages between them, they got along. It was a far cry from the life she shared with Andre, but she finally admitted—it was indeed a life.

She wrapped a towel around her neck and sat on the deck next to them. Tom managed to wiggle onto her lap and curled himself back into a ball indicating he was content and had no intention of moving. He might as well have sported a "Do Not Disturb" sign around his neck.

Often, she'd study Aldo. Admiring his sharply defined profile she noticed he was smiling more often. His body had filled out these last weeks since he was eating regularly with her. His hair, skin and beard were freshly washed, as always.

The only odor she could ever detect on him was a pleasant masculine musk mixed with woodsy forest scents: cedar, eucalyptus, pine and lavender. Lenya had no idea hygiene was an important part of his religion. Dia decreed, as the temple of the soul, the body must be kept clean and healthy at all times; her consorts regularly anointed themselves with scented oils—part of the sacraments they performed.

He even looked as if he had trimmed his facial hair this morning. She wondered how he cut it. His hair was damp when he arrived, left lose to dry in the warming air. By the time she finished her exercise his hair had turned into curls and waves cascading around his face and down his back. As she watched, fascinated as always by his dexterity, his fingers began working the intricate braids. He had no mirror, but with a bone pick he separated strands into neat sections he then plaited with a deftness born of years of repetition. It was intensely erotic—strange how it never occurred to her, what it might feel like to watch a man braid his own hair. Whenever she saw him do it, the same thought always popped into her mind. How would those skillful hands feel on my body? A flash from a long forgotten dream came to mind...an unknown man making love to her, her body responding with abandon...*a cave?...chanting? Touch?* She shook her head and the images once again fled beyond her reach.

Her hands automatically did the one thing she'd wanted to do ever since she'd first met Aldo. She reached out to caress the red fur of his beard. Amazing. It was so soft. She'd expected it to be wiry and rough. Her hand continued, almost of its own accord, up the side of his face and then down the length of soft red whiskers. There was a tug in her heart, her breath came in short gulps as if she had run a distance, but try as she might, she couldn't break the connection between her hand and his hair. Aldo assumed a stillness so perfect she realized he was holding his breath. Tom sensed something and launched off her lap.

With a huge intake of air, Aldo groaned as his hands grasped her under her arms and lifted her from the deck onto his lap. Facing him, she could feel his breath against her cheek. *How had her legs wrapped around his waist?*

His arms were around her, holding her firmly to his chest as he stroked her back. His big hands felt warm—tender and strong. Blunt fingers worked knowingly along her spine, relaxing tense muscles while holding her against him. It was the most sensuous feeling she could remember. Her nose nestled into the softness of his hair as she melted against him and was enveloped in the fragrance of lavender, pine and immortelle. Her arms automatically embraced him. Tom snuggled down next to them.

Aldo's body cushioned her bottom from the hard deck, his arms protective around her. Silent...close...neither moved except for his hands on her back. They stayed for what seemed an eternity as she counted the beats of their hearts inches apart. At first her pulse fluttered and jittered like the wings of a captured moth, but as his hands continued their supple caress, slow pressure down her spine, gentling her, it slowed down to a regular beat. She had never felt so safe. Her body molded against his, trying to get closer—to fit his contours and angles.

Her brain roamed completely out of context into thoughts she had no control over. *He wouldn't leave me for a younger woman with a bare midriff and a belly ring; I wouldn't be his trophy wife; there's no baggage he brings into a relationship. I really am losing my mind—no—correction—I have lost my mind! ... a relationship with a...a...caveman?*

Relationship? What on earth am I thinking? ... a barely civilized Cro-Magnon and I'm thinking "relationship? Her mind jittered into self- protective mode *...he could have some strange diseases. What do I really know about him? What does he want from me?* All her innate defense mechanisms flew into action.

Then she felt his erection. My god, it feels like a baseball bat!

It was as if she had been splashed with cold water.

She sprang off his lap and scrambled upright with as much dignity as she could muster. He rolled onto his knees and took her hand in both of his before she could fly further away. Firmly, he turned her hand palm up and pressed his lips to it. The kiss was soft and lingered. Then his tongue flicked out and licked the center of her palm in a slow circle.

A shock went through her from palm to crotch. It was as if he had penetrated her. The soft beard and moustache, the lips pressing, his tongue; it all felt as if he had opened her up and set fire to her core. Moisture trickled down her thigh as she stormed into the cabin, slammed the door behind and locked it. *Why bother, I can't keep the real culprit out when it's me!*

Tom was curled on the deck. Aldo stroked the little animal as he tried to understand what had happened. He was sure Lenya wanted him. She had felt so soft and yielding in his lap. She was the one who reached out to him first. What went wrong? It was a stupid question to ask himself when he knew the answer—she was terrified. But of what? He had given her no cause for fear.

He looked down to the quickly retreating hardness he wanted to share with her. He imagined her soft skin, his hands soothing her body as their contours melted into one being, gifting Dia with the energy of their pleasure.

He shook his head in sorrow. They had been so close. But it was not to be.

After a few moments, he slid off the deck and went into the woods. Nothing but emptiness stared at him from the cabin windows when he turned once to look back. What had he done to upset her and how was he going to fix it?

Chapter 36
Surveying The Past

Inside the cabin, Lenya stormed around opening and closing cabinets and slamming drawers. There was nothing she could find to help her clear the thunderstorm clashing and boiling in her mind. She made a point to avoid the windows as she stomped into the bathroom—didn't want to know if he was there. Perhaps a cold shower, a very cold one, might help calm her down. Sweat pants, sweat shirt and underwear piled on the small rag rug as she ripped them off and hurled them aside. She stepped into the shower, heedless of the penetrating needles of frigid water.

After the first shock, her mind began to clear. Choices, she thought. I've been making choices all my life and look where they brought me. They were the safe choices, not like Lotte who goes for the gusto. Her sister was a risk taker, always the 'wild child'. Damn Lotte! She wouldn't have jumped up and run away.

Lenya thought back to Lotte's first boyfriend, a James Dean look-alike with a Japanese crotch-rocket. The image of Lotte's long hair streaming behind her as they rode off into the summer afternoons flooded back. Mother, screaming from the sidewalk for her to get back in the house. Lenya smiled to herself as she remembered Lotte's raised middle finger as the motorcycle screeched around the corner.

Motorcycle guy didn't last long and was followed by a tall, slender Greenwich Village poet who turned out to have a very angry, tall muscular wife, easily taken to violence when defending her marital rights. Lotte earned a black eye from the venture.

While getting her MBA, Lotte's next lover was a six foot six inch Sikh on sabbatical with a hot pink turban and a pedigree which included several billion Rupees.

From there she moved into millionaire Euro-trash, then a few Silicon Valley start-up new rich—as long as they had a bit of snap to them, otherwise, geeks were of no interest.

There was no doubt about it, Lotte took risks in love and business and was successful in both. True, she had never married, but she thoroughly enjoyed her life and always had some delightful man around to keep her company. Lotte was quick to tell Lenya her mantra—when she and her current beau ceased learning from each other, there was always a replacement somewhere on the horizon.

Lenya thought of her past choices. As the conservative sister, she never ventured off the safe path. Her boyfriends tended to be lawyers or doctors. She went wild once and dated a dentist. Marrying Andre, a charming French businessman, was the most daring thing she'd ever done, and she never doubted for a moment it was the right decision. But now? Maybe she'd been too cautious, always doing the right thing, being safe.

Drying her hair, she looked at her image in the mirror. A woman stared back at her, attractive, the first bloom off the rose, but acceptable. She turned and looked at her butt. It was still in place, thank you Tai Chi.

Her eyes were haunted, even to her. What was inside them? Fear? Not wanting to cross to the wild side? She thought about her life, always purposefully choosing the path Lotte never took, being the 'good twin' who never got into trouble, never crossed the line. Maybe it was finally time to kick over the traces as grandmother used to say? Maybe it was now her turn to be the 'wild child.'

She examined the tiny lines at the corners of her eyes. How long will I have before my shelf life expires? Do I want to spend the rest of my life alone? But it wasn't the issue at all. She was terrified of how attracted she was to this very different man. But was it only attraction? Was it more? Love? Only lust? There was certainly magic in his touch.

Falling in love? Where did come from? But it was a puzzle. How had this quiet ardor, this infatuation, become so strong? And for who? A man who was an enigma? One she was not sure she wanted to unveil.

She twisted the towel into a turban and turned from the mirror. Who did she think she was kidding? Lenya, get a grip! There is no chance of a 'relationship' with this guy. You're horny...the thrill of a good roll in the hay with a very appealing man..admit it...appealing!

It wouldn't be fair to Aldo. It might signal something more than she was willing to give. He was a man alone, out of time, looking for a companion. What was she looking for? A good fuck? There wasn't anything else possible with a man like him. Leading him on would be cruel.

Her lease on the cabin would be up, she'd pack her computer and head back to New York and civilization. She imagined the stories she could tell about her Corsican caveman at book launching parties. No, it wasn't fair to him. Angry with herself, she yanked on her clothes with more force than necessary. My fault! All my fault! He has always been the gentleman and I screwed everything up!

As she combed her drying hair, she looked at the deck, the scene of her crime. The sun setting over the mountains turned the light dusting of snow pink and lavender. Tom was asleep on the small rug in front of the sliding door. He must be chasing something, his paws twitched and he made small woofing sounds as he ran through his dream.

The deck was empty.

Lenya sat on the floor in front of the hearth and sobbed. The touch had been there, she had felt electricity, current blazing through her. She knew what it was...and ran from it? *How stupid can I be? What have I done?*

Chapter 37
How To Hunt

Three days passed. Aldo stayed away from the cabin. He was out of patience, frustrated, and furious with himself. And worst of all—puzzled All he could think about was the scent of Lenya's hair as she sat on his lap, the feel of her legs around his waist, her breath in his beard, the softness of her body as he held her against his chest and stroked her back while she melted against him. The feel of her skin. New moss on a rock in spring. The fur of a kit fox. Smooth. Enticing. The special spark between consort and goddess, man and his mate, earth and moon, had clearly sparked between them. Lenya was his other half.

He was confused about her fear of him. He had done nothing aggressive, nothing he could think of to cause such a reaction. He would not go to her again until he figured it out.

It would have been easy with a woman of the clan. Aldo knew the art of giving pleasure; every man of the clan learned about giving power to Dia as soon as they started growing hair around their genitals. And as consort to Dia, he was schooled in the mysteries of sex...more than the other boys. When he was thirteen and ready to begin his training in the sacred sex rites, to eventually take the place of Maître, to proclaim his devotion, he gave his offering to Dia. Far back in the reaches of time, he knew Dia's priests castrated themselves as a sign of love and fidelity to their goddess, but thankfully, custom changed over the centuries. The clan didn't have enough members to prevent the strongest young men from procreating. The foreskin became gift enough.

If Lenya had stayed, joined together he would have shown her what he knew, what he excelled at—the ritual moves of the sacred marriage. Dia would have her ecstasy. The clan women understood and know how to behave.

But what to do with this very strange woman? She touched him first and when he responded, even a little, she ran off. Was she angry with him? He shook his head in puzzlement. He couldn't stop his mind from going over the incident again and again.

Maybe he had only himself to blame. True, she was from a very different clan. Perhaps he misunderstood her signals and the way of her clan's rites. Could running away be part of her mating ritual?

He had to be sure she was to be his mate, or he had to move on. By the standards of the clan he was already an old man even though he didn't think he was much more than three sets of fingers. He was not sure exactly how many winters he had seen. Raina kept track for many years, but then she gave up counting, as she gave up the rest of her life. Aldo never considered age important enough to keep track of himself. He felt this coming winter in his bones like none before. Maybe his time was running out.

For several nights he tossed and turned in his sleep. Then, inspiration came. He remembered his father; teaching him how to train the small animals of the forest, and later the dogs and foxes who lived with the clan. The first rule was to gain their trust, show them you meant no harm. Then, it was a simple matter; let the animal come to you. He had done this with the small fox who was his nighttime companion and partner at so many meals.

Aldo remembered the lessons. Father took seeds and nuts in his big hand and placed them in a trail on the ground. Then, squatting a short distance from the offering he waited and watched. When a squirrel found the seeds, its bright eyes flicked in all directions. The creature knew death hid everywhere in the forest. Tail reaching for the air, it was ready to sprint into the underbrush at the first hint of danger. But Father knew stillness, no movement or indication other than quiet slow breathing. He blended with the underbrush; became a part of his surroundings.

The small animal crept up to the treats, eyes constantly moving in fear. But Father stayed immobile as the squirrel snatched the seeds or nuts, stuffed them into its cheeks and ran. The next day and the next, Father repeated the procedure.

When the squirrel was accustomed to the treats and accepted Father's presence, the ritual changed. The nuts and seeds remained on the ground, but bit by bit they were placed closer and closer. After many days of quiet waiting, a treat was in Father's hand and then up his arm. This was his way. How he trained many creatures.

Birds were always perched on Father's shoulders or on the top of his head; tiny squirrels and chipmunks climbed up his arm to hide in little pockets made by Aldo's mother. Aldo remembered those pockets, skins or rags sewn together with delicate stitches, thread made from thin slices of twisted leather. His mother created nests by filling the bottoms of the pockets with soft hair, nests to be homes for tiny birds, mice and squirrels—all his father's friends.

No one else in the clan had such talent. Father was called man-friend-of-animals. At meals with the clan, elders would tease saying he was "feeding his pocket again" as he took tiny morsels of food for his pocket friends to savor. At night, the pockets hung on pegs pounded into the wall near where he slept in the casteddu. Small creatures slept there soundly, close to Father, secure in the knowledge they were safe.

Aldo was taught to use similar methods hunting the animals the clan depended on. Father would find a herd of deer grazing, sit immobile for hours, blending with the foliage. Several days might pass until the animals became used to his scent and presence. Then, moving closer, he sought out the oldest and least vital animal to coax into becoming his target.

When the animal finally took food from his hand, Father reached out and slit its throat. His motion so swift death was almost painless. The animal fell, life drifted out with blood spilling from the wound. Aldo remembered Father catching the blood in his hands and raising it in thanks to Dia for the animal's gift of food to the clan and, in return for the gift, soothing the dying animal with a chant of homage to guide its spirit's journey safely into the next world.

Thinking back to those days helped Aldo devise a plan—but how to implement it? He walked over to the wall and looked out into the distance. The fog had rolled in from the coast and up to the base of the mountains. Looking over the parapet, the world below had disappeared into a soup of mist. He shivered involuntarily. It was as if he was alone on his mountaintop, the last person alive, everything silent, all sound hidden on the other side, the side he couldn't see through to. Maybe Lenya was like that too. Maybe he could only see so far into her being when he was with her, maybe the rest would always be impenetrable to him. The reflection made him despondent.

He rubbed his arms against the cold air and moved back from the parapet. There was no point in such thoughts—negative thinking. He had to try again. He gathered twigs and made a desultory fire in his house to break the chill, thinking back once again to his father's knack for hunting.

The clan always said the best meat was when Father hunted. They teased him for seducing the animal so well it gave its life willingly. The meat was always tender and tasty, even if the animal was old.

When other hunters brought back their game, they bragged about how long they chased it through the woods. Aldo knew the animals were often almost dead from fright before the hunter dealt the final blow. The meat tasted gamey—a rank quality to it. Maybe how one hunted did make a difference. He didn't know. Now he was going to try his father's lessons on a different kind of game. The biggest hunt of his life.

Aldo strained to remember. As the memories flowed, he planned how best to use them with such a woman as Lenya. He thought of the fear in her eyes as she ran into her house and slammed the door. It was no different from the fear he saw in the wide eye of so many creatures his father eventually tamed. He stared at the ceiling long into the night, lost in thought, remembering ancient hunters flickering in firelight, chasing their game into eternity. As he thought of his frightened quarry, he stroked the soft fur of the small pregnant fox snuggled up and sleeping safely at his side.

Chapter 38
Softly, Softly Catches...

It was a week since Lenya had run from Aldo. She hadn't seen him nor had he left his usual nosegays. She didn't want to admit it had been one of the more miserable weeks in her life.

Christmas was closing in she tried to convince herself she was morose because she was going to spend the holiday alone. Terrence was in Asia and wasn't going to show up this time with a turkey or a ham.

But she knew it was all a lie. She only wanted Aldo to return. He had become such an integral part of her life she was lost without his presence. She had no heart for Tai Chi, practically dragging herself outside in the mornings. There was no joy in the motions of the forms. She couldn't stop thinking about Aldo. No matter what she did, she was obsessed by the memory of his tongue on her palm. Furious at herself, at her failure to admit how much she depended on his company. Now she didn't' have it and realized she wanted so much more from him than companionship. While she was busy castigating herself about how she screwed everything up with her idiotic reaction she also worried about whether she was a sex maniac, a cougar or maybe just horny. The only thing she was sure of was her embarrassment …and stupidity...and the probability she was falling in...no...not the 'L'-word...maybe lust?… with a man she couldn't understand...didn't even know? Her reaction to Aldo terrified her.

On the morning of December 21st Aldo strode up to the cabin. He stood tall, shoulders set with determination, not his usual loose stroll. Lenya stopped her Tai Chi forms as soon as she saw him, her spirits lifting even though she flushed with embarrassment at how pleased she was.

During the past week, her mental battles had been exhausting. *Crap! I had an orgasm when a caveman kissed my hand! How bizarre?*

But even her snarky thoughts couldn't deny the truth of her feelings. Every time Tom became alert, she hoped it was Aldo. Several times she went out onto the deck to see if he had left her anything. When the spot where he usually placed his offering was empty, she felt a stab of regret.

Lenya had no idea where he lived or how she could find him, or even if she wanted to. Before, he seemed to appear when she thought of him; it had never been an issue. This week she was so distraught she even considered combing the woods for him. Then she'd mentally beat herself up. *Now tell me I'm not nuts? Imagine the sub-title for book, 'In Search Of The Neanderthal.' Okay, maybe only Cro-Magnon, but I'm still nuts!*

There was no way she would have asked Sirio where to find Aldo. Sirio would take one look at her and know something was up. So she stayed in the cabin and stewed, muttering to herself about her reaction to him, her dammed upbringing, her false chastity—and last but not least—her prideful refusal to admit how much Aldo meant to her.

Aldo was spiffed up. His beard was fluffed and curled freely around his chin and the sides of his face, framing it in the morning sunlight with a shining bronze aura. It made him seem bigger than usual. His hair wasn't pulled back into his usual intricate braid, instead, a cascade of waves and curls like a cloud of saffron trailed down his back. The urge to touch him was almost painful but she refused to run to him. She couldn't stop herself from thinking how beautiful he was, how much the image of raw and unadorned masculinity. Her hands ached and trembled with the need to touch his skin, his hair—him.

But something was different. He looked both formidable...and *business-like?*

Tom frisked out to greet him with his usual joy at seeing a friend. Lenya hung back, unsure how to act. Her hesitant smile showed him she was glad he was there.

Aldo's chest was almost hidden behind a large armful of eucalyptus, pine branches hung with cones, and mistletoe. He held the foliage out to her—an offering. Nested in the middle was a small, rotund figure, carved from wood. Motioning and smiling at Lenya, he moved back as she took his gift.

The figure was a small woman with protuberant belly, pendulous breasts and prominent vaginal cleft. Topped by a round face, it was a simple rendering like the Venus of Villendorf, one of the earliest representations of the earth goddess, Lenya had seen her photograph many times in art books.

Aldo watched as she studied the figure. He pointed to himself and made carving motions and then pointed at her. At first, she was horrified. Had he meant it to represent her, enlarged vagina and all? Is this the way he sees me—making nude statues as a way to ask for sex? She had no clue what to say or do other than stand in breathless shock as her face and neck reddened.

But he knew what to do. He raised his palms to her in a gesture of offering and pointed to the statue, *"e Dia....regalo per te."* With relief, she understood. He had carved a representation of his goddess for her—a gift.

Breathing once again, she examined the gift. The wood was buffed, the figurine soft to the touch, almost feeling like skin. Hair was indicated by both delicate carving and the placement of the grain. A lot of time and work had been spent on this little woman. She was carved with the skill of an artist. *Did it mean she was forgiven?*

To indicate her pleasure, she took time to admire the figure, turning it over and over in her hands and smiling.

"Grazie por queste regalo. Me piace molto." It was the most Italian she could manage. He beamed in understanding as she reverently placed the figure on the table.

He pointed at the deck. *"Permisso?"* he asked, inclining his head.

"*Si*," she said, and pointed to one of the two chairs. Aldo climbed the stairs and took a seat on the deck instead.

She went inside, indicating for him to stay seated. Putting food on a plate and, arranging the branches in a vase, she noticed the magnetic calendar on the refrigerator—it was the winter solstice, the shortest day of the year. Could he have known and brought gifts to celebrate? Somewhere she remembered pagan celebrations sometimes included sex rites.

She mentally slapped herself. *Can't I think of anything other than sex with this man? What have you gotten yourself into this time, my girl? What is he expecting?* She shook her head in anger at herself as she arranged food for a snack and realized how joyful she was at his forgiveness. *I couldn't stand to have lost him.* It was a difficult admission for her to make.

She returned with the vase in one hand, a plate in the other filled with salami and bread. Placing both near the enigmatic goddess, who appeared to be very comfortable commanding the low side table, Lenya offered the food. He smiled and took a taste.

Do I have to say something to him? Apologize, and if so...for what...? This is going to be really awkward.

But it wasn't. Aldo had brought a small flute that looked hand made. She gestured to the instrument, made wood carving motions and pointed at him. He smiled and gestured back to her with the same motions and pointed at himself. So far so good. She didn't have to talk, explain herself, apologize for anything.

He played his flute. The haunting melodies flowing from the simple instrument seemed to echo the sounds of the forests, the mountains and the water bubbling through the endless creeks and waterfalls. He kept time with his foot to rhythms both compelling and primal. The music reminded her of something—something she couldn't quite remember.

The foliage surrounded her with scents of pine and earth and wood while his music slow-danced across her mind. The warp and weft of sounds and aromas created a visceral energy, stirring genetic recollections as old or perhaps even older than the menhirs. Encircled and energized by the magical weave and the closeness of Aldo, Lenya relaxed.

She imagined another time when she knew these woods, his melodies and the gods of it all. It was a time and place far different from the one she came from, but for the moment, she felt it's familiarity.

She had no idea how long they sat on the deck together. When he was tired playing, he took more salami and bread. She brought out juice and they drank in unison. They communicated by signs and words. She spoke to him in French and some words and phrases she knew in Italian. He spoke to her in his usual mixture of Italian and French, surprising her with an occasional word in English. They got along, understanding each other no matter what language the actual spoken words happened to be in.

When she asked him where he lived he pointed to the woods and turned his hand over a few times to indicate distance. Sirio's right; he's smart; he knows how to get his point across better than I do.

The light on the deck changed from full sun to slanting shadows, the air cooling in anticipation of nightfall, but the pull of their companionship kept Lenya warm.

At dusk he got up, climbed down from the deck and surprised her by saying *"Caio, a domani...tomorrow."* Smiling, he waved to her as he turned and left. Lenya felt a twinge of sadness as he faded into the forest.

The next morning he was sitting on her deck when she went out to do her exercises. He grinned and pulled some apples from his pockets, bit into one and offered her another. It was small and gnarly looking like the last ones he brought, she rubbed it on her pants to shine it up before bitting into it. The apples were tart, crisp, and juice dripped down their chins. They laughed at each other as they ate.

Lenya finished her apple and did stretching exercises. Aldo sat watching with Tom in their usual spot, until she began the Tai Chi forms, then he took out his flute and began to play a melody, almost in time to her movements. The music was once again primal, but this time with stronger rhythmical undertones, embracing—encouraging her motions to flow, energy and serenity coursing through her muscles—the chi. Tiny hairs on her arms stood on end and emotions tumbled out with the power she felt. Her nose began to sting; she was afraid she was going to cry, but she did not. The music stopped for a moment, then continued with its fragile familiarity, fingers of sounds caressing her from the recesses of memory.

Toweling off later, she knew it was the most astonishing workout she'd ever had and then shivered at the thought. Before she had time to say anything, he nodded to her and walked off into the woods with a smile and a wave.

For a long time she sat at her computer, staring at the flying patterns of the screen saver. Something was different, something had changed, like tectonic plates moving within her, rubbing up against each other, but she wasn't sure what it meant. Different. Not unpleasant. Maybe...unexpected.

The next day he came again, this time with berries. They were tart and made her face crinkle up. They laughed together at her expressions. When she began her Tai Chi, he stood next to her and copied her movements. She did them slowly so he could follow and was surprised how quickly he learned. Within two days he was doing the forms next to her as if he had done them all his life. She didn't know he'd been watching her for months, practicing the movements on his own.

He seemed to especially like some of the forms, like stealing the black pearl, the Yellow River with its turns, the crane, and stretching in the salute to the sun. He was light on his feet and graceful. Unexpected. Doing the movements with him was a powerful experience, and when she found they could do a mirror of movements together, it increased the power of chi between them, building a bond, an invisible rope binding them together. Afterwards, he sat for a while on the deck with Tom when she went inside to take her shower and work. He left before she returned, smiling to himself on the walk back to his home.

Aldo was in no hurry. He'd made it back to the deck and was pleased by his progress. She seemed to have little fear of him, but obviously wanted to keep her distance. What he couldn't know was she was actually more afraid of herself.

❦

Late at night, when she was alone, she called Lotte on Skype. She turned off the video, she didn't want to see her sister's face, or show hers. The conversation was going to be a bit too personal. She desperately needed someone to talk to. Lenya lived a very ordered life. Self-disciplined by years of getting her writing done on time, she had become internally imprisoned by deadlines. Now her concentration was shot; all she wanted was to be with Aldo. *Am I obsessed? This is not me! Definitely not me! But then, who is it?*

The internal conflict was tearing her apart and a sounding board might help. Her sister might appear as a ditz to the outside world, but Lenya knew otherwise. Many times over the years she relied on Lotte's judgment and cool approach to life. This time, she felt her life depended on it.

The twins had great respect for each other, getting over the rough spots in their lives together. They knew there was always a sympathetic ear to bend when needed. Lenya really needed ear.

It started off simply enough. Lotte was brimming over with news about the new man she recently met. "...and can you imagine, he has a home in Cap d'Antibes. I told him you were in Corsica... we're coming... visit you after the holidays."

Lenya groaned. She heard the "we." Just what she didn't need, Lotte and a fancy boyfriend with a home on the Cote d'Azure. She got a quick picture of introducing Aldo wearing his skins and homemade moccasins; the other guy in Armani and Rolex. *Shit! Sure, they'll get along fine...discussing mergers and acquisitions. I'm not saying a word to her...no way!*

"Great Lotte! I'll look forward to seeing you both, but my place is very small. Let me know when you're coming and I'll make reservations at a nice hotel in town." *This is going to be dicey...and ugly...real ugly!*

"Oh don't worry, we'll take care of it ourselves. He has some friends who own a castle in Corsica. I'll check out where it is."

Yeah, yeah, blah-blah a castle? Sure, even worse than I thought. What will I do if she arrives with il Signore Armani?

After a bit more gossip and chit-chat Lenya managed an excuse to get off the phone. She had given up. There was no way to say anything to Lotte. She'd never understand. This was something she'd have to decide on her own intuition, and something inside kept telling her it was right.

Maybe it was the damn voice she heard when she first came to Corsica? Was it Dia who was speaking to her? *Now I'm not only having conversations with my dead husband, but with a caveman's goddess too? I don't need a shrink; I need some really some good meds. Yeah, strong meds!...real heavy-duty...*

Lenya climbed up the stairs to her loft, but she didn't feel the usual joy—she felt very alone.

After a few hours of tossing, she clicked on Skype. When her contacts list came up, Lotte was off-line. With the six hour time difference it was 9:30 PM in New York. Lotte must be out for dinner.

As she got into bed again, she felt Tom snuggle in beside her. She picked him up and cradled him in her arms. Sleepless, she stared at the carved Venus figure she had placed on the table next to the bed.

Am I falling in love with this strange man? I don't know anything about him. Sirio said his wife had died? What does he think about, what is he really like?...and most important, what does he want from me? And finally... I really need help. The carved woman wasn't about to give her any answers.

Tom's presence comforted her, like her teddy bears when she couldn't get to sleep, worrying about her mother out late with a new boyfriend. *Maybe I should give sucking my thumb a try too? It used to work.*

She finally drifted off to sleep remembering the softness of Aldo's beard on her palm.

Chapter 39
Christmas Day

Lenya kept to her usual routine. Around noon she thought about lunch and remembered with a start—it was Christmas. Aldo was a no-show. Moping around the cabin, she cleaned the place even though it wasn't dirty. Then she sat at the computer and played solitaire. The will to work was nowhere in sight.

A few minutes after noon, she heard a car pull up the road.

As a car door slammed, Tom ran to the sliding door barking and leaping like a pup. Sophia was on the other side jumping up and down in unison. Tom's manic mirror image. Lenya laughed at the two of them as she patted her hair in place, adjusted her sweats. Congratulating herself on having showered and put on a clean tee-shirt in honor of the day, she went to greet her company.

There were the two of them, Sirio and Aldo, both grinning at her like they managed a neat trick. And they had. What a surprise, exactly what she needed.

Aldo held a large hunk of meat out to her. Not quite the kind of Christmas present she was used to but it suited her perfectly. She went over to the edge of the deck and watched as he pointed to the meat, made snorting noises and pawed the ground. It was a creditable imitation of a wild boar, or *sanglier*, plentiful on the island if you knew where to find them.

Sirio pointed at the meat. "Aldo is a great hunter. Especially with the *sanglier*. He came by and kidnapped me, I think not only for company but also to provide some wine, and here we are, time to celebrate the birth of the child, Jesu. Don't make too much about it though. For Aldo, it's a holiday for his Dia; the clan always celebrated the entire week after Winter Solstice."

"Please, please, come up, come in. Whatever holiday we are going to celebrate, I'm very happy to see you both." Now what was she going to do? There was nothing in the cabin large enough to cook such a piece of meat. She knew it was delicious; she had tried it several times in the local restaurants. So this was where he had been this morning, organizing a surprise.

Sirio must have seen her face and correctly interpreted her expression. "Don't worry my dear; you don't have to do a thing. Aldo is a great cook and has invited us both for holiday dinner. All you must do is provide dishes and glasses. Think of me as the sous chef and he—maître chef de cuisine!" A courtly bow, a radiant grin and a sweep of his arm accompanied the declaration.

What a treat! Company who brings and cooks their own dinner. Her loneliness fled. She was glowing, suddenly filled with joy at the idea of both good friends and good food. Even though it wasn't her usual Christmas ritual, it sounded like a great idea. Time to start a new tradition, she thought and then laughed to herself. She was thinking of Terrence and his Thanksgiving surprise. *What is there about me that makes men think I need to be fed?*

Aldo rooted around in his pockets and retrieved a clump of herbs. She recognized wild onion, garlic and rosemary. He rummaged again and brought out three large potatoes. He pointed to himself, and the meat, and then pantomimed eating as if he planned on eating the whole thing himself. Then he broke into laughter at his joke.

"Don't let him tease you, Lenya. He showed up at the winery with everything ready for a feast. I think he's out to impress you." Sirio couldn't resist a wink as he put his finger alongside his nose.

"Well, he's certainly on the right track. I've never seen anyone so prepared. But I don't know how or where he expects to cook such a large piece of meat."

"You can ask him. But don't worry...he knows exactly what to do."

Lenya was delighted. Talk about something special for Christmas—dinner al fresco cooked by a caveman; oops, I mean my new gentleman caller. She couldn't wait to tell Lotte. But she remembered Lotte's fancy new *il Signore Armani*. Maybe I'll keep it to myself for the moment.

Aldo spread all the ingredients for the feast on the deck, but Lenya removed the meat to the kitchen as soon as she saw Tom and Sophia heading over to take a sniff. Aldo gently shooed the dogs away and aimed make-believe arrows at them and laughed. How on earth and where is he going to cook this thing, does he even have any idea how to use a stove? This is going to be interesting.

When she came back from the kitchen, she found Aldo walking around the edge of the woods collecting rocks and wood and pointing things out to Sirio. She went to assist in the search for smallish twigs and branches and rounded egg-sized rocks. She went in one direction and the men went in another as they foraged outside her clearing. When their hands were full they all piled their treasures on a flat spot he'd selected. It was a cleared area away from both the house and the forest.

Aldo moved three deck chairs over to the clearing. With a motion like a courtier, he indicated Lenya was to sit on one of them and Sirio on another. Luckily, the weather accommodated; it was warm for the time of year and the sun was brilliant. A perfect day to sit outside and enjoy a barbeque.

While Sirio and Lenya chatted, Aldo dug a circular hole in the ground with a small shovel he took from the truck, and placed smaller rocks carefully around it, building up a small wall. Lenya was entranced by the play of muscles across his back and down his arms as he worked. She noted his hair was twisted into a sort of bun secured in place with what looked like bone picks. As Aldo worked, tendrils loosened and curled around his face and neck. They must have tickled him because he harrumphed and stopped for a moment. Wiping his hands on his pants, he stretched his arms backward to release the topknot. A flame of red and auburn curls cascading down his back caught Lenya's eye. She couldn't control her sharp intake of breath.

Sirio, sitting nearby, slid his eyes towards her with a sly smile and nodded to himself. So, he thought, my dear Lenya is not immune to Aldo's charms after all.

After tying his hair back with a piece of leather and re-securing his topknot, Aldo filled in the bottom of the pit with the rounded stones and then with dried grasses and smaller twigs. Next, he measured and broke branches to place inside, one on top of the other like a miniature log cabin. He took a few steps away, nodded and smiled.

Two stout tree branches, forked on top, he secured firmly upright in the ground and then stood aside surveying his work, arched his back in a good stretch after so much bending and went into the forest again. Lenya heard a sharp crack and he came into the clearing with a sturdy but supple green branch he handed to her, indicating she was to peel off the bark. *Wow, he's making a very cool barbeque.*

Watching Aldo move around was more than sufficient entertainment for Lenya. She had to pull her attention away to help Sirio bring several different bottles of wine from his truck. *Do cavemen drink wine?* She thought of all the terrible stories about the white man introducing fire-water to the Native Americans and the resulting violence. But then, Lenya was sure Sirio wouldn't have brought the bottles if he thought it might be a problem. She came out on the deck with glasses as Sirio opened a bottle.

"We shall have some nicely chilled white wine for aperitif and then move to red with the meat—that is, if it's all right with the lady of the house?" Sirio bowed in Lenya's direction.

"Whatever the gentlemen desire is fine with me." *Okay, the three of them could play the courtly game. It reminded her of Andre and for a split second she felt a pang. But I'm trying the wines of Corsica, she mentally told Andre. As soon as she did, she felt warm. It was almost as if he approved of her Christmas celebration.*

Soon the fire was lit. Aldo added larger pieces of wood until it glowed. She felt the warmth on her face and arms as she curled up in her chair with her feet towards the blaze.

When the flames died down, Aldo motioned for the meat, then rubbed it with the herbs and garlic before threading it on the branch she'd peeled. He placed the branch with meat in between the forks of the two upright sticks and, with a sigh of accomplishment, sat down in his chair.

Sirio handed Aldo a glass of the wine. After he took a sip, he slapped his head and went over to the deck. Coming back with the potatoes he placed them in the center of the fire where the fat from the meat would drip on them.

Lenya brought out a platter of goat cheese and crackers accompanied by homemade salami from the open market to hold them while the meat cooked.

They sat munching and sipping wine as the haunch began to brown. Lenya inhaled deeply, the meat gave off a heady aroma of succulence as it sizzled in the heat.

Tom and Sophia sniffed and explored, then joined their humans in the warmth from the fire. Aldo took out his flute and played some melodies reminiscent of several local bird calls. He accompanied himself with rhythms tapped with his foot. She was astounded, as always, by the sophistication of the music he played from the small instrument.

Also astounding was the play of the fire on his hair, flame upon flame she thought. After completing his work, he freed it to fall past his shoulders. Lenya couldn't suppress a slight gasp. After her second glass of wine she began imagining her nose foraging through Aldo's curls as they trailed across his broad shoulders. By the time she finished her third glass she was wondering if his collar and cuffs matched. She mentally slapped herself—lately, a disturbing habit.

She turned to Sirio, time for some distraction. "I'm fascinated by the music he plays, it feels so organic...reminds me of something I can't remember. Do you know anything about it."

"Why don't you ask him?" Sirio suggested.

Lenya raised her eyebrows and turned. "Aldo," she asked in English, "where did you learn the music you play?"

He put the flute down and thought for a moment. *"E musica antica, una tradizione tramandata dal padre ai figli. Ma, ho imparato dal mio Maître."*

"Did you understand him, Lenya?" Sirio asked.

"Yes. It's ancient music usually passed from father to son. But he said he learned from his Maître? What or who is a Maître?"

"Simple definition, a master, a holy man as Aldo means. Let's leave it at that for the moment. And are you surprised he understood your question? You asked him in English."

"I didn't even realize which language I was speaking. Too much good wine...your fault Sirio."

She got a laugh back in response. She was about to ask another question, but Aldo was busy with his barbeque so she turned to Sirio. "Do you have any idea how old the music is?"

"It might date back to Neolithic Man." He turned and looked at Aldo who had picked up his flute once again, so at peace and contented with his fire, his music and his friends. "A few years ago, a music historian paid us a visit. He was interested in our polyphonic singers. I asked Aldo to come and play some of the songs of the clan. The historian was amazed. The tonal combinations were so ancient, he thought Aldo was probably playing the first music passed down through history...maybe thousands of years old...probably Neolithic." Sirio got up and refilled their glasses.

Aldo stopped playing to turn the meat... sip wine. She noted he twisted his hair into a tight roll behind his back before he got near the fire. There's something about his hands, so facile and knowing when he handles his hair. She couldn't put her finger on it, but she was entranced.

When Aldo picked up his flute again, he was accompanied by renewed sizzling of fresh fat dripping on the hot coals. Lenya's stomach growled in harmony. By now the wine had mellowed her and she couldn't stop her mind roving to a new take on the old saw—I don't know what the rest of the world is doing tonight—but for me, it can't be any better than this. She laughed to herself. *You rock Corsica!*

Sirio opened a bottle of red wine this time. She hadn't been aware so much time had passed as she noted two empty bottles of white wine on the deck.

Aldo stood in front of her holding out a steaming piece of meat dangling from the end of a small knife. He bowed and handed it to her with a lopsided grin. *"Signorina,"* he announced, "your dinner is...*prêt*... no... ready." As Lenya took the offering, she realized he'd started in Italian, went to English, threw in a word in French but finished in English again. She laughed in astonishment while he hacked off another piece of meat and repeated his performance for Sirio.

Sirio laughed. "There Lenya, you have your second surprise for the day. Aldo is learning English with me. When he was a boy, I often read to him in English and he learned many words, but then lost interest as he grew. He's been practicing for a few weeks now and is an amazingly adept student."

Before Lenya could ask more questions, conversation stopped as the three of them attacked the steaming pork with gusto. It was delicious and tender with the seasoning adding a perfect savory touch with a hint of wildness. They ate with fingers and knives, cutting and picking off pieces of the hot meat and stuffing it into their mouths as they licked dripping juice from their fingers.

Aldo showed her how to peel the crisp blackened skin off the potato and eat the steaming white inside with her knife. As the second bottle of red wine emptied, she was relieved to note Aldo drank like a gentleman and behaved like one as well. She, however, was a bit tipsy and didn't know if it was from the wine or the magic of the evening.

When they finished, Aldo insisted Lenya and Sirio sit by the fire with blankets wrapped around their shoulders against the evening chill.

"Je vous invite pour your dinner, *oggi* you sit and warm *é io..."* He gave up and looked around as if for help, then made motions like he was washing dishes. It might all have been spoken in a combination of languages, now including English, but the meaning was abundantly clear.

Tom and Sophia ate meat and potato scraps Aldo saved for them before he dumped the rest into the smoldering fire. He puttered around cleaning up the mess on the deck, taking empty wine bottles and plastic glasses to the trash. Lenya didn't register when he went into the cabin to wash and put away the utensils she had brought outside.

Once Aldo was inside for the first time, he looked around as if to memorize every detail. He gazed longingly upwards to the loft. He knew it was where she slept. Stepping on the first tread, he rubbed his hand up and down the banister, then turned around and went into the kitchen to finish cleaning.

Lazy and warm sitting around the dying embers outside, the smell of burning wood was as soporific as aromatherapy and soon Lenya and Sirio were dozing, heads nodding with contentment, food and wine.

When everything was put away, Aldo found the outside water spigot and a bucket to douse the fire. The abrupt sizzling of the fire dying and the loud sound of cracking rocks broke the spell.

In the midst of sputter and smoke, Lenya felt Aldo's hand on her arm as he helped her out of her chair and guided her safely into the cabin. She had to admit she was a bit wobbly in the legs. Note to self, no more than three glasses next time, she forgot Corsican wine was stronger than most.

Tom followed and once she was inside, Aldo and Sirio replaced the chairs on the deck, waved goodbye and climbed into the truck with Sophia's head stuck out of the open window. The truck coughed to life and, heading down the track, Lenya watched the night fold them in darkness long before the sound of the motor was no longer audible in the silent woods.

If Aldo had been alone with her, she would have wanted him to stay longer. Perhaps it was good Sirio had been there. Otherwise, she might have signaled she wanted more… something…although, when she thought about it… maybe not…

Lenya came back out on the deck with the blanket swaddling her, reluctant to let the evening end. As she inhaled the cool night air, it was vibrant with the snap of ozone and the promise of events to come and her shiver was not from the cold.

As she thought back to the evening, there had been a lot of conversation between the three of them. Aldo was not very vocal, but he contributed when he wanted and in an understandable way. It occurred to her his sparse conversation was probably the result of living alone for so long rather than an inability to express himself. It was clear he understood the entire conversation, no matter what language it had been in. His face, when he sat in the glow of the flames, spoke volumes of his pleasure to be with people again. She realized he looked much younger than she had previously thought.

I've really sold him short. He's complex... and certainly more intelligent than I could have imagined.

It was so like her, she mused. If someone was attracted to her, she assumed he must not be anything special. She wondered how those thoughts had come into her life? Being the younger twin? Following in her flamboyant sister's footsteps? It had always seemed she was the second choice. If they couldn't have Lotte, there was always good old Lenya. Andre had been the one exception.

As she looked at the night sky, the clarity of the stars again amazed her. *Because I hadn't seen them so bright before doesn't mean they don't exist like that.*

It was time to learn new things.

Chapter 40
Meeting The Family

Aldo had arrived every day since Christmas. It was now their usual routine and they slipped into it easily. New Year's Day Aldo appeared and they did Tai Chi together.

Afterwards, when she went to take a shower, he pointed to the forest and her. "Caminamos?" he asked. "Do you want ...walk?"

As she looked at him he made a walking motion with his fingers and then pointed at himself, Lenya and Tom. Sign language was really no longer necessary; but they often used it for fun rather than necessity. They had developed an odd combination of languages that served them well. She had picked up more French and Italian and he was quickly learning English..

"Let me get a few things," she put her palm up in a "stay" motion. He sat with Tom while she went into the cabin to grab her walking stick/mop handle and a warm jacket to tie around her waist. The shower could wait. He was right; it was a good day for a walk. As winter progressed, cold, rain and more snow would make walking difficult in the weeks to come.

Aldo led the way through the forest. She was able to keep up, but he kept looking back to make sure she was there, and if it was difficult going, he stopped to take her hand and help her.

After an hour, they came to a stream where he motioned her to sit down on a nearby rock, then silently gestured with a finger across his mouth, "Don't make any noise."

She sat quietly. He picked up Tom and handed him to her, indicating she should hold him in her arms. This time he made the "stay" motion to her, and slipped away into the woods, only to return holding a tiny fox. Tom growled and Lenya shushed him by tapping him on the muzzle. She took his leash out of her pocket and fastened it to his collar in case he slipped out of her arms. There was no way she was going to let his terrier instinct take over to harm this sweet baby fox.

Aldo sat close to her with the fox; she reached out to pet its soft fur. She looked at him and pointed to the fox with a lift of her shoulders in question, afraid to break the silence with words.

"Recuerde momma?" He asked.

"Yes, I do," she whispered. Of course, she remembered the little one's mother.

The pup's fur was a bright orange, tiny black down marked the tips of its ears. Lenya yearned to take it in her hands and put her cheek against its baby softness. But she sat making sure Tom was securely clutched in her arms. He seemed to understand it was a baby and paid no attention to it.

A few minutes later momma fox slipped out of the underbrush and came over to stand by Aldo. Tom growled a bit at the larger fox but quieted when Lenya tapped him on the nose again. She could swear the fox gave him a dirty look. He gave a snuffle and half growl. Typical terrier, had to have the last word. Then he shut up. Lenya felt around in her pocket and came up with two dog biscuits she passed to Aldo. This time she wasn't empty handed for a visit with his friend.

Aldo gave one to Tom and broke the other in half, giving a piece each to momma and baby. Momma knew what to do with it, but baby dropped it on the forest floor only to have it snatched by momma. I guess motherly love only goes so far, Lenya mused as the two red creatures disappeared back into the woods, the kit bouncing with an unsteady gait behind momma fox. When Aldo had leaned over to feed his friends, she couldn't help noticing the hair on his chest was almost the same color as the fox fur...and it looked as soft.

He took her by the arm, and motioned to continue their walk. Lenya was anxious to see what was next on this journey.

When they came to the top of a rise he pointed off to the right. She looked but saw only more mountains and boulders, but after her eyes adjusted to the rock shapes peeking out of the shrubbery, she was able to make out a veritable forest of menhirs. They were standing almost in military formation on the side of a slope. She recalled his warning of the one she had found toppled near her grotto. Pointing at the array she asked "Evil gods...*peligrosi?*"

He shook his head. "No, beautiful Dia... *Dia mia...é...*soldiers?" He took her hand again and guided her on the trek over the rocks to visit with his goddess and her warriors.

The menhirs faced another range of mountains across a long valley. She was astounded such a breathtaking view existed so close to her cabin and she had never seen it before. The guide books placed most of the menhirs in the southern part of the island. As she looked down, she saw a tiny lake below, brilliant turquoise, lighter around the edges and dark in the center. The air had a different smell, a bit of salt from the ocean, mixed with the odd fragrance of the immortelle growing nearby. But it was mixed with something else as well. The scent was familiar, and when she looked far down below into the valley there it was, a field of purple lavender.

She thought she could smell the sun on the rocks as she inhaled hot dry air, different from the moist cooling breeze blowing up from the ocean.

"Grazie, Aldo, grazie per questa..." She couldn't finish the sentence. How do you thank someone for showing you history...mystery...beauty? She clasped her hands to her chest and inhaled again. No words could express her joy at such a view. She walked over to the closest of the standing rocks and laid her hand on the weather worn façade, touching the remnants of a face carved on the rounded top of the stone.

She thought the sense of familiarity was déjà vu until she remembered actually doing the same thing the first week she was on the island—the very moment she realized she had to leave the tour and stay. Once again she felt thrill go through her as she touched something carved thousands of years ago.

Aldo looked at her seriously.*"E la mia famiglia que gli ha facciando...* my family ...did these." She pulled her hand back as tiny hairs stood up on her arms. It was a blinding recognition of a universal connection. For a moment she couldn't catch her breath. My god! He really is a Neolithic remnant. He's telling me he's descended from the people who made these statues?

She had to know—where was his family now? "Aldo, *dove e...*" she pointed at his chest "...*famiglia?*"

He turned to her. *"Tutti morti. Io sono l'ultimo...*my...no, I—the last."

His truth was there. He was alone. Everyone else... dead. Sirio had told her this, but the expression on Aldo's face gave the words such powerful emotion...her breath caught in her throat. At least Lenya had people... friends... someone she could call... talk to...if she was lonely... most of the time.

"E la sua moglie? Dove?"

"Morte. Piu de un anni fa." His wife was dead, about a year ago. Again, she had known he was a widower, but the pain on his face told her more than the simple fact.

Oh heavens, his wife died about the same time Andre did. She reached over, took his hand and patted his arm. Then she started to cry. *"Il mio esposo...anche morte...*the same time."

He put his arms around her. Grief was shared, as they stood together on top of a mountain surrounded by ancient monuments to long forgotten gods and goddesses.

She handed him a Kleenex from a pack she had in her pocket and he looked at her, wondering what to do with such a thing. Realizing his problem, she took one herself and wiped her tears, then blew her nose. He did the same, and put the damp paper scrap in his pocket when he finished.

On the way back, he took them on a different path. This part of the forest was dense and filled with pines needles carpeting the ground for them, softer than rocks but slippery. It was getting to be late afternoon and she knew it would soon be dark. She hoped he didn't expect this to be an overnight trip. Her idea of camping was at least a Motel 6.

They made their way to a small clearing. Rocks were piled in a mound at first glance looked like a slide. Closer, Lenya realized the rocks were placed in a pattern—smaller stones filling in holes between larger ones to create walls, and on top, a huge rectangular stone. She couldn't imagine how a primitive people could have placed such a massive piece on top of the structure below. It must have taken many men with a lot of muscle to lug such a heavy boulder around, let alone lift it into position. It's a necropolis, she realized with a start. Neolithic. She had seen photos of them in the guide books.

Aldo took her to the front opening of the small dark man-made cave. He pointed to the dark interior, *"Famiglia, tribu, moglie...tutti."* The final resting place of his family, his wife, the tribe, everyone.

Her heart was beating so hard it seemed determined to escape from her chest.

He had brought her to meet his family.

Chapter 41
Over The Threshold

Back at the cabin, Aldo escorted Lenya to the deck and left without a word. She was surprised. She thought she might invite him inside for something to eat, but he turned and walked off—not even his usual wave or smile. Maybe it was too emotional for him? It was understandable. To be so alone in the world must be terrifying.

Alone now too, she stood on the deck for a moment, silent and staring out into the dense trees and brush. The mist from the low clouds was heavy on her and she touched her hair, surprised to find it wet. She hugged herself and gave an involuntary shiver. As soon as the sun was gone and the mist came in, the temperature dropped ten to twenty degrees. It went from lovely to dismal in no time and tonight, it suited her mood.

Tom sat close to her ankle looking with her into the woods. He always sat in an odd Jack Russell manner with his hind legs off to the side. Thank goodness for Tom, she thought, he keeps me from going out of my mind with loneliness. But it would be nice to have a slightly bigger companion in bed. She laughed to herself as she went inside. Maybe I'm ready for a little more horny snuggling. It's been a while.

She opened her computer to find an e-mail from Terrence. Speaking of horny snuggling. They had been e-mailing as he made his way across Asia, and she knew he was due to arrive back home in Los Angeles.

At first glance it didn't look like an e-mail from him, not his usual two or three lines. Breezy. Funny and to the point.

He never pushed her, but always made sure she knew he was thinking of her. It was a nice touch. She kept her e-mails to him in the same light-hearted tone. This one looked very different.

BevHlsGamaster:

Hey Babe, how are things?

It's been difficult here.

'member the woman I was living with? Seems she didn't marry the guy after all while I was away. They had a fight—he knocked her around and she split...still had the key to my place and when I got home, é voilá, there she was—black eye and all! ... not a pleasant surprise.

After an hour or so of pissed off conversation on my end, I relented and said she could stay for a few weeks until she found her own place; but you know how that goes... I'm three days back and she wants to cozy up permanently— guess she figures an old disinterested guy with a few bucks is better than a broke stoned young one with anger management problems.

I'm not up for it and playing a dead hand.

The time you and I had together showed me what I really want in a woman— the sex was fabulous, but companionship even better. Am I getting to be an old fart? Anyway, no pressure babe... wanted to keep you current on local complications.

Any chance you'll be coming back to the USA in the near future? I hear the last book is going gangbusters. Yeah! One for the good guys!

How are things going with you and your caveman? I'm bummed I didn't get a chance to see him. I don't want to hear you've given up society and moved into his cave with him. Tom will miss his fancy gourmet biscuits...☺

Miss you! T.

Lenyascribe:

Hey to you big T! Looks like you have a little mess on your hands, but I've faith in you to solve it. All is well here, had Christmas dinner cooked by Sirio and my local neighborhood "caveman"—sanglier no less! ...built a lovely barbeque in the clearing...

Tom sends you a big sloppy kiss. The book is coming along, need lots more research but plot moving pretty well.

Stay cool this new year! Lenya

Okay, maybe I could have been a little more familiar—more— lovey? Nah!

She read Terrence's e-mail for a second time with some relief. He hadn't found other women on his trip, but there was a mess at home he had to clean up—or not. Her attention was focused on Aldo, she really didn't want to deal with Terrence or any possibility of a future relationship.

She opened up the file for her book. Her heart wasn't in it. Without Aldo around, she couldn't seem to gather her concentration to write.

She played spider solitaire for a while, checked out what was on satellite television—the usual hundreds of channels in a myriad of languages—none of which interested her. She punched buttons on the remote... how bizarre is my life? Here I sit, in the middle of a plethora of mass communication—satellites, the internet, computers and cell phones—can't work 'cause I miss a...a...caveman?

As soon as she thought it, she realized she no longer thought of Aldo as a "caveman." She was beginning to see him in his complexities and understand their cultural differences. But it was a challenge for her to figure out, even to herself, how she could refer to him. He was certainly more than a friend. Not a lover, but, deep inside, she knew what was to come, no matter how hard she tried to deny—perhaps even avoid it.

Chapter 42

Friends Lost

It was three days before she saw Aldo again. He walked up while she was doing Tai Chi. When she motioned for him to join in he shook his head and sat on the edge of the deck, taking Tom into his arms.

She sat next to him. *"Que successo?"* "What's up?" she asked.

He reached behind his back and produced two fox tails, one large and one small; fashioned together into...something? She was shocked. His pet fox and her baby were dead? Could he have killed them...and made...a gift? As soon as the thought passed her mind she knew it couldn't be, the fox was his beloved companion.

She raised her hands palms up in question.

He shook his head. *"Orso... mangiagli... laschati solo questi."*

Tears filled her eyes. The two foxes had been eaten...by a bear? Only the tails and bones were left, nothing to eat on them.

He pointed toward the cabin, *"trope persone, orsi...* hungry...too many people, bears no much...eat." The encroachment of civilization hurt wildlife everywhere—even in Connecticut as she remembered the rail thin coyotes she often saw in her back yard.

He handed her the two bushy tails and she reluctantly took them in her hand.

"... buona fortuna ... ponga en cazu." She had trouble understanding, his speech had more dialect, accents and pain entwined in it, but she made out "good luck" and "put in the house." As she inspected the forlorn remains of the creatures, she saw he had fashioned them into a talisman. There were three images carved from bone: momma and baby fox, and a bear.

The carvings were strung with feathers on leather thongs; another thong with sea shells bound them to the tails. It wasn't as ghoulish as she feared. And after all, they were dear friends remembered fondly. She pictured the kit fox, so small in his big hands when he proudly showed it off to her, and the momma fox, so trusting, pressing against his leg in companionship. Nature could be so damn cruel sometimes, but it was wilderness … death was as common as life.

She accepted the two tails, and took him by the hand, leading him into the cabin. Holding the gift up in the air, she gestured where he would like them placed. He looked around the house. He studied the fireplace, went over and inspected the rock fascia and the mantelpiece. One of the rocks protruded to create a natural hook; he took the tails and fastened them there. *"…erano amici Lenya, i loro spiriti proteggere voi e la vostra casa"* They were friends and their spirits now protect you…and your house." He didn't add he hoped these friendly spirits watched over her when he wasn't around.

She wondered if the bear fetish was to loan her its strength, similar the Native American belief.

"Grazie Aldo, I will keep their memories close to my heart." She gestured towards the couch, indicating he was to sit, and as soon as he did, Tom jumped up and curled into a tight ball in his lap to share his grief. Maybe Tom had liked the little foxes too.

She knew Aldo was sad. The mother fox had been his companion, like Tom. It must be lonely back at his home she thought, now his friend was gone. He seemed to perk up a bit sitting on her couch with Tom in his lap. We all need companionship.

After a while, Aldo began playing his flute. She went to her computer. He watched her work in a silence broken only by the soft melodies he played. No words necessary. It was pleasant to have him nearby. She realized she had never invited him in the cabin before.

His presence was calming, easier for her to concentrate. With Aldo and Tom near, she realized she felt at peace. It was something she had refused to acknowledge. She was not one of those women who needed a man to complete her, but he added a special quality to her life.

The fog rolling in over the deck muted and softened the colors of the trees outside. It looks like an impressionist painting, a particularly personal artists view of life smoothed into the essence of their vision. Inhaling the woody scent of the cabin, she found it now highlighted with a soft odor of male, Neolithic style, nicely blended with notes of pine, immortelle and lavender. And she recognized an intense feeling of joy: Where she was, who she was, and who she was with.

Her fingers sped over the keyboard in wild rhythms of creativity.

When dusk came, Aldo left without a word, blending into the mist as she watched through the window.

Chapter 43
The Artist Emerges

The next day Aldo walked onto the deck and up to the door. He stood tall, a gentleman proudly awaiting his invitation to enter. The sun behind him shined through his hair like a halo of dark copper tinged with twenty-four carat gold. *Hmmm, no braid today.* Even his beard seemed to glitter with touches of brilliant metals. It was a decided counterpoint to his angular and very masculine features.

Lenya almost gasped. He wasn't handsome in the way of movie stars or male models, plastic surgery to fix noses, raise cheekbones, butt implants, gym molded abs, pumped up biceps. No, he was simply male, the beauty of man in its most basic and primal form.

She had begun to accept how civilized he was, in his own way and within his own time and culture It was not easy for her to bridge the gap of a lifetime of prejudices to truly understand and accept that other cultures could be as civilized as her own. Perhaps even more so—in ways she had not known before.

Understanding required an open mind. Intricate. Especially for someone born and educated into the Anglo tradition of arrogance, secure in the knowledge there was only one right way. Their way. Andre, and accepting his French sensibilities, had been her first step towards opening her mind. Her journey to understand Aldo might require a leap to bridge the gap between them.

Feeling her heart surge with pleasure at the sight of him, she opened the door and invited him in.

The night before, lying sleepless in bed, she had an inspiration. Now she was anxious to put it to the test.

During the days he visited, he sat on the sofa, playing occasional music on his flute while she worked. She didn't want him bored, to lose interest in staying close to her. He was a natural artist, she was positive when she remembered his use of light and shadow with her camera.

She indicated he sit at the dining table next to a stack of white paper and a plastic pack holding a variety of markers. Then she added a few pencils. "I thought you might like to use these." She had remembered his carving—Dia, his flute and the talismans he made from the fox tails and wondered what he would do with paper and some color.

Amused, he picked up the pencils to try on the paper. At first he ignored the rest. He didn't seem interested in the colored markers until she picked several up and made random curlicues to show how they worked. For a few moments he was thoughtful, then his expression changed to pleasure.

"These are gifts—*regali*—for you," she said. His smile widened as if they were gifts of great magnificence.

She thought back to the nosegays of flowers, bouquets of greens, the Venus carving he made for her. The fruits he brought—meat for Christmas. He seldom arrived empty handed, and she had given him nothing but suspicion. She felt like the Dutch giving the natives twenty-four dollars worth of trashy beads for the Island of Manhattan.

Aldo held up the paper, almost measuring its density before examining the colored markers, taking the tops on and off, on and off, one at a time. He tested colors on his hands. Lenya left him to his discoveries and went back to work. For the rest of the morning his flute was silent.

Later, when she fixed a lunch of bread, cheese and fruit, she noticed pages filled with colors. She was reluctant to disturb the works in progress by looking closer so she pushed a plate of food and a glass of wine towards him on the table and left.

Hours later, the cabin was getting dark as the sun fell low behind the trees. She moved to put on the lights and passed the table. Aldo was still at work and so intent he didn't stop as she looked over his shoulder.

The table was filled with riotous color and incredible images. Birds and flowers filled some pages; others were populated by creatures of the woods. A raccoon family sedately washed their food in a stream while deer watched from the other side. An eagle in flight had a small animal in its mouth. The one that caught her attention was a secluded glen with two foxes, a mother guarding a smaller one. Both momma and kit seemed to be filled with life again as they looked out from his drawing.

Some of the drawings were unfinished, simple lines clearly conveying images. Others more detailed in certain areas as if he wanted to make sure some of the images were obvious while other parts of the same drawing might only be sketchy background. It was as if he wanted to put down as much as he could as fast as he could, anxious to try and draw whatever came into his mind lest he forget.

Hunters chased their prey across several pages, rendered in the ochre, brown and black of cave paintings. Another was of a campfire, people sitting around staring into the flames. They were dressed in the same rags and skins as Aldo. Special attention had been given to one woman, young, slim and beautiful with dark hair. She wore a floral dress in an old style. The young woman caught her eye and Aldo saw her looking. He turned and pointed, *"Raina...moglie...morte... picatto."*

Lenya remembered *"moglie,"* strange Italian word for "wife." This drawing was of those he loved, those no longer here. She related to his need to re-create memories. She wished she had the skill to bring Andre back like this. Words were always her way; she spoke to Andre, knowing full well he was no longer there. She had his cell phone so she could hear his voice, dear French accent requesting a message or a call back.

That night, Aldo didn't leave. After dinner, exhausted by creativity, he fell asleep on the couch, his precious drawings spread out in front of him on the long coffee table. He was careful to make no move towards her; he had no intention of spoiling the progress he was making. After all, he was finally sleeping inside.

Painting might have entertained him for a while, but he wasn't about to be sidetracked from his purpose. This woman was going to be his mate. He was more sure of it than ever.

She went upstairs as usual to her bed in the loft. All night long she could hear him breathing and turning. It was good to hear the sounds of another human being. It made her feel vital. A part of something larger? Not so alone in the world? She wondered if he felt the same. Is this the way he felt in the clan? *Do I snore?*

The next day she was going to Calvi for shopping. Before she left, she turned to Aldo, *"Je vais au Calvi maintenant, voulez vous m'acompagner?"* Would he like to go with her? He had arrived Christmas Eve with Sirio in his truck. He wasn't put off by automobiles.

He looked at her for a moment and then back at the cabin where his drawings and paper were spread out on the table. He looked reluctant, like he was longing to get back to drawing.

She sighed. "You can stay here, *si vous voulez,* you don't have to come." She learned if she accompanied her English with some sign language and occasional words in French or Italian he understood her perfectly.

He looked relieved and bent down towards Tom. "...and yes, you can keep Tom with you for company." He grinned at her as he picked up the dog and held him protectively in the crook of his arm. While he didn't speak much, she didn't mind as long as he was with her.

The city was almost empty, most of the shops closed for the winter months and waiting for the tourists to return. After making her purchases, Lenya decided to have lunch at one of the restaurants around the harbor, take the time to enjoy the clear air warming in the sun. She chose the busiest, assuming it was the best one since the people left in town were mainly locals.

She was sorry she hadn't called Sirio to join her, and as soon as she had the inspiration, dialed his number on her cell. When she heard his voice, she was glad she had called.

"Lenya, it's a pleasure to hear you. What are you doing this precious day?"

"I'm in Calvi at the port and about to have lunch. Are you able to join me—I can have an aperitif while I wait for you." It wasn't a long drive from the winery to the port.

"Absolutely! I'm bored—tired of sitting waiting for visitors who don't come. I'll be there before you order your second Kir."

"How did you know I'll order a Kir?"

"Because it is your favorite. I'm not psychic. Also, I have a small present for you."

"Sirio, you know your company is present enough. I'll be at the place that turns into the disco at night, outside enjoying the weather and admiring the view across the water."

"I'm on my way."

True to his word, Sirio arrived while there was some Kir left in her glass. He was dressed in his old flannel shirt, jean jacket and boots. He waved and smiled as he came to her table. "See how anxious I was to see you? I didn't even change my clothes. Since the tourists are gone, there is no one to impress... you take me as I am." He thrust a wrinkled paper bag into her hands.

She could feel the shape of a bottle and peeked inside. "Oh Sirio, thank you, it's my favorite." There was a bottle of orange wine.

"It's the new vintage...finished bottling yesterday. I hope you approve."

"I can't wait to try it." She put it back into the bag and stuffed it in her large shopping bag.

"How are things at home, Lenya?"

"Everything is fine...my book is accepted and I'm doing some last minute tinkering on it. It means enough money to remain here as long as I want." She did not mention Aldo was now sleeping in the cabin.

A young man arrived with menus. "Hello Sirio, good to see you here. Nice to see you dressed for the occasion." He poked Sirio in the arm and then bent down to give him a hug. "I forgive you since you have a beautiful woman to decorate the patio."

"Lenya, this is Armand, the son of my good friend. I remember this kid since he was in diapers and now he's fresh with me." The two men smiled at each other.

"I see your taste in women is improving." Armand winked at Lenya.

"Don't mind him Lenya, this mere youth obviously has an eye for the ladies...at least the attractive ones."

Lenya laughed.

"What's best today? I want something fresh and wonderful—your mother at her finest." Sirio poked back at the young man.

"We have a cous-cous with lamb and chicken she made this morning. It's been popular, let me see if there's any left." He turned and went back into the restaurant.

"His mother is the best cook in the city. As usual you have made the right choice, my dear." Sirio leaned in and gave Lenya a friendly hug.

Armand returned. "We have cous-cous and also some *moules* I highly recommend either or both."

"Not a wonderful combination to have together, but let's have an order of each, that is, if it's all right with my companion."

"It's fine, whatever you want. You know I will eat almost anything." Lenya was pleased with herself. It had been a good idea to call Sirio.

"Armand, if you could serve the *moules* first with a nice demi of white wine, and after the cous-cous another demi, this one rosé. But please, give us some time in between the two to digest a bit." Sirio liked to take charge. Armand smiled and saluted as he went to the kitchen.

Sirio sighed and stretched as he sat back in the chair. He turned and looked around the port to the citadel and across to Lumio. It was warm in the sun with a gentle breeze off the water making the temperature perfect for sitting outside. "Here we are, another day alive to enjoy this isle of beauty." Lenya could almost hear him purr. "And how are you getting on with my friend Aldo?"

"You certainly come right to the point."

"We both know he is in love with you. It is obvious, isn't it? The question is—what you feel in return?"

"I honestly don't know. He's very attractive. I enjoy his company, but we are from such different worlds...minds... experiences. I can't get my head around the way he has lived, how he was brought up."

"There are times in life when you have to take things on faith. Trust to your heart, your instincts." He turned and looked toward the harbor again. She could tell he was collecting his thoughts. "You must understand about the clan. They were not savages...not by any means. They may have lived in a crude or...perhaps a better word is 'ancient' manner, but they had a sophisticated society. Their children were carefully educated... in the old ways. They were a religious and righteous people, perhaps not as those terms are known now, but as they were in distant times."

He took a sip of wine and leaned over to pat her hand. "Aldo is cultured in a manner unknown today. His knowledge about many things—nature, seasons, holistic healing, herbal medicines, spirituality and sensuality, all the ancient sacred knowledge passed down through the centuries. He's lived and survived on instinct, as his clan had done since time beyond memory."

He took out his pipe and started to fill it with tobacco. Lenya recognized it as his way to have some time to think about how he wanted to express himself. "I always trust his feelings. The clan trained him as both Maître and Signadori, a kind of shaman—consort of the goddess. He is a holy man, recognized as such not only by the clan, but those left who respect, even adhere to the old ways." He stopped for a moment while Armand set a basket of crusty bread in front of them.

"While he might not have much experience with different women because of the small population of the clan, he has the ancient knowledge...the mysteries." Puffing on his pipe for a moment, he looked off to the far mountains. There was a very slight upward turn at the corner of his mouth. "Yes, I would not be concerned, I think he knows exactly what he is doing."

Lenya squirmed in her chair. This conversation was not easy for her; she found it difficult to talk about her feelings, her emotions. The touchy-feely stuff was never her forte. But she wasn't ready to change the topic. "You understand I have to go back to my life; to leave? Someday. I don't know when, but the day will come. I cannot be here for Aldo in the long term and I don't want to deceive him, to mislead him into thinking I will stay in Corsica forever. No matter how sophisticated he might be, if he is looking for a mate—I'm not it. He will be alone again when I leave, and I know he wants a...a...family? I see it in his drawings, in his face. If we go on like this, it will not be fair to him when I must go."

Sirio saw her distress, but he also had faith in his friend. "Pardon my asking, but has he made love to you yet?"

Lenya almost fell off her chair. Her face began to flame red.

"I'm sorry for asking. I see this has made you uncomfortable." He couldn't suppress a crooked grin. "The reason I'm asking is because Aldo, as a consort of the goddess, has been extremely well trained in erotica—sexual secrets. The clan believed when a man and woman join together, the woman becomes a vessel for the goddess to...to share her pleasure. When the woman achieves orgasm, the goddess is with her, sharing her power."

This was more information than Lenya wanted. Not only was she blushing, she also felt a surge of arousal. Luckily, Armand arrived with the *moules* in time to end the conversation. As he set the steaming bowl piled with mussels and golden broth fragrant with saffron between them, she managed to gain control of her wildly running imagination. It all entailed making passionate love...forget love...wild sex...with Aldo... and what the hell secrets was Sirio talking about?

Get a grip Lenya, stop this fantasizing...do it now! She managed to breathe again, and felt the red receding from her face. *Crap, this was not what I needed to hear.*

There was no way she was going to speak about sex and what she and Aldo were or were not doing. "The *moules* look wonderful, I'm so glad you thought to order them." She picked up one of the shining black shells, and, as she had been taught by her husband, ate the *moules* using the empty shell as pinchers. Her pink tongue curled over the succulent golden flesh as she slurped them into her mouth.

Sirio was amused. She obviously had no idea of how sexual her attack on the *moules* was. He thought Aldo would probably have lost his mind seeing her dexterous tongue grasp and suck the small orange and black creatures with such authority.

They ate in silence. She felt her composure returning. Note to self, do not talk about sex with this man.

The cous-cous was as delicious as the *moules*. Sirio was right, they were really not a great combination, but enough time passed between courses to allow proper digestion. All through the meal, she couldn't help but notice the snarky smiles Sirio was having trouble suppressing. Damn the man, he knows something's up no matter what I say. *Damn him!*

Lenya had other topics on her agenda she wanted to discuss and she was desperate to deflect the conversation away from Aldo and his sex education. "Are there any of the standing stones in this area?"

"Not so many I know of. They are mainly in the south, but we do have dolmens here. If you check the guide books, they will tell you where to find them. I suggest going to Sarténe if you want to see dolmens and menhirs—not a pretty place, but there is supposed to be a good museum nearby, and several places to see the best alignments." He placed a sugar cube in his mouth and sipped his coffee around it.

"Why do you say the city is not pretty?"

"It's dreary, especially this time of year. No tourists. Most of the city is closed. In the old days it was referred to as 'the city filled with demons' because of its bloody history."

"What was that about?"

"There were many vendettas, blood feuds. So many, in fact, the feuding families put their main doors on the second floor so they could defend the houses like castles. Can you imagine having to climb a ladder every time you brought food or water into the house?"

"Sounds pretty creepy to me." She rolled some bread crumbs around the table. "When's the best time to go there?"

"I'd save the trip for the spring. It can rain and snow in the winter. I know you don't like nasty narrow roads winding up the mountains... odd, by the way, since you live on one of worst of them."

"I fell in love with the cabin...decided the road was a minor inconvenience."

"Women!" Sirio figured was enough of an explanation.

As they relaxed with an espresso, she wanted to talk about Aldo again, but sex was off limits. "Did you know Aldo is an artist?"

"No, not exactly, but I know he's very creative and makes beautiful things with his hands." He paused for a moment and looked at her out of the corner of his eye. "As a matter of fact, I imagine he can do the most amazing things with his hands." There was no way he could stop himself from enjoying her flush red again. It said a lot. "Aldo's a man of many talents." The devil made him say it—no chance to hide his smirk. He tried gallantly by sipping his espresso through his sugar cube, but the tiny cup was too small to be a good hiding place. It took all his will power not to laugh out loud, but he didn't want to embarrass Lenya further. Finally taking pity on her, he continued in a different vein. "Now I think of it, I've seen things he's carved. Yes, he has many talents and a good eye for beauty in all living things." The devil was much too powerful to resist, but at least he winked at her this time.

She willed herself not to blush. "I sat him down at my dinner table the other day with paper, pencils and colored markers. He stayed there for hours, until well after dark. You can't imagine the beautiful pictures he drew."

"Actually, I can. He's not had much of an opportunity to express what he has inside his head. The clan had little paper or paints. Early man needed no such things. They made do with pigments from nature and stone walls. I don't recall him ever being interested in doing wall paintings and I imagine he must have greatly enjoyed the freedom of having such tools as you made available to him."

"It was amazing. There were things he drew from memory—the clan, his wife, his parents...even mama and baby fox." Her face lit up talking about him.

Sirio saw in her excitement feelings she was reluctant to admit to herself. She obviously had pride both in Aldo and his work. He speculated she might have seen his skill as a kind of confirmation of his worth, a validation of her feelings for him.

Sirio settled the bill over Lenya protesting she had invited him to lunch. He would have none of it. "It was my great pleasure to see you my dear one, and for the bit of torture I subjected you to, it is also my pleasure to pay." And with that, he gave her a hug and got into his truck.

As he drove back to the winery he was deep in thought. Perhaps, no matter how strange the melding of their two personalities might seem, his friend might have truly found his mate.

Chapter 44
Lenya Home From Calvi

Lenya pulled up to the cabin late in the day to find Aldo sitting on the deck with Tom. He had some papers on his lap and was scrutinizing the foliage near the deck. She had bought him presents—different size pads of sketch paper, a set of watercolors and several art books, two with illustrated instructions on the human body, light and perspective. He appeared very pleased as she handed her purchases to him. While she unloaded groceries from the SUV, he sat immobile on the deck, holding the gifts in his arms for a few minutes before going inside and spreading his treasures out across the dining room table. He was so busy examining his gifts he forgot to help her unload the Rav.

She put the groceries away, and told him about calling Sirio and meeting him for lunch. They both wished Aldo had come too. He nodded indifferently. Lenya saw he was obviously not at all sorry about staying home when he nodded at the pictures spread out on every surface around the cabin.

They sat on the couch after dinner and he showed her the pieces he worked on while she was gone. She noticed Tom now chose to sleep on his lap. So, you fickle beast, you've chosen him over me. We'll see who feeds you treats from now on.

Aldo slept in the house again and Tom slept at his feet instead of hers.

Lenya lay sleepless in her solitary bed in the loft wondering exactly what Sirio meant—how Aldo was trained? Consort of the goddess? What did that entail and what old secrets were passed down on how to please a woman? To give Dia power... ecstasy?

Dwelling on those thoughts kept her up most of the night tossing.

◦✇◦

Downstairs on the couch, Aldo dreamt. Stories he could tell in pictures moved across his mind like the ancient hunters chasing game. They wouldn't be forever pictures, like the ones on the walls of a cave, but he could tell Lenya who he was, tell her about the clan, and most of important of all, how much he desired and loved her—and not only for Dia's sake.

⚒

Three days later, Sirio's truck came up the drive while Lenya and Aldo were finishing up Tai Chi.

Sophia was the first to visit, followed by Sirio carrying a stout looking plastic bag.

"Hello my friends. I've brought you a gift—a favorite of Lenya's, I know." He fished a dripping net bag filled with black shining *moules* out of the plastic one. "I hope you know how to cook them my dear." He had a mischievous twinkle in his eye as he looked towards Aldo. If it was a joke, Aldo didn't seem to know the punch line.

"Thank you so much, you know they are my favorite." Lenya looked delighted. "If I remember correctly, I sauté shallots, parsley and garlic in butter, add some white wine and drop the cleaned mussels in when the both reaches a rolling boil., take them out when they open and serve with crunchy baguettes? Sound right?"

Sirio nodded his approval. "Exactly my dear. You know everything."

"I wish I did, but having a French husband taught me a little about cooking. I'll have to go on-line for the proportions, it's been a while since I've cooked these little guys." She took the bag and went inside to put them in the refrigerator, leaving the two men chatting companionably on the deck.

When she came back, she looked at Sirio, "I have fresh baguettes and all the rest of the ingredients. How about staying for lunch?"

"Thank you for the kind invitation, but I have to visit the finance department in Calvi and since they keep typical bureaucrat hours, I must catch them before they break for lunch. I leave you both to enjoy the *moules* at your pleasure." He whistled to Sophia to get into the truck and they were off.

Lenya eyed Aldo and tilted her head in question, "... *moules* for lunch...*maintenant?*"

"*Ah oui, bien sur, j'aime les moules.*"

An hour later, Lenya had finely chopped parsley, garlic and shallots sautéing in butter with a little salt and pepper. A few minutes more and the mussels were open and ladled into big bowls next to chunks of warm baguettes.

Another ten minutes and Aldo thought he could no longer contain himself. He was watching Lenya prise the plump orange, black and yellow bodies free and pop them into her waiting mouth with an empty set of the shiny black shells she used as pincers. The problem was the shape of the *moules,* smooth and open, rimmed with a delicate dark tracery like a beckoning vagina. That alone was enough to make him squirm in his current state of deprivation.

But nothing could have prepared him for the sight of Lenya's deft pink tongue teasing the dangling *moules* as she slurped them into her mouth with gusto. He found himself twitching in his seat as he watched her, tongue darting in and out, *moules* submissive under her ministrations, and he, imagining all the wonderful things she could do with such a facile organ...and what he could do to her *moule* if given half a chance. He tore his eyes away and couldn't suppress a groan.

She looked at him with head tilted. Is he in pain? she wondered.

He was looking down in his bowl where the damned offending mussels rested in their saucy pool. It seemed they were all angled toward him with soft satiny plump lips wide open to display the delicious morsel hidden inside. As he looked at them, they reminded him of...of...never mind. He was finding it difficult to breath and had to catch his breath.

Had Sirio seen her do this—old rascal?

Then he laughed out loud as he pictured Sirio driving away in the sure knowledge of the torture he'd inflicted on his good friend. I'll get even with him someday, he vowed and the spell was broken. He could breathe again.

He plowed into the remaining mussels...all the while making sure to keep his eyes as far away from Lenya as possible.

Chapter 45
At Home

The next week Aldo slept five out of seven nights in the cabin. He left early every morning, came back later in the day and stood in the door. Lenya always invited him in. The days he didn't come, she waited for him. When he failed to appear by lunch time, she was angry at herself for missing him.

On the seventh night, he didn't stay in the cabin, but went back to the casteddu, to his home to sleep. He knew she cared for him, it was obvious when he returned each day. The softness in her eyes spoke to his heart, but she kept some unseen wall between them. Was it fear?

What could she fear from him now? Didn't she know him enough to understand he cared for and protected her? The more he thought about her, the more determined he became. He would not give up, he was so close. Looking out the window of the casteddu, he saw the mist moving to cover the top of the mountain, shrouding Venus, hiding her up in her sky perch as it dampened everything below.

His sleep was fitful, tossing in the now unfamiliar skins. He dreamt of a velvet black night pierced by the light of Venus, hanging brilliant above the mountain. The night was also pierced by needing to understand what made Lenya hold back, what she wanted from him. What signals was he missing?

In his dream, he saw a shadow, a figure, push open his door.

A figure enters. Closer, he sees a woman, tall and slender. He senses her strength—muscular shoulders and arms. Naked save for a gauzy drape, her nakedness is worn with dignity and pride. Shocked for a moment within his dream, he knows her, she is his goddess, come to demand his gift...his energy, demand he make good his vows. He turns and thrashes about, speaking aloud in the ancient tongue.

Closer, she moves to him, and touches his beard. It is as if both lightening and ice caress him. He sees her face—it is Lenya, come to him as supplicant, and as lover—Dia's willing vessel. Joy fills him, his heart grows in his chest as he reaches for her. Elusive, she is no longer close, but once again at the window, her back to him, her body clear in glowing silhouette against the night sky.

His yearning for her is overpowering. He desires to begin the sacred marriage... to massage her feet with scented oils...run his tongue along her spine as he inhales the fragrance of her. He can almost feel the firmness of her body under his hands as they flex in the hallowed massage. The rite is about to begin.

He moves to lie to her right side, as he should to begin the ritual of love, pleased his skills as consort are finally called into use once again. And then, she is no longer there. Again she has fled.

He turns in his dream, his voice hoarse as he calls her name, "Dia," then "Lenya."

She is with him once more...the gauze is gone...her beauty unveiled. He tries to bring her close, yearning to press his face into her triangle, tease her with his tongue until the lily of her sex opens fully...to let him pierce her with his love... push against the secret place inside until she releases her sacred nectar, the goddess' gift of heavenly power. He is now both supplicant and consort. His hands grasp for her but find emptiness...he sees her, beyond reach. As he watches, she changes from Dia, strong features, dark, long flowing tangled hair, to Lenya with her neat blonde cap, and then again to Dia, smiling at him as she fades from sight.

His hands grasp empty air as his voice echoing off the walls wake him. Daylight has arrived. She is gone.

Later, when he returned to the cabin, he walked in without waiting for an invitation. From then on, he stayed every night, and when he left, on his return he entered the cabin without a word. They never spoke about it, but he understood she wanted him there, to stay with her. It was clear in her eyes, in the way she looked at him and the way she smiled.

He made no move towards her, willing her to come to him. He knew it was destined to happen—Dia's gift. He was could wait as long as it took, and she would come to him...as her Maître and consort.

They took turns cooking, she in the kitchen, he outside on the fire pit he made for their Christmas feast. Together, they spent nights on the deck sipping wine and looking at the stars. They taught each other songs to sing together. His were chants to Dia in some archaic language she suspected might be ancient Ligurian, and he laughed at her accent and difficulty in learning the words and sounds.

She came up with songs she learned at sleep-away camp, like "She'll Be Commin' 'Round The Mountain When She Comes," and "Ninety-Nine Bottles of Beer In the Wall." And then there were songs they discovered they both knew, the round "Frere Jacques" and "Compagnie de la Marjolaine." Those were their favorites.

Sometimes she used the signs she had trained Tom with, and when he saw the dog react, he understood what they meant. He taught her the signs the hunters had used, similar hand signals of stay back, go left or right, don't move, be quiet, come this way, and Lenya understood. In between, there were facial expressions and body language. He was improving his English by listening to the BBC on television and radio while he worked and when she spoke to Tom or on Skype to her sister. His English was already better than either her French or Italian.

They got along amazingly well. Lenya was surprised one day as she realized they were having a rather complicated discussion about religion. Aldo wanted her to understand about Dia.

"Dia is Goddess of nature—of woman—of life and death... birth." Lenya listened with interest as he spoke in his rough, almost guttural, voice. "Dia gets power from life, love...when man and woman join together Dia make love with her consort in our bodies...they join with... no...become?..us." Interesting. What Sirio had been trying to tell her. Time to research goddess religions. She felt something inside her begin to throb.

Lenya knew the feminine deity religions were very powerful around the Mediterranean in the pre-Judeo-Christian era. These religions were eventually forbidden in the areas where the Hebrews settled. Since Judaism was a matrilineal religion, the Hebrews did not want their women worshipping the goddess by giving sexual favors to strangers in her temple. It confused the inheritance of real property and businesses which were passed on through the line of the mother. The death knell for the goddess cults was sounded once the Jesus cults took over, the only remnant left were the various beliefs in the Virgin Mary.

Since Lenya was not religious, in the past it had been interesting to her only from an intellectual point of view. Now, anything important to Aldo was something she wanted to know more about. It was a way to help her understand him; a window into his head. Sirio's passing question about whether or not they had made love kept coming back to haunt her. What had he meant about Aldo being 'consort?' What did it entail?

As the days passed, they drew closer and closer—almost like a long married husband and wife, but there were differences, very important ones.

Her body and space was her own. He never touched her or went near. If she wanted to be close, he made sure she came to him.

At night, she climbed to her loft alone while he curled up on the couch. He knew when she fell asleep because Tom trotted downstairs to finish the night with him.

He knew he was making progress, albeit slowly. Once, sitting at her machine she stretched her back and rolled her neck. For a moment he forgot his resolve to not touch her and put his hands on her shoulders. Slowly, he began massaging her sore muscles as his mother taught him. It was a natural response. Raina had loved it; she spent her days washing and working, always bent over and his hands knew how to give her relief.

Lenya moaned a bit and moved her head from side to side in pleasure. When he remembered his plan of no touching, he patted her shoulder, stopped the massage and walked away. She didn't say anything but turned and looked at him. He saw she was sorry he stopped. Grinning to himself, he didn't go back.

Lenya soon realized he had a very meager wardrobe and needed washing almost every day. She bought him several tee-shirts a chambray shirt and some jeans on one of her trips to town. Undergarments were not on her list, she had no idea if he wore such things, but figured he probably went commando. His clothes still needed regular washing and she wondered how he took care of them as they were always clean and fresh smelling. One morning she walked with him to a stream and watched while he stopped to wash a small bundle he carried under his arm. When he got up from his work, he stretched and rubbed his back in pain.

The next day, she picked up the clothes he had worn. He didn't want to give them to her, it was not her job to go to the stream. She worked at her computer writing machine. Lenya insisted. He relented when she waggled her finger at him to stop trying to take the bundle from her. Motioning for him to follow, she went outside to the back porch of the cabin. The place he had crawled into for shelter.

There, she put his clothes into the large white box-like machine. The one he once slept around. It seemed a very long time ago. Now he often listened to it making very unpleasant grunts and groans but hadn't paid much attention to it otherwise.

She picked up her soiled clothes too and put them inside the machine with his, measured, and added blue powder. After pushing a few buttons, the contraption rumbled around making its terrible noises. Taking his arm, they walked away and left the machine to its moaning and sloshing. After a while the noise stopped and when she took the clothes out; they were wet and clean.

He quickly took all of them from her and spread them outside on nearby bushes to dry in the sun. It was a better way to dry things than the other machine in the cabin. His clothes always smelled fresh like the air while hers smelled of chemicals and the dryer.

From then on, she washed and he dried. He liked doing this chore because her clothes were soft and reminded him of her, he liked to feel them as he spread them out to dry. Now they both had fresh smelling clean clothes to put on, and his back didn't scream anymore.

They adapted to the customs of each other. They each studied how the other did things and often managed to combine the two ways, the old and the new, like the wash—picking and choosing a bit of both as it suited them. They were becoming a clan.

Aldo learned how to turn on the shower and wash with warm water when it was cold outside. At first, he burned himself. With a little practice he became master of the gods living in the silver handles—the ones who controlled water temperature. He looked forward to the warm water on his body, it soothed some of the pains the cold left in his joints.

He enjoyed the soap in bottles Lenya used and he liked to make shapes with the bubbles when he washed his hair and beard. Fashioning a big headdress of white foam, he came out naked and dripping to show her one afternoon. She laughed at first, then shooed him back into the bathroom. She seemed embarrassed as soon as she looked down his exposed body. He thought she was very odd. Nakedness was taken for granted in the clan.

Aldo continued to use fragrant oils, made from herbs he dried, to perfume his hair and beard. It was the way of Dia's consort, and he preferred the scents of nature—the lavender, immortelle, saffron, mint and eucalyptus, to the ones in the bottle—but he was very fond of the bubbles.

Cold days were particularly good. On those days Lenya took a small machine to blow warm air and dry his hair and beard after he bathed. At first he hadn't known what she was doing and didn't like the heat blowing on him. Then he found it had other benefits.

He sat on a chair and felt her nearness and sometimes the soft press of her body as she leaned into her work. He saw the way she looked at him when she ran her fingers through his curls, pushing them under the warm air. He smiled at her as she moved around him with the warming machine. It was the closest to her he allowed himself. What he really wanted to do was unbutton her shirt slowly and kiss her nipples, tonguing them until she screamed for him to move to other parts of her body. Some day, he thought to himself, and tried to not become erect and frighten her again.

Sometimes he took his flute out and played one of the melodies she knew and she hummed along. Sometimes he taught her more Italian or French. She was a fast learner too and it allowed them to communicate more. Sometimes she taught him names of things in English, modern things, things he had no words for and she didn't know the words in either Italian or French. It developed into a game they played.

He pointed to his knife as he was dressing some game.

"*Coltello*" she said.

He pointed the knife at the hare lying on the counter."

"*Lepre, yummm—con aglio*." He knew she liked the hare rubbed with garlic before he roasted it.

He sat on the chair while she dried his hair and pointed to the warm air machine.

"Blow dryer," he announced.

Then she pointed to the shower.

"*Doccia*, shower."

She held out one of his dark red curls for him to see in the mirror.

"Aldo's curly hair."

She wanted to hug him, but she didn't.

One day he was looking at himself in the mirror when she passed by.

"*Uomo bello*," she couldn't stop herself from saying.

Aldo broke out in a huge grin and puffed his chest a little. She thought he was handsome.

Aldo marveled at mirrors. He explored his face and body as if it they were novel inventions. The best use of mirrors was to study an unsuspecting Lenya when she dried her hair or put on her makeup. For these chores, she always put on her bathrobe and opened the bathroom door to let out the steam from her shower. It was one of his favorite pastimes, other than drawing.

Every day he experimented a little bit more with his art, understanding how to create things he pictured in his head. At first, the figures he drew were stick-like as in cave drawings. Then he spent days studying his own body and hers, how they moved, how muscles reacted as they did certain movements. Then he looked at the art books Lenya brought and how other artists rendered these things. He discovered how to make his pictures more life-like, figured how to add perspective and distance. He knew animals bodies and muscles from hunting and preparing his game. He experimented with drawing how birds looked when they flew or ran. He drew game in flight with new details and surety. The drawings had power.

Always fascinated with light and shadow, when he applied them to his drawings, different feelings, sometimes enhanced motion came to life. Every day was a new discovery.

As his personal style developed, a large carton arrived by post. It was from Amazon.com in Paris. Lenya had ordered a history of art series for him. Aldo opened the first book to see pictures—like those in the clan cave—hunter chasing game across stone walls! How could a book have these pictures? Like things the clan made so many years ago. On closer inspection he saw they were not exactly the same, but so close—what tribe? Where? He wanted to ask Lenya where they were from and when they had been made, but he kept forgetting to ask. He became more and more immersed in his artwork.

Every day he took one of the books out to the deck and, sitting with his feet dangling over the side and Tom on his lap, he studied the book intently, wanting to understand how those artists created so many different moods and perspectives. The things he liked he tried in his own works, other things he forgot about.

He saw the books as things to learn from, not to copy. He was energized. Living with a mate he believed Dia had chosen for him, albeit under very unusual circumstances, any hint of his old sadness fled and he regained his usual supreme confidence—after all, he was le Maître .

Some of the art he found disturbing—like the injured man, hung on the upright stick with his arms nailed outspread on a cross bar. Sirio told him years ago the man's name was Jesus and he was commonly believed to be the son of god. Jesus wore thorns around his head and bled from the cuts and a wound in his side. Aldo wondered what Jesus had done to deserve such punishment—must have done terrible things. Jesus was pictured in almost all of the books, every time enduring torture. Aldo had seen him many times before, many of the local villages had buildings with his picture too.

Aldo didn't know which god Jesus was the son of, but was certain he wasn't the son of Dia. She'd never let her son be treated in this way, no matter how evil or vicious he might have been. It was especially puzzling because Jesus' face always looked sad and kind, not bad at all. No matter what he might have done, Aldo felt sorry for him. Why didn't his father god save him from such suffering? Was he mad at his offspring? Perhaps Dia might have helped if Jesus had prayed to her.

What Lenya said was "Modern Art" left Aldo cold. There was nothing that spoke to him in the angles, squares and boxes. Some of the splashes of colors he enjoyed, they made him feel happy, but on the whole, there was no passion. Those books he put away in the bookcase, nothing he wanted to study in them.

He liked hunting scenes, men on horseback in red coats, dogs running alongside. The battle scenes showed dying men in strange poses; he snorted in disgust; obviously the artists never saw anyone dying. They didn't have those plaintive looks on their faces, eyes lifted to the sky.

The rounded lazy women with rosy bodies were amusing to look at. The way the artists rendered the backgrounds and the animals in the paintings were interesting; but best of all were nature scenes, baskets of fruits and vegetables, vases of flowers, scenes with many animals.

With practice and patience, Aldo's skills developed. He went back to some of his early pictures to change a shadow or add perspective, create a different ambiance. His favorite was of a family sitting in a cave around a fire. The man's face was seamed and there was white in his beard, his body thin and muscular. On one shoulder was a squirrel and on the other a bird. The woman laughed as she stirred a pot over the fire; a small boy with red hair looked on with a dreamy expression.

After staring at the large watercolor for a while he'd add a shadow, or something remembered. One time he added an earthen bowl, another time a bow and arrow leaning against the wall. Cave drawings decorated the space behind the figures. He was cataloguing his memories, lest he forget.

Lenya once asked who the people were.

"La mia famiglia—papa, mamma ed io," Aldo answered. They were his family-mother, father and himself.

Then he drew a picture of the cabin. Lenya sitting at the table, a man with long red hair and a beard across from her, a small tri-colored dog on the floor. Light streamed in through sliding glass doors. They were his two families: the first painting what he missed and the second what he now had, for however long he might have it. It was the only way he could express to Lenya how important they were to each other. The first time she saw the paintings together, Aldo saw her eyes grow shiny. Tacit understanding.

Once he was satisfied with his skill, he started painting Dia and her consort. He wanted to show Lenya the rites of celebration, the clan's homage to Dia. Their gift of the *hieros gamos*, the sacred marriage when priest and lover became living embodiments of goddess and consort. Someday, he thought. Someday.

When Lenya saw his painting of the summer solstice celebration and the fertility rite with its overt eroticism, he was shocked to see her grimace and go red. It was clear to him she found it hard to see the celebrants intertwined on the carpet of grass under a full moon.

Aldo was sick at heart when she turned away from his goddess and their ages old manner of worship. Perhaps Lenya didn't understand. They communicated, more each day, but explaining cultural differences and attitudes was often far beyond his ability.

He wanted to tell her about Attis' love for Cybele and the gift to her of his manhood...a gift of eternal fidelity modified over ages by the clan to be the gift of a foreskin rather than the entire shaft. Then he thought about it some more. Perhaps it might frighten or upset her. She seemed very peculiar about the union between a man and a woman—things, natural things, to do with certain body parts—more of their differences?

What Aldo couldn't know was why Lenya reacted so strongly to those particular pictures. As soon as she saw them, the dream of the cave, her first night at the cabin, came back to her with clarity. The cave, the strange man making love to her, her body responding with wild abandon. It was Aldo. It had always been Aldo, and Dia had given her permission. Lenya, astonished at the revelation she suspected but not acknowledged, felt herself go red as she remembered her reaction to this man she loved. It was time to let him know.

After almost two months of living together in close proximity, it was clear to both of them they were not only happy in each other's company, they depended on each other in ways needing no communication, no words of confirmation. The transition had been seamless. This was now their life, every day and night spent together. But they kept their distance.

How had he become such an integral part of...of...me? I don't think I could go back to living without him. Lenya pushed the thought away. She worried how long Aldo would stay with her under the present circumstances, no sex, no contact. Unnatural between a man and woman as close as they had become. But no matter how much she longed for him, she couldn't force herself to change the dynamic. She didn't know how.

Aldo didn't think about it at all. In his mind, it was simply the way things were. He enjoyed her closeness and ached for the day they would make love. Someday. He knew it would happen, he hoped it wouldn't be too much longer.

Chapter 46
The Casteddu

Aldo took her hand and pulled her away from her computer, pushing her out the door into the sunlight. It was a perfect day to be outside. As usual, when he wanted her to accompany him on a long walk, he shooed Tom out of his bed and put her trusty mop handle cum walking stick in her hand. They were going to celebrate spring. A hint of winter cold and damp hung over the woods, but he knew with certainty the Mediterranean sun would warm and dry the island within an hour or two. Even the air smelled different, carrying the sharp tang of tender leaves not unfurled, buds ready to bloom, but not quite .

As Lenya started down the road from the cabin, she noticed how much more rutted it had become —winter rains carving small gullies waved down the mountain like hollow snakes. She must remember to take care with the SUV not to have it catch a tire in one of those ruts. They could easily turn the boxy vehicle over and tumble it down the steep track.

Damn, I'm such a worry wart! Here is this magical day and I'm obsessing about turning the car over. She looked over at the man walking beside her. Blue jeans and a tee shirt under the old rabbit vest couldn't hide his sturdy body. He had filled out with both of them taking turns cooking, and moved about more freely since he had been doing Tai Chi with her in the mornings. It must be helping his mobility, she thought, or perhaps it's sleeping out of the cold air.

She glanced over at his broad chest, wiry-muscled legs and strong arms. An errant thought arose of slithering all over him and rubbing her nose in the soft red fur on his chest. She imagined it would feel like cashmere. She mentally shook her head, gotta' get my act together, inhaled deeply and followed him as he turned off the road into the brush.

They had spent most of the winter working inside, each at their own creations. When it was particularly warm and sunny they sat on the deck or exercised outside, always taking advantage of good weather.

She wondered if he had spent such a winter before, and doubted it. She hadn't seen where he lived, but she didn't imagine he had a cozy fire and a big table to spread out his drawings. When they first started living together, she was concerned he would interfere with her writing. Now, she was more concerned she might interfere with his painting.

Lenya was a thoughtful tenant and didn't want to abuse her kind landlords by returning a cabin with splashes of paint all over the floor. They had spread a large tarpaulin out on one side of the cabin; the area became his studio.

Aldo now had an easel, a palette and paints he was learning how to blend into the colors of nature he so loved. He no longer turned out the frenzy of drawings, but was currently into teaching himself techniques of both oil and acrylic. He saw they allowed him to reproduce in more detail his interpretation of the nature he knew and the stories and legends of the clan. Lenya was so proud of him and his delight and obsession she spared no expense to provide him with materials. For her, it was a pittance. For him—miraculous.

The past week, Sirio had braved the rutted track to come for dinner. When he saw the myriad paintings, sketches and drawings around the cabin, he was amazed by his friend.

"Lenya, I don't know what you've done to this man, but I can't believe my own eyes. Either he's been hiding this talent, or you knew what buttons to push to let it out."

"Honestly, it was an accident. When it was cold, he liked to sit in the cabin with me and, selfishly, I wanted him occupied so I could get on with my writing. Remember, I told you a few months ago I handed him some paper, pencils and colored markers—this was the result." She turned and gestured towards the riot of color and life on the cabin walls as if she was a circus ringleader introducing a lion tamer. "It was like turning a key to unlock a hidden door inside him."

She was pleased with Sirio's response to Aldo's art. While Lenya was convinced Aldo had real talent, it was good to see someone else did too, confirming that her growing love for Aldo wasn't blinding her.

When Sirio was leaving, he turned and asked quietly, "May I bring a friend of mine who owns an art gallery in Bastia to look at Aldo's work?"

Lenya was reluctant. "I think it's too early. We must give him more time to experiment, to find his own style." She looked over at the tiny kitchen where Aldo was washing dishes, Tom and Sophia sitting hopeful at his feet, knowing any scrap off a plate would be theirs. With the water running, Aldo couldn't hear their conversation. "At the moment he's having fun. Sometimes he does things in the manner of other artists to see how they do it. He'll find his own approach if we leave him alone—like he found his way when he first started." She led Sirio over to a pile of papers stacked on a bookcase; showed him the first drawings Aldo had made.

"My God, you're right. Look at the difference, but even at the beginning, you can see he's a natural." Sirio held up one of the older drawings to compare it to an oil on the wall. "Even when he began, he was not a primitive. Look—an instinctual use of light and shadow to give dimension."

"Yes, you see it too. I don't want to rush him. He's doing this for pleasure and to exorcise his own demons—and preserving his memories. Leave him alone for now. When he's ready and has his own style, we'll know, and so will he. That will be the time."

As she said the words, Sirio looked in her eyes and saw a shine. Emotion? Pride? Love? Fear? Maybe all together, he decided.

Since then she'd been thinking about her refusal to let Sirio's friend see Aldo's work. Sometime she worried she'd reacted for selfish reasons. Maybe she wasn't ready to share him with the world. Maybe she was afraid she'd lose him. They hadn't made love. He never pressed her. And now, she was too uncertain to make the first move.

After her stupid scene when she ran from him, she was afraid he didn't look at her as being desirable. Maybe he saw her as an older woman, less interesting as a lover, fine as a friend...a roommate. When she looked at his work, she felt unworthy. If the world saw him, then women would be all over him. He was certainly both attractive and talented. *Those bitchy celebrity fuckers wouldn't let him alone. Crap! Maybe I'm selfish?*

Striding down the track alongside of her, she noticed even his walk had changed; no longer walking with his usual surety, he walked with more determination, Tom trotting between the two of them. She wanted to take Aldo's hand. Something deep inside her wouldn't allow her to do it. Pride? Fear? Idiocy? Probably all three.

He moved onto a narrow path winding through dense woods and up a steep slope. After an hour, Lenya was getting tired. In the fall it wouldn't have bothered her, she'd been walking all over the nearby mountains. But confined to the cabin for most of the winter, her legs felt leaden and she was cranky. Aldo must have sensed something as he pointed up to the top of the next rise. "Casteddu there." His hand swept the vistas. "My house to welcome...," he said with a big grin. He was taking her to where he lived—enough to energize her into movement again.

They walked through underbrush and up precarious trails seemingly crisscrossing the mountain. The wind blew stronger with every uphill footstep and Lenya was sorry she hadn't brought a warm jacket. Aldo didn't seem to mind the cold, grinning in enjoyment as his cheeks turned pink from the freshening air.

He pointed and she saw stone ruins at the top of the next peak. It didn't look much further but she knew distances could be deceiving in the mountains. The last part of the climb was very steep and Aldo stood behind her to make sure she didn't slip as she climbed a sheer face of rock with hidden toeholds he pointed out. She wondered how Tom was going to make it up but to her surprise, the dog waited for her at the top. He seemed to find narrow places where small animals before him had climbed without having to scale the sheer faces of the mountain. Lenya worried. Going up was one thing. Getting down quite another.

When she was about to give up and call it quits, Aldo nodded towards walls made of large stones hewn into rough blocks and smoothed by the weather. It was an opening topped by a lintel—a gate—to a Neolithic village. She'd seen photos of such places in the museums she'd visited in France and on the island. Most of the buildings were roofless, as if deserted for millennia. On the far wall of the village, across a central square, one remaining structure seemed habitable. They headed towards it.

Made of stone like the rest, this one was much higher and bigger. The roof was made of wooden beams and crude shingles fastened with wooden pegs A rounded archway indicated an entrance closed by a wooden door artfully made of twigs and branches woven on crosspieces on one side and a skin fastened on the inside. Okay, she thought as she studied the contraption, it's like a storm door to keep out the winter wind from roaring through the cracks, and you can take the skin off in summer to get the cooling breezes.

Aldo pointed at the door and himself. *"Il mio casa,"* he announced, pushing the door open. She smiled at the reference to his home.

Lenya looked around before going inside. Two stone steps led up to a carved threshold. The house was slightly raised to keep the inside free from water rushing by during heavy rains. The windows had outside shutters painted in the same blue as the Mediterranean coves, what Lenya always thought of as Pigna-blue, like the shutters of the magical village.

Inside, the place was neat, the smooth rock floor swept clean, almost polished from centuries of human feet wearing it to a shine. Clean reeds provided a partial covering. She thought the place must be freezing in the winter until she saw leather hides stacked up in the corner and realized they probably covered the floor to keep some of the cold back. Perhaps they also covered the inside of the windows to keep out the wind.

A handmade table and four mismatched chairs carefully mended to hold their burdens were the centerpiece of the room. She knew Aldo lived alone. The four chairs were remnants from the old days—life with his parents and wife. She felt a pang at the emptiness he must feel coming home. No wonder he was content in the cabin.

A stone shelf ran the length of the house on an unbroken wall. It had several bowls, a cracked coffee mug, some utensils and a jug. A small framed photograph of several people hung askew on the same wall as the window, faded woven hangings hung on the other walls. As she watched, he walked over and straightened the photograph.

A platform chipped out of solid rock was in one corner, piled with more skins, these with soft looking fur must be where he slept.

She was surprised at the smell. If she had thought about it, she would have imagined a musty smell redolent of human sweat, old cooked meat and animals sleeping on the floor. Instead it smelled fresh, like the maquis but sweeter and mixed with smoke from the fireplace in one corner. Looking up, she saw bunches of immortelle and lavender—herbs and leaves hanging from the beams beneath the roof. She recognized pines, rosemary and eucalyptus, but many were unknown. The place smelled of Aldo. She suddenly felt at home.

Tom sniffed around and with one leap landed on top of the sleeping platform, made himself at home in the pile of skins, almost disappearing into the fur of the one on top. Lenya thought it might have been bear.

In a corner of the house there was an ancient bow against a wall next to a leather and fur quiver of arrows, several spears and a large axe with a stone blade. They all looked unused for generations and next to them was more modern hunting gear, but it was all oiled, glistening, spotless, like the rest of the place. As she looked at the shelf with the utensils, she saw some objects she realized were jewelry. Aldo saw her looking and pointed at them, *"Mama ed Raina—bijoux."* She understood but was surprised he used the French word for jewelry. Odd.

They left the house and walked outside to the edge of the cast-eddu, bounded by the tall stone ramparts protecting the casa from much of the blustery weather in winter months.

Over the ramparts and far, far below, the sea sparkled in the sun and tiny cars motoring along the RN looked like cockroaches. It seemed to be another world, another century—no, she stopped herself. It was another millennium.

The wind picked up carrying a chill with it. Aldo came and stood behind her. She felt his warmth on her back. Slowly, he put his arms around her and held her close. She made no move to get away, no flinch, no pulling back. She moved closer to him, fitting her back to his chest, her butt in the curve of his groin, her thighs against his. As the wind whistled around them it was the safest she'd ever felt.

They stayed melded into one person for several minutes. Then, he abruptly turned her around, took her hand and began to lead her down the mountain, back to the cabin.

She made it down with no problem; he held her hand all the way.

Chapter 47

Spring

Aldo and Lenya sat on the deck, laughing at the raucous bird song, a cacophonic paean in celebration of the season. The early spring air was filled with new life, the joy of surviving another winter, the scents of sun on dry rocks and tender green shoots, furled and hinting at a summer soon to come. Expectation and fecundity joined bright sun and a breath of the last coolness brushed through the air.

Filled with such a longing and love for this man who lived beside her, she knew she couldn't stand it much longer. Every time she looked at him, her throat clenched and she was afraid she would cry from the strength of her emotions.

She understood Aldo would make no move towards her. She must come to him when she was ready. Somewhere deep inside old forgotten insecurities kept floating up, she was both embarrassed and terrified of taking the step. *What if he doesn't want me anymore? What if he thinks I'm too old? What if we're only friends?...what if he turns me down?*

The more she obsessed over her fears, the more she wanted him. At night she fell asleep and immediately dreamed of feeling his body against her, inside her. She longed for the tickle of his beard on her neck.

Lenya packed a light lunch and folded herself into a crossed leg position next to Aldo, sitting on the deck, intent knitted brows hovering over his pencil and sketch book.

Knit yoga pants and a white tee shirt closely molded the curves of her body. She held the basket in front of him enticingly. "Lunch?" she asked.

He smiled at her. *"Dove?"*

"How about the grotto?" It was cooler there and the day was showing signs of being a scorcher.

"Va bene," he said as he put aside his implements and reached for the picnic basket. She picked up two blankets and a tablecloth.

The grotto lived up to its promise, cooler than the cabin, quiet unbroken by even the hint of a breeze. Lenya spread the blankets and blue and red checkered cloth on the rock they called their *"tavola."* Wine, cheese, several apples and bread, two knives and napkins completed a feast fit for royalty in a setting close to paradise.

Lunch half over, wine consumed, she was filled with fear. *How am I going to do this? How do I tell...show...this man how I feel about him. It's now or never, old girl.*

She reached out for a piece of bread and Aldo brushed against her hand, taking it in his. As soon as their skin touched, panic struck her.

Trembling, she almost flinched—her first thought to flee—to run like the wind. The simple graze of his skin made her weak and aggressively strong at the same time.

She saw a flicker of hurt in his eyes, but instead of running this time, or even pulling away, she squeezed his hand.

Heart beating as if trying to fly out of her body, she wouldn't let him go. The power between them excited her and this time, she drew his hand to her and she kissed his palm, flicking her tongue around and across before reaching out put both of her hands on his face. She twined her fingers through his long, soft hair and he put his hands over hers. He was motionless as they stared silently into each others' eyes, only the space of a breath between them.

She wanted to tell him she had no intention of running this time but instead of words, she leaned towards him and placed her lips over his as the soft auburn strands of his beard caressed her face.

She heard rumbling sounds deep in his throat, felt the vibrations in his facial muscles, but couldn't make out words or distinct sounds. His body became rigid; she had been afraid she'd see fear, disgust, anything but love. She had started this, it was in her hands now. His eyes slowly closed and an expression she could only interpret as bliss spread across his face as she heard repetition in the unfamiliar sounds he was making, and, intuitively, she knew it was an ancient chant to Dia.

He needed Dia's help to show this woman how much he loved her...desired her...wanted nothing more than to gift her with pleasure.

When her hands left his face, he moaned in despair. She wasn't going to run again, was she? Her lips were still soft against his but she was moving her body. Twisting about. It was odd. Then he understood—she was throwing her clothes off—thanks be to Dia! He didn't know how his clothes came off but he knew they were finally in each other's arms on the *tavola*, skin pressed against skin the length of their bodies. The way it should be.

Her arms were around his neck, her nose in his hair, he had washed as usual with the sacred oils: lemon verbena, immortelle, and lavender—had taken the time, as consort, to always be prepared.

Lenya relaxed in his arms, supple, yielding—it was time to honor Dia. He felt a small nudge of doubt. As much time as he had spent with her, he had some concerns. Lenya wasn't a woman of the clan. Could she be different in her responses? Clan women were grateful for his knowledge, his gentle hands and knowing tongue. Would she permit him to love her in the ways he knew?

He pressed her body to his and felt their hearts beating in unison. His senses were filled with the scents of her shampoo, perfume and the underlying deep musk of a woman's passion. His fears dissipated when she moved her body against his. She clearly wanted him. He felt himself harden. It was time to bring her to goddess.

Pulling away for a moment, he first wanted to look at her, to revere this woman he had desired, had hunted with so much determination. She was beautiful, her muscles defined beneath skin not scarred by the harshness of life nor coarsened by sleeping in caves. His hands trailed over her smoothness, approving the creams she applied when she thought he wasn't looking. Thank Dia again for mirrors.

Then he lay her body on the blanket and bent to her. It was time to awaken the lotus.

Lenya squinched her eyes closed. In fear? Expectation? Shame? She not only desired Aldo, but her body sang a song of pleasure to him as his hands played her with light feathered caresses. She felt him with all her senses, wanted him to join with her, take her. Right now! Take her as she now knew he had in her dream.

Aldo moved to her right, his breath fluttering like a moth on her eyelids. Stopping to press his lips against her forehead, he breathed in the fragrance of her. His mouth exploring her shoulders, tracing her arm, the inner soft skin and, taking her fingers in his mouth one at a time, his tongue was soft against the place where fingers conjoin.

Tenderness moved over her hand, and when she felt a gentle press against the center of her palm, she remembered the first time and, catching her breath, relaxed, melting against him.

Turning her head she tasted his skin, fragrant with herbs, and salty on her tongue. A bead of sweat threatened to escape from behind his ear, and she caught the precious drop with a sigh.

He moved to her breasts, tracing circles around and around her nipple, sucking until she moaned, thrusting against him, and then he suckled once more before moving to the center of nerves where arm meets body. She inhaled the sweet musk of him, it was as if the earth itself in all its glory had taken her over.

Lenya thought she would die with the feel of his beard mapping her body as he moved across her ribs, down her abdomen and then brushing against the crease where thigh and triangle converge. Suddenly she felt a flow of warmth and he bent to taste the nectar. She didn't know he believed the fluid embodied the power of a woman—her most precious gift to him. As he looked upwards, he was thanking Dia and Lenya realized there were many things about him she didn't know, but she was finally willing to learn.

He moved further down her leg, caressing her thigh and calf, pressing the arch of each foot with silent and gentle knowledge, then sucking each of her toes in turn. Lenya was afraid she was going to faint, her pleasure dizzying. She felt the soft silk of his beard brush between her thighs. Her back arched as he began slowly to tease open the lotus as she offered him her rapture.

Nothing in Lenya's life before had prepared her for this harmony. She tried to understand what was happening to her heart, her mind and her body as this man she loved worked magic on her with finesse and tenderness. His love came through every touch and she trembled with its power. Well beyond her realm of understanding, she felt herself transported to a different plane of ecstasy.

What the hell? This is fancy fucking!. The only recognizable thought penetrating her consciousness, shocked her with its snarky profanity, her last attempt to claw her way back to earth. Too late.

She heard a low rumble—he was chanting again.

She made out some words *"Dia, Dia... do vito... seme."* He was offering his goddess... life...his seed...?

It didn't matter; she was in an altered state—a totality of pleasure... wanted it to continue...please...don't stop. But at the same time she wasn't sure she could stand more as her mind rocketed around a phrase she once read somewhere, "unendurable pleasure indefinitely prolonged."

She felt him rock hard and pressing against her leg. Lenya squirmed around... reached for him. Her hands found...*he was circumcised?* How could it be?

Twisting and writhing, she yearned to feel his hardness in her mouth but he held her firmly in place as he searched her core..

"Un altra volta,"...another time...she heard him mutter seconds before her ecstatic screams filled the air. Shoulders pressing against the rock, she convulsed over and over again.

It was too much, the pleasure...more than she could bear. She couldn't catch her breath, found herself helplessly gasping "no, no, please!..stop!" At the same time, her body ached to join with his.

Frantic, grabbing his hair and beard, she roughly yanked him from between her legs, and wrangled her way underneath him, frenzied, squirming, desperate with longing to feel his length within her. *"Venga con mi... venga, venga subito!"* She found enough Italian to shout she wanted him to come with her...and quickly!

Aldo's joy was complete. Power—the greatest gift of the gods—the joining of man and woman—what he had waited, longed for, was his. He offered his seed to Dia in the old words as he slowly began to slide his length into her home, Lenya's sacred triangle.

Lenya felt him slow and firm as she opened to him. Joyful! It felt so wonderful she wanted more—bucking and grabbing his buttocks to try and force him as deep inside as possible.

But he refused to relinquish control, filling her deftly, then slowly emerging to the tip, only to tease her again....his own pace...Maître in control...measured. She was engulfed in wave after wave of pleasure. But it was too slow and gentle for her; she wanted him rough... fast...knocking hard on her internal door. Frantic! Feral!

He, however, was unhurried, leisurely. Not to be rushed. Eyes closed, his face radiated pleasure and bliss. He wanted to savor, enjoy the moment to its fullest as he continued his steady rhythm while she rose to ecstasy time and again. When she could stand no more, she wrapped her arms and legs around him and, clinging to him like a monkey, tried to set the pace harder and faster.

Aldo laughed. He couldn't help himself—it was so wonderful and joyful the laughter bubbled out of him to join with Lenya's howls. He had his desire, his true sun and moon mate, the woman who filled his heart. His woman to spend the rest of his life pleasing.

A rush of his fluids mixed with hers—their offering. This time, the scream was his too as it soared out into the trees. Together they made a melody of homage to Dia.

Aldo drifted on the cusp of sleep with Lenya curled against him. He felt completely whole for the first time in his life. They were joined— two pieces of eternity, goddess and consort, players in the eternal dance of man and woman, sun and moon, earth and seed, lover and Maître. He stroked her hair, felt her move closer into the circle of his arms as sleep finally overtook him .

Later, she awoke with the rock hard beneath her, their bodies stuck together. Tom was spooned up against Aldo's hip. Aldo, asleep and serene, lay partially off to the side, entwined...and yes, his chest hair did feel like cashmere as she imagined. She gave a flex of strong vaginal muscles and felt an answering twitch from him. Silent and awake, he instantly awoke inside her. She was happier than she had ever been. Life is good after all, she thought. His beard, against her face, smelled of lemon verbena, lavender, immortelle, and her.

As she moved against him he cupped her head with one hand, the other her buttocks, and pressed her tight against his body.

"Grazie, Dia," he roared into the cooling evening air.

Chapter 48
Rhythms of Life

Time seemed to fly by. Lenya couldn't believe it was already a year since she rented the cabin. She signed a lease for a second year in the same real estate office, grateful she wasn't faced with the necessity of looking for another place to live.

It would not have been easy to find another location where Aldo could be at ease. He had no concern for creature comforts, but he was uncomfortable around new people. Aldo had seen enough television by now to have no interest in coping with the 21st century.

Lenya wasn't about to move into the casteddu without internet, telephone and television, let alone the rest of the comforts she was used to. Those modern conveniences were an umbilical cord to her world. She knew without Skype, her sister would be on the first plane out of Kennedy and whacking through the brush of Corsica to find her.

Lenya and Aldo created their own life, their unique style of living. Simple, close to nature, unencumbered with crowds, elevators, social networking, skyscrapers, taxis, deadlines, people—strangers.

Every day she woke with delight, looking forward to another day. Aldo had taught her magic—the art of living in the now. Taking life every day and enjoying the pleasures offered as they came. Before, she worked hard, but worried about deadlines, traffic jams, strangers robbing her, getting in an accident, gaining weight, having a bad hair day, breaking a fingernail. All those insignificant and nonsensical myriad of worries.

It saddened her to remember sex with Andre while wondering if she paid the electric bill, accepted friends' dinner invitation, or hurrying him along so she could get back to work, instead of gifting him with her undivided attention.

Making love with Aldo was like creating their own paradise, their own space in time. She turned herself over to him completely, her mind steeped in their pleasure, her body his instrument to play as he wished. They were two people in complete harmony. Time had no meaning, nothing more important than the pleasures of the love.

He gave her the gift of serenity. She gave him the gift of her desire to understand.

She worked at the computer and he drew, painted, carved and played his flute. They took joy in each other's work.

They were like a tiny clan. Both their needs were filled.

Often Aldo took off into the woods for hours at a time, only to return with skinned rabbits or some birds he'd later cook for her on the open fire. Sometimes Tom went along with him, but most of the time he stayed in the cabin with Lenya... old age creeping up.

Lenya could never have imagined her life. She was used to entertaining... traveling...big cities with plenty of plans, movement...traffic...people ...horns blaring...noise...a social life...filled Day Planners and Blackberries...the whirl of literary parties. Had the fullness of life been an elaborate illusion to disguise its emptiness? Like a misplaced menhir guarding something of little consequence? She had complete contentment in their small and quiet world.

Aldo slept with her in the loft, his arms comforting her and his breath in her hair a reminder she wasn't alone. And the lovemaking—he never seemed to tire of her, always ready, always gentle and always determined to satisfy her needs in every way. She reciprocated wholeheartedly.

Her estrangement from Lotte was a problem. It was impossible for Lenya to tell her twin how she felt about Aldo. How do you explain to a dyed in the wool New York playgirl life in the woods with a throwback to a Neolithic age is wonderful? It doesn't play at lunch chatter at the Palm Court in the Plaza.. What would Lotte say when socialite friends asked how her brilliant writer sister was doing? Lotte was always on her case to come home and Lenya feared her sister was going to show up at her door any time. And...probably with her new gentleman friend... 'Signore Armani' as she thought of him.

She wanted no one interfering in her life with Aldo. A life she knew as a series of miracles.

Aldo watched Lenya work at the computer. Her face twisted into frowns and exasperation as she fought with a chapter—couldn't seem to get the scene she wanted right—not quite writers block, but close. Intuitively, he took her hand and pulled her from the desk, almost dragging her outside into the soft summer afternoon. She didn't protest. He handed her the trusty mop handle, the signal they were going for a long walk. It was a perfect time to get away, no point brooding at the screen as if words would jump out at her. From long experience, she knew it was a futile hope.

As they left the cabin, the air was filled with the sweet scent of wild flowers—asphodel and sea lavender peeking out through the maquis shrubs. Tree branches were tufted with generous green. Bees buzzed in endless quest for pollen while small critters scuttled through underbrush making rustling sounds as they searched for food. Birds exchanged exciting gossip overhead.

He set a fast pace, not stopping to enjoy the bursts of natures plenty coming at them from all directions until she pulled him to a stop to admire some butterfly orchids and dark red hooded serapias.

At one point, he dodged into the underbrush, looked around and signaled she join him. Two bulls quietly grazed off in the corner of a large open field. A dirt trail crossed the verdant pasture and disappeared beyond a rise. No one else was in sight. The bulls paid no attention as two humans invaded their territory and continued their grazing, heads and horns together as if in intimate dialogue.

Aldo pointed across the pasture to some tall objects barely visible over a crude fence, but it was too far away for her to make out what they were. As they trekked through tall grasses towards the fence, the bulls sauntered over to investigate their progress. Aldo signaled her to move slowly and make no noise. Lenya was frightened, the bulls were formidable, but she slowed down and moved quietly. After a few minutes, the animals lost interest again and went back to their grazing.

An alignment of standing stones, the menhirs, were in front of her, sharing the field with the bulls. Lenya was breathless when she realized where Aldo had taken her. There they were, eight stone warriors in the middle of nowhere. She knew from her reading about the island they had maintained their silent sentry duty for millennia; no one sure when they were placed on the island, anywhere from four to eight thousand years ago, depending on the scholars you were reading. As she moved around the stones, she could make out some vague and weathered facial features, one with a sword hung around its neck.

Aldo pointed at one of them and then gestured to his own genitals and she saw the faint shadow of the ancient warrior's family jewels. They were sized rather large for the size of the stone, she noted. Some things never change. *Men!*

She took out her camera and was about to press the button when Aldo reached out for the camera, motioning her to stand next to the menhir. As she did, he began to take photos from different angles. She'd forgotten how much he liked cameras and wondered if he was experimenting with light and shadows to enhance the photos as he did with his paintings. After a few minutes she was getting bored posing and as he was positioning her to catch the light, she reached out and, grabbing for the ancient warrior's balls, stuck out her tongue. The next thing she knew they were both on the ground laughing and rolling in the grass. She hoped the bulls hadn't left them any presents in the same spot, and then decided there were more interesting things to think about.

As they got up and brushed themselves off a while later, Aldo pointed at the menhirs genitals and shook his head "No, no, no!" Then he pointed at his own and laughed. *"Solo questi!"*

Okay, she got the point and laughed too. He was one jealous caveman.

They continued on for more than an hour of steady climbing and pushing through dense maquis. Lenya was tired, hot, chafing and sticky from sex and sweat. Dried grass decorated her usually neat hair and pricked at her through her shirt. Something had bitten her ankle while they rolled on the grass. This wasn't so much fun anymore and she was about to suggest they return home when Aldo stood back and pointed.

A flat clearing in the cleft of the mountain sheltered a natural pool of brilliant turquoise surrounded by rocks, long grass and trees. Ferns and wild orchids in a profusion of colors decorated the edges of the water. It was perfect privacy, a hidden spot she had never been to before. They were both tired from their exertion and the pool beckoned with an offer of cool refreshment. Almost in the pose of a maitre d' bowing to suggest a prime table, he gestured in the direction of the water. As they approached, she saw the small stream running from the crest of the mountain into the pond, meandering out on the other side through a cluster of wildflowers to drip as a tiny waterfall, creating nature's perfect filtering system. Like her beloved grotto, but much bigger.

Aldo's clothes were off in a second. Jumping into the middle of the pool he waved for her to join him. Soon they were splashing and laughing like kids in a swimming hole. The water was crystal clear and blindingly cold at first, but after a few minutes they felt refreshed rather than freezing.

Later, Lenya was mesmerized by rivulets of water dripping down Aldo's chest and tracing paths along the muscles of his shoulders and arms, running over his abdomen down into the red fur of his groin. I never seem to be able to get enough of looking at him, she thought, as she leaned over to lick a small stream of water trickling down his neck.

Drying off on the warmth of the surrounding boulders, they made love again. Lenya took pleasure in the smoothness of his skin, the feel of his hardening length in her mouth, the fragility of his genitals in her hands. She craved to give him pleasure too, and while he was trained in the arts of lovemaking, she was not. As they made love, she was learning from the nuances of his movements and the speed of his breathing to find things that gave him the most enjoyment. Their bodies pressed against each other, cool damp skin against skin making the heat of their joining all the more powerful. Hot and cold. Yin and yang. Breathtaking.

Afterwards, Lenya snuggled her butt up against his warm groin in the cooling afternoon air. It was hard to believe they weren't the last two people on earth—like Adam and Eve. And I thought I knew what love was...I guess I did, but this is way different... or is this the lust of a horny middle aged woman? Yeah... I don't really care...and why do I always have such negative thoughts?

Aldo was asleep, his hand flopping across her hip to rest on her belly. Her body was so attuned to his a mere touch caused her to flood with warmth. He was the same. She turned to him at night if she couldn't sleep and running her fingers in his chest hair he would be ready. When she looked at her image in the cabin mirror, she saw a happy, younger looking woman grinning back at her. Amazing what fabulous sex can do. But then, is it really only sex?

And the strangest part was it seemed to show in her work. Ellie called after receiving several new chapters. "Lenya, I think you must be happy. Have you finally found yourself a new man?" The voice on the phone almost bowled her over. How on earth could Ellie have suspected anything? She hadn't said much to Lotte and nothing at all to Ellie.

"I am happy, Ellie. What's the problem?"

"Nothing dear, it shows in your work. If I were going to give you a color, in the old days I would have said your work was dark maroon and brown with flashes of color jolting the reader. Now I see a mauve with a patina of purple passion and flashes of bright azure and fire-engine red. You wake the reader up, but with a sensual power, almost a throbbing. I can't exactly explain."

"Don't forget, it's a different type of book...requires a new style of writing."

"Yes, I agree, but...hmmm...it's something more than ."

Lenya needed to change the subject, "Okay, but are the chapters I sent acceptable? Do you think the editor will like the direction I've been taking?"

"I'm sure she will…the chapters aren't only brilliant, they have a heart and a heat to them I've never seen before. You're a great writer, but this is a new you…a *veritas*…gives me the chills. It's the way you're nailing emotions." The phone was silent for a moment, but Lenya could tell Ellie was there.

"Don't let me be too analytic…don't want to interfere with your flow." Ellie continued after another brief pause, "You got it girl…keep it coming."

Chapter 49

Unhiding

They were both at work, she writing, or at least trying to put words on pages. Aldo was musing over his latest painting—an ancient hunt for mountain goat in snow covered mountains. Lenya thought it was one of his best, the soft grey of the rockscape and snow made the browns and beiges of the men and their quarry seem small and poignant.

The barking at the door was unmistakable. Sirio and Sophia were outside, looking anxiously in through the sliding glass doors.

Aldo laughed as he opened the door and grabbed Sirio into a bear hug. He had been so busy with his painting and art as well as his life with Lenya he had lost track of time—hadn't seen his old friend recently. As soon as he stood back to look at the older man, he realized how much he missed him.

Lenya came running to embrace Sirio, pausing only to grab a handful of biscuits from the kitchen to treat her littlest guest.

"I have come to visit you, my children, since you seem to be so busy with each other you cannot spare the time to let an old man into your lives."

Both Lenya and Aldo felt chastened. It had been weeks since they has seen him. When they had each been alone, they turned to Sirio for companionship, now they unintentionally had excluded him from their life together.

Guilt showed in Lenya's eyes. "I'm so sorry, believe me, the time has flown by. We never meant...please...understand."

Aldo looked stricken. He clasped his old friend in his arms and hugged him again like he had no intention of letting him go.

Sirio had to push him away to speak. "Stop, I forgive you. I remember what it was like to be young and in love." He smiled and put his finger alongside his nose.

Aldo mock punched him in the arm. "You were never in love, you never stayed with a woman long enough. You lie! You were always anxious to get on to the next one...maybe she'll be a better cook or a better... something." They both laughed.

"I was never lucky enough to find a woman like Lenya. Always my problem." He looked down at his shoes for a moment. "Maybe I would have married and had some children and grandchildren to watch as I grow old."

"Come, sit, have a drink with us." Aldo steered him over to the couch.

"I see your English is improving, my friend. The old saw is true—the best place to learn a language is on the pillow. You are a testament to its verity."

Aldo laughed. "Almost so, but television also helps... the BBC...I like very much."

Lenya came back into the room with a tray of tiny Monaco crackers and an open bottle of red wine she set on the low table in front of their guest.

Sirio took a glass of the offered wine and several of the crackers. "My dears, actually, I have come to speak to you about something not so easy. It's been bothering me for some years" He looked at Aldo with concern, "since you are now with Lenya, and I'm growing older, I think it's a matter we need to take care of before it becomes too late."

He looked very serious, not his usual demeanor. "Aldo, there is a problem you have never had to think about, but the time has come when I believe you must. The casteddu, where you live, is rightfully yours as the last living member of the clan. Your rights extend back much further than living memory, but you have no paper in your hand to prove it's yours." He had suddenly caught their interest. This was unexpected.

"You have no birth certificate or paper to show you are a citizen of this country. As far as the damn French bureaucrats know, you don't exist."

Aldo got up and looked out the window, something he did when troubled, then started pacing around the room. Lenya saw his hands were trembling. It never occurred to her. She knew the only thing he feared were the French, especially anything to do with government or bureaucracy. This was ingrained within the clan. Hidden is safe. Exposure is death. Their mantra.

Before Aldo could stop him, Sirio held up his hand. "You must listen to me... even though I know you don't want to. Remaining hidden worked for the clan for centuries, and for you, up to now. I know. I understand, believe me. But it must change."

Aldo paled and stood once again at the window shaking his head. Lenya was afraid he'd bolt out of the cabin at any moment. Dealing with government regulations wasn't possible for Aldo. It was something too foreign...he had no comprehension of how to react. She sat in silence. Ice churned in her stomach. Unknowingly, her head was moving side to side in time with Aldo's.

"Don't shake your head at me Lenya. I know what you are thinking." Sirio continued. "But I have been giving this much thought and I think I have a solution for our 'little' problem.

Lenya turned to him. Hope was clear in her eyes.

"Remember our friend Rapha? Well, he wants to build an exclusive boutique hotel down at the bottom of Aldo's mountain. Problem— he can't get title to the land. When his attorney checked land records to see who holds title, it's nowhere to be found. The parcel is not recorded, nor is any of the clan territory. Anywhere. It's shown in the ancient surveys but there is no owner indicated and no parcel numbers. Since nothing was ever recorded, the land never appeared on the tax rolls. I think whoever was in charge when the original records were created several hundred years ago knew it was the home of the clan and left it off all the rolls, sort of thumbing his nose with a 'try and find this' to the French tax authority."

As Sirio paused to fiddle with his pipe, he saw Lenya look towards Aldo. Her brow was furrowed and the usual sparkle left her eyes. For once she was silent as he continued. "Since no one has ever claimed it, or even seems to know of its existence, it might be considered part of the French National property, but it's not listed in their inventory of properties either, so even if they might own it, they don't know about it."

He started to laugh. "I think it was meant as one of our good Corsican jokes. But now it might become a problem. Another Corsican mystery?"

Aldo returned from the window and sat next to Lenya on the sofa. She reached over to take his hand in hers. Sirio saw her tender concern. His friend made a good choice after all.

Sirio continued. "In trying to solve this puzzle, Rapha's attorney thinks someone with unbroken, open, notorious, and continuous use of the property for a long period of time, hence the legal right, could assert a claim of adverse possession to get title. That someone might then sell the parcel to Rapha. It started me thinking."

He took more wine Lenya offered. "What if Aldo makes an arrangement with Rapha? I've devised a scheme to work it out to everyone's advantage." He looked over at Aldo, who, frowning, got up and began pacing again. Sirio knew this was not a conversation pleasing to his friend and wondered if Aldo was even following him..

"Here's the plan I've arrived at. I've already discussed it with Rapha and he agrees if Aldo does."

There was a sound almost like a growl from the window. Aldo was looking outside, his body tense as if ready to flee, but he looked over at Lenya and, seeing she was listening intently, came back to sit at the table this time.

"As the last of the clan, Aldo has the right to claim several thousand hectares—including his mountain, the flatland where Rapha wants to put the hotel, the casteddu, the cave, the dolmen and grotto as well as the forest almost up to this cabin. That is the 'hidden' property— a sizable and extremely valuable piece of real estate." Sirio stopped for a moment to catch his breath. He now had both their rapt attention.

"Aldo's claim is based on centuries of open, notorious, and continuous use and occupation." They both had their mouths open.

Sirio couldn't help a huge grin. "My idea is to have Rapha's attorney, who, by the way, happens to be his grandson, handle all the legal work. It must include a birth certificate for Aldo, a ruling from a local judge he is absolved from military service for something, such as, well... whatever ...health...elder care...reasons, and clear up all possible legal questions. Rapha will pay whatever costs are involved.

"In return, Aldo would deed him the piece he wants for his hotel, the ten hectares, and at no cost. Oh, and Rapha would agree to pay all property taxes on the entire parcel for the next several hundred years, or as long as legally possible... unless you or your heirs decide to sell it." He took a deep breath and leaned back on the sofa. "This way, you never have to worry; the property will always belong to you and your family." He looked towards Aldo and grinned. "Not too bad an idea for a crafty old man, eh?" he said as he poked Lenya in the arm.

"Is all this possible?" she asked. Her constant fear was what might happen if people found out about Aldo. She had no idea about the legal ramifications attached to his home, but this seemed to be a solution to so many potential problems.

"Anything is possible with the right connections...and enough money. I won't say more, you can figure the rest for yourself."

"So you have already spoken to Rapha about this?"

"We had a brief discussion. I think he would be amenable to almost anything if he can get property. He thinks of it as his 'retirement nest egg.' Trust me, not like he needs one. But he has become attached to the idea. Especially since he knows about the clan. Making Aldo secure for the rest of his life would give Rapha great pleasure. Truly, he told me it would be his honor to do so." Sirio nodded towards Aldo who had been thoughtful and silent throughout the discussion, but clearly understood what had been said.

Sirio continued. "Rapha is of the old Corsican families. You have to know their mentality...many times throughout history his ancestors found refuge with the clan...vendettas...a romance or two with the wrong family...mob takeovers...even pirates I am told. They always knew they had a safe place to go. You get the picture." He nodded at Lenya. "He considers this an honorable way for his family to pay back their debt for several hundred years of clan kindness and generosity." His finger was back next to his nose. "In fact, I think Rapha also availed himself of clan hospitality one time over some small incident involving a married woman and angry husband... when he was much younger, of course." He leaned back and laughed remembering the incident. "So, my friends, what do you think of my idea?"

Aldo got up, again pacing around the room. It was hard for him to stay calm, the urge for flight was strong. "You know how I feel about making the clan known." He was shaking his head at Sirio.

But the older man was having none of it. "What must be faced, my friend, is this—if the property eventually comes to the attention of the fucking bureaucrats without anyone filing a legal claim, it will escheat to the French government. End of story. So far, you have been lucky and it's remained as hidden as the clan. But, with the economy tanking, the government is in need of every Euro they can get their hands on. We have heard they are going to start reviewing tax rolls and creating new surveys. With satellites, aerial photography, digital imaging and new survey methods, you won't be so lucky in the future if some young and eager clerk, very proficient with computers, checks the tax rolls against the new surveys and sees a nice piece of land with no owner."

There is was. Plain and simple. He was going to be discovered no matter what. Civilization was finally catching up with the clan. Lenya understood the ramifications and her stomach clenched.

"How can I do this, this breach of tradition...we...the clan, has remained secret since time began. It is our way." Aldo looked like he had been struck.

"Yes, all is true. But now you are the clan...all that is left of it. It is up to you alone to decide its future." As soon as he said it, Sirio was sorry he had to speak such words.

Aldo looked like he had been punched. He sat down quickly and put his head in his hands, rubbing his forehead and sighing. "But you know I don't know how to act...talk, with these people, the offices, the villages...French...I don't understand anything...know how it works...."

"*É voilá*—the beauty of my plan. The only one you will have to speak with is Rapha's grandson, Manno. He will give you a paper to sign allowing him to represent you, and all the work will be his... attend all the necessary meetings on your behalf." Sirio could see he wasn't convinced.

"At least let Manno explain everything to you. Then you can decide." He knew it was hard for his friend. After so many generations of being removed from the world outside, the culture of paranoia was not easy to put aside. The clan had been frozen in a web of fear for millennia.

In fact, Sirio was both amazed and pleased Aldo had opened up sufficiently to let Lenya into his life—to have even moved from the cast-eddu and into the cabin with her, as it was obvious he had. Perhaps this wouldn't be so difficult for him with Lenya by his side.

Chapter 50
Decision Put Off

Aldo sat for a while on the deck, trying to clear his head and calm himself. The weather was warm in the late afternoon and showed signs of being a balmy evening. It had been a while since they had been to the grotto, but he was certain it would be warm enough for what he had in mind.

Circumstances were forcing him to make grave decisions. Even Dia couldn't hold back change.

The clan was finished. It was now time to make choices for himself. Living alone in the casteddu was out of the question. Life with Lenya gave him the simple joy of spending every day, every waking hour, with a person he loved. His precious gift from Dia. Daily he prayed to be worthy.

Although Aldo grew up in what might have been another millennium, he was smart and a fast learner. He understood the legal problems flowing from the clan remaining hidden for so long—certainly a cause for concern, but he was sure those things would be skillfully handled by Rapha's grandson; especially under the watchful eyes of both Sirio and Lenya.

What caused him grave worry was the future and possible trouble that might arise from the vastness of the gulf between his life experiences and Lenya's. Watching television, hearing newscasts, seeing the progression of time so clearly displayed in the art books he poured over, their differences repeatedly smacked him in the face.

He and Lenya existed in harmony in the world they created for themselves in the cabin, the grotto, visiting the casteddu—but once they ventured out of their special world, he'd have to face the objects of his fears—the current century and everything came with it.

Technology he couldn't hope to understand. Different religions insisting on supremacy. Terror. Politics. Crimes. Hate. Massive wealth and hopeless poverty stripped people of all dignity. Others hungering to amass unimportant things, new inventions and tidal waves of information assailing life from all directions. Social interactions by machines rather than speaking directly to another's face, a breath apart.

Modern life enfolded in front of him. He forced himself to watch newscasts—unbelievable; senseless killings, devastating fires, tornados, floods, bombings. To Aldo it was both repugnant and horrifying.

He wanted no part of this present, but he'd have to face it in order to be with Lenya. She was not meant to exist alone with him in the cabin, and he didn't expect her to, even though she seemed happy enough for the moment.

Aldo looked to Dia for help in understanding this momentous— terrifying and joyful—change in his life. Like the earth's crusts shifting to shake the island, followed by the inevitable tidal wave washing away all that existed before—there was no stopping it.

While he hunted and yearned for Lenya, he had given no thought to what would happen after he caught her. They'd been dancing together in bliss these past months with little thought to the future, existing solely in the now. As his mother had often told him, there always comes a time to pay the piper. But he needed more time to think.

He hugged Sirio as he left, and thanked him for his concern, but said it was something he and Lenya must discuss together and think about.

Sirio nodded and clasped his friend in his arms before leaving. Sirio was well aware of the turbulent changes Aldo would soon have to face.

Aldo went into the cabin, kissed Lenya goodbye on her forehead and asked her to meet him at the grotto at dusk with a bottle of wine and some bread and cheese. She was busy with her writing and nodded absentmindedly. He poked her in the arm to get her attention. She looked up at him, "Okay, I got it...dusk...wine...cheese...grotto. You got a date...and I always pay attention to you." They smiled at each other and he grabbed her in a bear hug. As usual, she melted into his arms.

By the time she arrived, he had arranged the grotto to his satisfaction. The large bear skin from the casteddu covered the altar where Lenya liked her picnics. The place where they first made love.

Around the skin, groups of wildflowers were artfully arranged in a profusion of yellows, purples and pinks mixed with branches of strawberry tree, eucalyptus and sandalwood, immortelle, sprigs of rosemary, thyme and bay leaves. The fragrant mixture accompanied Lenya's strides long before she arrived.

Handmade candles fixed in melted wax topped surrounding boulders to light the grotto with flickering lights. She stopped and tried to take it all in. Magical.

The natural splendor of the grotto was something she always appreciated, but the transformation was stunning. Her man had created a fairy circle—the most exquisite thing she'd ever seen. That is, until Aldo stepped from the shadows into the light. His was garbed only in a wreath of braided greens encircling his head. Lenya caught her breath— the light from the candles caressed his body like lovers, giving definition to the broadness of his chest, muscles of calves, thighs and arms, hollows beneath cheekbones, veins visible on hands held out to her. It was too much, too much love and emotion, she found it difficult to breathe. The hair on her arms stood on end in expectation as he stepped closer and put his arms around her once more, echoing the bear hug before he left the cabin earlier. He kissed her eyes, his tongue tasting salt as he unbuttoned her shirt. She stood silently and let him do what he wanted. He was le Maître, in command. When her clothes pooled around her feet, he placed a wreath of fragrant star jasmine around her head, then picked her up in his arms and gently laid her on the bear skin.

Summer solstice arrived, time to honor Dia. Lenya thought she knew what to expect when Aldo made love to her, but this night exceeded anything she ever imagined. His strong hands touched her body with a gentle firmness speaking of a love transmitted through her skin to her soul. It was as if she was in a dream of desire, love and fantasy she never wanted to wake from. His lips, his tongue, his beard...caressing, gentling, rousing her. Her breath caught with emotion as her body responded to him.

By now, she had learned not to rush him; to put her upbringing aside and let him love her in the way he wanted, in the moment, relishing every touch, every contact between them, letting him take pleasure from pleasuring her, and she in turn savoring the feel of his body with her mouth, her fingers, her skin. He taught her to slow down, relax— luxuriate in his skill. It was like the enjoyment of a fine wine, don't gulp it down, roll it around in your mouth so the taste buds get the full sensation.

There was no need to rush to climax, only slow down and experience the power of being together, exploring each other's body, giving each other the delight of two people in love.

Dia got her fill.

They awoke together when dawn lit the grotto bathing them in the soft pink and orange of first light. They had slept in each other's arms, bodies locked together as yin and yang,.

Aldo had made his decision. Dia had shown him the way. He would do anything in his power to stay with Lenya, even if it meant facing the unknown world outside.

What he didn't know was Lenya had made a decision too. She would do whatever it took to protect this man she loved from having to deal with a hostile world that might bring him harm. She knew that together they could solve any problem.

Chapter 51
E-Mails

Aldo looked at Lenya with a tenderness he knew well. It was the way he remembered his father looking at his mother, the way a man looks at the woman who completes him.

He had been shocked when Lenya told him the customs and beliefs she had been taught as a child. She had grown up in a culture of shame, guilt and covering up sex, treating it as an unsavory adventure.

He remembered laughing when she explained what her mother had told her what a woman should do during sex, "Look at the ceiling, darling, and think of England."

But then he realized it wasn't funny. It was sad to think a woman's pleasure should be so ignored. Sad to grow up in a culture that reduced the beauty of the union between two people to 'fucking' or 'hooking up'—like a connection between two animals, or worse—mechanical devices. He visualized two dogs rutting and 'hooked' together. There was no appreciation of the harmony between lovers or the power of the act. From what Lenya said, her relations with her husband had been satisfying for her, Aldo was glad it had been so, rather than as her mother explained. And now Lenya was learning still more ways of pleasure, the ways he could show her—exploring together the power of the sensual.

When he watched television to learn more English, he was horrified at the sexual habits he saw. He found it hard to understand young people rutting with no thought, no emotion. Aldo knew sex rites in ancient times were performed between priestesses and the consort, often strangers to each other, sacraments in homage to Dia—rituals between believers performed in accordance with tradition. Always, the principle was veneration of the power when man and woman join, and the acceptance of its profound role in the universe.

Learning English was important, but not important enough to suffer through such trash as "Jersey Shore." It both sickened him and made him sad. He harrumphed and went outside. Fresh air was sometimes very necessary to clear the head.

Lenya wasn't feeling well. She was queasy in the mornings and threw up, but it didn't last long and soon went away. Her breasts were sensitive to the touch, nipples feeling like they were on fire when Aldo caressed them, and it wasn't a pleasant sensation. It was odd to her as she loved him to touch her, but for some reason, breasts were off limit for the moment. *Maybe I'm allergic to something? And they seem to be growing? What's that about...too much massaging? Too much sex? Too bad!*

Next time I go into town I'll make an appointment with a local doctor and see what they have to say. She missed her period, but she had been irregular for the last year, probably perimenopause. The thought had occurred to her she might be pregnant. But after eighteen years with Andre and no birth control, she didn't believe it was possible. In any event, she was probably too old. She pushed the thought out of her mind.

But Aldo knew. He hoped Lenya could bear a child to term. He knew all the signs, even the scent of her changed with the growth of new life inside. Lush, fertile...woman. He didn't think she was aware of it. He knew she had never bred before. Her sister had no children, so maybe she didn't know what to look for. He thought back and reckoned she might be about two, maybe three, moons along. It could have happened at the summer solstice, maybe earlier. Life was good. His love was bearing his child.

Lenya told Lotte her Skype video camera broke when it fell off her desk so she had privacy at least. Lotte kept nudging here to get a new one but she was able to stave her off by pleading she was too busy to go into Ajaccio to the computer store. Her usual pleasant and funny chats with Lotte took a different turn.

Lotte469:

Are you avoiding me? Is there something you're not telling me? Are you all right? Is Tom all right? Have you stopped work on the book? Talk to me! Love, L1, remember me?...your big sister in case you forgot

Lenyascribe:
Okay, I'll answer in order of questions.
No, I'm not avoiding you.
No, there is nothing I'm not telling you.
I'm fine.
Tom is fine.
I'm working on the book like a slave. Ask Ellie, she'll tell you I'm sending her pages almost every day. She loved the last chapters.
How's your new beau? Hanging in?

Lotte469:
New beau is fine. I'm coming to see you. I smell a rat all the way over here. Don't forget, twins are psychic with each other.

The next day there was another chat request.

Lotte469
I spoke to Ellie and she says she thinks you're in love because of the way you're writing has changed. She likes it, by the way.
Is it true?
Who with?
I'm booking my ticket and want to see for myself.

Lenyascribe:
Don't be getting your knickers in a twist and hopping on a plane. I'm fine,
writing and for god's sake, I'm happy.
Can't you deal with that?

Lotte469:
I'm happy you're happy!
But with whom?
I have to look him over and give my stamp of approval.

Lenyascribe:
Okay already, you can come, but please, please come alone. You can see
your new swain after you come here, but don't bring him.
I want this to be you and me please...a two sis meet-up. And, if you're
good, you can meet him.

Lotte469:
Meet who?

Lenyascribe:
Him.

Lotte469:
If this is a caveman he better be good, and I mean real good!

Lenyascribe:
I think you'll like him if you give him a chance.
We'll have time to talk about it when you're here.

Lotte469:
I'm booking my ticket as soon as I stop writing to you.
Bye for now, love, me.

It seemed she couldn't open her mail box without a batch of mail waiting for her.

Another day, the first was from Terrence.

BevHlsGamaster:

Hey Babe! How are things? Sorry you haven't heard from me in a while, been in a bit of conflict here. First the lady, you remember, wanted to stay with me...she decided... we should be parents. I never mentioned to you since it didn't matter, but I'm sterile...mumps as a kid. Oh well, used to want a family but decided not to be for me. Anyway, then she wanted a sperm donor...didn't need a script to imagine how that played. No thanks!

Went a few rounds, she aims low, and the short of it is - she's back with the guy who socked her...seems he's got sperm.

The locksmith just left and the locks are now woman proof! ...but not if you might want to come and visit... stay for a while, decide to move to LA... whatever...

Love, T

Lenyascribe:

Hi T! Sorry to hear about the continuing mess but seems like you got it figured out...good for you!

Busy working on the new book and they seem to like it in the Apple.

The caveman moved in and it's working out fine for now, but who knows? Will keep you posted.

By the way, he's quite an artist, here's one of his works I scanned...his woodland friends.

I admit it's an odd relationship but seems to be working for now. We'll see.

No plans at the moment to come to the States but will certainly be there in the foreseeable future. Maybe we can be on the same coast at the same time.

Cheers! Lenya (or Ugga-Wugga as I'm now known)

As she pushed the button for "send" she had a moment of conflicting emotions. Did she really need to have Terrence know she was living

with Aldo? ...and the snide comment about my "cavewoman" name...
how bitchy was that?

Too late, the mail was on its way. Would he tell Lotte? She didn't
think they were in touch, but he might tell his sister. She's got to find
out sometime anyway. Then she felt guilty she'd told Terrence.

She felt a very slight flutter in her abdomen. Something was moving a tiny bit in there. Okay Lenya girl, time to give it up....and she
admitted for sure what she had been suspecting. She was pregnant.
There was no more denial, no way to ignore the signs. Her hands found
their way over her belly, moving together of their own accord to hug her
own special new bloom in a gentle embrace. "Hello down there" she said
out loud as she caressed the bump growing inside her...hers and Aldos.

She was so filled with joy she thought her heart was going to burst
out of her chest.

Chapter 52
Thank You Amazon

The cardboard box with the smile was propped on the sliding glass doors when Lenya returned to the cabin after a trip to town for groceries. Tom and Aldo were off on some adventure. The cabin was empty. Good, now I can have the place to myself and see what I can learn to surprise Aldo. She had been waiting anxiously for this particular package.

Opening the box, she picked out the books she had ordered:, "Sacred Sex," and the "Kama Sutra."

Okay, they might not be exactly goddess worship, but they should give me some ideas. She thumbed through the illustrated pages with interest. Lenya had been satisfied with her sex life with Andre and thought they knew it all, after a few months with Aldo, she realized she was less than a neophyte.

For Aldo, sex was a sacred experience, every possible joy to be explored and gloried in, every bit of energy an offering to his goddess. Nothing was too intimate, no place on her body unexplored in the event it might offer her some pleasure.

In the past, she had looked at sex as very pleasurable, but not a holy act. It was time for her to study up on the more esoteric pleasures. She knew she would never be able to turn love making into an art as Aldo did, but perhaps she could offer him some tiny bit of interesting artistry as well. After on-line research, she realized there wasn't much written on ancient sacred sexual practices other than Tantric yoga. She had learned how to give some awesome oral sex, and laughed over an on-line lesson on how to put on a condom with your mouth. It reminded her of afternoons sitting in a college bar with her girlfriends tying cherry stems in knots with their tongues and howling with laughter.

The books gave her some interesting historical insights. Some experts speculated Tantric practices had probably made their way to the Mediterranean to become incorporated in the rites of goddess worship. Others thought the reverse might have been the case. Lenya didn't care which came first, she wanted to know what they did and how they did it.

After a little more reading, she realized many of the intricate positions Aldo used for lovemaking were in the Kama Sutra. Coincidence or an accident of natural lovemaking? She didn't know.

Aldo returned home to find the cabin scented with basil, ginger and bergamot, fragrant incense burning in holders placed next to bouquets of greens and ferns.

A low fire burned in the fireplace, cushions and quilts arranged on the floor nearby. The strains of I Muvrini with their distinctive primitive and sensual harmonies played in the background. The gentle voices of five hundred choristers blending with strings and wind instruments for "Sara," the majestic and commanding beat of "A Voce Rivolta," after the haunting bagpipes of "Rispondimi Ie" filled the air. The primitive and mystical sounds of Corsica.

Lenya studied his face with apprehension as he took in the scene she had set. He nodded approval at her naked body, softly visible beneath a flowing saffron silk caftan and his hand was warm, strong and electric to her touch as she led him to recline on the nest of pillows. He couldn't suppress his pleasure as she undressed him, lightly caressing his body as she removed piece after piece. Kneeling, she bathed him from head to toe with warm washcloths fragrant with scented lavender water and lilac. Gratified, she watched him relax under her ministrations while she patted him dry. He was almost purring.

She massaged first his hands and then his feet with oil she mixed from patchouli, musk and sandalwood, the scents blending to suffuse the air with magic. Her hands spoke to him of her love greater than words could express as she moved slowly the length of calves, massaging hard muscle into pliability, then up to his thighs, taking time to enjoy the feel of him beneath her palms. He tried to speak but she placed her finger on his lips. Silence. Then she tapped the head of his manhood and shook her finger at it. No. Not yet. You be quiet too, she thought as she slipped her mouth slowly over the velvet skin, savoring every difference in texture. He reached to massage her neck and head as he groaned beneath her.

This was her game, and she exalted in the bliss of her mouth and lips surrounding him, taking him into her. She realized she given this gift in the past more as a duty than a joy, she hadn't minded, but misunderstood the gentle connection from the act of giving this most intimate of pleasures. She inhaled the dizzying musky maleness of him, nuzzled her cheeks, her nose, in the soft hair on his body, like a cat purring in contentment as she luxuriated in the feel of her man.

Remembering the various positions and illustrations she had studied and tried to memorize, she moved to recreate some of the postures described in the sacred rites. Many of the forms looked awkward to her, arms and legs entwined oddly, but together, they moved seamlessly into them, Aldo seeming to be familiar with Tantric Yoga as he guided legs and arms through the most complicated positions. In the Lotus position, impaled on him, ankles crossed at his back and thrilled at the feel of him so deeply inside her, she moaned as muscles moved of their own accord and she lost herself in pleasure while looking into the depths of his grey-blue eyes, inhaling the delight of his breath.

Hours and ecstasies later they awoke, entwined.

Slipping out of his embrace, she returned with a tray laden with shining red grapes, apricots, satin skinned plums of purple and green, dried dates and figs from Africa; Casinca, A Filetta and crumbly white Brocciu cheeses; a long baguette, crispy and fragrant from the boulangerie, sliced prosciutto and local dried Fegatelli salami. Shooing a nosey Tom away, she filled two glasses with Sirio's special reserve Sciacarello and proceeded to hand feed her love the choicest morsels from the feast while he grinned at her.

After a while, he rolled over and kissed her on the navel, his hands gently massaging the small mound growing inside. Then he touched her on the lips. Her turn to be quiet. "This is last like this, no more deep... hard until baby comes, not to bend his nose. We do other...things...for this time." He gave her a wide smirky grin. "I learn...many other ways." He nipped at her earlobe on his way to give her breast a quick tongue flick.

He had known about the baby all along. They would be making love very carefully until their child was born.

She had often thought he was much smarter than she was in many ways. Now she knew for sure.

Chapter 53
Lotte Arrives

Lenya waited at the Calvi airport with Tom for support. This is not going to be easy, but it had to be done. Lotte and Aldo together? Just the thought made her fidgety.

She had no idea how her sister would react to Aldo. And can they even relate to each other? Aldo's English was improving daily, but French and Italian were interspersed when he couldn't find the English word.

Lotte had studied a little French in high school as far as Lenya remembered. Languages were of no interest, only business and how to make money, an odd calling for such a free spirit. Lenya shrugged her shoulders. No use worrying now.

Tom was restless. His sight and hearing were both failing, milling people now made him uncomfortable, more so when the waiting crowd began to push toward the gate, anxious to greet loved ones or clients.

Lenya looked outside and above to the range of mountains surrounding the airport on three sides, sunlight bathed the craggy peaks, softening the brilliant green of the maquis along the slopes. The long terminal was filled with people coming and going from airports throughout Europe. Summer brought tourists to crawl all over the island. Lenya saw them rushing by with luggage filled with hiking shoes and poles and she laughed as she thought of her personal hiking equipment, a pair of open back clog-type sneakers and a mop handle. *Chacun á son goût,* each to his own taste.

Over the heads of the river of people arriving, she saw a red gloved hand waiving in the air. It had to be Lotte. Who else would wear red kid gloves to Corsica? The rest of the crowd was dressed in jeans and tee-shirts or casual business attire. Lotte emerged from the crowd in a black Dior suit with a red silk rose on the shoulder to match the gloves and brilliant red lipstick and red soles of her Christian Louboutin patent leather pumps. I love her dearly, *but damn*!... she is predictable!

As soon as Lenya hugged her sister, the tension lifted. We've gotten through a lot more difficult things than this together. She'll do fine.

They pushed and shoved to load the SUV with Lotte's four large suitcases.

Lenya couldn't resist. "I'll bet you overweight cost was more than the cost of the flight."

Lotte laughed. "Yeah, I guess it was, but remember, you're not my only stop. I'm going to visit Mauricio in Cap d'Antibes for a week. Gotta' look spiffy for a new beau."

The sisters laughed.

"I hope you brought some hiking gear with you, we do a lot of it around here." Lenya couldn't repress giggles at the thought of Lotte's red soles sloshing up the muddy driveway or tottering on spike heeled Jimmy Choo's at the grotto.

"Don't worry about a thing, I got it covered. Brought two different wardrobes, one for cavemen in the woods, the other for the new beau—*soigné accoutrement* for the enticement and enjoyment of very well-heeled international lover boys." Lotte laughed and tossed her long hair out of her face. "But you have a point, probably would have been cheaper to buy the woods-woman trekking gear here...or borrow yours. That is, if you wear anything in the woods." It was impossible for her to resist a meaningful double eyebrow twitch.

Lenya couldn't resist a light punch at her sister's arm. They were back to their usual teasing banter; easy familiarity relaxed them both.

When Lenya pulled the car into the clearing at the cabin, Aldo was standing at the open door with a brilliant smile. The unadorned deck Lenya had driven away from was now resplendent. Bouquets of flowers and greens overflowed in close to a dozen cans and buckets. It looked like a pastoral celebration about to take place. As they opened the car doors, the smell of meat cooking on the open barbeque wafted along with the smoke of burning oak. Had he really gotten out the fatted calf for Lotte? My man knows how to make a good impression... why do I keep selling him short?

Lotte seemed suitably impressed as Aldo walked towards them. He was neatly dressed in un-ripped jeans and a bright cobalt blue golf shirt that strained a bit at the biceps. His blue-gray eyes twinkled while he took in the close resemblance between the two women.

When Lotte got out of the car, he took her hand to assist. As soon as she was standing, he bowed and placed his lips slightly above the top of her hand. Lenya was stunned. *I didn't know he was such a gentleman. Where did he learn such courtly manners?*

The day was clear, the sun highlighting Aldo's dark copper hair. His beard had two thin braids at the sides, the rest gathered and tied about two inches past his chin with a piece of leather. Two more braids framed his face and were pulled back into a thick, shining plait trailing down the center of his back to end in a soft brush of curls.

Lotte's mouth was open, admiring Aldo's muscles flex as he hauled her heavy suitcases out of the car, the glow from the sun creating a bronze aura around him. He wasn't any pumped up body-builder, but a naturally powerful man.

Lenya hadn't truly acknowledged how stunning he was until she saw him through her sister's eyes...couldn't help the feeling of pride as she saw Lotte's reaction. *Hah! Bet her fancy Armani-wearer doesn't have kind of physique...or hair.* Lenya mentally slapped herself. This was her twin, she had to stop gloating.

Aldo left the women alone in the cabin to catch up and went outside to tend to his cooking. Lotte looked around approvingly. "You have a nice cozy set-up here. I like it. And WOW!...you sure found yourself a yummy guy! And he cooks too!" Lotte shook her head as she peeled off the gloves and tossed them on top of her travel bag.

Do I detect a hint of envy? Lenya thought as she said, "Why don't you change into something fitting for a barbeque, then we'll go outside and open a bottle of wine."

Lotte nodded, looking around the living area. "Where are you going to put me? This place looks awfully small. I don't want to cramp your style." She couldn't resist the naughty single eyebrow raise.

"Don't worry, there's a guest room we've fixed up for you. It's not the Ritz, but I think you'll manage for a few days," Lenya said as she opened the door to the small room. A single bed was covered in a colorful patchwork quilt, a few bright pillows scattered on top.

One wall was graced by a window opening to the brilliant green forest beyond. "What a view to wake up to!" Lotte said.

The walls were a rough wood redolent of cedar. A bouquet of flowers and greens dominated a night table; mixing with the wood scent they perfumed the small space better than any Parisian room fragrance. Lenya smiled as she realized Aldo had added the bouquet while she was at the airport. He wanted her sister to feel at home.

"This is fine...more than fine—perfect. Thanks sis...." Lotte paused—looked around again "...and did you put the flowers there or did he?"

Lotte caught on pretty fast, Lenya thought. She's already beginning to understand Aldo. "He did."

"Thought so. Hmmm... I've got the feeling you've found a real live one."

Lenya nodded, feeling the knot in her stomach begin to dissolve. The visit might turn out okay after all.

The three of them sat on the deck and killed a bottle of wine while Aldo played his flute in between preparing his favorite meal—*sanglier* accompanied by zucchini, peppers, onions and garlic tossed in olive oil and roasted in a pot over the fire. A salad of mixed greens dressed with salt, pepper, Dijon mustard, local olive oil and fresh lemons was the final touch. After they had eaten until they groaned, they lay on the deck like they used to when they were kids and looked up at the stars, so brilliant in the black night with no artificial lights to dim their beauty.

Lotte took another sip of wine, "I don't think I've seen stars so bright since Mom took us to the East Hampton cottage in the summer."

"I know, isn't it spectacular? We spend most evenings out here... beats TV all to heck."

The sounds of Aldo's flute drifted over the deck. "I think you've stumbled into paradise. Be happy and enjoy." Lotte had dropped her usual New York banter, Lenya heard the sincerity in her voice.

The days passed in a blur of hikes through the forest and the good-natured bitching always accompanying Lotte's attempt at exercise. But at the end, she admitted she enjoyed the walks, especially lunch at the grotto and visiting the menhirs. Aldo didn't take her to the necropolis, and Lenya never mentioned it.

One afternoon they went swimming in their private mountain pool. This time the sisters wore bathing suits and Aldo got the message and jumped in wearing cut-off jeans.

Lotte was fascinated by Aldo's paintings. She spent hours studying his work and having him explain the various subjects to her. They seemed to understand each other quite well, evolving their own common language.

One morning when Aldo had gone on one of his rambles, Lotte got Lenya aside.

"Your man has real genius. He's self-taught but his work is sophisticated. It gives glimpse of a past I couldn't imagine. Think Grandma Moses times fifty, both in talent and the lifestyle he portrays." She rummaged on the table for a certain picture. "I'll bet a gallery in New York would get a bundle for some of these." She held up a watercolor of the clan holding spears and hunting a large brown bear.

Lenya looked at her sister as if she were daft. "There's no way his work can get out on the market—they'd want to know who he was and how he knew all the things he does...investigations...trying to call him a fraud...not a hornet's nest I want to stir."

"But honey, think of the money he could make, the fame he could have. He's unique, one of a kind, nothing like this anywhere in the world. Do you have the right to make such a decision for him?"

"Yeah, and can you imagine the investigative reporters digging into the new art sensation I found in the backwoods of Corsica? No way would I put him through all that ...not going to happen!" Lenya spun around and walked away from her sister. *She doesn't get it. He can't face what we call civilization.*

Turning back again, Lenya implored, "...and if you have any fondness for him, you won't tell anyone...I mean anyone...not even the new beau. I don't want the sharks capitalizing on Aldo; he has no defenses against the outside world, he'd never survive our idea of fame."

"Okay, okay—I get it, sis. Mum's the word. But I think he's a diamond in the rough, an undiscovered genius."

"Let's keep him that way." But as soon as the words came out, she wondered how long their secret would remain safe after all the paperwork Sirio told them had to be done.

Begging for a break from hikes, Lotte insisted on a day at home with no exercise. Lenya was happy to be back at work writing. Lotte and Aldo were outside on the deck relaxing together in the sun. Her peace and quiet was suddenly shattered by Lotte screaming, Aldo howling and loud slapping noises. *Ohmigod, there's no way he's hitting Lotte! He's much too gentle. Did she lose her temper at him?*

Lenya ran to the deck, not knowing what to expect. What she saw was her sister and Aldo laughing at each other with a deck of cards between them.

"What are you doing to him? Did you hit him? Did he hit you?"

"Naw, don't get nervous... taught him how to play Slap-Jack. He's good at it ...but excitable."

Aldo had a huge grin on his face as he held up cards to show her he had taken the pile.

Lenya shook her head at them and went back to work. All during the next hour she heard laughter, slaps, groans and howls from the deck. *What will my sister think of next? It sounds like I've already got two kids playing outside.* But she knew in her heart how important the simple game was in solidifying the bonds of family between her love and her twin. Lotte had intuitively made the right move with the silly game. She had been accepted into the clan.

Lenya had finally confided to Lotte, admitting she was pregnant. Surprised, she watched as her twin burst into tears. "I'm sorry, but I can't believe it. I thought we were going to be the last of our family...neither one of us ever pregnant...figured it would all end with us.

"Oh my god! I'm going to be an aunt! Auntie Lotte! What is it? What are you going to name it...him...her?" Lenya laughed and put up her hand. Her sister was going to kill her with questions.

"Rein it in cowgirl! I'm glad you're happy, but we're doing this the old fashioned way. I'm not going to find out if it's a boy or a girl. We are not going to bombard this child with sonograms, x-rays or what-have-you before it's born. And for your information, my baby is going to be born at home with its mother and father—together with a mid-wife of course. Aldo has delivered many babies. His family has always been Signadori, healers, for the clan, but he also wants a mid-wife he knows and trust to assist. We have spoken about this and it is decided.

Lenya saw Lotte understood how important this was to her and let the subject be, but not all the way. She had to get the last word or a thousand in. "Of course you have made up your mind, but make sure you check out the vitamins and diet you should be on, it's all on the Internet anyway. Let me know if you need anything. Oh, and if there is any sign of trouble, I expect you to high-tail it to the nearest doctor... and you certainly have found a good obstetrician on the island. Right?" The concern was loud and clear in her voice, as was the underlying order.

Lenya knew when to capitulate. "I promise I'll check out a good doctor and keep his number in my cell, but don't worry, everything is going to be fine."

Lotte hugged her again, and when she let go, she ran her hand over her twins slowly growing bump. "Well, I'm glad to meet you little one. I'm your Auntie Lotte and I promise to spoil the heck out of you." She backed up and looked at the slight mound and tapped it twice with her finger, "...and if your mom and dad don't treat you right, like make you live in a cave or something,... you can always run away to live with me." The twins hugged again and laughed.

One afternoon Aldo took them to one of the many caves in the mountains—one Lenya hadn't been to before. Entering the darkened space he motioned for the women to sit down. The cave was dry and pleasant but the air inside held a faint musty odor of habitation, old cooking, long dead fires, musk redolent of bodies and animals. The scents of many lives lived within its confines. It was the ancient home of Aldo's clan. Before the casteddu had been built.

He carried some dried branches inside and started a small fire. As the flames leapt high the twins saw long dead hunters chasing their game across the walls. Shades of ochre, carnelian, black and browns fading to buff flickered in the light giving life and movement to the fleeing animals. They were looking at something from the far reaches of time, a memory of distant millennia, a story of life left by a long forgotten artist.

Waving his hand over his shoulder backwards several times so they understood it was from the distant past, Aldo explained "My family...long... long...many...many ago." The sisters shivered as they thought of how many years—perhaps four or five thousand...maybe more?

Later evening, Lotte again tried to press her point. "He has first-hand knowledge about life in a time no one knows anything about, and the rare talent to show it in living color. Lenya, are you sure you don't want to share this?"

"I'm sure. I only want to protect him. I know I'm right."

"I respect your wishes, but if you change your mind..."

Lenya shook her head. There was no way she was going to expose Aldo to the prying, prodding, doubting and angry world she came from and realized that she was picking up the paranoia of the clan. She also understood how quickly things could change.

When it was time for Lotte to leave, Aldo presented her with a roll of canvas. His going-away gift. As she spread it on the table, the canvas opened to the three of them sitting on one of the boulders lining the mountain lake. The two women faced forward and looked alike, the only difference was one had long hair and wore a loose flowing off-the-shoulder blouse, the other had a short haircut and typical L.L. Bean clothing. The man sat in three-quarter profile, bare-chested with a red beard and long red hair trailing down his back. A small dog, white with brown and black spots, sat on the man's lap.

The expressions on their faces showed how content and happy they were together. The sky was clear soft blue and sun glistened on the water and their hair—a memory of a perfect day. Lotte held it to her heart and then gave him a kiss on the cheek. "Mercie, Aldo. I will treasure this always, I promise you."

He was glowing as he patted her with a one arm bear-hug.

Under her breath, Lenya muttered, "...and you keep it in your house, to yourself...no explanations to anyone.... It only shows us in modern clothing and a man with long hair and a beard in jeans...could be any artist...easy...explain it away."

Lotte nodded assent.

The sisters couldn't convince him to go to the airport with them. Lotte tried to tease him into coming but to no avail. She knew he didn't mind the car as they had all taken drives together. When he shied back at her suggestion, she realized he didn't like the idea of being with crowds, and also, maybe he didn't want to say 'goodbye.' Lenya suspected he was giving them this last time alone.

Lotte now understood her sister's reluctance to share Aldo with the world they came from...a world he didn't understand... and had no interest in. His discovery might impact their unborn child as well. It finally made sense to her.

Chapter 54
Book Accepted

News travels at the speed of light in this new millennium, sometimes too fast. Lenya stared at the e-mail from Ellie.

Dear Lenya:

I'm delighted to be the one to give you the good news. Arbor Island House has accepted the manuscript. The terms are very generous considering the marketplace at the moment. They are willing to pay a guarantee of $750,000 for the trilogy as long as they represent all rights – TV, films, new media, etc. Considering what I've been seeing lately, it's a stunning deal and I suggest you move quickly before they change their minds.

They have a few questions, such as, where did you find the letters between Napoleon and Josephine? Did you make them up or are they accurate translations? There are a few other historical references they want back-up for or will take the work as fiction rather than historical. Their main interest is the reader will learn something based on fact along with enjoying the story. Can this be done?

Let me know when you will be back in the states to attend to all the details.

And of course, let me know if you are interested in the terms. If so, I suggest a speedy response and I'll prepare a deal memo for everyone to sign. I have your power of attorney but I'd like a fax confirmation once you see the memo.

And by the way, the payment on submission of first draft is $100,000. Go have a nice glass of wine and relax. Things are looking up!
Ellie

Lenya's triumph was short-lived. Ellie had submitted the outline and the first ten chapters, now she had to finish the damn thing!

Lenya read and re-read Ellie's message. It meant a lot of work, more research and travel. There was a new contract to draw up with negotiations about advances, royalties, rights—much to think about. Her lawyer would take care of most of it, but she had to be in on the bargaining. As Lenya was always aware, this could be her last book and she needed to secure her future. Instead of herself, there were now going to be two more people to worry about and on Corsica life was expensive, not only because of a sinking dollar and higher Euro.

She had to give Ellie an idea of when the book would be delivered. Lenya knew there were incredible amounts of research she kept putting off. The island didn't have enough resources to supply what she needed and not everything was available on the internet. Since Ellie had pointed out the publisher was specifically interested because of the historical accuracy, there was no getting around it.

The Bibliothéque National de France de Arsenal where the Mandregore collection resided was a must. It housed thousands of illuminated manuscripts she wanted to study in order to maintain the accuracy of her descriptions—the clothes, living conditions and customs for each of the epochs she covered in the books. While much of the historic factual materials were available on-line, these illuminations were crucial for her to breathe reality into her characters and the conditions under which they survived. Lenya found the digitalized versions didn't quite convey the same feel the originals did. It was the difference between seeing the original "Mona Lisa" and a print.

She spent hours on line wading through the lists of manuscripts and historic factual materials but it was a time consuming process. To streamline the time needed to get through the morass of information, she had to go to Paris and speak with some of the librarians and historians connected with the Bibliothéque, the Louvre and the Sorbonne. Hopefully, someone at one of the institution might be able to direct her to a student or two, happy for some additional income, who could assist in the mind boggling research —to at least point her in the right direction.

Many times Ellie had stressed the detail Lenya provided in her books made them come alive. It was the element set her off from the rest of the writers in her genre. For the new series it would be even more important. The facts and dates of history were easily found. But they gave little indication of what life was actually like for those enmeshed in living and making history.

What did the peasants eat for dinner? ... the nobles? What were their clothes made out of? How often did they bathe? What did the nobility wear under their lace and silks? Where did they go to the bathroom? How often were they able to take a bath? Did they brush their teeth?

How many people worked in a typical manor house? What kind of furnishings were found in the homes of the nobility?... the merchant class?...the peasants? What did they sit on?...hang on the walls What kind of animals did they keep and where?

How often did markets convene? What kind of cooking implements did people use? Were there traveling merchants? ...and on and on with an endless list of the questions needed to fill in warp and weft of the fabric of life clothing the bare facts of history.

It meant she had to leave Aldo, at least for a while as she poured over hundreds of illuminated manuscript pages and paintings at both the Bibliothéque and the Louve or, until she found research assistants. Unless Aldo came along...the thought lasted for less than a nanosecond. He didn't like crowds; he'd never been off the island, or in a city. She couldn't picture him on the Metro. So far, she'd only been able to convince him to get into an automobile, probably because he was used to riding with Sirio. An airplane was out of the question.

Maybe she could sit him at a table in the library and he could sketch? But what if he went out and got lost? He'd wander around Paris, she wasn't even sure he could cross a street in traffic.

On Corsica, she went to shop at the market alone, went to town by herself, and if she had the urge to go to a restaurant, it was strictly a table for one unless Sirio was available. Lenya couldn't help it, the idea of leaving him made her tearful, and the thought of subjecting him to the insanity of modern life did the same. She was trapped in her own personal catch 22.

She made her decision—go alone to Paris, eat in some of her favorite restaurants and get the research done in little more than a week, two at most. She'd be home with him before he even had a chance to miss her. He would understand she wasn't leaving him forever.

Motivated to get everything done as soon as possible, she sent notes to the head librarian at the Bibliothéque, the Louvre and the Sorbonne asking if they knew of any students interested in doing research, and if not, would they post a notice. Then she began the arduous job of lining up exactly where to go for her research, and how to get it done quickly. It was a start.

As Lenya fretted over the trip to Paris, she knew she would eventually have to go back to New York City too. It would be a much longer trip and she dreaded it so much she didn't want to even think about it.

She had been away more than a year and a half. There were too many things to attend to on the other side of the world, not the least of which was to see if her house was standing. But she couldn't leave Aldo—no, she wouldn't leave him. The thought was painful, even considering it gave her a pang of fear? Regret? When she could no longer avoid the issue, bracing herself to deal with it gave her inspiration.

A plan started to emerge. He could come to New York with her. They would go by ocean liner; he might even enjoy the trip. They'd be together and he'd have some understanding of the world she came from. She imagined he might be fascinated by the sights of the city. Another thought that lasted for a few seconds.

He'd have to have a passport to get into the United States, and with European Economic Community citizenship he was entitled to a visa waiver. If Rapha's lawyer was able to get him a birth certificate, problem would be solved. But how about the rest of the problems: taxes, military service, land ownership? What if the government thought he was hiding because he was a terrorist?

Or even worse, "they" or whoever "they" might be, might want to study him. He could be prodded or poked, examined and possibly debunked as a fake. No government wants to graciously admit a whole clan had been living within their country in secret for millennia. What kind of a hornet's nest would open up?

Lenya cringed at the idea their baby might be the subject of study. Poked and pinched, DNA analyzed. What if she had to deny Aldo was the father? She knew Aldo considered this child to be a gift from Dia— the continuation of the clan.

Lenya turned the problems over and over in her mind for nights on end. Aldo couldn't help her solve this conundrum; he had no experience with governments, administrations, functionaries or petty official-dom. Lenya shuddered at the thought.

One night she woke up in a cold sweat after a nightmare. In her dream Aldo was held in a cement room like a prison. Tubes were attached to him and his fluids were being drained into bags. His eyes were wide open and staring at nothing—hair and beard matted and drab. She called out to him in the dream and he tried to turn to her, but his head was held immobile in some contraption with screws penetrating his skull. A glass wall separated them and she pounded on it in rage, but it didn't break and she ended up weeping on the floor in an antiseptic white corridor, helpless as she watched his life flow into the tubes. Weak and vulnerable, tears were flowing down her cheeks as she woke.

Shaken, she recalled similar scenes from movies she had seen. An involuntary shiver overcame her. There had to be a better way.

In the world of terrorists and post-9/11, life wasn't so easy anymore, at least not for people without a criminal mentality.

Sleepless, she rolled over in bed, and looked at Aldo's profile. The sharpness of his nose, the slight brow overhang and the startling red of his beard comforted her. He snuffled in his sleep, turned and flung an arm over her waist. Then he buried his head in the curve of her neck and shoulder. *Screw it, there's no way I'm leaving.* They could get on without her in Manhattan!

She couldn't sleep. Crawling out from under Aldo's arm she went downstairs to her computer. Skype opened up and she saw the little green telephone receiver indicating Lotte was on-line. Lenya called and the familiar voice answered on the other end.

"Hey sis, what's up in the boondocks? How's the hunky caveman doing?"

"Don't be snotty; you know you liked it here."

"Don't mind me; I'm sitting here watching the market tanking and my retirement going up in smoke. Pardon the gloom."

"I'm a little gloomy too." Lenya explained the problem with Aldo's non-existence and Sirio's plan to fix it.

"Please, don't worry, it's going to be all right. It sounds like Sirio's come up with a great solution."

"I know, but I've been so worried. I don't want to leave him."

"Now you don't have to. Buck up kid!" Lotte paused for a second or two, "...and if Sirio's scheme doesn't work, I think my Signore Armani might be able to offer some help. He has a brace of lawyers all over Europe who seem to be able to fix anything. He thinks I'm his Venus and would certainly do such a little thing for me." She pursued her lips, making a *moué* at the screen as she fluttered her lashes.

Lenya laughed and shook her head. One thing about her twin, she sure didn't lack confidence.

Later, Lenya thought up another scenario as a fallback. How about having Lotte impersonate her at meetings in New York? It might work...if she would even do it. Lenya could prep her in advance, give her power of attorney to sign the contracts. Something else to consider. Lots of information from the books would have to be learned, but maybe... darn!... no way...as Lenya fell asleep.

Chapter 55
Aldo's Business

The ringing of the land line annoyed Lenya. She and Aldo were in the midst of Tai Chi on the deck and the phone rang. Probably a French telemarketer. But maybe it was Sirio? She dashed inside to answer.

A strange voice asked for her in lightly accented English. "Yes, this is Mrs. Lecroix. What do you want?" She knew it was rude, but too bad. They were in France, after all.

"Nice to speak to you. Glad I caught you today. This is Manno, Rapha's grandson...the avocat, sorry...attorney?"

"Oh, hello Manno. Sorry, I wasn't expecting anyone to call. It's nice to speak to you too." She had the good grace to sound at least a bit apologetic.

"I'd like to set up a time to meet with you and Aldo...as soon as possible. We need to get started on this...project...my grandfather's been...talking about." He sounded reluctant to say anything more definite. "Can you come to my office tomorrow afternoon? Is three o'clock convenient?"

She realized his English wasn't quite American but had some British intonations as well, an appealing mix with the French. He also sounded very young over the phone, but voices can be misleading. "Yes, fine with us. Give me directions and we'll be there."

"No need. I've also asked Sirio to join us...as he is a long time friend of both Rapha and Aldo—I thought he could help if we need to explain legal terms to Aldo. I understand they converse in Corsican as well as French and Italian...and now some English."

That's an excellent idea." Lenya agreed. "Please go on."

"I'm afraid I'm of the new generation who understands a little Corsican but can't speak much. Rapha, my grandfather, suggested Sirio being here might make the visit easier for Aldo."

"Very considerate of you both."

"I've been advised Aldo's not used to being in big cities or crowds... although my office is hardly where he would find either." He laughed before continuing. "Sirio's agreed to pick you both up and bring you here."

"Thank you, I appreciate your concern." Lenya was impressed by the sensitivity of the young man as well as his obvious ability to take charge. He didn't sound like what she'd expected from a mob attorney, but then, she'd never dealt with one before. She'd been dreading taking Aldo to a lawyer's office and having him face all the machinations of the French legal system.

Maybe it won't be so bad after all.

The next day at one o'clock Sirio and Sophia arrived. Sirio bounced out of the truck with almost as much energy as Sophia. "Halooo you!" He shouted as he came up onto the deck. "I came early so we can have lunch near the law office. There's a bistro that serves a very nice plate of *moules* and we can sit outside in the sun." The word *'moules'* was followed by a wink at Aldo. He stretched his hands out, palms to the sky as he looked around at the beautiful day, light breeze, clear sky and typically comfortable Mediterranean temperature.

The drive to L'Île-Rousse on the RN followed the sparkling coast-line part of the way, the water turquoise and blues in coves and beaches. Sirio parked in the tree shaded parking in the center of town. They walked past the local market where Lenya came to buy *saucisson* and cheese, now deserted and packed up for the day with the exception of one lone vendor flogging various flavored honeys. Lenya followed behind Sirio, one hand with a death grip on Aldo and the other holding Tom's leash. Sophia trotted alongside Sirio with no leash or inclination to leave his ankle and dart into traffic.

Aldo seemed to be taking everything in stride; there weren't many people around. She wanted to breathe a sigh of relief but thought it might be premature until Sirio turned to her. "Don't worry about him, he's fine here. He often comes with me to this *marché* to sell our sausages."

As the words left his mouth, the honey vendor caught sight of Aldo. He stopped packing his wares and turning, he waved and smiled as he yelled "Alloo Aldooo!" Aldo waved back with a broad grin.

She hissed at Sirio, "I thought you said he was afraid of cities?"

"He is—strange cities. This one isn't strange."

She wanted to punch his nose. There were other things she could have spent her time worrying about. All the past night she fretted and tossed in bed, fearful about making the journey with Aldo. She chided herself about grumping as Sirio turned up a small street and headed toward the water. He turned and walked into the doorway of one of the first restaurants on the right.

Aldo and Lenya waited outside in the sun. Tom and Sophia joined two big dogs facing the entrance to a nearby *boulangerie*, the four sitting in a line looking hopeful some kind departing customer might drop a cookie or two on the way out of the store. Sirio motioned them all to join him at an outside table under an awning. There were four chairs, Tom and Sophia jumping onto the empty one and curling up together as French canine manners dictated. The waiter handed them menus and Aldo took his and put it down on the table.

"Do you know what you want already?" Sirio asked.

"Yes. You said we would have *moules*." Aldo flashed his most brilliant smile. Both Sirio and Lenya were taken off guard. They had been nervous about Aldo's reaction to this outing, but he was not only taking the trip in stride, he appeared to be having fun.

Lenya snuck a glance at him. His red hair glistened in the sun like a polished bronze shield and she noted he had fastened it back with carved bone and a leather thong. He wore an open neck black cotton safari style shirt, black jeans and sandals...all things she had bought him in Calvi when she knew Lotte was coming. If he added sunglasses, he could easily pass for a male model specializing in romance novel covers...or underwear ads, she thought with a smirk. As she looked around at the other tables, it was clear every other woman in sight agreed with her. He paid no attention to the stir he was causing, and smiled at his friends as if he had lunch at sidewalk cafes every day of the week.

Okay, now I can breathe, Lenya thought.

When lunch was served, Aldo seemed pleased by the *moules* as he pinched the meat out with a set of empty shells and dipped his bread in the savory sauce they were cooked in. This time he wasn't distracted by Lenya's facile tongue, he was now fully acquainted with its many talents. He displayed a plate of empty shells all neatly lined up one inside the next in a close procession around his plate like a cross section of a Chambered Nautilus. Always the artist.

Next came a salad and dessert, both of which met with approval. This is wonderful, Lenya thought. Perhaps now we can go out for dinner in Calvi once in a while.

❧❦❧

What she hadn't realized was Aldo was carefully observing everything and everyone around them, on guard to protect her from the smallest hint of danger. He hid his apprehension from her, wanting to please her, to let her know he could accept her world once in a while—when it was necessary.

❧❦❧

Lenya paid the bill and they followed Sirio further along the opposite side of the street to a narrow four story building. Like all its neighbors it had a stone facade, tile roof, and a small store occupying the street level. They entered by a side door and climbed a steep staircase from the *rez-de-chausée* to the first floor. There was one door, glistening paneled wood with brass fittings and a simple brass plaque announcing 'Manno Rizzoni - Avocat'.

Lenya pushed a polished brass button and they heard a ring inside. Shortly, the door was opened by a tall young man with short black hair,

- 346 -

hazel eyes and an appealing smile bracketed with dimples. Cute, makes him look even younger then he sounded, Lenya thought.

As he ushered them inside, Lenya noted he was wearing tan slacks looking suspiciously like L.L. Bean and a bright turquoise cotton knit shirt with the ever present Polo logo on the breast. His Topsiders completed the picture of an East Coast yuppie-preppy. Her eyes must have telegraphed her question or Manno was a mind reader as he whispered in her ear as she walked past, "Preparatory school in England, Yale undergrad and Harvard Law, Sorbonne Law too—love the states and go back every year to stay with friends. I understand you're an East Coaster." Lenya nodded. She was so surprised she had no words.

Sirio made the introductions. As he began to introduce Aldo to Manno, the young man bent to place one knee on the ground, bowed his head and took Aldo's hand in both of his. "Maître, thank you for gracing me with your presence. Please give me your blessings as consort."

Lenya's mouth dropped. Sirio grinned at her. She looked back at him with one eyebrow raised as he nodded towards Aldo, who was taking it in stride. Placing his other hand on the young man's head he intoned the words of the blessing—*"Via con Dia en tutti gli affari ed vita."*

"Grazi Maître é Dia. I am honored to have you in my office." Manno said as he bowed his head once again before standing.

Sirio nodded to Manno and whispered to an awestruck Lenya. "Manno is schooled in the old ways as well as the new. His family can trace their roots almost as far back as the clan. He shows his respect for Aldo as consort of the goddess, Maître, Signadori...or holy man if you will. Aldo has offered his blessings and Dia's on both Manno and his office." He paused for a moment as he looked at the two men, so modern looking, so much of the present, and shook his head as he nudged her through the reception area. "Never mind, now we can get down to business."

Lenya was speechless as she followed them into Manno's office.

They seated themselves in front of a large antique partner's desk with a luminous finish. When Lenya reached out to put her purse down, she brushed the surface with her hand—a good hand rubbed wood finish. She almost missed the opening business pleasantries until Manno brought her attention back to the present.

Then she realized they were having the meeting in French. She was able to understand most of it as Manno continued. The two dogs lay down on the floor beside her, one muzzle touching each of Lenya's feet as if in solidarity and comfort.

"Maître, I am missing your full name and birthday. Also the names of your parents. Then I can get on with preparing the papers."

Aldo looked over to Sirio. "My parents were Ronaldo and Lucia. The name of the clan was Borgo. I don't know where the name came from other than it only means 'town' or 'village.' I have never known another. Clan members used the name 'Borgo' as their patronymic. So, I think my name would be Ronaldo Borgo."

Sirio and Manno looked at each other and shrugged their shoulders. Both raised their palms in the typical Italian "who knows?" The name was as common as 'Smith' or 'Brown' in English...not very convincing for what had to be done.

"I guess one name is as good as another." Sirio ventured.

Manno rubbed his forefinger over his lips and looked out the window. He was humming a little tune in thought.

Aldo was calm as he leaned forward in his chair. "If the name isn't so...good for the...the papers...maybe then we use 'De Manzino'? It's a name I am very familiar with and...okay, I like very much the people who bear it." He gave a punch at Sirio who looked like he had won the lottery.

"Fine then, let's go with De Manzino. All right with you Sirio?" Manno looked over to the older man and grinned.

"I am touched beyond speech, my dear Aldo. It is a great joy to me to finally have a son, even if I did not have the pleasure of raising him myself." Sirio turned to Manno, rubbing his finger alongside his nose as he looked downward for a moment before looking directly at the young attorney and continuing. "No matter, it is well with me to take the fruits of someone else's vineyard as my own...like buying grapes from the neighbors crop and putting my own special touch into the wine. I have always wanted a family, and now it seems I might even have a grandchild quite soon." He glanced at Lenya before looking back at Aldo, both men laughing.

Two hours later Lenya felt assured everything was in good hands. Despite his youthful looks, Manno had shown himself to be well versed in the French legal system and the laws on adverse possession. He felt their position was strong and already had a plan to proceed.

Bringing Aldo into the present was a trickier problem. Manno knew of no precedent for a hidden clan. There were those who had never been registered at birth, families not on the rolls for a generation or so but still part of the community.

In Aldo's case, his family had been unknown for more than just centuries. How to have him acknowledged as a French citizen? Manno decided it was a matter to take up with the local magistrate and already arranged an appointment to discuss the matter. The magistrate was also from one of the old Corsican families, and, strangely enough—named Rizzoni.

Manno was formulating a petition asking the magistrate to make a extraordinary ruling as to Aldo's status. There was no French law to rely on.

Remembering a procedure Manno learned at Yale to determine real property boundaries of land that had been in families for hundreds of years, he thought he might bend it a bit for use in this matter. Title guaranty companies were reluctant to write title insurance when the original descriptions were in rods, metes and bounds based on land-marks no longer existing. The way around the problem was to have the boundaries attested to by elderly long-time residents who relied on their own memory as well as word of mouth from other family members and neighbors.

He'd read cases where ninety year old grandmothers remembered swings hanging on branches of boundary marker oak trees on a neighbor's property. Their memory of the location of the tree was accepted and designated as the starting point for boundaries, even though the tree had been gone for more than half a century. He figured if it could work with real property, why not try it with people?

His petition would include affidavits by elderly locals able to attest to knowledge of the clan since childhood. Some even could state the knowledge had been known to their family for generations past.

Manno had a list of names from Rapha of the old Corsican families and some members who his grandfather thought might be alive. Manno hoped at least a few would remember Aldo, the clan and what land had always been known to be clan property. He had contacted a few families before their meeting to test his theory.

Manno bowed his head once again to Aldo as he reported what he discovered. "Maître, I found many from the old families eager to attest to the clan holdings. I always thought some of our early religious beliefs must be alive, but I had no idea how many remained hidden, existing side by side with the new religions. Especially in the more isolated villages on the island. More surprising to me, however, is the number of people in the more populated, modern areas who were aware of the clan." His audience stared at him in astonishment as he continued.

"Aldo, le Maître, consort of the Goddess, and the only survivor of the clan, is not only remembered, but is considered to be a very powerful and revered holy man. The few I have contacted consider it a great honor to assist le Maître in this matter."

Lenya took it all in. She saw Aldo understood the discussion. For a man who had spent most of his life hiding in a Neolithic village, she was finally realizing he was very sharp. The meeting had brought her to an understanding of what she didn't know about this man she loved and whose child she was carrying. To begin with, she hadn't even known his name. The rest had her mind reeling.

They said their goodbyes to Manno. He would prepare all the papers and affidavits and they would meet again in ten days to have Aldo sign whatever was necessary for presentation to the magistrate. At the same time, Manno would speak with a friend in the local *mairie* to see if there was a way to have Aldo's birth certificate recorded now, or have him apply for a new one.

Manno could supply affidavits attesting to his client's birth, who his parents were and where he lived. Aldo would be able to take the name he chose. The only thing Manno was concerned about was Aldo had never done military service or paid taxes. However, he also had never worked at a regular job or had an income. It would be touch and go to clear it up, but he was confident he'd find a way.

On the way home, Sirio turned to Aldo. "My dear friend, what do you think about our day?...how it went?"

Aldo thought for a moment or two. He gave Lenya a long look. "For my woman I go...do...whatever necessary. Even a trip to a big city... many people...but I did like the *moules*...and the ice cream."

For the rest of the journey home Aldo sat quietly and looked out the window. Silent. Holding Tom in his lap. But his mind worked non-stop. He had been taken aback by Manno's show of sincere respect. After spending most of the last year and a half between the casteddu and the cabin, he had little contact with the villages or the villagers. Lenya brought him clothes and magazines, newspapers, food and art supplies from Calvi when she went shopping. Foraging no longer was necessary. He was rarely at the casteddu and would not have known if any villagers had come to see him. Le Maître.

When the clan still had elders, people often arrived to show their respect, ask for healing, or a blessing from Dia, and to remove the evil eye or other curses from *streghe*. Visits dwindled when the clan members dwindled. As he listened to Manno, at first it had pleased him to know Dia was still venerated. Then he became concerned.

His father's father remembered a time in his youth when well over a hundred villagers would arrive to join in Dia's celebrations.

Then, every year, fewer villagers came as the new religions' priests went from village to village shouting 'blasphemy' at the mere idea of following the ancient traditions, calling the followers of the old ways the spawn of Satan. The Inquisition had made a strong imprint on Corsica. Anyone who openly believed was reviled.

By Aldo's childhood, the celebrations stopped.

Now Aldo began to consider he might have been wrong. Perhaps Dia was not forgotten. Was he still needed as le Maître, as her consort?

Had he been shirking his duties? The image of Manno kneeling before him—asking for the consort's blessing—kept coming back to him. He had neglected the position he had been born into, foretold by the *strega maschia* and trained by his father to follow as le Maître. Consort of the goddess. *A man of honor, of status.*

Shame overcame him and then resolve. He must undertake once again his duties to his goddess and her followers—however small a group they might be.

Lenya's heart sank as she watched Aldo in deep thought. This sight of him was breathtaking in his modern metro-sexual black casual clothes, hair shining like a saffron crown. But re-hashing the meeting, she thought his angst didn't concern business affairs. She intuited a spiritual power had reached out to him across the millennia to touch him deeply.

All she wanted to do was put her arms around him. But he was clearly shaken. A hug wouldn't be enough.

Chapter 56
Aldo's Temper

The legal documentation proceeded at an amazing pace. Especially considering the horror stories about paperwork bogged down for years in the morass of French bureaucracy.

Lenya and Sirio visited Manno at his office several times, Aldo preferring to leave the legal wrangling to them. Much as he liked Manno, the trips to the law office seemed to annoy him. More than ever, he stayed on familiar territory.

Since the first meeting with Manno, Aldo had taken to going back to the casteddu regularly. He had spruced it up, fresh reeds on the floor, shook out the skins and burned rosemary and sage to cleanse the inside air of both spirits and spiders. His mind was in constant motion. Should he be staying there? Be Dia's consort to those who needed the comfort of the old ways? Leave Lenya and the cabin? Would she move to the casteddu with him?

Perhaps he had been selfish, only thinking of himself as he stayed with Lenya, leaving the ways of the clan, immersing himself in his painting and drawing, neglecting his duties as consort and Maître?

It was a conundrum occupying his mind so much he found it influencing his painting. Bit by bit he brought art supplies to the casteddu and found it gratifying to sit at the old table and paint subjects the ruins brought to mind.

Manno's research alerted the villagers Aldo was alive and still at the casteddu from time to time. A trickle of people once again began to make their way up the steep track to find him.

After several weeks, he realized he had over a dozen visitors. While he waited, he had worked on his art. Canvases and drawings were stacked against the wall, on the table, every available shelf—images of villagers asking for blessings of Dia, a triptych of a Mazzeru on a dream hunt. The first panel was the Mazzeru stalking his prey, the second was the kill, a wild goose falling to the ground at his feet, the stock of his antique gun carved with ducks, geese and quail. The last depicted the Mazzeru turning over the carcass and jolting back in surprise when he recognized the face of a woman.

Aldo missed Lenya when he worked at the casteddu, but he was conflicted. He was Dia's consort with obligations far beyond the ecstasy he shared with her. How could he have forgotten them for so long? What if someone needed him, his blessings, his healing hands, his ability to lift the evil eye. He had comforted many in the past, solely by keeping alive the knowledge of the old ways. But what if someone came to him for comfort and he was not there? He never knew when someone might be in need. At the cabin, no one could find him.

So engrossed in his work, he often forgot the time. When it became dark, he stayed in the casteddu, going to the cabin in the morning to wake Lenya with a kiss. Then he made love to her, caressing her tousled hair, inhaling the sleep smell of her body as he explored it with his lips, tickling her awake with his beard and arousing her with kisses. Touching his cheek to her swollen belly, he blessed the tiny life he could feel moving beneath the taut skin. Their child.

When Lenya looked for him at the cabin, he was often gone. He'd leave in the morning and be back late in the day, sometimes not until the next morning. She was stricken. First, she worried about him and if he was all right. Perhaps something or someone upset him?

When she could not think of any incidents, nor had he said anything to her, her thoughts became darker, more fearful. Was he finished with me? Did he not love me anymore? Since I'm pregnant am I no longer appealing?

One thing she was sure of. She wasn't going to play the role of a jealous lover and had no intention of asking him to account to her where he went and what he did. When he didn't come home at night, she cried herself to sleep. But then, the next morning, he'd be there, waking her with his gentle lovemaking. She didn't understand. What was wrong? Was something wrong?

Aldo knew he had disrupted his life with Lenya. She looked upset whenever he left. He was trying to be at both the cabin and the casteddu and it wasn't working. Frustration was building within him. There were too many things he had to deal with, things he hadn't thought about or considered before. He wasn't used to complications in his life.

On top of his duties for Dia and his love for Lenya, now he also had to think about bizarre legal problems impacting both his home and the home of the clan, even possible jeopardy with the French government. He had spent his whole life outside the system; now trying to understand it angered and terrified him.

He'd been working in the cabin on a painting of Tom with momma fox and kit, all three sleeping together in front of a bonfire. In it, he and Lenya sat side by side, holding hands as they watched the animals. He imagined the animals together—different but similar species, hunter and hunted, finally able to make friends. Perhaps on the other side when Tom made his last journey, the fox and kit would be waiting for him. It was a gift Aldo hoped Dia might give. He knew Lenya loved the three animals and he thought she might like the painting—a gift to show how much he loved her. Better than words he wasn't sure he could express correctly.

As he put the final strokes to the painting, adding glints of light on the brilliant saffron coat of the fox, his brush slipped, streaking across the canvas. A small slip easily remedied, but as he bent to pick up the brush, his shoulder knocked the canvas to the ground, smearing all the wet pigments into a mass of colors. Aldo's control was already fragile. The dam broke.

He threw the canvas across the room. Venting his frustration felt so good, he picked up the easel and threw it too, followed by the palette, the wooden box filled with tubes of paint, and any other canvas near to hand. Finally he swept his arm across the dining room table tossing stacks of drawings on the floor. Those he stomped on as he howled and screamed his fury, his rage at the conundrum he had to face. The threats to the life he and Lenya had made together.

Tom hid under the bed in the loft trembling with fear. Aldo never raised his voice.

Lenya had been at the Sparr and was pulling into the driveway when she saw Aldo running from the house into the woods. As she stood in the open sliding glass doorway, chaos greeted her. The place was a shambles. What had he done? What could have caused it?

Fear traced its fingers up her spine as she entered. Was this disaster caused by her sweet and gentle lover? Had some stranger broken into the cabin and wrecked Aldo's work, now strewn all over the floor? A robber?

A quick perusal told her laptop and desktop computers were intact, her small stash of jewelry next to nightgowns she no longer wore.

Thinking of nightgowns given up for the pleasure of her body naked and spooned against his, Lenya felt a stab of fear as she bent to gather his drawings, trying as best she could remember to sort them into the same piles as he had. Then she gathered the paint tubes and placed them in the wooden box where they normally resided. Within a short time she had restored the cabin more or less to its normal state.

She set the easel up as usual and looked for the canvas Aldo had been working on when she left. She found the dog and fox canvas face down in a corner behind one of the club chairs, the stretcher bars twisted and broken. As she looked at the painting, she saw the smear of colors and the detective in her figured out the scene of the crime. Something had gone wrong while he was painting and Aldo had a temper tantrum. Lenya had seen tension mounting in him. He must have hit critical mass.

What was bothering Aldo? Was it something she had done unsuspectingly? Could there be another woman? She couldn't imagine it, but then, as she had learned, in life, anything was possible.

Chapter 57

Remorse

Aldo returned to the cabin the day after his explosion. He was surprised Lenya had put everything in order. He was ashamed of his loss of control but he had no words to explain to her how he felt. All he could do was embrace her, his face in her hair, inhaling her familiar scent.

Afterwards, Lenya kept a subtle distance from him and asked no questions. She didn't reject him, but didn't reach out to touch him as before. It was time for him to clear the air.

Lenya ran the old ride-on lawnmower out of the shed behind the cabin. As usual, she started it up with a little gas and a lot of perseverance. Rather than have the real estate agent send someone to mow the grass, she'd agreed to run the mower around the perimeter of the deck and sides of the drive when the grass got too high .

Aldo thought if he learned to command this thing he could get her to laugh again, laughter being in short supply since his temper exploded. Words were not in his vocabulary to apologize for such a loss of control.

Instead, he was going to save his pregnant woman the task of mowing the lawn. Perhaps the simple act would help?

The mower sat in the middle of the clearing chugging in neutral, waiting for Aldo to get on the seat. As he walked over to it, he had no idea why he had to mow anything. The grass grew in the spring and summer and died in the winter. Why interfere with the cycle?

Reaching over, he touched a pipe emerging from the chugging part. It was hot and he drew his hand back. He walked around looking at the protruding levers and buttons and sticks. He wasn't sure he remembered exactly what she explained each of those things did. The round thing was for steering, he understood from riding in cars.

It can't be so hard. He had seen people commanding bigger machines, cars and trucks. They drove them fast on the road and killed animals in their way. He hoped Tom was safe.

At the thought, he took Tom under his arm and put him in the back bedroom of the cabin with the door closed.

As Lenya explained, he put his foot on one of the metal pedals, moved one of the sticks and the monster lurched forward.

He took his foot off one of the floor pedals and onto the other. The lurching stopped but now he was moving much faster than he was comfortable with. He tried to command the thing to go slower, but kept pressing his foot down harder. Thinking he might turn the wheel to make it slow down, he found he was going in a circle.

Looking back at Lenya for help, he crashed into the boulders around the fire pit. Thank Dia he held on and didn't fall into the rocks.

The machine made terrible noises, coughed and then was quiet. He climbed off and shook himself.

When he looked around, Lenya was laughing so hard she was holding her stomach while tears ran down her cheeks.

Harrumphing, Aldo kicked the iron beast before walking over to the deck. He had no need for machines.

Lenya stopped laughing long enough to put her arms around his neck and hug him. It was all right, she wanted him—and she was hugging him. Good things. Maybe the monster was really dead and he wouldn't have to get on it again. As he leaned against her, he could smell the foul burn odor on his shirt. No animal was ever difficult...or nasty! But his idea worked, he could still feel her laughing as he held her against his heart.

Okay, so he'll never be comfortable with a lot of modern things, Lenya thought.

He adapted to Skype and liked to stand in front of the embedded camera to smile and wave at Lotte. Lenya remembered him taking pictures with her camera one of the first times they met. There might be a way to get him more comfortable, introduce him to some smaller gadgets, less daunting. He had, after all, made friends with the clothes washer and refrigerator.

Later in the day, she went into the cabin and, rummaging around in a drawer, found her iPod. It was loaded with music, classical, rock and roll and country as well as several international groups. I Muvrini, and Corsican polyphonic music were their favorites.

Aldo was back at work sitting in front of his easel.

Setting the iPod to play some haunting Corsican sounds, she put one earbud in her ear and sat on his lap. Aldo looked surprised. She put the other earbud in one of his ears and smiled at him.

Instinctively, he pulled away when he first heard the sounds. Lenya stayed where she was and showed him the tiny player. He pointed to his ear. She nodded, "Do you like the music?"

Without her prodding, he picked up the iPod and examined it, turning the shiny object over and over. He pointed at her earbud and she took it out and put it in his other ear. This time he smiled. *"Mi piace."* He liked it. She got off his lap and left him to enjoy the music while he worked.

Chapter 58
Consort, Maître, Signadori

Sirio honked his horn promptly at nine AM as promised. Lenya climbed into the passenger seat and handed him a go-cup of strong coffee. "Thought you might use a little high octane fuel to get through the morning."

"Thank you my dear one, you always correctly second guess me. I was going to invite you for some coffee and croissant on the way. Now all we need are croissants."

They had an appointment at Manno's office. Once again, Aldo declined to go with them. However, he seemed to be interested in the proceedings and always asked them to tell him in detail what happened when they returned.

When Manno greeted them, it was obvious he had news he couldn't wait to share. "Come in, come in." He waved a handful of papers at them. "You won't believe what I've discovered... amazing." Lenya smiled to herself. He was rattling on like she did when she was excited.

"Look at what I have—see all these?" He was shoving a stack of papers at them.

Lenya took them from him and looked at the one on the top. It was an affidavit from a woman; her age was given as ninety-six, born and raised in a tiny village Lenya had never heard of.

Sirio read over her shoulder. "Manno, this place is far from here, close to Sarténe, isn't it? How would someone know him from there?"

"Read" he commanded. "Sirio, you won't believe it."

The affidavit was in French, Lenya could have made out the gist of it but Sirio read the document, translating aloud for her.

"When the woman was a teenager, she contracted polio. Her parents took her to many doctors on the island, but none could help them.

Her father heard of the clan, remembered hearing of a healer there, and even though it was a long and dangerous journey by mule, he brought her to the Signadori."

Manno looked at Lenya, saw the confusion on her face. "Aldo is Le Maître of the clan, as you know. But you need to understand a bit about ancient, probably Neolithic, Corsican mysteries. There are several different types of people who commune with the unknown. There are the Mazzeri, the Dream Hunters, who in nocturnal dream hunts see who next will die. They deal with the dark side and our interest in death.

"Then there are the Signadori, and they are the healers, the ones who can take away the evil eye of the witches, they have ancient medical—homeopathic—knowledge, like a mid-wife can deliver babies. They are those in the light and deal with life. Aldo is a Signadori, hence his title as Le Maître. It is a gift passed on to him when he became the consort of Dia."

Lenya nodded, but her head was spinning with this new knowledge.

Sirio continued reading, "While the Signadori couldn't heal her, he put her on a diet of vegetables and herbal teas made from the special rosemary that grows only on the island. The disease progressed no further. The woman even remembered the name of the Signadori—Le Maître Ronaldo—great grandfather of Aldo."

The affidavit went on to explain how the clan welcomed them, the family stayed for several weeks while Ronaldo gave the girl massages with herbal oils and taught her some exercises to ease the pain and build up other muscles to help her get about in spite of her twisted limbs. He gave her hope to go on with her life even after she and her father made the long journey back home.

Another document was from a man who fled from a vendetta caused when his dog killed a neighbors chickens. Six members of his family had been murdered in the crazy quest for honor. His distraught mother sent him, her last son, to live with the clan where he remained hidden for eight years until vendettas were finally outlawed.

The documents went on and on. They told of a history of herbal healing, setting of bones, children delivered, lifting of spells, marital problems solved, special diets for children's behavior—detailing cures and ancient remedies from his grandfather, his father and then from Aldo himself.

The story was told in well over a hundred affidavits from all over the Balagne and as far north and east as Bastia and Corte. The number was astounding, more than they ever dreamt possible. Aldo was a man still held in great esteem.

Lenya was silent, sitting in a corner of the office taking everything in.

Once again, she was appalled at herself for not recognizing the stature of her lover. The underestimation, how she had belittled him in her mind, made her flush with shame. She was a perfect example of those who looked askance at aboriginal knowledge. Arrogantly assuming those who came before had nothing worth learning and passing along. How could she have been so blind?

Manno must have sensed something was wrong. He got up from his desk and took her hand. "Lenya, I can see this is a shock for you. What's wrong?"

"I had no idea. I am so ashamed of myself. I can't even tell you how much I underestimated him; the word itself is way too mild."

"Who did you think he was? What had Aldo told you about himself?"

"Obviously not as much as he should have." She was beginning to adjust to an entirely new understanding of the man she loved.

"Perhaps it was hard for Aldo to explain his upbringing, the honor given to his position within the clan. After all, the clan was gone and he was a man alone. He probably thought there was no one left who respected him."

"But he is so smart, and talented. And I thought of him as a Cro-Magnon caveman. How stupid and arrogant I've been!"

Sirio had to intercede. "It's hard to understand, I know. I have tried to explain to you—he is a most civilized man, but in ways far different from those accepted by your culture. What none of us can comprehend, or are willing to accept, is the brain of the Cro-Magnon, if those are really who he is descended from, has been found to be substantially larger and probably superior to the brain of modern man.

"Today's scientists tell us our brain has many parts still unused. Can you imagine what might be lurking in Aldo's brain?" Sirio shook his head. "We have to make sure the damned scientists don't get their hands on him. We don't want them cutting him up to have a look." His agitation held him prisoner as he stomped around the office.

"Don't even give it a thought." Manno added. "No one will touch him as long as I'm around. He has the same rights as any other man and I'll make sure they are respected."

As they left the office, Lenya realized it was time to heal the breach between them.

She had also made an important decision. No longer would she try to bring him to New York. She finally understood, not in her mind, but viscerally and in her heart—he *was* Corsica, and belonged to the island, as much a part of it as the menhirs and dolmens. Dia's last living warrior.

Chapter 59
Making Amends

The next morning Lenya was determined to find out where Aldo went, and why. Her reluctance to speak, to face his disappearances, widened the gap between them. Stupid, she knew.

He sat at the table looking over his sketches and drinking a tiny cup of espresso. She came up behind him and laced her arms around his neck, breathing in his ear. "Where are you going today? Wherever it is, can I come with you? Please?"

He turned and gave her a brilliant smile before kissing her full on the lips, his tongue tickling as it circled hers. *"Bien sur, amor."* Sometimes he liked French better when he felt loving. She could see he was truly pleased by her suggestion.

"Where are we going?"

"To the casteddu. I work and wait there. Come and bring little computer." He liked her brand new netbook, it was light and made her more mobile.

"What do you wait for?"

"Maybe you will see. Maybe someone comes today. I never know."

He was being very secretive, at the same time, he was open and happy to have her come with him. Whatever the secrets were, they were nothing he wanted to hide from her.

She had broken the ice. It was time to see how deep the water below was. She gathered her netbook and her mop-cum-walking-stick. A small flutter from her midsection assured her the baby was fine as she handed Aldo a backpack filled with bread, cheese, and salami, biscuits and water. It never hurt to be prepared.

The walk to the casteddu was always a challenge, up steep sides of the mountain, the path treacherous, but she was hardened by past months of exercise, and Aldo took her hand when she felt unsteady. When they reached the large flat rock breaching the opening in the stone wall, even pregnant and a little unwieldy, she made the journey with much less huffing than when she had first been there.

As they entered Aldo's living quarters, she saw it had been re-arranged into a studio, some of his paints and other art supplies were in evidence; many canvases stacked along the walls. He came here to paint? Is he moving away from me piece by piece? He didn't seem to be hiding any-thing from her and she had the good grace to feel ashamed of her suspicions.

Her shame was complete as she looked at the subject matter he was working on. Dia. The clan. All the legends he told her, and many more, were depicted in the riot of color spreading over canvases.

Dia sitting on a throne of lions, her consort washing her feet, then rubbing them with the contents of a small oil amphora Lenya knew was filled with aromatic oils to massage the goddess—as she read in her research.

Other paintings showed the consort bending to caress the god-dess, initiating the act of love; goddess and consort joined in passion. The consort holding informal audience with supplicants, his hand placed on the head of an infant. So many were familiar to her. And in the paint-ings, she, Lenya, was the personification of his goddess—her face was Dias. She flushed with emotion.

Walking over to the wall, she thumbed through the canvases. Each one depicted a different part of the rites of Dia: ecstatic dancing, making of holy oils, massage, what looked to be blessing of an infant, rituals of hygiene—the castration of Attis—long forbidden within the clan, thank goddess!

She was about to pull out one of the canvases to have a clearer look, when the sound of gravel and stones moving outside alerted some-one was coming. Tom growled low in his throat. As he grew older, he liked strangers less and less.

Lenya hastily put the painting back into its place. The sound of feet crunching pebbles was enriched by light female voices chatting in Corsican. Women? What did they want here in the casteddu?

Pregnancy heated hormones flamed an instant flash of jealousy. Were they here to join with Aldo to give Dia some fucking power? Is this why he's been leaving me so often? As fast as the thoughts came, she dismissed them as unworthy. Why am I such a jerk?

The branches and twigs of the door to Aldo's house shook with tentative knocking. *"Permisso?"* A young sounding woman's voice floated through the wood and skins covering the door. Lenya could hear what sounded like whispering and then giggles. Two women. ...*ménage à trois?* *Stop that*—she thought with self-anger.

Aldo looked over at Lenya and smiled, putting up his hand. "Now you will see," he said as he opened the door. Standing aside, two young women entered, both carrying infants in slings across their chests, one also with a toddler holding her hand. The entourage was red faced and puffing from the exertion of climbing the steep and treacherous path to the casteddu.

When they entered, Aldo pointed to the table and chairs, offering a place to sit and rest for a moment, but the women, in unison, knelt in front of him, the one pulling the toddler to his knees as well. *"Maitre, s'il vous plait, votre benediction."* Aldo placed a hand on each head in turn, muttering something in a language Lenya couldn't understand. Then he lit a small herbal cluster and, as it smoked, waved it over their heads before letting it burn itself out in an earthen bowl.

The women appeared satisfied. They got up, went to the table and relieved themselves of the slings as they put the infants on their laps. Both of them sliding questioning looks towards Lenya. The woman without the toddler produced a large canvas grocery bag she had slung over her shoulder and handed it to Aldo. He bowed his head in gratitude. *"Je vous en prie,"* and as he handed the bag to Lenya, introduced her to the women *"puis-je présenter ma femme, Lenya."* He spoke in French so Lenya could understand.

The two women smiled at her and relaxed as she bent to examine the contents of the bag. It was filled with home grown vegetables—plump red tomatoes, zucchini, several onions, a bunch of carrots tied with a bright red ribbon, and mushrooms Lenya was not familiar with.

So this was why he brought so many vegetables home lately. Payments. *"Mercie beaucoups,"* she said to the women.

They smiled at her in return, mumbling in unison, *"Je vous en prie."*

Then she realized how he had introduced her—*"ma femme,"* my woman—it meant she was his wife.

All the anger and fear she had bottled up flushed away in a rush. Just as if my mind had been a toilet, she thought with relief as the tightness in her chest relaxed and she breathed again with both joy and ease. She finally understood—le Maître at work.

The toddler was becoming fractious. The walk had been long and the child was grumpy and tired. Aldo bent and picked the him up and placed him on the bed on top of the pile of furs. He kissed the child on his forehead, and was rewarded with a giggle as Aldo's soft beard brushed his face. Delighted, the boy stuck his thumb in his mouth and was asleep almost immediately.

The women then asked for Aldo's assistance. It was in Corsican, but Lenya understood enough to get the gist of the problem.

The two women were sisters. Their mother was ill and could the Maître give his blessing for her health? They hoped it would keep the Mazzeru from seeing their mother's face in his dream hunt. Also, if she had been the victim of the evil eye rather than a normal malady, would he be able to get rid of the curse?

Aldo explained he would certainly give his blessing, but he had no influence over a Mazzeru and if the dream was to come, it would come. He could, however, combat an evil eye. and pray if the dream hunter came for their mother, her journey would be an easy one. The women both nodded in understanding. He reached for another small bundle of herbs to burn, the smoke this time acrid and less fragrant as he waved it while speaking some of the ancient words while he walked around the small group.

Handing them what looked like a thong made of dark leather with something hanging from it, he told them to have their mother keep it close to her.

Lenya, curious, moved closer to see what it was. The dangling charm was a small woman, face serene and smiling, pendulous breasts and protruding stomach, but charming for all the grotesqueness of her body.

A Venus statue like he made for me—Dia.

Aldo placed his hand on the caved image and recited something in the same language as before. Lenya could tell by the expressions of relief on their faces they were satisfied as they turned and bowed once more before leaving. There were no guarantees, but then, there are none in life.

Lenya had found acceptance. She too had what she came for. Once Manno began seeking people for the affidavits he required, it had become commonly known in the villages that Aldo was alive, and through him, the clan—Dia. The old ways, always there on the island, but hidden, continued. Aldo had only been doing his duties as le Maître—Signadori, priest, consort, shaman, holy man...whatever she wanted to call it.

Her acceptance was replaced by both shame and anger—self directed. *What crappy self-esteem I have, or is it self-obsession, to be so sure it was all about me? At least I have the good grace to accept I was the one who screwed-up.* At the realization of her mistakes, she let out a sigh of relief.

She turned and saw Aldo looking at her with the wonderful expression she knew showed how much he loved her. *How could I have been stupid enough to have doubted him?* She stood and put her arms around his neck and whispered in his ear, "Do you think you'll have more visitors today or are your duties done for a while?"

He replied by kissing her neck and running his tongue under her ear as he picked her up and carried her to the bed. It was warm on top of the furs where the toddler had been sleeping. She felt a small internal twitch of approval as she turned to receive her man.

Chapter 60
A New Level

The rain poured down on the cabin as if angry gods above decided to empty their celestial swimming hole—all at once. Aldo looked at the water coursing down the windows and plopping in heavy drops on the deck only to rebound into stalagmite-like forms.

The cabin was nice and dry and there was food in the cold box, fire to be had on the cooking machine. He didn't have to hunt outside in the torrential rain. No one in their right mind would brave this weather to visit the casteddu. Aldo enjoyed the feeling of loosening his back muscles as he stretched in the soft light from the fireplace.

Lenya was across the room looking morosely at the screen on her computer. Warmth filled his heart and rose in bumps along the surface of his arms as he realized all he wanted to do was spend this day listening to the rain on the cabin roof as a counterpoint to some nice music from his tiny beloved iPod. He also had a few other things on his mind.

He could bask in the warm glow of the fire while he experimented with new ways to please Lenya. There must be something he hadn't tried; something new to bring her pleasure, and it was an excellent day to attend to this most important task. He could feel certain parts of himself agreeing to his project as soon as he considered it.

Perhaps it was a change in his breathing, or some new electricity in the air, because suddenly Lenya turned to look at him. Something in her eyes told him she had the same ideas. He ambled over and began to stroke her back while he bent down and ran his beard over her ear and neck. This time, she was the one who attained a perfect stillness as tiny bumps rose on her arm, the fine hairs standing on end. He smiled to himself. She didn't want him to stop.

One button at a time, he unfastened her shirt. Wonderful, nothing holding her breasts tight today. He gave up on her ear and neck to kneel beside her chair and open her shirt—all the better tickle her with his beard and breath. Her silence was broken by a groan of pleasure. I have all her attention now, he thought.

She leaned towards him and he lowered her to the floor next to him. Pleased she was in the same mood, he began his exploration of new and delightful ways to make his woman sigh, howl, and groan with pleasure. He couldn't imagine a more blissful way to spend a rainy day.

By the time he had run through all the Tai Chi moves he thought might be useful—the crane posture as he tucked his face under her outstretched leg, her arms splayed to the side, fingers touching thumbs; then moved on to stepping over the snake, her thighs over his shoulders while he earnestly searched her, probing earnestly to see if the snake might be hiding somewhere inside her.

He couldn't hold back his laughter as she yanked him in a very fine imitation of grabbing the tiger by the ears and pulled him away from her while she howled her joy to the skies.

Later in the afternoon, it seemed Lenya had another plan in mind. She wanted to play too and his sweet gentle woman turned into a very exacting mistress.

Finally, exhausted and drained in the most wonderful way, he smiled at the recollection of Lenya taking charge of his body, intent on the same sort of experimentation he had tried.

He was a most willing sex object when she poked him awake and rolled him over onto his back, taking both his arms and pulling them over his head and told him he wasn't allowed to move in the game she had in mind.

It sounded like fun, so he lay immobile as she searched and probed his body with her tongue and fingers, finding spots he hadn't even realized could bring him pleasure.

The soft skin behind his knees gave him a start, he hadn't thought an erogenous zone might be hiding there. But when she pushed him on his side, he thrilled as goose bumps rose all his body when she snuffled her nose into a tuft of hair at the tip of his spine, her breath and then her tongue creating a marvel of pleasure.

Now she was sound asleep, her head on his arm, one leg sprawled over his hip, and snoring…his love was snoring in a soft and rhythmic sound. It was so innocent sounding; he had to control himself not to laugh. He didn't want to wake her, but there was something he wanted to do.

Prising himself out from under Lenya, he covered her back with a soft throw from the couch and took up his sketch pad. It was something he had been thinking about doing for several weeks, and now he had the chance.

His pencil flew over the page, and then the next and the next. It was a chronicle of their love for each other, sacred positions to please the goddess, erotica, the joy of each one bringing the other to fulfillment. What pleased him the most was the soft rounding of her abdomen, the new fullness of her breasts, signs of the life they had created together. Dia's gift.

He didn't know the right words to tell Lenya how he felt about her, the ecstasy he felt in his spirit when their bodies completed the eternal circle of life. The joy of the new life blooming. These drawings would be his words. But he didn't want her to see until he was finished, totally pleased with his work, sure they expressed what was in his heart.

After a while, when he saw the signs of her awakening, he left and hid the drawings inside the cover of a sketch pad. As she awoke, he reached down and took her hand to help her up. She smiled and stretched her back, the arc of the baby more prominent. Once again, his heart filled with joy at the sight of this beautiful woman—his mate. "Thank you Dia," he sighed to himself in the ancient language.

Twining her arms around his neck, Lenya kissed him as she whispered in his ear. "Would you like something to eat?" she asked. He looked down at her suggestively with a slight tilt to his head and she put her hands over her crotch, slapping him very lightly as she did so.

This time he did laugh out loud as he put his arms around her and picked her up off the floor to twirl her around.

An hour later they were at the table finishing a pasta dinner and sipping one of the hearty Corsican red wines. She had her allotted glass. He reached over to take her hand, and was gratified by the look in her eyes. Tom snored as he slept in his bed near the hearth.

The fire died down to warm red embers, leaving a hint of pine smoke in the air as the rain continued to pelt down on the roof of the cabin.

This is the way life is supposed to be, Aldo thought. Maybe it'll rain tomorrow too. He was hopeful. And maybe there were more Tai Chi moves to try. He'd have to give it some thought.

As Lenya got into bed, thinking of the exquisite day they spent together, she had an epiphany. It was almost painful as the truth hit her.

How wonderful to spend a day making love and playing with another adult person! Memories of days full of work, things she had to do, to get done...study...research ...damn deadlines. My God! Her mind reeled at the thoughts that tumbled out: I've missed a whole part of life, the pleasure of being with someone I love, enjoying their body while they enjoy mine. It took her breath away. Something of great value she hadn't understood, lost because the thought of idleness made her feel guilty. Duty ingrained from childhood.

The greatest gift Aldo gave her was learning to be in the "now," to take the pleasure he gave her, without guilt, without pushing him away because of something else she thought she had to do.

Then another realization came to her. What she had not been able to wrap her mind around before was the idea of *hieros gamos,* the rite of the sacred marriage, the transference from god/goddess to man/woman. It was the "apotheosis," the idea of man and woman becoming one with the gods that made the sex act holy. And then she finally got the true meaning of it. What could possibly be more godlike than the ability to create life during an act of love?

It was the first time she even came close to accepting there might be a god, a goddess, a supreme being.

Dia, as Aldo described her, wasn't demanding, punishing and jealous, insisting on man's obedience and self denial, but instead, Dia recognized and accepted man's joy in the natural act of love as an offering of energy...power...a gift. Lenya smiled for a moment as she thought—after all these years of being atheist, when I finally find a religion I really understand and like—it's pagan.

She spooned her naked rump up to Aldo's belly; he mumbled in his sleep and put an arm over her, holding her close. Nothing better than this, she thought as she finally fell asleep.

Chapter 61
The Caveman Returns

Lenya was antsy. Every time she looked at her computer she had a sick feeling in the pit of her stomach. It was only a matter of time before she would have to leave Aldo, at least for a little while.

He sat on the deck with his back against the cabin, a large flat piece of plywood across his lap as a make-shift desk. Tom plastered up against his thigh, asleep in the warmth of the sun. As she came outside, both man and dog looked up at her. She could swear they both smiled.

Walking over with her mop handle ready for a hike, she took Aldo's hand, pulling him up go with her. When he put the drawing aside, she saw it was a sketch of Tom sleeping. It had an unusual quality, generally his drawings were serious, but this had humor as it showed the soft charm of the little dog.

"Dove andaremus?" "Where will we go?" he asked.

"I don't know. Let's just walk." she replied as they headed for the woods.

It was starting to turn cool again, and after they walked up the side of the mountain into the denser area of forest, she could feel the chill and smell the fresh ozone scent. God I hate the fall, she thought. It always feels like death. And then she remembered it was when her father died—over twenty years ago, and she still got the willies at the same time each year.

She reached over to take Aldo's hand so he could help her over a pile of rocks. He held his hand out and then froze in position. Something caught his attention. He put his finger over his lips to silence her. Even Tom was locked in place.

Aldo motioned her to stay back as he reached down for Tom and handed him to her while slitting his eyes to focus on something she couldn't see. She heard nothing, but a low growl came from Tom, more a vibration she could feel as she held him tight in her arms. Aldo took her by the elbow and moved her behind a large tree, motioning her to stand with her back against it. He took the mop handle from her.

She watched as he crouched in front of the tree, the mop held like a spear. A knife suddenly appeared in his other hand. The hairs on her neck and arms stood at attention as she saw his lips pull back in a snarl. Something was threatening them and she had no idea what it was.

The forest was like a vacuum, no sound, even the usual bird chatter and small critter rustling in the underbrush was sucked into the silence. Lenya heard her heart beat like a roaring in her ears.

Aldo, motionless, poised for something...battle? But with what?

Once again Lenya's brain reeled back to the Early Man diorama at the New York Museum of Natural History—a hunter ready to kill his prey. All Aldo needed was to change his jeans for a fur loincloth.

Fierce snarling filled the air as a large brownish grey blur hurled itself into sight.

It was huge, a more than a quarter ton of death on hooves. Lenya heard snarling and shrieking drown out the thrashing charge...some of the snarls from Aldo. His knees were bent—poised for battle. Muscles corded in tension, he was directly in the path of the charge. At the last possible moment he stepped aside with the skill of a matador ready for the kill.

Glimpses of his arms flashed in front of her. His teeth were bared. White tusks flashed by as the mop handle crashed into the skull. Momentarily stunned, the animal looked around as Aldo leapt onto its back. The knife rose and fell. Blood geysered into the air, splashing her arm and turning a slash of Tom's white fur a brilliant red. She felt the ground shake as something crashed, seemingly at her feet. She looked up and Aldo too was covered in blood as he stood over a huge twitching body.

Lenya was screaming, she didn't know where the blood was from or what happened. Everything moved so fast all she knew was her heart was pounding and Tom trembled in her arms.

As she looked again, she saw Aldo kneeling over the dark, fur covered body. He reached out and swiftly slit the animal's throat, then bowed his head. It looked like he was praying. His mouth moved but all she heard was "...Dia."

The large creature shuddered once and was gone. *"Sanglier,"* Aldo growled, adrenalin pumping through his voice. *"Mamma, ma dove e bambini?"* ... okay it was, a sow, a female, where were her babies? *"Va bene Lenya, non ha paura."* It was all right, she didn't have to be frightened. His English had deserted him and he lapsed into Italian.

Her back against the tree, Lenya slid down to the ground, ignoring the scratching of the rough bark and clutching Tom in her arms. Tom had calmed down a bit and wasn't shaking as much, but she trembled and felt weak as the rush of adrenalin left her.

Aldo wiped his knife against his jeans and poked around in the underbrush. She realized he was looking for the piglets. He motioned for her to put Tom down. Maybe he thinks Tom will help him find the babies? Tom immediately started sniffing the large boar and then around in the dense growth. He stopped at a large pile of rocks almost obscured by maquis and began to bark.

Aldo crouched as he pushed the brush aside with the mop handle, his knife poised and ready. There was no telling how large they were. Then squealing from the rocks gave the piglets away. Lenya moved over to see them when Aldo motioned it was safe.

There were four of them, none bigger than Tom. Two were pink and two were a dark brindle, all obviously terrified. It was hard to imagine the little creatures would grow into something as large as the mother.

She looked back at the large body of the sow and felt a wash of sorrow for the brave mother who defended her babies to the death.

Her mind flashed back to the mother raccoon attacking Tom when Aldo saved him. Momma fox and her kit. Families. Protecting their loved ones, their young.

With absolute certainty, she now understood completely who Aldo was: hunter, protector of his clan and family, willing to fight for her. My lover. She kept seeing his face at the moment of the kill, lips pulled back, teeth bared, and muscles corded for attack. It was not the Aldo she knew but a savage who stood in front of her, ready with a mop handle, a knife and his need to protect. A different creature, a throwback to millennia past, to the cave paintings she remembered with vivid clarity. Like the sow with her young. Protect to the death. *Take it or leave it girl.*

And then Lenya knew nothing had changed with time, the same savage lived within her too; if necessary, she would also defend her child, her love, her family, to the death. Nature—it's most basic law—protect and guard those you love.

Aldo took the piglets, one by one, and removed them from their hiding place. *"Tropo jovene, no posso vivere."* They were too young to survive by themselves.

Lenya looked at the small squirming and squeaking lives. She pointed at herself and Aldo, *"Posso mama é papa?"* Could they be the babies' mom and dad?

He laughed at her. *"Va bene, mas non é facile."* She agreed, it wasn't going to be easy, then shrugged and reached out for one of the piglets. Nothing in life ever is.

Bending over the dead sow, he proceeded to gut and clean it. He wasn't going to waste the meat and she was sure they'd be eating pork for weeks.

It was a sobering lesson. I'll have to give this a lot of thought, and she picked up two of the piglets to carry back to the cabin. He followed with the other two, and she knew he'd go back to bring his kill home in time for dinner.

It would be a few weeks of bottle feeding before the piglets would be strong enough to eat on their own. Lenya mentally made a list of powdered milk, puppy food and pabulum she'd buy on her next trip to the market.

Aldo returned to the cabin a few hours later dragging a large burlap bag filled with meat. He took it over to the outside spigot and washed off the excess blood from both the meat and himself. He was dividing the meat in several piles. She came over and watched him working.

"Sirio" he said as he pointed to a haunch.

"Salciche per mercado," and he pointed to a pile with the intestines and large pieces of meat.

"Per noi!" and he pointed to ribs, the other haunch and what looked like filet mignon of *sanglier.*

The last pile had the head and some roasts. *"Pour Rapha, le tête et deux roti."* Lenya smiled at his change of language.

She managed to pack the meat he had put aside for them into the refrigerator and the freezer. The largest portion for the market he placed into a carton and put in the SUV, came back for the portions he indicated were for Sirio and Rapha, put them in the SUV too, and sat in the passenger seat with Tom on his lap.

Okay, so he was fine with going places in the car when it suited him, Lenya thought as she got her keys and handbag and locked the cabin. The piglets were huddled together on a corner of the deck on an old blanket she had found. Nearby were bowls of water and softened kibble. She didn't think her charges were going to wander off.

As soon as she started the engine, he turned to her and grinned. "Sirio," he announced, and off they went.

When they arrived at the winery, Sirio and Sophia came to greet them. Sophia and Tom were immediately off on a chase, Tom manfully keeping up as best he could, at least for a while. Sirio hugged both Aldo and Lenya as he asked, "What have I done to deserve this wonderful surprise?"

Aldo grinned. Lenya answered. "Aldo is my hero. We were attacked by a *sanglier.* He killed it...a sow...we have the babies at the cabin... meat in the car." She stopped to catch her breath before continuing, "Honestly Sirio, I never heard a thing but Aldo stopped us, handed me Tom and killed the thing as it charged us. He saved our lives—and it was huge!!"

"Well children, it seems you've had a most exciting day."

"Exciting? We were almost killed and would have been without Aldo. I've been walking those woods since I arrived...how stupid... never realized the danger in them."

"Lenya, you never knew it, but Aldo was always there, protecting you. Since the first day he saw you."

"Really?"

"Yes, my dear. He fell madly in love with you—at first sight. You've never been in any danger with him around."

The men carried the boxes of meat from the car. She was torn between love and a very creepy feeling. Aldo had been stalking her for months and she had no idea. She wasn't sure she was okay with it; there was an inherent manipulation she'd have to think about before she forgave him completely.

And what had he thought about Terrence? Neither of them had ever mentioned him.

Sirio must have understood some of her feelings. He held her arm, and whispered to her, "You can't hold this against him. It is in his upbringing to protect that which is dear...as you are to him. It would be a very different thing in a modern man. You must take my word on this."

She did understand what Sirio was telling her. There was a huge difference between a nut-case stalker of celebrities or an obsessive love object they fantasized about, and a man whose culture stressed the need to protect the people of their clan, those who were important to them. She did understand, still...

Sirio came over and handed her a glass of red wine. "Let me explain what Aldo and I will now do. When we have a *sanglier*, the two of us make ham and sausage from it. It takes months to cure. After we prepare and season it, we hang it in the storeroom with the wine. When it is dry and cured, we sell it at the local markets. We also have some customers from the local restaurants. We've done this for many years and are known to the locals for our good meat...oh, and that's how the honey man at the Marché knew Aldo."

Early the next morning they were back at Sirio's, ready to start on the curing process. A familiar black SUV was already in the parking area.

Sirio greeted them wearing a long leather apron and a pair of rubber gloves, waving one of the hams over his head. "Come, have some coffee, we have croissants and a baguette as well as some visitors, as you can already see." He nodded in the direction of the black SUV.

On the table behind the winery sat a large thermos of coffee, cups and a platter overflowing with croissants and sweet rolls. Rapha and Michaele were drinking coffee and eating. Michaele even looked happy.

"Can you believe Rapha and Michaele were here by seven AM this morning? I called him last night after you left and told him about Aldo's hunt. He's delighted with his present and stayed to thank you in person for the roasts and the head." Sirio said.

Rapha stood and embraced her. Then he started to kneel, a bit stiffly Lenya noted, in front of Aldo, who immediately bent before the older man and, grasping him around the chest, lifted him into an embrace as he whispered something in his ear.

Lenya couldn't make out all the words in Corsican, but she thought it was something like, "Old friends don't kneel for me, from them I prefer a good embrace." Both of them were laughing and patting each other on the back. Finally Aldo released Rapha who seemed grateful go back to his chair.

"Thank you both for thinking of me with this excellent gift. My chef makes a wonderful head cheese, one of my favorite meals. Michaele will bring some to you when it is done and I will expect a sausage or two when they are ready." Rapha looked like he had concluded a big deal.

Aldo nodded in appreciation.

Rapha continued, "I'm also very pleased with the progress Manno has been making on the paperwork. It looks like everything is going smoothly, so much so I've already hired an architect to begin the plans for the hotel. My dear Aldo, it seems all your concerns will soon be over. I know you prefer the old ways of the clan—to remain hidden from the modern world, but now, at least, you will be safe. You can come and go as you wish." He looked over at Aldo, standing behind Lenya with his hand on her shoulder.

"And as for you, my dear friend and famous writer, it seems soon you will providing a new addition to the clan." As Rapha finished, she found herself blushing from head to toe.

"I guess our secret is out." She glared over at Sirio who had his back to her, busy fiddling with the coffee cups. "It will be several more months before our new clan member arrives, but we are very pleased." She patted Aldo's hand resting lightly on her shoulder, and looked up at him. As usual when he thought of their child, his pleasure was obvious.

Looking directly at Lenya, Rapha spoke. "You can't know all the old ways, even though I'm sure Aldo has told you much. But you must be aware how important it is for us all to know his line will continue. And most significant is you have added your new blood, and modern ways to the clan. It is almost a miracle when I think of it. This mixing of the old and the new between such strong and intelligent people as yourselves. It has given me great hope for the future."

She was speechless. The combination of their diverse genes was something she never considered. All she could do was lean over and hug Rapha. Words weren't necessary, he had given his blessing.

Rapha stood and nodded to Michaele. "We will leave you all to your work. I know it takes a lot of time to prepare such a large amount of meat properly, and I don't want to interfere with the process."

After hugs and goodbyes, Michaele hefted the large box of meat, their gift, nodded at the group and started to the black SUV, careful to walk within grabbing distance of Rapha in case of a slip or trip.

For the rest of the afternoon, Aldo and Sirio occupied themselves with cutting and organizing the meat and supplies. At first Lenya sat under the large olive tree in front of the vineyard office, watching and working on her laptop. Then she went inside to see how the sausage makers were doing and curiosity overcame her. "Can I help too? I'd like to learn the process?"

Lenya rolled up her sleeves, washed her hands and went over to the table where the meat was spread out. Salt, sugar and herbs were placed next to an old hand cranked meat grinder and an odd shaped funnel like-contraption used to stuff the sausage into the casing of intestines.

Pointing to the herbs on the table, Sirio listed, "Sage, rosemary, garlic and savory. Aldo brings them from the forest. I always have the salt and brown sugar on hand to use in the curing process."

Lenya spent the rest of the afternoon and into the evening watching and volunteering when needed.

Her final job was to carefully twist the casing into the individual sausages while Sirio and Aldo wrapped the haunches in cheesecloth before hanging them from the rafters near the chains of sausage. Sirio explained, "The cheesecloth is to keep any inquiring animals off the ham while it cures. Flies can be very bad, carry many diseases and as you know, their larva, maggots, destroy the meat. We must throw it away if they get into it."

"The temperature here is quite even all year long, and it is the correct amount of humidity to keep bad mold from growing on the meat." Sirio told her.

Lenya nodded and he continued. "We have almost finished with the first part. The next is to wait—months. Everything must air dry until all the moisture is gone. Not quickly with machines like commercial charcuterie nowadays." Sirio laughed. "Here comes the best part. Follow us." They went into the tasting room of the winery and sat at the small table. Sirio removed the winery advertisements to the counter and they set down their wine glasses.

A large piece of pork was trimmed and seasoned, a fire set in a stone fireplace. Aldo had already threaded the meat onto a long iron rod hung over the fire. The meat sizzled as the fat dripped and flamed.

Shades of Christmas, Lenya thought. The dogs were curled together outside under the olive tree, the men bustling around making a salad and setting the table.

Dinner was delicious and she was so full she could hardly keep her eyes open on the treacherous drive home. They could have stayed overnight with Sirio, but now they had four hungry babies to feed.

The next weeks they spent feeding baby pigs, first with doll bottles and then graduating to normal size. They laughed at the greedy little critters and ended up giving them names. Porky, Sadie, Jake and Daisy grew quickly on their new diet. They were so cute and friendly she wanted to bring them inside the house but Aldo insisted they be kept outside.

The piglets quickly learned to come to the cabin for meals, the rest of the time they explored the woods. Nights they slept cuddled together under the deck in a nest Aldo made for them of the old blanket and dried leaves.

Each day the piglets went a little bit further away. After a month, Lenya understood why Aldo insisted they remain outside. They were showing signs of growing as large as or larger than their mother, and Tom, dwarfed by them already, was wily enough to keep his distance.

When she woke up one morning, all the piglets were gone. So was Aldo.

When he came back alone, she asked "Where are the babies?" He shrugged and pointed to the forest. "*A casa.*" They were home. He had taken them into the woods and put them back in their cave. They were big enough to survive on their own.

Chapter 62
Journey To Paris

Lenya woke with a heavy heart. She was so conflicted she wanted to stay in bed and pull the covers over her head. It was time for her to go to Paris. On her own. She didn't want to leave Aldo. Something in the pit of her stomach made her anxious and told her to stay.

On the other hand, her old life was calling out to her, demanding attention. Now. The list of things she had to attend to kept growing and she lay in bed obsessing. The new book had to be finished and research had to be done first. Lotte was on her case to come back and take care of her house, sell it, rent it...something. The baby was growing and it would be good to go to her regular ob/gyn in Connecticut. There have to be plenty of good doctors on the island, she could tend to that problem without leaving. The publisher wanted to set up a tour for the release of her last book as a trade paperback. She wanted none of it, just stay here in the cabin with Aldo and live her life. Have their child.

Skype called out to her as she brushed her teeth. Damn thing, it only brings more bad news!

Slouching over to her computer, she punched the mouse over the green receiver. It was her editor! And there Lenya sat in the tank top of her pajamas with bed head and a toothbrush sticking out of her mouth. Shit! What's she doing? Gotta be o'dark thirty in NYC...doesn't she ever sleep?

Then Lenya looked at the bottom of the computer screen. It was 1:30 in the afternoon in Corsica and 7:30 in the morning in Manhattan. How did I sleep so late?

The computer screen displayed a Chanel suit, a single strand of large white bubble-gum size pearls topping a jewel neck blouse in what could only be lush silk. A little camera adjustment and a face came into view. It was disapproving.

"Lenya, it's got to be afternoon in Corsica...time to get going my dear."

Lenya hated when she called her 'my dear,' it was always the prelude to a chewing out. She knew she shouldn't care, she was a big girl now! But a tiny pang of insecurity began to carve a hollow spot in her gut.

"Yeah, didn't get to bed until late last night...working on a new twist for one of the chapters." *Why do I even bother to lie...*

"Yes, well it's good you're working but don't exhaust yourself. You're looking a bit peaked."

"I'm fine, working along. Did you get the last version?"

"I did and liked it, but when are you going to do the research? We ran a test market and everyone liked the idea readers would also learn something. You need to be an expert in the period."

"I'm going to Paris—the Bibliothéque Nationale de France. The Mandragore Collection houses their illustrated manuscripts and I've made arrangements to be allowed in to do research. I'm also interviewing research assistants...next week"

"Good, I'm glad you're on it. Call or e-mail me when you've got the next draft ready...and Lenya, are you gaining weight? You look a little bigger...broader...might be the video...or the pj's"

"Yeah, maybe put on a few pounds...great French and Italian food in Corsica ...need to work out more." She had noticed a little weight gain herself. Happiness sometimes caused some expansion and pregnancy certainly did. Especially around the chest and waist. Paying attention to her calorie count was not her first concern these days.

The voice trilled over Skype, "Remember dear, over forty it becomes harder to lose and everything sticks to the hips."

"...mmm, I know, working on it." And to herself, a mental note to disable the damn video camera as soon as she hung up.

Chapter 63
Research Awaits

Lenya packed her laptop and Tom into the Rav while Aldo wrangled her suitcase into the way-back. It was only a quick trip, she consoled herself, but she hugged him like she was never going to let him go. The flight to Paris was short and she'd be back in less than two weeks, maybe ten days. The more she thought about it, the shorter her trip became.

Aldo would be fine without her. But there was no arguing with the sick feeling in the pit of her stomach. She didn't want to go and was fighting with herself. She knew she had to get a grip, interview researchers, only a few days away. *He got along without you for years, why the angst? It's probably hormones from the pregnancy.* But she couldn't shake the feelings of anxiety and foreboding as she pulled out of the driveway and waved goodbye. *Or was it really despair?* She knew this was only a presage to her trip to New York.

Aldo understood she was only going to be gone a little while, he had his paintings and Sirio to occupy his time for two weeks...no problem.

What plagued Lenya was how to explain going to New York for months without him? She had to travel soon; she might not be permitted on the airplane without doctor's permission after thirty-two weeks. Their baby might then be born in an American hospital without it's father. Unthinkable! But how could she wait until after the baby was born and then take Aldo's child away from him? Would he believe it was only for several months?

The flight to Paris was short and sweet. Tom slept in his travel case under the seat in front of her. A pleasant gentleman wrestled her carry-on from the overhead compartment and she exited the familiar Orly Terminal. Before catching a taxi to her hotel, Tom stopped at his favorite spot to leave one more pee-mail message to the poodles of France. They were on their way—one day less before they could go back home.

Her guess on how get researchers had paid off. When she arrived at the Bibliothéque nationale de France, or BnF, as it was referred to, she was greeted by Madam Sevigine, her contact to find assistants. She was even more accommodating in person than her friendly e-mails.

"Welcome Madam Lecroix. We have all been waiting for you."

Lenya wondered about the plural address and if it was an idiosyncrasy in a language not the woman's own. Her misconception was soon corrected as Madam Sevigine continued. "I have found seven people quite eager to assist a famous American author. When you advised me of your arrival, they wanted to meet you as soon as possible and are waiting for you now. Please come this way."

When Lenya entered a modern and serviceable conference room, she was greeted by seven bright looking young people. Introductions were made around and Madam Sevigine suggested Lenya conduct the one-on-one interviews in her office.

After several hours of discussions, three of the applicants, two men and a woman, seemed most suited for her needs. Amie, a tall and willowy brunette, was working on her doctorate in medieval psychology. Her paper was on the damage done to families from the stress of living in times filled with the unrest of political strife, the black plague and general lawlessness. Laurent's research dealt with military machinery He was trying to discover if the new inventions had concomitant applications to mechanize life in the 15th Century. So far he was disappointed to find most of the future applications were used mainly to kill more people at a time.

Simon was studying the hierarchy of life on medieval estates and how it differed from country to country. His side study was the lingering of the old religions in the peasant class, even as the Catholic Church began to make it's stranglehold felt throughout Europe. Lenya was very interested in his findings. Perhaps one day I can give him some insight too, she thought.

She made arrangements to meet with them later to chat informally. The other four she thanked for their time and interest and let them go.

Lenya was reluctant to turn over the research, she always enjoyed searching through the illuminated manuscripts herself, but now every moment away from home was painful. Time to let go.

On the way back to her hotel, she browsed through the offerings of the used booksellers along the Seine and found a well preserved copy of "Les Très Riches Heures du Duc de Berry," her favorite depiction of 15th Century life. This led her to search for Skira art books on the Middle Ages and found several she would take back to Corsica.

The next day, at the BnF, Lenya wanted a few hours to enjoy the pleasure of paper beneath her fingers, the personal connection with ancient scribes. The originals were kept under lock and key for preservation, but their copies provided a closer feel than digitized versions. Technology, with such perfect and brilliant reproductions, made the distance between reader and creator mechanical, no humanity involved. The ability to place your hand over lines someone else had drawn so many years ago, the idea their sweat might have fallen on the page as they worked, made the connection real.

While Lenya sat reviewing the material Madam Sevigine placed in front of her, the woman at the next table was sneezing and coughing. Lenya didn't want to expose the baby to any germs so she moved to get as far away as possible. Damn, she thought, I need to get out of here before I come down with something too, I'd hate to catch the new flu the television has been warning about.

In the late afternoon, she took a break at the bar a short distance from the Mandragore collection. It was a typical French establishment with a worn wooden bar running down one side of the narrow space, ornate mirror behind bottles of every size and description, overhead fans and ubiquitous handles for *pression*—draft beer. A row of small beat-up wooden tables and chairs opposite were filled with people chatting and drinking.

She was occasionally nauseous from the pregnancy and appreciated the current French no-smoking rules—amazing to her they were actually obeyed. The researchers from the Bibliothéque she had hired were sitting with some other people she had seen in the library.

One of the young men stood next to her at the bar for a refill on his beer. He nodded at her and waved for her to join them. "Come, sit with us." She took her coffee over to the group. There were five of them crowded around a postage stamp table, laughing and talking with their hands. The familiar faces gave her welcoming smiles.

"So, tell us, what are you researching?" a long-haired young Frenchman she had not met, asked in very charmingly British accented English as he held a chair for her. She had seen him several times at the library.

"I need to have a feeling for clothing, weapons, food...the ordinary things of daily living in various periods for a series of novels I'm working on...middle ages, Renaissance."

"But why here?" he asked with a smile.

"Looking at illuminated manuscripts, seeing how life of the various historical periods are shown, customs...what the people look like, what they did at their everyday tasks. The drawings tell me much more than words ever could."

"You don't have to be at the library—now most everything is on-line. Google what you want and you'll find it."

She explained her theory about finding things not so readily available to the average researcher. His response was a Gallic sound between a "pfufff" and a "fhuff" with face tilted upward and the expression one of disbelief. How could someone could be so thick? "It doesn't matter; the people who read novels today don't begin to understand those subtle differences anyway." He was probably right.

A tall skinny woman joined in with less perfect English and a more cheerful face. "I'm here because I like to hang out in Paris," the skinny woman, unasked, chimed in with a laugh. "I'm Louise, from Belgium. I can find everything I need there, but it's a good excuse to be in Paris." The twinkle in her eye was impossible to miss.

Two of the researchers she had hired, Ami and Laurent, introduced her around.

It was nice to be with a group she could so freely converse with. Lenya loved Aldo, but she had to admit, sometimes their conversation was limited.

They all started talking at once, telling her about the various projects they were working on. She found herself enjoying these people and didn't want to leave.

"What kind of novels do you write?" Louise asked.

"I've been writing romance, had some published but want to get into more serious stuff," Lenya replied.

She had an immediate audience. Louise was the first to ask, "What are the titles of some of your books? Would we know you in Europe?"

Lenya's books were translated into over twenty languages, from Afrakaans to Zulu, as she often joked, and of course, French. "I know they're available in French, Spanish and Italian. My name is Lenya Lecroix." Everyone stopped talking.

Louisa took a breath, "You wrote "La Verité d'Amor?"

Lenya had to think a minute about the name in French. In English it was "The Truth Of Love," not a book she was very proud of, but it was a best seller. "Yes, it's one of my books" she admitted.

The long haired young Frenchman turned out to be named Roger, and he hurried over with a carafe of red wine and a handful of glasses. "Well, well. Now we must celebrate. We have a famous American author in our midst." He pulled a wry smile as he put his index finger at the side of his nose and wiggled his eyebrows, shades of Sergio, and the right touch to tell Lenya he was teasing her as much as celebrating.

To get into the spirit, Lenya took the carafe and began pouring wine and handing glasses all around. She signaled for the waiter to bring another carafe and put it on her tab. Tom showed his gentlemanly spirit by moving from lap to lap around the table and snagging a few odd peanuts and a crust or two of bread as they talked.

After the third carafe was emptied, Lenya was afraid to drink much more than her allotted small glass of wine. It was probably time to go and she felt the wine had gone to her head. Was it really bad during pregnancy? She had read conflicting opinions and studies on-line. What do French women do?

She expressed her concern. They all assured her wine wouldn't hurt the baby or there would be no children born in France. The men promised to accompany her safely back to her hotel if she stayed. Three hours and one more glass of wine for Lenya later, they all stumbled out of the café, holding on to each other. One of the young men broke into the words to a song Lenya thought was something like *"Cheri je t'aime, Cherie je t'adore, comme la sauce de pomador."* "Darling I love you, I adore you, like tomato sauce?"

The tipsy crowd were curious why she was so anxious to get home, and not stay a few extra days to enjoy with them the pleasure of Paris. "Tell your husband or boyfriend, or whatever he is, to come join us. We'll show you both parts of Paris you've never seen before." Roger had a loopy smile on his face as he clapped his hands and spread them out in an *'et voila'* motion at the end of his invitation.

Seeing no way out, Lenya decided to come clean. "I live in Corsica in the mountains outside of Calvi. Had to leave my man behind— he's never been to a city or off the island. I don't think he'd travel well."

They looked at her in surprise. Not at all what they expected from an American author. But he was Corsican, like Napoleon, so, after a fight about the pros and cons of Napoleon, they decided she was one of them. Whether the Corsicans liked it or not, they were French. And after all, if she was crazy enough to live in the mountains, let alone with a Corsican, she had to be all right. *If they only knew.*

œWithin twenty-four hours she and Tom were at Orly for the trip back to Calvi. Between her new friends and the three students she had hired, the problem of research was handled. As she sat in the lounge waiting for her flight to be called, she felt some of the bands clenching her stomach begin to loosen.

Smiling to herself, she caught the irony of her trip. Since she had been off in the woods with Aldo, technology had made her worries groundless. The internet and digital advances now meant she could stay in the cabin and have the world information highway available to her at a click.

Tom was on her lap, her computer and new information securely between her feet. She could breathe a sigh of relief. Her world was secure again.

Sneezing, Lenya cursed to herself. Damn, I've picked up something from the woman across from me. Home with a cup of hot tea with honey and I'll be fine, she thought as she felt the first chill begin to take hold. She wrapped her jacket tighter around her shoulder as the plane took off.

By the time she pulled up in front of the cabin, she knew she had more than a passing cold. Her shoulders and neck ached and she felt feverish. It's off to bed as soon as I get inside. She didn't want anything to affect the baby.

Aldo was so happy to see her he wouldn't let her go. The days she was gone seemed endless to him. He kept looking at the empty spot where the laptop usually resided, no dog to sit on his lap, no woman buzzing around him, talking, laughing, tapping on her computer. Once again he felt the loneliness of being the last of his clan. The table wasn't covered as usual with his artwork. A few unfinished drawings were scattered around, but he didn't have the heart to work. He'd gone hunting, and prepared a rabbit stew for her homecoming.

Lenya looked at the stew and her stomach lurched. There was no way she could eat anything. She insisted on keeping him company, sipping a Coke while he ate, even though she longed to be in bed, securely under a pile of covers. She missed him so much even feeling as sick and weak as she was, she wanted to sit and look at him.

Her shivering got worse. She had her flu shot before she left for Corsica and hoped it would be working after almost two years. It was too late to worry about it now. After dinner she climbed to the loft and crawled into bed. Two hours later she awoke to Aldo handing her a cup of steaming herbal tea laced generously with cognac and honey. It was soothing and she fell asleep immediately.

When he got into bed, she spooned up to his back and twined her fingers in the hair on his chest. He was much more satisfying to snuggle with than her old teddy bear, or even Tom for matter.

It was a week before she could work. The first five days she was curled in bed like a cooked shrimp, never moving other than to pile more covers on or go to the bathroom in the bucket Aldo had brought up for her. She was so weak the stairs were more than she could manage.

Aldo was frantic trying to get her to eat, but her stomach clenched at the thought of food. He insisted she drink water, herbal teas and a thin broth with vegetables he made for her. She knew he was right to push liquids so she forced herself to keep hydrated and she had to eat for the baby.

She felt so sorry for the worry she was causing him. He would stand beside the bed and look down at her with his brows furrowed. Tom sat on the bed and stared at her with the same worried look, although now his brown eyebrows were frosted with white. She hadn't noticed it before.

On the sixth day, she rose from the bed and made her way downstairs by herself, hanging onto the railing for fear of falling. It was hard to realize how weak she was after only a few days of being sick.

Aldo looked up from his painting and there she stood, disheveled, smelly and in the grungy bathrobe she hadn't taken off for days. He held his hand out to help her but she shook her head and shuffled off to the bathroom.

Brushing her teeth was heaven. Off came her robe and nightgown. Oh my god, I really stink! She thought, now I know what going without bathing smells like.

The hot shower beat down on her sore shoulders and back, streaming through unwashed hair and over a body covered with multiple layers of dried sickness-sweat. Paradise couldn't possibly offer more bliss. She shampooed, scrubbed every inch of her body with a back brush, and finally, satisfied she was clean, turned off the shower.

Reaching for the towel caused her to sweat again. It was clear she wasn't finished with the nasty bug, but clean was certainly better. When she was dry, she donned a fresh pair of yoga pants and a tee-shirt Aldo left out for her. Putting them on made her weak but she refused to give in.

When she left the bathroom, she saw he had made a small lunch for her—a soup thick with meat, rice and veggies and toast. A throw was over the back of her chair and a pair of clean warm socks were folded next to her napkin. My man thinks of everything, I'm not used to someone taking care of me, she mused.

Not that Andre wasn't loving, but it was different. They were lovers and friends...but equals. Aldo cared for her, protected her, she was his mate.

After soup and toast, she felt better and called Lotte on Skype. Asking her to get in touch with Ellie—please, no one was to nag her about work or send her nasty e-mails. They had to leave her alone until she had her strength back and her mind clear enough to get back to work. For now her brain was muzzy from the fever and chills, all she wanted was to crawl back upstairs to huddle under the covers and sleep.

She graciously took Aldo's offered help and found he had changed the bed linen too. Touched by his thoughtfulness, she hadn't wanted to get back into sheets she'd been sweating into for days, but at the same time didn't want to ask him to change them. She knew she didn't have the strength to do it herself.

For a few more days Aldo hovered solicitously. He insisted she drink the herbal teas, hearty soups and a vile smelling broth he made from something Lenya was afraid to ask about. The rest of the time he tried to keep her warm and quiet and bring her whatever she felt like eating. At night she slept in his arms and was at peace.

On the ninth day she knew the worst had passed and came downstairs with a bounce in her step. After a hot shower and a change of clothes, she almost felt like her old self again. But when she tried to do much, the effort made her weak and dizzy.

Life looked bright, the sun shone in the sky, she could smell the scent of Corsica and she was ready to get back to work as soon as possible.

It was not to be.

As soon as Lenya felt like she'd live, Aldo got sick.

Chapter 64
Aldo

Lenya kept a protesting Aldo in bed and gave him aspirin and tea. It had worked wonders for her. But he got sicker. While she suffered what she was beginning to understand was a mild case of the flu, he worsened with every passing hour.

His nose ran and he coughed up great gouts of green phlegm. A rattle developed in his chest. Every breath he took had a wheeze in it. He burned with fever.

Death tolls from global a influenza pandemic screaming out from the television were worrisome. She Googled what to do to treat him. WebMD strongly suggested a doctor before it turned into something worse, like pneumonia.

On Skype to Lotte, Lenya was frantic. "I don't know how to take care of him. He's getting worse every day and refuses to go to a doctor... and in a way I don't blame him. What if they want to know who he is and where he's from?

"Don't be such a fraidy-cat. Call a doc and get him to come over and look at Aldo." Lotte never worried in advance. She went straight to the point.

"I'm afraid he has no immunity for this kind of thing. Remember, he's been with his clan in the woods all his life."

"You might be right, he didn't have the chance to develop the immunities the rest of us have from being exposed to every piece of crap in the universe...especially growing up in the Big Apple."

Lotte was right. They rode the subway as kids, were in department stores, touched everything, ate from hot dog and pretzel vendors on the street, took buses, rarely washed their hands until they were home. What on earth had they not been exposed to?

But Aldo was different, he'd led a very sheltered life with the Clan...never had a flu shot, and probably never had the flu. "How can I make sure he gets the right treatment? What can I do for him?"

Lotte heard hysteria begin to rise in her sister's voice. And with the hysteria was an unspoken guilt—she'd brought this sickness home to him, unthinking of the consequences it could have for a system with no resistance. All Lenya had worried about was the baby. How could she have even remotely thought of such a thing? It was completely foreign to her experience.

"Lenya, you need to call Sirio. He must know of a local doctor who can be trusted."

Lenya was reluctant. She lived in fear. Word of Aldo might get out—he'd become an object of study...an oddity. The images from her nightmare returned, but Lotte'd have none of it.

Muddled, weak and still feverish herself, it hadn't even occurred to her to call Sirio before. She dialed him immediately.

Chapter 65

The Fight Is On

Sirio didn't answer. Lenya thought he might be with a customer, or in the vineyard. She'd wait a few minutes and call back again, even though she had left a message on his answering machine. Maybe he didn't check his messages often.

While she waited, she looked at Aldo's artwork, out of order and not put neatly away as usual. Something was wrong, she thought as she bent over the drawings. He must have left them there for her to see.

As the subject matter became clear, her heart started to beat faster and she clutched the drawings to her chest. He had left her instructions. He must have felt the sickness taking hold and understood the danger.

There they were on the dining room table, clearly there for her to find. Aldo's finished art was always neatly stacked and put away but these few were not in their place. Sobbing, she went through the brilliant colored paintings. They were so alive—the wildflowers, forest creatures, brilliant sunsets, birds in flight, Tom on the deck watching squirrels.

A drawing of Aldo was set aside by itself. He was overlooking the mountains of Corsica, the little A-frame cabin beneath him as he sat on a cloud in the sky at the feet of a beautiful woman with long flowing dark hair. Dia. Lenya understood, this was where he believed he would go when he...she couldn't even bring herself to think the words. As she moved the drawing, she found others beneath—what he had put out for her to find. The way of the clan to honor their dead.

There were four paintings together—a blueprint for her to send him on his journey. The first showed him in his bed with Lenya and Sirio standing beside him, each holding a hand. The second showed a funeral pyre in the sacred cave, his body encased in flames. The third had the removal and cleaning of bones and the last was the dolmen ossuary with bones inside.

Lenya sank to the floor and sobbed. Still weakened by her own sickness and beyond panic, she fell into a dreamlike state.

Leaning over his motionless body, she wrapped him tight in the sheets he lay on, dragged him off the bed and bumped his body down the stairs from the loft. She repeated the act several times, banging his heavy body down the stairs again and again. Her back protested but she refused to listen and kept at it.

Once, she bent and washed him—she knew he must be clean to meet Dia. She washed and dried his hair, but it no longer shined the same as it did in life. She refused to cry even as the thought repeated.

Outside, in a beautiful sunny day, she gathered armloads of firewood to fill the fire pit. It was impossible to drag him to the sacred cave...too heavy, too far.

He lay on the pyre, how he got there she didn't know, but she saw him silent as she placed a bouquet of flowers and herbs in his hands and crossed his arms over his chest as best she could. His body was stiff and unyielding.

Standing back as the flames from the fire enveloped him she cried her grief to the skies. Tom howled. The rest of the forest was silent. For once she couldn't hear the sounds of chattering birds or small creatures rustling in the underbrush.

Moaning, she continually stoked the blazing fire as the scene looped over and over again. She knew she didn't have the courage to scrape remains of flesh off the bones so she kept the flames going until nothing remained but charred bits.

When the fire cooled, with a pair of tongs from the kitchen she pried out as many bones as she could find and placed them in a sack made from two pillowcases, one inside the other. When she thought she had them all, she placed the empty skull on top and tied the makeshift sack with some gaily colored ribbons she found in the cabin.

Walking mop handle in hand, bag sometimes slung over her shoulder, sometimes dragged behind, she and Tom took off into the forest. At first she was surprised how light his bones were, but they became heavier and heavier as they made their painful way up the mountain to the necropolis. She had to take him home to Dia.

There was a banging in the kitchen. Startled, she awoke. Cramped from sleeping where she fell to the floor, and unwieldy with pregnancy, she got up.

Lenya was angry, angrier then she had ever been in her life. Powered by her rage, she screamed at the memory of the fading dream. "Damn it Dia, you can't have him yet! He's mine!"

Who was she yelling at? She must be losing her mind; as she shook her head to clear it, the banging started up again. Tom, pushing his water bowl around the kitchen, making a racket on the tile floor, waking her up to her responsibilities. He needed water and food. Aldo needed more.

She quickly filled the Tom's water dish, set out some kibble, and was on her way upstairs to Aldo. She had left her laptop on the dining table and pushed aside some papers to get to it.

Underneath was one of Aldo's sketch pads with a few pages poking out. When she moved it, drawings tumbled out—portraits of her sleeping, brushing her hair, Tai Chi on the deck, details of her body drawn with careful and loving detail. Beneath, there were quick sketches of their lovemaking, their bodies entwined in every possible position. The joy in each other was so clear she couldn't bear the pain.

The possibility of loss was so frightening it almost crippled her, and she had important things to do.

Chapter 66
How To Take Care Of Him?

Lenya reached over and felt Aldo's forehead. He was burning up, sweat soaking the sheets around him. What do I do? How can I keep him alive? Helplessness overwhelmed her.

And then something inside her snapped.

I'm not going to let him die!! This man will not die, he's the father of our child and he will fucking well live to play with his son!

Anger can be a wonderful thing. It slashed away doubt, leaving in its wake a cold determination and adrenalin pumping. Her mind regained its clarity. I'm NOT going to build a fucking funeral pyre. My man is NOT going to die!

Calm and cold, she knew what to do. She called Sirio once again. This time he answered. He had been outside with customers and had forgotten to check his answering machine. He was so sorry he hadn't been there for her as soon as she explained Aldo's condition.

He said he'd be right over to give her a hand, and bring a friend who would help them.

Relieved, she went to the loft and bathed Aldo's forehead. The sheets were soaking wet.

It was hard to change to dry sheets. He couldn't stand and she could only roll him to one side, fold the wet sheet up and roll him over it onto the dry one, and then repeat the process on the other side. By the time she finished, her back was screaming but the bed was dry and clean. She thought he might be delirious, but he was only dreaming.

❧

Aldo's eyelids moved and twitched. It was his dream hunt now; he followed the vision.

The ancient legend of the clan came alive; it was the War of the Mandrache—the war fought as the Mazzeru of each village and clan battled to defeat each other. The battle prophesized how many of their people would die in the coming year, the victor always relieved because it meant less would be taken, the vanquished suffering the most deaths.

Like all battles it was bloody, but this even more so as the Mazzeri battled to the death with swords and long rifles, blood showering them as they died, one after the other.

Aldo tossed, moaning, moving his fists and mumbling as he gave support to his champion, encouraging him in the battle.

Long dead Mazzeri gathered on the familiar mountain peaks near the necropolis. Aldo saw knives, gun barrels and spears shine in the moonlight. In slow motion, silent mouths screamed empty sounds into the night air, weapons flashed, bodies clashed and withdrew to clash again and again.

He watched swords rendering flesh with slashing fury. Blood flew through the night air in endless gouts of gore.

Aldo panted, grunted as sweat poured off him when his fever and heart rate climbed. He couldn't speak. Words wouldn't come as he tried to tell Lenya what was happening when she leaned over him to wipe his brow with a cool washcloth. He gripped her wrist, holding her as if she were his lifeline to reality and out of the dream, but she pulled away. He realized he might have hurt her but the thought passed in the power of the dream and he could only moan.

Phantom avatars streamed with blood as they plunged knife and spear in wild directions, arms raised both in protection and attack. They stumbled over bodies on the ground but got up to fight again.

Aldo's arms flailed, almost hitting Lenya in his zeal.

Was he fighting the battle alongside the Mazzeri, or was he a Mazzeru too?

He didn't know—had he passed from spectator to combatant? It was becoming hard for him to breathe, it was as if there was a weight on his chest, and he tossed the covers off onto the floor.

Tom had been pressed against him, but the wild movements frightened the dog so much he leaped aside to crouch under the bed as it moved and heaved with Aldo's fight.

The tide turned in the battle. Unfamiliar Mazzeri stormed the peak where the clan had taken its stand. Mazzeri tumbled to their death, broken bodies in long robes bouncing off rocks on their way to the bottom. The dream hunters continued their battle. Aldo tossed and moaned. Soon the mountain peak was slick with blood; he could see it glisten.

He watched the ancient Mazzeri of the clan dwindle. Knives slashed once again, making patterns as their slicing movements caught fractions of moonbeams. Rocks appeared only as dark holes in the fabric of his vision as they hurled through the night to strike skulls, crushed before his dreaming eyes.

His breathing was shallow and rushed as he panted his fear through the raging battle. Sweat poured to once again soak the dry sheets.

He felt Lenya bend over him. Whispering she would be back soon. No words came as he tried to speak; a rush of foul air. His eyes constantly moved sightless beneath closed lids to follow the battle. The scent of Lenya's fear came to him though the power of the dream. He felt a terrible sorrow at leaving her but was powerless to stop.

Sirio had called from the road. His car had broken down in a ditch off the RN. He had to dodge an oncoming car—luckily he wasn't hurt but he was angry and shaken. Lenya must come pick him up and on the way back to the cabin, they were to stop and pick up a friend, Rapha's personal physician, Dr. Farrone. He was retired, but available to Rapha or his family and friends. Help at last. "And don't worry, Lenya. No one need know more than they should about Aldo. Dr. Farrone is a man of discretion, and also from one of the old families." Sirio was well aware of her concerns.

She breathed a sigh of relief. This was to be a doctor who knew how to keep his mouth shut. Aldo would be in good hands.

Tom refused to come down from the loft. He wouldn't leave Aldo. "Okay old boy, you stay and be nurse for a while." She didn't want to leave either, but she had no choice and the thought of Tom staying by Aldo was comforting.

The last Mazzeru of the clan clutched his heart and, in slow motion it seemed, toppled off the mountain peak. Aldo let out a long breath and fought violently, punching the empty air as his soul tried to rush to join with the falling man. He hadn't been sure if he was the falling man or was it another? It was time for him to take this last journey but he was resisting with all his might.

Sirio was in the car as soon as Lenya slowed down. They raced to their next stop. Doctor Farrone was standing in the street in front of his house. Elderly and still spry, he jumped into the car and directed them to the local pharmacist. He had already called in for supplies and a carton was waiting.

Lenya felt a little calmer when she understood the doctor was taking no chances, covering all bases. Sirio must have done a lot of explaining.

Pulling the car in front of the cabin, she ran across the deck to open the door as Sirio and the doctor followed close behind.

Tom hadn't come down to bark at the sound of the car pulling up in front of the cabin. It wasn't a good sign.

Everything was quiet. She couldn't hear labored breathing as she ran upstairs to the loft. She placed her head to Aldo's chest—heartbeat—faint. Tom trembled against Aldo. Everything was too quiet. She grabbed Aldo and shook him. "You can't leave me! I won't let you go." She slapped his face hard and pounded on his chest.

The doctor leaned over the bed as Sirio pulled her away, holding her in his arms to try and quiet her. Her shaking was uncontrollable.

Lenya dropped to the floor. In the far recesses of her mind she knew this was something she had done before. *But can I survive this time?* She needed to lie next to Aldo, to hold him in her arms. On her knees, she pushed at his body to make room. Neither Sirio nor the doctor tried to stop her this time as she squeezed next to him, holding him. The doctor readied a hypodermic and injected something into Aldo's arm.

Lenya leaned over to glance into the carton from the pharmacy Sirio had carried upstairs. It was filled with humidifier and a bag full of decongestants, plastic bags of fluids, needles, tubing, lozenges, she recognized an Epipen, small boxes labled Doxycycline, Ciprofloxin and penicillin. The doctor noted her interest and patted his large black bag, "Just in case, I brought more fluid bags, steroids, tubing...intra-venous needles. We never know...he could be very dehydrated...I know he wouldn't want to go to a hospital so I brought the hospital to him." Lenya breathed another sigh of relief. Aldo was finally in the hands of someone who knew what he was doing.

Aldo had thought it was the end for him when he fell over the precipice. But a new dream began when he heard Lenya shouting and she punched him in the chest as he was falling. The fighting around him stopped as he slipped into a new vision.

The Mazzeri looked on in horror at a woman standing on one of the mountain tops. Her long black hair blew out in a tangle behind her and around her face as if caught in a gale wind. She held a long bloody sword upraised as she stood in the classic hero's stance.

Aldo couldn't see her clearly and wasn't sure if he was looking at Lenya or Dia as her hair changed from black to golden and then back.

A long gown whipped around her strong body...changed to Tai Chi work-out garb ...her hair became short and blonde. The only thing he clearly saw were muscles flexing in her arms and shoulders.

The men around her stopped fighting, blood ceased flowing from the mountaintop. Now there were two women standing together, tall, strong, back to back on top of the mountain, one in a long diaphanous robe and the other in yoga pants and tee-shirt. Both of them held swords, threatening the Mazzeri who had been fighting. His women. He sighed in relief.

Aldo's viewpoint changed. No longer at the bottom of the mountain, he was at the top...standing between his women as each clasped one of his hands in hers, the other hand holding a bloody sword aloft.

He looked down, eyes roving over bodies strewn across rock and field... he saw a fallen stag in the grass below. The old Mazzeru from the clan...but hadn't he been killed already?...bent to the animal's head and started to turn it over. Aldo felt his heart sink, fearful his face was to be the one revealed.

For once, Aldo feared death. There was too much to live for, Lenya—the love he always wanted, his painting—as important to him as the breath of life, his unborn child—fulfillment of his need to continue the clan. He moaned and fitfully thrashed out. The child needed to know of the clan, the old ways...must learn...

But the dream pulled him...relentless. Aldo sighed and started to slip away, his body cooling off from the fever wracking him...and felt himself yanked fiercely back from his dream.

Lenya had her arms around him, pulling him... holding him so tight it was almost hard to breathe. The dream faded. Something pinched him in the arm, then a sharp pain and he felt his arm was tied down so he couldn't move it.

He opened his eyes and there she was—lying next to him—arms around him, holding him quiet. Sitting at the bedside was Sirio and some strange man with glasses holding a bag filled with clear fluid. It felt cool as it flowed through the arm he couldn't move and he looked down to see a needle in his vein attached to the bag by a long strand of something. He didn't care. He was in Lenya's arms. Everything must be all right. He understood. Her turn. To protect.

He pushed the thought of his dream behind. Safe in her arms, he fell into a peaceful sleep, exhausted after days of fear, sickness and emotion. When he woke, she was asleep spooned against him, her arm draped over his chest. The two men were gone. He wasn't sure who saved him, Lenya or Dia, but then, maybe they were really one and the same.

The thought made him smile as he drifted back off to sleep.

As twilight drifted into dark, Lenya sat on the deck, exhausted and drained. Tom pushed next to her. The two of them motionless as the embers died in the fire she made to burn the linens and sheets from the sickbed. No way was she taking any chances. Her man was alive. He was going to live.

Chapter 67
Offering To Dia

Lenya realized how close Aldo had come to death, how close she had come to losing him as she watched him get his strength back. Almost a month of slow progress, gut-wrenching for her. Thinking of her panic and failure to realize the danger he had been in sent her into frozen fear. To move on, she had to push those thoughts back into the recesses of her brain. So close. Too close.

She knew deep within her heart how she and Aldo completed each other—soul mates finding each other across time, cultures and continents.

Each moment of their life together was filled with anticipation of the impending birth. Lenya grew large with their child, delighted at every movement inside her. Aldo slept at night with his hand on the taut skin covering the child he had prayed for. Protecting. As always.

When the time came, Rapha sent Doctor Farrone once again, this time to assist Aldo in the birth of their child.

Lenya always mentally shook her head as she remembered that day. Three men, Aldo, Sirio and Doctor Farrone, all taking part in the delivery. At least she was in good and loving hands.

The men considered the birth uneventful. They had told her so when it was over.

Fine, Lenya thought, it might have been for you guys, but it was far from uneventful for me. Fuzzy memories of pain during delivery were obscured by the sharp, bright joy of holding their son in her arms for the first time. A healthy boy, robust and full of energy as he howled a welcome to the world.

The most brilliant memory she had was of the bliss on Aldo's face as he held the squalling infant. His son. Strong!

Now Lenya had something to do, something she needed to do by herself. It was winter once again, but the sun was warm on her back as she made her way up into the mountains. The baby was snug on her back, papoose style, her mop handle for both protection and balance. Tom trotted along at her side.

The necropolis was easier to find than she had feared. Once she and Tom arrived, she saw wilted and dried flowers gracing the opening to the dark interior. Tears came again as she recognized Aldo's gift to his clan. She had a gift too, but it was different.

The fresh air was a relief after the difficult trek through the forest and up the side of the mountain. She sat on a flat rock to catch her breath and looked across the valley to the peaks on the other side as she cradled their son in her arms.

Tom licked her face and looked at her with his usual quizzical expression. The baby howled. Ronnie—Ronaldo after his father—was hungry. She freed her swollen breast as little hands reached greedily for a nipple to put into his waiting mouth. Red-orange wisps of hair glittered in the bright sunlight. "Hungry little bugger, aren't you?" The only reply she got was a slurping sound.

As the baby fed, she brought out the small offering of flowers she'd gathered on the way up to the dolmen and pushed them inside the ossuary. "I know it was you Dia, you saved him...for me...to let him see his son...for those who believe in you and need your consort...to let him express himself in his art....and to let him bring his special joy into all our lives. I wanted to come to you myself, to show you our child—your gift—and thank you in my own way." She couldn't stop the tears as she realized the truth in her words.

Lenya scrabbled around in the diaper bag and pulled out a small replica of the Venus of Villendorf she'd found in the artisan knife shop near the supermarket in Calvi. She pushed it into the dolmen next to the flowers. "I'm sorry it's not a more flattering representation of you—I'll bet you're really quite a stunner with no protruding belly or pendulous breasts, but it's the best I could find. I really didn't think Wonder Woman or a Barbie doll was an appropriate offering for you."

Now what do I say, Lenya thought. This was probably a really bad idea, but she was going to finish what she had started. She realized Ronnie had fallen asleep at her breast. He heaved a sigh of contentment as he dozed. Long red eyelashes fanned towards rosy cheeks. Her heart ached with joy.

Standing, she breathed in the unspoiled Corsican air and continued. "Well Dia, thank you for letting me have Aldo for a while more. I'm sure you know he loves you. I have no idea how to pray, but I think, if you can hear me, you already know he's a good man who worships you above all else. He'll be yours to take care of eventually, but his son and I, and those who revere you, need him for a while longer and...well...human time probably doesn't mean much to you. Oh, and please... when he must go, make sure he has a smooth journey to the other side."

As she took out a tissue to blow her nose, she remembered the first time Aldo took her to the necropolis; how he put the tissue she gave him away as if it were a treasure. She knew he was her real treasure.

The air blew across the rocks and through the trees below her. She thought she heard in its susurrus the same whispering voice she heard when she arrived on the island.

Maybe it's been Dia all along.

Epilogue
Eight Years Later – Corsica

The door to the cabin banged open and a small fury topped by red curls hurled itself across the deck and into the dense underbrush. The boy was chased by a ball of black and white fur nipping at his heels. Once motion stopped, Lenya looked at their red-headed son and the Jack Russell and poodle mix puppy—Sophia's naughty grandson named Tommy. The two of them raced around the clearing, the boy laughing and Tommy play growling.

As the two rolled around on the grass in their mock fight, she did Tai Chi on the deck, the sunlight shining on the streaks of silver in her golden hair. Sirio sat on a lounge chair watching her do the strikes and sweeps, Sophia now content to sit on his lap and take in the action.

Okay, so I'm a little slower than I used to be, she admitted. She was also slightly thicker around the middle, but prided herself on keeping in shape.

Her books were selling well, the last a series about a prehistoric clan living in hiding on a made-up island in the Mediterranean. She didn't want anyone poking around Corsica thinking it was true to life.

It was the Ronnie's school vacation and they always spent holidays at the cabin. Lenya wanted her son to know his father and they spent as much time as possible together.

She finished the forms and wrapped a towel around her neck as she headed into the cabin. "Get in here you guys, it's time for lunch. Ronnie, don't rip your pants...they're the last decent ones you have left."

She couldn't help smiling at the boy, he not only walked and looked like his father, he always seemed to be dressed in tattered clothes as well.

"Okay mom, wait a sec. I gotta' feed Loco first." He bent down to brush the grass and leaves off his shirt and pants and grabbed the black and white puppy firmly in his arms. He whistled a long chirp sound, and a squirrel came out of hiding and, looking around to make sure it was safe, and the puppy firmly in control, before it snatched the peanuts the boy had placed on the ground. Tommy was quiet and didn't growl as the squirrel made off with its lunch.

She stood on the deck and watched. Their son had a knack with animals too... gentle as he eased them into friendship like his father and grandfather before him.

He was so like Aldo. There was the hint of a beetle brow to come. She thought she could almost detect the slightly protruding upper frontal jaw, but time would tell. It was still too early to see his father's sharp cheekbones in the child's rounded face.

"Can we go to the cave this afternoon and see the paintings again?" he asked.

"Anything you like Ronnie, as long as you eat all your lunch."

"Let's picnic...eat in the grotto."

"...'kay, let me pack it up and we'll go.

Sirio was bending over rubbing his back with Sophia at his side. "I think my friend and I will stay to guard the house. You young and energetic ones can make the damned trek through the woods." He ruffled Sophia's ears and she looked up at him as if in agreement. Sophia wasn't ready for a long walk either.

"Of course you can stay. Make yourself comfortable. Is there anything special I can find for you on the satellite?"

"We will be fine. Don't worry, sleeping at our age is always a suitable entertainment."

"Enjoy your rest. I left your sandwich on the counter next to a bottle of wine."

Sirio often stayed at the cabin, better than the treacherous drive back to the winery. There was an addition built behind the original structure with enough room for their extended family to stay whenever they wanted.

She left the cabin mostly in its original state with some upgrading and new furniture to suit their tastes. After all, this is where I was reborn, she thought.

Lenya walked through the cabin admiring, as always, the artwork filling the walls with vibrant color and life. She had Aldo's works framed and many hung both in the cabin and at home in Los Angeles. Several art experts had seen them over the years; each one asked if she would consider an exhibition. Her answer was always the same, "These belong to our son Ronaldo, his inheritance from his father. When he's an adult, it's up to him to decide what he wants to do—keep them for his family, or share them with the world." She knew Aldo agreed. He had no interest in fame or money, his objective was to keep the story of the clan alive for his son to know.

The drawings of their lovemaking were for her alone. They were safely placed in a vault with only one key. She wasn't sure she would ever want to share them with anyone. Maybe someday. Every so often she visited the vault in Los Angeles and cried over the drawings. It wasn't as if her life was unpleasant—quite the contrary.

No one could ever take his place in her heart. But life moves on, she thought, and we are its survivors, doing what we are obliged to do.

Lenya and Ronnie trekked through the woods accompanied by a bouncing Tommy, armed with a flashlight, small backpack and her trusty old mop handle, a bit dented after the fight with the *sanglier* years ago, but useable. As they spread their lunch on the giant flat rock, she unconsciously looked around for a small offering of flowers and herbs. There they were, placed as usual in a corner.

The boy turned to her. "I didn't know dad was going to join us?"

"Of course I am. You don't think I'm going to leave you two alone in the woods with only tiny Tommy to guard you?" Aldo said as he stepped out of the grotto shadows. The silence of the cool air was rent by the boy's laugh accompanied by puppy yaps as Aldo stooped to hug his son and his woman. She felt Tom present in spirit, enjoying with Dia the energy of this new generation.

As she looked at Aldo, she was, as always, breathless. The shining bronze hair, neatly French braided as he liked, now had threads of gray and white. He too was a little thicker around the chest and middle, but his face was carved artfully by age, the high cheekbones and deep set eyes showing clear traces of the ancient shaping of the bones beneath. Tattered pants and rabbit vest had given way to well worn jeans and soft chambray shirt. Her man.

⌖

Later, as was their ritual, Ronnie and Lenya sat with Aldo in the sacred cave, admiring the wall paintings left by the ancient artists. Hunters in pursuit of their prey chased across the stone walls in the light from their small fire. Ocher, brown, buff and black animals fled from the raised spears of the boy's ancestors. Prehistoric handprints spoke of man's desire to be remembered, an existence to be recognized throughout time.

Aldo's voice took on the tone of a storyteller as he spoke with reverence of Dia. "...and the clan was on this land, in this very cave, long before Corsica was an island...before the great flood filled the waters of the Mediterranean and separated us from the mainland."

"Was it the time when they made the stone warriors?" Ronnie asked.

"No one knows for sure, but the clan believes they are the warriors of Dia. Dia is the Magna Mater, the mother of us all. It is Dia who controls life and death and whether or not children are born.

"It is also Dia who taught woman how to tame all men so women could live with them, not have them wild like the beasts of the maquis." Ronnie always laughed. This was currently his favorite work for Dia.

Lenya liked to chime in at this point, "Dia certainly has her hands full with this particular task. Sometimes I think it's more than even she can handle. The men of today seem to be as warlike and untamed as ever." She nodded at her two men.

Aldo smiled at her. "Well my dear one, it seems to me you have tamed this man." His chest expanded with pride at his woman.

"Not really, I think 'this man' has just made me wilder." She punctuated the remark with an upward quirk of eyebrow, and Aldo had the good grace to respond with a slight blush. Maybe only the reflection of a red beard? The spark between them had intensified over time, ready to ignite at any moment.

Ronnie cut in. "Is Dia why we don't cut our hair, dad?"

"Yes. It is to honor Dia. To preserve our strength, to serve her as her consort. As someday, hopefully, you will too.

"Dia has many names, different in many of the countries of the world, but always she is Dia—woman, powerful and—beautiful like your mother." Aldo turned to look at Lenya and smile before going on.

"She is known as Athena, Venus, Cybele, Demeter, Frigga, Hera and perhaps hundreds more, but she is the same. To me, to the clan, she is always Dia. Goddess."

His voice continued. Lenya dozed off, but Ronnie always listened, mesmerized as he committed to memory his link with the past.

Reverently the man and boy examined, as they did every time they came, the ancient artifacts on the shelf above the crude living area, and, like hundreds of generations before them, the son recited back to the father those legends of the clan already memorized. The stories about surviving an Ice Age, the clan almost totally decimated until they found the cave to protect them from the killing cold. And then, when the great ice melted and spilled into the ocean, how, once again, the cave saved them from the floods.

Stories about great hunts. Ronnie's favorite of all the hunt stories, was when Lenya told how his father saved them from the *sanglier*.

When she was finished, Ronnie always asked, "Did you ever see the piglets again—Daisy, Jake, Porky and Sadie?"

"No, we never did. But I'm sure they are here on the mountain somewhere with their own families. Your father put them back in their cave to be safe."

Aldo continued, the flames flickering over his face. "Your great, great, great grandfather, over a hundred or more generations ago, was one of those who painted these figures on the walls. He painted them for you, so you would know what life was like for him, and for you to pass it on to your children and your children's children. The same way I am telling you. He even left his handprints for you—to know he was here."

There were no computers, tablets, netbooks or iPads to record the clan stories, only the oral histories in the same way they were passed down for millennia. Now spoken in English, later Aldo hoped his son would be able to recite them as he had when a boy, in the ancient tongue.

Lenya was glad she purchased the cabin and the several acres around it up to the boundary of the clan territory.

Manno had worked his brand of magic and Aldo now legally owned the casteddu and all the land settled by the clan except for Raffa's hotel. The home of the clan was safe, it couldn't be disturbed. Eventually, everything would be passed down to their son. Aldo was content. He only hoped Ronnie would be more fruitful than he had been. It would be a great gift to have many grandchildren. Dia's decision.

Later, when they returned to the cabin, Lenya's iPhone sang her sisters melody. Lotte's face appeared on-screen when she answered.

"Hey sis, can you pick me up at the airport? I'll be on the six o'clock from Nice tomorrow. . . if there's no problem. Mauricio is driving in from Cap d'Antibes. . .we'll meet at the airport to fly to Calvi together. . . and tell both the little and the big caveman to behave. They're supposed to take care of you when I'm not around." Same old sister, always trying to be my caretaker, Lenya thought.

Senor Armani—Mauricio—turned out to be a good man—a keeper. He and Lotte were still lovers, now more than a decade, both with no visible intention of ever getting married, but enjoying being together—when it suited them.

Even Lenya had to admit she liked the man. Aldo, Sirio and Mauricio had all become very unusual and close friends. Mauricio had no living family of his own, and sorely missed their loss. He often came to the island to visit, sometimes to stay for a few days even when Lotte wasn't around. Another addition to their clan, Lenya thought. Growing, as life, once again stranger than fiction, moves on.

❧

Her two men were rooting around in the freezer. She looked at the long shining bronze hair, so distinctive and beautiful on them both.

Turning the iPhone camera to the kitchen she put it on video. "Look at those two guys, snooping around in the fridge together. You'd think they were starving." Lotte laughed on the other end.

Ronnie's voice was loud and clear, "Hey Aunt Lotte, don't worry, I've made sure mom's kept away from the chocolate ice cream. I ate it all!" Ronnie stuck out his stomach as far as he could and chuckled.

Aldo laughed and waved toward the phone as he leaned down and patted his son's tummy.

Sirio was up from his nap and crowded into to the kitchen to get in on the confusion.

Lenya smiled and got back to business. "We'll be there, don't worry…call if you're delayed."

Lotte waved goodbye to everyone. Her family too. Part of the clan.

Lenya felt her heart flood with happiness. She loved Aldo unconditionally; he and their son pre-empted her heart.

Life didn't allow them to be together all the time. Lenya had duties in Los Angeles for the next year or two consulting on films based on her novels.

Aldo wouldn't leave his duties to the people who believed in him and the old ways. Dia still needed her consort. He was content to live at the cabin and certain days take the long hike to the studio he built for himself at the casteddu. His own responsibilities to attend to.

When she was away, Sirio often stayed with Aldo and the two men cooked dinner together, talked about the old days and drank a bottle or two of good Corsican wine. Rapha and Michaele made frequent trips from the hotel to join them, bringing surprise cartons filled with excellent Italian cuisine.

Manno came too. He came alone at first, later with his wife, and two merry little boys with round dark eyes and fat cheeks no one could resist pinching. Adding more family and life. Their clan. Growing a new generation. Soon Manno's boys would be old enough to go with Aldo and Ronnie to the cave and learn the legends and stories—their history too.

Aldo and Lenya agreed their son must understand both sides of his heritage. Duty and obligations might separate them all from time to time, but they knew what bound them together—their love—their clan. It could bridge anything, even centuries and cultures, once they had learned to understand and respect each other.

Lenya looked out the open doors past the deck to the clearing and forest beyond. Her island now. On it, she found the most special gifts of all—her mate, her family, her life.

The Corsican breeze sang through the branches and, listening carefully, Lenya was sure she heard once again a familiar and special voice. Smiling, she whispered back to it, "Thank you, Dia."

Author's Notes

This is a work of fiction. All names, people, commercial places and characters are fictional. Any resemblance to actual people, living or dead, is purely coincidental. While some locations on Corsica are real, they are used fictionally.

There are many menhirs, dolmens and Neolithic ruins dotting the island. I've called on literary license to move a few about for the sake of the story.

To my knowledge, there is not now and has never been a clan as described on the island; they are purely a figment of my imagination as is Dia, a generic name for goddess. Many of the old ways and beliefs are a fiction compiled from research, taking into account ancient artifacts found on the island, European Neolithic peoples and settlements, goddess worship, and prehistoric religions.

However, the beliefs in the Mazzeru or Dream Hunters, is particular to Corsica, although other cultures have references to dream warriors, dream parades and predictions. Also related to ancient Corsican beliefs are the Signadori, a type of shaman or healer who can lift the evil eye believed cast by witches, male or female.

The term 'le Maître' means simply 'the master' and is commonly used to refer to anyone skilled in their craft. In ancient times, the term often referred to religious leaders. The author felt the word "priest," although used for male celebrants of ancient goddess religions, might be confusing if applied to Aldo as consort of the goddess because of its use in modern religions.

Goddess worship is believed to date from early prehistory. Tantric yoga is thought by some scholars to have been practiced as part of the sacred rites of goddess religions. There is little clarity in regard to which beliefs came first, tantric or female deities.

There is very little concrete historical proof of goddess religions being practiced on the island of Corsica, other than "Venus" artifacts and some of the menhirs depict females, whether warrior or goddess is unknown.

Goddess religions were commonly practiced for millennia under many names and in many places around the Mediterranean until they were stamped out by the advent of the Judeo-Christian belief systems.

These newer religions sought to obliterate all belief in the goddess, by whatever name she was recognized. Followers were debased as whores and catamites, and the practices were considered abominations. In many countries, the beliefs were considered blasphemous and punishable by torture and death.

When the Age of Enlightenment became popular in Europe during the 1700's, Jesuit position against the movement resulted in their wholesale expulsion. In the course of several months, under an edict of King Charles III, they were rounded up, herded onto ships and exiled to Corsica. They brought the Inquisition to Corsica with a vengeance and left a painful mark, forcing original beliefs further into the shadows, where many have remained to the present day.

19th and 20th century archeologists and historians have been hampered by the bias of modern faiths. Therefore, little credence has been given to the importance of the goddess in European history. Current discoveries point to evidence indicating the power and influence of goddess beliefs were denied or discounted. Several popular authors have recently stirred interest in the relationship between goddess worship and the cult of the Virgin Mary.

Scholars of the last several decades are more receptive to the acceptance of the possibility our ancestors might have had knowledge of value to pass along and history might be quite different from what had first been thought.

Lenya had trouble with the concept too, but she was open-minded enough to be an apt student.

I Muverini is a Corsican musical group famous for both resurrecting and keeping alive polyphonic music, the haunting melodies of the island. I Muverini has no connection in any manner with the characters, story or places in this book. The author just happens to be a devoted fan of their music.

For more information on the mysteries of Corsica, prehistoric man, goddess religions and sacred sex:

"Dream Hunters" by Dorothy Carrington

"When God Was A Woman" by Merlin Stone

"Sexual Secrets, The Alchemy of Ecstasy" by Nik Douglas and Penny Slinger

"The Kama Sutra"

"Cro-Magnon – How The Ice Age Gave Birth To The First Modern Humans" by Brian Fagan

About the Author

Alice R. Donenfeld-Vernoux spent her professional life in the entertainment business. After practicing copyright and corporate law in Manhattan, she was Vice President of Marvel Comics and Executive Vice President of Filmation Studios where she launched world television and merchandise licensing of "He-Man and the Masters of the Universe" among many other wildly successful animated series. Her companies— Alice Entertainment, Inc. and Alice4TV.com, were producers and creators of over a hundred television episodes, as well as distributors, consultants and exhibitors in world television markets.

She has been involved in all phases of the entertainment business from Broadway, films, international program distribution and television to New Media. A respected entertainment business expert, she served as an instructor at UCLA and a frequent speaker at industry events.

This is her first novel.

Currently she is at work on several new books:

"The Abandoned" a collection of short stories,

"Out Of The Chute" a novel of the modern west, and

"Behind the Spandex: Globetrotting With Superheroes" a memoir spanning her time with superstars the likes of "Spiderman," "He-Man," "Fat Albert and the Cosby Kids," "She-Ra Princess of Power," and "The Incredible Hulk," and a prequel to "Cave Dreams."

She lives in Baja California, Mexico and Orange County, California with her four dogs and can often be found in local French restaurants enjoying a *kir vin blanc* and in search of the perfect red wine to go with *sanglier*.